A LOVE SONG ANTHOLOGY

Elle Kennedy

K.L. Kreig

Leslie McAdam

Lynda Aicher

Mara White

Marni Mann

Nikki Sloane

Rebecca Shea

Saffron A. Kent

Sierra Simone

Veronica Larsen

Xio Axelrod

foreword written by
Laurelin Paige

Copyright

Foreword. Copyright © 2019 by Laurelin Paige
All I Want. Copyright © 2019 by Mara White
Broken Hallelujah. Copyright © 2019 by Sierra Simone
Guys My Age. Copyright © 2019 by Saffron Kent
Kiss Me. Copyright © 2019 by Lynda Aicher
Lush. Copyright © 2019 by Marni Mann
Moment of Truth. Copyright © 2019 by Veronica Larsen
Say it First. Copyright © 2019 by Nikki Sloane
Say Yes. Copyright © 2019 by Elle Kennedy
Think I'm in Love. Copyright © 2019 by Leslie McAdam
Toothpaste Kisses. Copyright © 2019 by Xio Axelrod
Wild Pitch. Copyright © 2019 by Rebecca Shea
Your Everything. Copyright © 2019 by KL Kreig

Cover photography. Copyright © 2019 by
WANDER AGUIAR PHOTOGRAPHY

Cover design. Copyright © 2019 by SHADY CREEK PUBLISHING

ISBN. 978-1-949409-99-4

All rights reserved. No part of this publication may be reproduced, distributed, or transmitted in any form or by any means, including photocopying, recording, or other electronic or mechanical methods, without the prior written permission of the publisher, except in the case of brief quotations embodied in critical reviews and certain other noncommercial uses permitted by copyright law. For permission requests, write to the author.

This book is a work of fiction. The characters, events, and places portrayed in this book are products of the author's imagination and are either fictitious or are used fictitiously. Any similarity to real persons, living or dead, is purely coincidental and not intended by the author.

Contents

Laurelin Paige: Foreword . . . .*i*

♪

Saffron A. Kent: "Guys My Age" 1

Nikki Sloane: "Say It First" 51

Sierra Simone: "Broken Hallelujah" 103

Elle Kennedy: "Say Yes" 139

Mara White: "All I Want" 191

Xio Axelrod: "Toothpaste Kisses" 233

Rebecca Shea: "Wild Pitch" 287

K. L. Kreig: "Your Everything" 317

Leslie McAdam: "Think I'm in Love" 363

Veronica Larsen: "Moment of Truth" 407

Marni Mann: "Lush" 455

Lynda Aicher: "Kiss Me" 487

Foreword

It was the fall of 2001. I was three years out from graduating from college with a Bachelor's degree in Musical Theater, a degree I'd done nothing with beyond a couple of community shows. I worked for an eye doctor's office, a job that involved sitting behind a desk all day billing insurance companies. While the work had earned me enough to buy my first condo in Denver, it was a hollow success. There were things that filled my cup—songwriting, acting—but they were fleeting. The shows always ended. The songs were unheard.

I had very little going on socially. I was an introvert who craved deep one-on-one interactions, and I was fortunate enough to meet some amazing friends through the plays, but those sorts of relationships are more than not quick burns—deeply passionate and over by the time the next cast list was posted. The few men I'd been involved with were the same—narcissistic in nature, men looking for temporary feel-good situations. My head always knew the story going in. My heart broke over and over again anyway.

I'd made it into the Actor's Studio in New York for a Master's program, but I needed a year to save money. So I postponed entrance and got a job moonlighting at a movie theater in a rich area of Denver. It was work I'd done for many years through college and a time after which made it easy. It was depressing, though, going back to a job behind the concessions stand when I'd been a manager for so long. I filled popcorn buckets and pushed the next size up alongside sixteen-year old kids who were only using the job to get spending money for designer jeans.

Then September 11th happened, and no one felt safe or happy anymore. Customers spit on Abdul, the brown-skinned forty-year-old man who cleaned the theaters between showings. He was the hardest working employee in the place. He'd been a medical doctor in India, and, here, he cleaned up puke and picked off gum from the bottom of theater seats for less than six dollars an hour. He ate the curry-flavored foods he brought from home alone in the break room and didn't flinch at the slew of racist comments he encountered on a daily basis.

I watched him more than I should have. He made me wonder what things were happening to my father's family back in Utah, where I grew up. They were all immigrants from Iran, and though they weren't big on practicing, they were also Muslim. I'd been estranged from them for years and didn't feel like I could reach out and ask, but I thought about them. A lot.

It was a time of heavy melancholy. Gloom covered the country like a weighted blanket. Personally, I was sad and lonely and restless. The projectionist at work flirted with me, but he was hot and cold and made me doubt everything about myself. I was optimistic that something better lay ahead for me, for our world, but it felt like I was trudging through mud to get there. I was tired. Too tired to expend a lot of energy on hope.

Then a new manager took over the theater.

Within weeks, a rumor floated through the grapevine that he had a crush on me. He was annoying as a boss—too strict, too uptight—but I agreed to go on a date with him, mostly because I hoped it would make the projectionist jealous. Yeah, I was that girl.

Thank god, I was, too.

It was a typical first date. A movie at a sister theater—that was free since we worked for the company, and we were both dirt poor—followed by hot chocolate at Denny's. We sat at that Denny's for hours and talked and talked and talked. We connected on everything, and the things we didn't we still enjoyed discussing. Both of us felt isolated and alone. Both of us were searching for that elusive "more".

Soon, he was staring at my lips, and I was staring at his. The make-out session that followed in his car didn't have me declaring I was in love, but it didn't take many dates after that before I was ready. We were inseparable—meeting for stolen lunches, late-night hot chocolate, and movie watching. Hours were spent on the phone.

It felt like I barely slept. He worked late to close up the theater, and I had to be at the eye doctor's every morning by eight.

But I was happy. Over-the-moon full of joy.

One evening, determined to get a good night's sleep but desperate to see him, I met him outside the theater after he'd closed up around one in the morning. We turned on the car radio really loud, left the doors open so we could hear, and danced alone in the parking garage.

"This Year's Love" by David Gray came on. Do you know the song? I encourage you to Google it now if you don't. Listen to it. Read the lyrics. I can't quote it due to copyright law, but I'll give you the gist. It's a love song that's as woeful as it is happy. The singer recounts all the heartache from the past, the lies, the short affairs, and now he's in the arms of someone amazing and wonderful, someone who reassures him, and he yearns, he prays, he begs for this love to last. The basic chord structure, though in a major key, is simple and repetitive, and with the six-eight time, the listener gets the feeling of being on a merry-go-round. It feels circular and ongoing, like the string of disappointments the singer speaks of. But then, when the singer speaks about this year's love, the chord progression changes, and the listener begins to think, Oh, this might be different. Maybe there's hope here.

This song spilled out of the speakers, enveloped us in our dance, and It. Was. Me.

It was everything I'd been feeling—the tumult, the brokenness, the longing. The merry-go-round of heartache. The hope.

Was that the story David Gray had intended to write? A story of a lonely, lost, half-brown girl in the aftermath of the country's greatest terrorist attack, trying to find something deep and lasting with her movie theater boss? Is that what the song is about?

It could be.

It could be.

That's the thing about a good song—they tell a story, but they're just vignettes. They don't have all the details. They hit on universal emotions, specific enough that they can feel like they came from a page out of your soul's diary, but sparse enough that they can also be someone else's story.

About a million years ago, someone once asked me what I thought "Scenes from an Italian Restaurant" by Billy Joel was about. Well, duh. It's about a piano player (maybe a waiter) at an Italian restaurant remarking on all the different customers there for dinner that night. The song changes tempo and melody as it tells of a table where the couple dining is young and in love and another table where the couple has been together for a long time. A table where the couple is fighting. A table where the couple is on the verge of breaking up.

But my friend said, "For me, it's about me and my ex. All the 'scenes' are different times in our relationship."

Was that the song Billy Joel was trying to write? The one for my friend? Or did he intend the one that I'd imagined? Or something else entirely?

It could be any of those. Or all of those. It could be about a thousand other people's stories. It could be about you. It could be about a different you when you listen ten years later. It's the reason songs were the first stories I ever wrote, the reason I'm so in love with that format of storytelling—because they can be so many different tales at once.

That's what this Mixtape Anthology is all about—stories that could be. Each author included has taken a song that speaks to her and created a scenario around it or inspired by it. You might know the songs. These stories might not be what you imagine when you hear the songs, but I bet you'll hear the influence the music and lyrics had on the author. Tiffanie DeBartolo's forward in God-Shaped Hole tells how Jeff Buckley's album, Grace, was the inspiration to her debut novel. She recalls the first time she heard it, how it transformed her and moved her like no other collection of music. She played it on repeat when she wrote the book. Pieces of that album are sprinkled throughout God-Shaped Hole, including Buckley's famous version of Leonard Cohen's Hallelujah. That song fits that book so completely. It also completely fits Sierra Simone's story in this anthology, also based on that song.

What story does that song really tell? Tiffanie DeBartolo's or Sierra Simone's?

Both of them.

And your Hallelujah story.

And mine.

A year and a half after that night with my boss in the parking garage, we played This Year's Love as our first dance at our wedding. My mother said she thought the song was perfect because it was about two people saying their love—this year's love—was going to last forever.

Is that really the story David Gray meant to tell with his song? It could be.

Laurelin Paige

New York Times Bestselling Author

WWW.LAURELINPAIGE.COM

Guys My Age

SAFFRON A. KENT

CHAPTER ONE

Fallon

Fifteen years ago, I asked a boy to marry me.

I was three and he was seventeen. Apparently, that's a big age difference. I didn't know that at the time. I didn't know he was older or what it meant even if he was.

All I knew was this boy gave me the best piggyback rides and brought me candies all the time. He played with me, read me stories, taught me to climb trees and ride my bike. He was always the one to wipe away my tears.

When I told him I was going to marry him and that my wedding dress would be made out of all my favorite Harry Potter quotes, he laughed. Then, he kissed my forehead and told me I'd feel differently when I grew up. I told him I wouldn't. And I think we bet on it — I don't remember that part well.

In fact, I shouldn't remember any of it; I was three for God's sake. But somehow, I do.

I remember everything about him. I remember growing up with him by my side. I remember him living a few streets over and coming to dinner at our house most nights with his sister. I remember my dad and my mom loving him as their own son. I remember my mom saying she's never seen a friendship like this, like ours. A boy of seventeen being best friends with a three-year-old girl.

Most of all, I remember him always making me happy. Or at the very least, making my sadness not so sad. Because not being sad has always been very difficult for me.

But I'm not going to think about it right now. I'm not going to think about how hard things are or how different I am from everyone else. Because he's here.

Dean.

My best friend and the love of my life.

From the top of the stairs that lead up to my college dorm, I notice him standing across the cement pathway.

He's waiting for me.

Over our last phone call, we'd agreed to meet here at 9 A.M. sharp and he's early. Like always. Dean loves to be early. He loves to go the extra mile. He's very much like my dad in that way. Always working, always trying to prove himself.

Anyway, I'm never early but today I am.

Because I'm excited. I've been excited about this morning for days now. Besides, I haven't seen him in weeks and I don't want to waste even a single second of our time together.

Dean hasn't seen me yet. His head is bent over his cellphone and his fingers are flying on the keypad, and I imagine him typing up high-level, lawyerly things. He is one of the best prosecutors in L.A. That means he never has time to see me. All we ever do is talk on the phone, and that's it.

But finally, he's here. So again, I'm not gonna think about how much it hurts knowing that my best friend, the man I'm in love with, doesn't have time for me.

"Dean!" I call out his name, grinning.

His head snaps up from his phone and his eyes settle on me. Dark and gorgeous, just like his hair.

I begin panting, pulling huge amounts of air into my lungs that suddenly feel starved under his gaze. Dean takes me in, his eyes boring into mine, then sliding over my face so thoroughly. Slowly and rapidly, both at the same time. Like, he needs to make sure that I'm really here.

A few moments later, his lips pull up at the side and the lines bracketing his mouth deepen. My breath hitches as his smile comes into view. The smile that I see in my dreams.

He doesn't stop there, though. He opens his arms, his thick, corded arms, and I feel a jolt in my chest. An onslaught of memories that fill every corner of my body, leaving space for nothing else but him. Not even air.

I'll wait for you, Tiny. Right outside the school gates, he'd tell me, when I threw tantrums about going to school. Mingling with people, studying, lessons. All these things that might come naturally to other people have always been hard for me. Dean was the only one who could get me to go.

I'd ask him teary-eyed, *Promise?*

Yes.

Will you also hug me? Like, really tight? Like, when I get sad and I don't know why.

He'd smile and his eyes would go all liquidy and soft. *Yeah, I will. I'll hug you for as long as you want.*

He always kept his promise. He'd wait for me just outside the school gates, and as soon as he saw me, he'd kneel on the ground and open his arms for me so I had a place to run to.

That's what I do now, too.

I rush down the steps, and like always, I run to him.

But the heel of my sandal twists on something — knowing me, I'd say it could be a crack in the ground — and instead of going straight into Dean's arms, I'm flailing my arms so I don't faceplant on the ground.

I don't. Faceplant, that is.

Because someone saves me. That someone steps into my space, grabs hold of my waist and my arm so I collide with his massive chest instead of with the ground.

I'm so thankful and generally, so happy in this moment I don't have it in me to be embarrassed. Gulping in air, I look up at Dean.

"T—Thank you," I breathe out.

He smirks. "You've still got two left feet, Tiny."

I shake my head at him. "It could happen to anyone."

"No. Not really. Only you."

"It was an accident."

"Sure, it was."

"That thing from the ground came out of nowhere."

"Sure, it did."

His smirk is still in place, and I can't decide if I want to smack it off his face or kiss it. I settle on narrowing my eyes. "You know, I don't wanna fight with you today. So, you're in luck. Or I would've kicked your ass for pointing out my coordination flaws."

Dean chuckles and strangely, it vibrates through my own chest. "Lucky me."

I take a moment to absorb him, absorb his nearness. He's warm and strong. So solid. Dreams of him pale in comparison to the reality of him. In my dreams, I can't smell his citrusy scent or touch the softness of his t-shirt. Or notice the nuances of his brown eyes.

"Hey, Dean," I whisper.

"Hey, Tiny," he whispers back.

I love it when he calls me that — Tiny. It makes me feel cherished. It makes me believe that I really am tiny. That I don't have massive issues for which I take a pill every day.

"You're early," he murmurs.

I let his rumbly voice wash over me, seep through my clothes and into my skin. Winding my arms around his waist, I bury my face in his chest and nod. "I know."

He lowers his face and his lips seem so close to my forehead I'm disappointed when they don't touch me as he says, "You're never early."

Closing my eyes, I smile. "I know. But I couldn't sleep last night."

His arms tighten around me in concern. "Why not?"

I burrow my face even more, rubbing my nose against the tight arch of his chest. "Because of you. Because I was excited to see you. Be with you."

"You need to sleep, Fallon. Are you sleeping well otherwise? Eating?" he asks, rubbing his clean-shaven jaw over my hair, concern still evident in his voice.

I sigh.

God, why does he have to be so wonderful? So caring and protective? It just makes all of this so much more difficult. It makes not kissing him and declaring my love for him even more agonizing.

Soon though. It's gonna happen soon. I *think*. And hope.

Moving away, I look up at him. At his high, sculpted cheekbones and his soft lips. I gauge the distance between our lips. I'm shorter than him and I will have to stretch my legs, going up on my tiptoes to reach the height where I can put my lips over his.

I wonder over his reaction. What will he do if I kiss him out of nowhere? I wonder if he'll kiss me back.

I wonder if he'll finally admit we're more than friends.

Biting my lip, I ask, "Aww. Are you worried about me, Dean?"

"Was that not obvious?"

"You've always been worried about me, haven't you?"

Studying me, he frowns. "Am I supposed to answer that?"

I swallow and fist his t-shirt. "Answer me this. Why?"

"Why, what?"

"Why have you always been worried about me?"

His eyes rove over my face. My silver hair that I get from my mom and my gray eyes that I get from my dad. Dean takes me in like he was doing earlier but this time, his perusal feels intimate. So intimate my body breaks out in goosebumps.

Then, his gaze drops to my lips. My *lips*.

Is he studying my lips? Oh God, has he ever done that before?

The tingles I feel along the seam of them makes me think that yes—yes, he has. Only, I've never caught him in the act. He's never been this blatant, this intent. This close to me. So close all I can see is him. All I can smell is him.

I can't help but tilt my face up, leaning more into his body. But as soon as I do that, he moves away.

Letting go of me, he says in a roughened voice, "Because you have a habit of not taking care of yourself and *that* worries me."

I'm a little dazed and a lot disappointed. The breeze wafting over my body feels cold without his heat warming me up. It's not as if I'm unfamiliar with this disappointment. I've been feeling this ever since Dean moved away from New York, our home, to California two years ago.

Sighing, I give him a look. "I'm fine. Everything is fine. As it was when you called me last Tuesday."

Dean calls me every Tuesday at 8:30 P.M. sharp. Not to chat—Dean doesn't have time to chat anymore, apparently—but to check up on me. How my classes are. If I'm taking care of myself. If someone is bothering me.

"Good. Glad to hear it."

"You do know I'm not a little girl, right? Not anymore." My words sound frustrated but I don't care right now.

At this, something flashes across his face. A shadow that jumps out under the sunny sky. It goes away quickly and his lips twitch as he reaches forward to tuck a fly-away strand behind my ear. "Little hard to forget that when I was the one picking you up from playdates and kindergarten."

Is it sick that the tender look in his eyes makes my heart race? Actually, it makes my heart race *and* it makes me wanna shake him until he realizes how tremulous my heartbeats are.

I fold my arms across my chest and cock my hip out. "Well, then I'm glad we're doing this thing. It will give me a chance to show you that I don't go to Kindergarten anymore and I don't need playdates to amuse me. I know a few games of my own that keep me pretty happy."

Dean thrusts his hands into his pockets and arches his eyebrows. "Is that why you came up with the insane idea of driving three thousand miles back to New York, instead of taking a six-hour flight? Because you wanted to show me how grown-up you are."

Bingo.

Yeah, that's why. I mean, it wasn't planned or anything. Last Tuesday when he called me and told me there was a chance he'd be going back to New York for Christmas, I suggested that we go together.

There was a bit of a silence on his side but he agreed. He told me he'd get plane tickets and then, before I could stop it, I told him we should make a trip out of it. It took a little convincing but here we are, ready to start our three-thousand-mile, five-day journey back home.

And hopefully, back to each other.

Because I can't take this distance anymore. I can't hide my feelings for him anymore, either. So, I've got a plan.

Keeping my eyes connected to his, I close the space between us.

I feel the air turning static, thick and heated, saturated with all of these emotions inside me.

"No. I came up with the insane idea of driving three thousand miles back because I wanted to spend time with you. Because you never seem to have time for me anymore," I say in a soft, low voice, sanded over with craving for him.

"That's because I have this thing. It's called a job," he says, his voice full of amusement. Although, amusement is hardly the emotion reflected in his gaze or on his expression. It's too intense, too penetrating for that.

"Oh, I know. You're this bigshot lawyer now, right?"

"Right."

"Are you sure they're gonna survive without you at the firm?"

"I think they'll manage. For once."

I nod once, trying to hide my smile at the arrogance in his voice. "My mom's gonna be happy to see you."

Though not as happy as I am right now. I'm bursting with happiness. Such a strange thing for me.

He smiles. "Yeah, it'll be good to see her."

My mom and Dean have always been close. So have my dad and Dean. But I guess, my mom's more eloquent and more open about it, than my dad. My dad is a closed book, very much like Dean.

"She thinks you work too much." *I do too.*

"Does she?"

"She thinks you have no life."

"No kidding."

"She thinks you need to slow down a little."

"She said that to you?"

"Yup."

No.

I mean, my mom and Dean's sister, Mia, they both do think Dean is working himself into the ground. But this is all me.

"She also said you need to loosen up a little," I continue, making stuff up; though to be fair, he does need that.

"Loosen up, huh?"

"So, I told her she should leave it to me."

"Leave it to you?"

"Uh-huh." I grin, and then, looking him in the eye, I declare, "I'm going to loosen you up, Dean."

With a slamming heart and buzzing skin, I wait for his reaction. Dean seems frozen for a few seconds. As if all he can do right now is stare at me.

But the moment breaks when he ducks his head and runs his fingers through his thick hair. "Thanks for the offer but you should tell your mom I'm doing just fine." Then, looking over my shoulders, he tips his chin. "That your luggage?"

He's probably referring to the giant magenta suitcase along with the floral handbag bulging at the seams with all the stuff I've packed for the coming days. I don't care enough to confirm. I'm more interested in him and his restrained reactions.

"Yup."

He takes a step toward it, but I stop him. I clutch the sleeve of his t-shirt and sort of barge into his space.

Dean's eyes are full of suspicion when I raise myself up on my tiptoes and lean in to place a soft kiss on his jaw. It ticks under my mouth and he goes completely still once again. But that doesn't deter me. I won't *let* it deter me.

"I missed you, Dean. I missed you so much," I whisper the words to the slant of his sculpted jaw, making him feel the words rather than hear them.

The said jaw ticks again and I step away.

Throwing me a glance that kinda looks frustrated—though, I can't be sure—he leaves to grab my luggage.

Even though his reaction was less than enthusiastic, I beam.

Nothing can dampen my excitement. He's here. We're going on a road trip and I have a plan.

Before this week is over, I'm going to tell Dean how I feel. And I'm going to convince him we belong together.

It doesn't matter that he's older—much older, and we've always been just friends. We have something special and I'm gonna make him realize it, too.

CHAPTER TWO

Fallon

When I suggested a road trip, I didn't know we'd be driving for ten hours on the first day.

I didn't know that Dean wouldn't let me drive his precious car. Some sleek convertible I hardly know the name of.

"You're a fucking control freak, you know that?" I tell him at his refusal.

"Hey, watch it, Tiny. Language," he growls from beside me.

He's sprawled in the seat, his strong thighs taking up the whole space with their largeness and masculinity. As I said, he's lucky I'm in a good mood or I'd take major offense at his high-handed tone.

As it is, I roll my eyes. "The only reason you're alive right now is because you're driving."

"And because you like me."

God, why does he have to be so confident? And why do those sunglasses look so sexy on him?

"On second thought, maybe I should kill you. That way I'll get to drive your stupid car."

"No abuse on the car, either."

Again, I roll my eyes and hand him a peeled orange, his favorite. I decided since Dean's mapping out the whole route and figuring out where we'll stay overnight, where we'll eat and whatnot, the least I can do is be in charge of the snacks. Somehow, he let me do that and so, I got his favorites.

"Well, if you're not going to let me drive, I'm gonna put on some music."

I lean forward and fiddle with the music system, and Lana Del Ray blasts from the speaker.

Right on cue, Dean groans. "Ah, fuck."

I tsk at him. "Language." Then, "She's awesome, Dean. She's the bomb."

He shoots me a glance and turns off the music. "Let's keep all kinds of explosives away, all right?"

I throw a piece of popcorn at him that collides with his chest and rolls down to settle on those sexy thighs. Smirking, he picks it up and pops it in his mouth.

Gah.

I can't even be mad at him. His smiles, his relaxed posture, they kill me every time. Mostly because they are all so rare.

Now, we're in Utah, Salt Lake City to be specific, and we've stopped for the night at a motel Dean had already picked out. I'm in my room, which is sadly separate from Dean's, when my phone rings. It's Mom.

"Hey, Mom," I say, lying on the bed.

"Hey, baby. How are you? Are you tired?"

Apart from Dean, my mom's always been my best friend. She understands me in a way that's rare and sometimes, spooky. When I was little, I used to think my mom could read minds. Turns out the only mind she can read is mine.

"No, I'm fine," I assure her.

"Did you take your meds?"

"When have I ever forgotten, Mom? I take it on time, every day."

And the reason she can read my mind is because she's me. Or I'm her.

We both suffer from clinical depression. I was medically diagnosed at thirteen. But I guess, my mom always knew about it. I feel like she blames herself sometimes. Although, my dad and me, we both tell her it's not her fault.

In fact, it's because of her that I'm so well-adjusted about my condition. Well, as well-adjusted as I can be. You know, when my brain isn't telling me I'm worthless and there's no hope for me.

"I'm just saying," Mom continues. "Mostly because I think you're a little too happy today."

"Is there anything wrong with being happy?"

"Nope. Not at all," she says in a grave voice because she knows how hard it is for people like us to be happy. "Just don't forget to take the pill, kiddo."

I chuckle. "He reminded me already, you know. Not that I would've forgotten but still."

Dean knows my schedule by heart. Even though we don't talk to each other every day, he still manages to remind me via text or email. Initially, I thought those texts meant a segue to chatting, but no. They were simple reminders about my medication. Sometimes he won't even look at my reply for hours. I know; I have checked.

I can hear my mom's smile. "He did, did he?"

I nod, smiling as well, as warmth pools in my chest. "Yup. He thinks I'm still a kid. Like you guys."

"Well, you're always gonna be my kid. And to be fair, compared to him you actually *are* a kid."

"I'm not," I snap, pursing my lips. "Stop saying that."

Mom laughs. "Ooh! A little bit touchy there. Should I know something?"

I bite my lip and dart my eyes around the room like I'm not alone. Like, Dean can hear me. "No."

"Really?"

Her tone suggests she already knows, and I get both nervous and relieved. We've never talked about how I feel about Dean. I mean, I only realized it two years ago myself.

Am I slow or what?

I've known the guy all my life, but I only realized I loved him when out of nowhere, he declared he was taking a job in Los Angeles.

I'll never forget his kiss at the airport. I was crying—sobbing really—and he hugged me so tightly I was surprised when the hug was broken, and we came apart as two different bodies, instead of one.

"Mom," I say, sitting up on the bed, fisting the sheet.

"What?"

"Don't try to play innocent."

"Oh, unlike you, you mean?"

"Mom," I whine like a kid. She reduces me to that sometimes, and I hate my voice like this.

She laughs harder. "All right, I know. I've always known."

"I'm not sure if we're talking about the same thing," I return cautiously, even as my eyes are scrunching shut and I'm crossing my fingers.

If I wanted someone to know before Dean, it would be my mom. She's the coolest.

"Okay. So, we're not talking about Dean and how you picked a college in L.A., so you can be close to him. And how you're driving to New York just so you can spend some time together. Because apparently, he's just always working," Mom says with a smile in her voice. "So, that's not what we're talking about, right?"

See, mind reader.

I fold my legs, crisscrossing them and chew on my nail. "How long have you known?"

"I'll tell you if you stop chewing on your nails."

I whip my finger out of my mouth. "God, you're spooky. Anyway, tell me. How long?"

She sighs. "Always."

"How? Even I didn't know."

"I've always known, Fallon. I guess, I have the sense for these things. And if it were someone else, then I probably would have a problem with it because, well, you're young and he's older—much older. But it's Dean, you know. He's like my other son and I know him. I've watched him grow up."

It's true. When Dean was twelve, he met my dad accidentally and since then, my dad has always tried to be there for Dean and his sister. Because Dean's own father has hardly been a part of their lives. From what I hear, his dad completely checked out when Dean's mom died, and he threw himself into his work.

My heart hurts for Dean and his sister. When I think of how lonely they must have felt, how the responsibility of bringing Mia up must have fallen on Dean's shoulders. Thank God for my mom and dad, stepping up and helping.

"Do you . . ." I bring my knees up and sit back against the headboard. "Do you think he loves me too?"

"What do you think?"

"I don't know. I mean, sometimes I feel that he does but . . . I don't know, Mom. What if he doesn't?"

"You're never going to know if you don't ask, honey. Besides, that's why you came up with this insane idea anyway, right?"

"Okay, why does everyone keep calling it an insane idea? People take road trips all the time, okay? It's not that insane."

"Yeah, tell that to your dad. He's losing his mind over here."

I gasp. "Mom, please don't tell Dad. Please don't tell him I love Dean. Please? He'll lose his shit."

"Language," she chastises. "And no. I'm not saying anything to your dad. Believe it or not, I'm kind of scared of him too."

"Oh please. Dad worships you. He can never be mad at you, like, ever."

"Well, yeah. Your dad does worship me."

She giggles at that. Apparently, Dad's the only person who can make her giggle.

They met in the unlikeliest of places: a psychiatric ward. When my mom was eighteen, she went through a major depressive episode that led to her attempting suicide. So, she was sent to Heartstone Psychiatric Hospital, where my dad worked as a lead psychiatrist.

I, for one, love their love story. I love how my silent, seemingly unemotional dad fell in love with my quirky, cute mom. I love how my dad, who hardly ever smiles, laughs when my mom is around. I can see it in his eyes, how much he loves her, how much he admires her.

Sometimes I feel like Dean looks at me that way but maybe it could be the imaginings of a lovesick girl.

"Mom? Everything's gonna be okay, right?"

"Yes. You know why? Because life's full of possibilities."

"Even for people like us?"

"Yes. Even for people like us."

I have tears in my eyes and I know she has them too. But then I hear my dad's voice in the background—he must have just come into the room—asking who my mom is talking to.

"Fallon?" My dad says when Mom passes the phone to him.

"Dad. Hey."

"Hey, kiddo. How are you?"

"I'm good."

"Did you eat?"

"Yup."

"Meds?"

I laugh. "I took them. I'm fine, I promise."

He sighs. I can imagine him straightening his glasses. "Where you're staying . . . Dean sent me the location. Is it a good place? I've been looking at it online—"

"Dad, I'm fine. I told you. Stop worrying. I'm having fun."

"Next time have fun on a plane, you understand? We've been worried. Five days, Fallon. That's not a joke. Especially when you can be here in six hours."

I go to say something, but I hear my mom reprimanding him. *Stop being such a hardass, Simon. Let her have fun.*

She can have just as much fun on a plane. Why does she have to drive three thousand miles to have fun? Do you have any idea the things that could happen on a road trip? I was reading this article online—

Gosh, you're such a nerd. Stop. It's fine.

Did you just call me a nerd, Willow?

Yes.

Yeah. I don't think I like that very much.

What're you gonna do about it?

You don't want to know.

I'm not afraid of you . . .

I can't hear anything after that because the phone's snatched by my brother, Brendan, who's four years younger than me. Brendan means 'son of a king,' and apparently, my mom used to call my dad, her psychiatrist, Ice King. So, she picked our names with that thought in mind.

"Ugh, Mom and Dad are being gross again," he says, forgoing his greeting.

I laugh. "When are they not being gross? But it's better than having parents who fight all the time."

"I guess . . ."

We talk for a little bit before I hang up and hug myself. Gosh, I miss my family. Moving to California was an easy decision for me. I was doing it for Dean. But actually living there, so far from the people I love, is hard.

The only person who can make it better is on the other side of this wall and I can't wait another second to be with him.

Mom's right. I'm never gonna know if I don't ask.

I'm going to go ask Dean. Although first, I need appropriate clothes. Giggling because apparently, Dean makes me a giggler too, I get to work.

He's not going to know what hit him.

CHAPTER THREE

Fallon

He's awake.

Good.

There's light under his door so I knock on it, trying to tamp down my excitement.

A few seconds later, Dean opens it and there's no use even trying to control my heartbeats. They're not going to slow down, no matter what I do. My heart isn't mine. It's his. It belongs to this man in front of me.

"Fallon?" Dean asks with a frown and a concerned voice.

"Hey," I breathe.

He looks up and down the brown-carpeted corridor. "Are you okay? What going on?"

For some strange reason, I've forgotten all my reasons for being here. All I can do is simply stare at him. At his rumpled hair and faded t-shirt. His bare feet with a sprinkling of dark hair on the toes, which makes it all the sexier. And his checkered pajamas.

Dean's always worn them. They make him look very straight-laced and mature. And now I realize, super sexy too.

"You still wear checkered pants?" I say, chuckling.

Dean's frown takes on a sort of offended turn. He looks down at himself, seemingly put out, and that only makes me laugh harder.

A second later though, I'm not laughing. He's stolen my laughter, my breaths even as he drags his gaze up and down my body, reminding me what I'm wearing.

It's my usual night clothes—a pair of shorts and a tank top—but a little shorter and a lot lacier. And black in color. Dean's favorite.

He runs his eyes from my feet, up my bare calves and thighs, to my stomach and up to my chest. He lingers in places, making those spots burn with longing. Making my stomach buzz and nipples bead inside my top.

I rub my feet together, feeling jittery and hot, wondering if he can see how his careful study is affecting me. If he can tell I picked this outfit, just for him.

All my musings evaporate when his gaze clashes with mine. There's so much heat in the depths of his eyes that his brown pupils seem burnt. They appear black, almost, and blown up.

The silence is too much to take so I whisper his name, "Dean..."

Without saying a single word to me, Dean grabs hold of my wrist and pulls me inside the room, making me squeak. I jump when he shuts the door behind me, still staring at me like he'll never stop.

"At least, it's better than what you're wearing," he says, at last, letting go of me.

I freeze in my spot. Does he not like it, my clothes?

"What's wrong with what I'm wearing?" I ask carefully.

Dean steps back from me without answering, and strides over to the bathroom.

Um... what was that?

I don't know what to think. I mean, I didn't expect him to jump my bones as soon as he saw me in these clothes, but I didn't expect him to literally leave the room, either. I was going for a little sexual tension here and I thought I got that. Right?

I go further into the room and notice his bed is messy and almost covered with files and documents and his computer. He must be working, as always. Maybe I interrupted something and now he's mad at me.

But damn it. When is he not working?

Dean comes out of the bathroom, looking like a man on a mission. "Nothing's wrong with what you're wearing except it shows more than it hides," he almost snaps, before throwing something fluffy and white toward me. "Put this on."

I pull the fabric off my face and realize it's a bathrobe. "What?"

"Put it on."

I look at the bathrobe and then, at him, all rigid and stern. I'm starting to feel a little self-conscious. I tug on the hem of my lacy tank top. "You're acting crazy."

"I'm serious."

I tug at my hem again but then stop. Even though he doesn't like my outfit because clearly, he looks super offended right now, *I* like it. I think it makes me look sexy. So, screw him. Although I know I'll probably agonize over it later in my room, I still hold my ground. "There's nothing wrong with my clothes. It's what I wear when I'm sleeping."

"Are you sleeping right now?"

"Well, no but—"

He tips his chin to the bathrobe in my hand. "So put it on."

Dean's eyebrows are arched and he's got this arrogant and authoritative look on his face. That look messes with my head, I swear. I can't decide if I want to tell him to cut it out or ask him why he doesn't like what I'm wearing. Or—yes, there's a third choice—kiss that soft mouth of his and shock him the fuck out.

As it is, I cross my arms and let the robe fall on the ground. "No. I think you're being stupid."

"I think you're being a little too naked."

"What?"

He grits his teeth, all angry and bothered. "You walked over to my room wearing that."

"Uh, yes . . ."

"Anyone could've seen you in . . ." He trails off, waving his hand in the general direction of me.

"That . . ." I open my mouth and close it before saying, "That would bother you? Someone seeing me like this?"

Dean takes a few seconds to answer and I rub my foot against the calf of my other leg. His angry eyes are making my skin buzz with an odd electricity.

"Yes," he replies at last, and something about his reluctant agreement makes me feel lighter.

Is he . . . Could he possibly be . . . jealous? Could his strong reaction be explained by jealousy?

"Are you—"

"Put the robe on, Fallon," he says in an impatient tone.

"Why? I'm not outside right now. I'm in your room. And you've seen me in my PJs lots of times."

"That was when you were a kid," he snaps.

I clench my thighs and I notice his gaze dropping to the tops of my bare legs before quickly moving away and up to my face. If I were smart, I'd be scared of how furious and how agitated he seems.

But I'm not smart. I'm in love and even his harsh expression and tight cheekbones can't scare me.

"Oh, so now you admit I'm not a kid anymore. A little too convenient, isn't it?" I prance over to the bed, plop down on it, careful not to touch any of his precious files.

Dean watches me for a few beats, standing in the middle of the room, as if stranded at sea, and he doesn't know what to do about it. "What do you want?"

"I wanted to see if you were sleeping."

"And now that you've seen that I'm clearly not?" he asks with clenched teeth.

I hide my smile at his irritated tone. "You know, I'm not gonna fight with you. It's been ages since we hung out together. And I'm *mature* enough to not waste my time over petty fights."

He watches me some more before sighing and raking his fingers through his hair. "I was working."

"Okay. Well, do you think you could take a little break?" I ask with hope. "Maybe watch a movie with me or something?"

I can see him debating the merits of watching a movie with me. Actually, the merits of watching a movie with a little-too-naked me.

Sighing again, he nods. "Okay, yeah."

I beam at him. "Awesome. Harry Potter? Chamber of Secrets?"

As soon as Dean sits beside me and the movie starts, I crawl over to him and fit myself in the crook of his arm. He turns rigid. I don't even think he's breathing as I lay my face on his strong, warm chest, my body flattening against his side.

Every part of me is touching every part of him and it's heaven. How did I not realize it before? How did it take me so long to come to the conclusion that I love him, that I've always loved him?

I hate that my nearness is making him uncomfortable. I hate that there's this awkwardness between us.

Suddenly, something occurs to me—I have seen my mom do this to my dad. I wrap my arm around him, bringing it up so I can reach his dark hair. I sink my fingers into it and rake my nails along the nape of his neck and his scalp.

"Fallon—"

I knew he'd protest so I cut him off, "Please, Dean. Please let me make you feel good."

"I don't need—"

"You do." I look up and into his eyes. "Please?"

Clenching his jaw, he throws me a small nod and I grin at him.

After that, he lets me play with his hair, massaging the tension in his neck and shoulders away. A few minutes into it, I feel him relaxing. His body goes liquid and I burrow into his chest even more. He even groans.

That intimate sound echoes in my chest. "See? You needed loosening up."

He chuckles. And then, he wraps his own arm around my back and brings me even closer, plastering my soft, malleable body against his hard, unforgiving one. I bite my lip and tighten my muscles to stop a major shiver from rolling through. It feels like my body is awake in all the different ways.

We stay like that for a little bit as the movie plays on his computer. I honestly don't know what's going on. All I know is him and the effect his body is having on me.

"Dean?"

"Hmm?"

"Do you . . . Do you have a girlfriend?"

"What?"

Okay, so, I don't know where that came from. But now it's out there. All the warmth and intimacy of the past half hour vanishes. I reluctantly move away from him and sit up.

I stare at the five-o-clock shadow on his jaw as I ask, "Girlfriend.

Do you have one?"

Someone who plays with your hair. Someone to massage the knots away from your shoulders. Someone you watch movies with.

"Why?"

I shrug and tuck my hair behind my ear. "I just . . . was wondering. Since you never mentioned anyone."

Dean follows my gesture with his eyes. "No."

Oh, thank God.

"Why not?" I ask, casually, trying to hide all the relief I'm feeling.

"I'm busy."

"With work?"

"With cases, yes."

I shake my head at him. "God, you and your work. It's okay to relax once in a while, you know. Go out. Have fun. Meet girls. I—"

I cut myself off because, hello? I don't want him meeting girls. I just want him to let loose a bit.

"I mean, meet people not girls. *People.* Like, you know, don't meet girls. Because you don't know how girls are. Especially, girls in L.A. They're not what you're looking for, trust me. You know? Yeah. Not those girls. Just trust me, Dean. You want a girl who would . . . you know . . ."

"No."

"What?"

"I don't know. A girl who would what?"

Suddenly, I realize his eyes are hooded. Kind of sleepy but not really. More like restrained. Similar to his body. His back is against the headboard, his legs straight and almost sprawled like they were in the car.

Even relaxed and lazy, Dean looks intimidating. Authoritative. Sexy.

Everything that's lethal to me, my heart. My love and my lust. I'm hypersensitive, tight in my skin and bursting at the seams. And all I want is for him to kiss me. Kiss this tightness, this ache away.

"Girl who would what, Fallon?" he asks again, lazily, like he has all the time in the world to stare at me, to pin me down with one look.

"Uh, a girl who would . . ." I lick my lip, feeling a tug in my lower belly, and he lowers his gaze to my mouth. "A—A girl who'd do anything for you."

"Anything, huh?"

"Yes."

"Like what?"

"Like . . ." I fist the bedsheet and try to ground myself in the moment, and not completely drown in his eyes or drown in this heavy, thick feeling. "Anything to just be close to you. Just to . . . just to be able to touch you. To smell you. Anything to look into your eyes when you smile, because they shine. A girl who'd do anything to be able to say to you that she l—loves you."

Love.

Gosh, I used the L word, didn't I? I fucking used the L word when I don't even know if he feels the same way.

Great going, Fallon.

Worse, he isn't saying anything. He's simply watching me.

I wring my hands together, breaking his gaze. Maybe it was too soon. I mean, we just reconnected. Maybe I should give it a few more days before I get to the main part. Namely, telling him I'm that girl. The girl who would do anything for him.

"I didn't mean l-love —"

"You don't have to worry about me meeting a girl, Tiny," he cuts me off.

"I—I don't?"

"No. Because I'm not interested in girls. They're a little too young for me. I'd rather be with a woman."

CHAPTER FOUR

Fallon

He's talking to her, the waitress.

I guess, you could call her a woman. She's tall and busty. Her face is made up and her blonde hair's shiny. She's wearing her uniform, a pair of black shorts and a white t-shirt. But even then, she's got a type of body that suggests she'll look good in a nice, sophisticated dress, as well. So basically, the complete opposite of my sneakers, Harry Potter t-shirts, and messy buns.

Ever since Dean said he likes women, not little girls, I've been a little pissed at him. We drove from Salt Lake City to Cheyenne in more or less complete silence. He let me pick the music and I had half a mind to force him to listen to Lana Del Ray. But I didn't. Because I'm mature enough not to.

We're three days into our journey, and the easy silences and comfortable conversation from day one have vanished. We've just reached Des Moines, Iowa. The land of corn and broad fields. Although, you can't see that right now because it's winter and everything is bare and frosty.

Kind of like my heart because he's talking—*flirting*—with a waitress.

I just came out of my room and was planning to ask him out to dinner. I even put on a nice pink dress to look more like a grown up. Although, I'm not liking the length of it. It barely drops down to my mid-thigh.

Anyway, I figured we could go eat at a decent place and we can get back to being friends. And I can get back to convincing him we belong together. I've already wasted a lot of time being pissed.

But it's not gonna happen. He's super engrossed in his conversation with the waitress, and that pisses me off so much I can barely handle it. She has her notepad out but instead of writing on it, she's laughing at what he's saying like he's the most hilarious guy ever.

A moment later, Dean laughs as well and I'm done. I can't take it.

He used to laugh with me like that. Before. Way before he left for L.A., and I didn't know the meaning of the things I felt for him. Now, it's too painful. He has hardly smiled since we started this road trip.

I whirl around, getting out of the dining area and follow the hallway back to where our rooms are located. I stumble along the way but there's no one to save me except the colorless wall I clash with and somehow, I manage to stay upright.

I have no idea how long I've been inside my room, trying not to cry but crying anyway, when a knock sounds. It's loud and confident. It can only belong to one person.

"Fallon," Dean calls out, confirming my guess. "You in there?"

Sighing, I wipe stray tears off my cheeks and get up to open the door to reveal an angry Dean.

"What's going on? I thought you said you were going to be down soon. I ordered for you," he says, all irritated and pissed off.

"Did you?" I can't stop myself from saying.

Was that what he was doing, just ordering? Oh please.

"What?"

I let go of the death grip on the door and sigh. "Nothing. I'm just not—"

"Are you crying?"

Damn it.

I move away from the door, hiding my face from him. "No."

"Why are you crying? What's wrong?"

"I'm fine. I'm not hungry though. So, you should go eat."

Turning away from him, I walk to the bathroom or at least, try to. But Dean grabs my hand, his fingers circling around my wrist. His touch is so hot I forget to breathe. I forget to do anything but feel his grip on my hand.

"What's going on, Fallon?" he asks, his chest awfully close to my back. To my trembling back, actually. Because I can't contain the things inside of me anymore. I can't take his nearness, his voice, his *smell* and be unaffected.

I face him, my eyes stinging with miserable tears. I compare how Dean looks now—tensed, concerned, his jaw tight—with how he looked with that waitress, carefree, laughing. Happy.

"You were flirting with her," I whisper.

"With who?"

"The waitress."

I'm met with silence and I don't know if he's heard me. In his defense, I did say it very softly. I was embarrassed. I *am* embarrassed. I don't do jealousy; I never have. Well, apparently not until him.

At last, Dean lets go of my wrist and draws away from me. The earlier tightness of his frame has nothing on how he looks now, aloof and cold.

"So?"

Like me, he speaks softly but I flinch all the same. His casually-asked question hits me somewhere deep in my gut. My soul, even.

"So . . ." I fist my hands before admitting, "I didn't like that. In fact, I hated it."

A pulse runs through his face. "Why?"

"Are you really asking me that?"

"Yes. Because from where I'm standing it doesn't look like it's any of your business who I flirt with."

Anger bubbles up inside me. Anger and something very close to despair. So far, I've been holding onto the hope maybe Dean feels the same for me. Maybe he hasn't realized it yet. It took me years as well, to come to the conclusion that I love him. So, I can't really blame him for his ignorance.

But maybe I was deluding myself. Even so, I can't stop the words coming out of my mouth.

"Not my business?"

"Yes."

"God, you're so . . ." I grit my teeth and practically vibrate with fury while he appears to be unruffled, watching me with a blank face. "You're such an idiot. I love you, Dean. I'm in love with you. Don't you know that? I've been in love with you all my life."

My words sound like a gunshot. An explosion, even. They are probably louder than any other words I've spoken in my entire life. They have rattled me, quickened my breaths, my heartbeats. But apparently, they have had no effect whatsoever on this man in front of me.

"No, you don't," he says, a dangerous, angry glint in his eyes.

I'm not afraid of it, though. I'm not afraid of the danger lurking in his gaze. All my secrets are out. I'm exposed. I've got nothing to fear or lose.

"What?"

"You don't love me."

"Wh . . . What the hell are you talking about?"

"You don't love me," he repeats, though this time his mouth seems pinched. "You *think* you love me. There's a difference."

"Oh yeah? Why don't you enlighten me? Tell me about this difference."

Contrary to the ruckus inside my body, I sound so calm to my ears. So put together, like I'm not falling apart with every second he simply stands there, looking like none of this matters to him. Like, I don't matter to him.

He sighs impatiently and runs his fingers through his gorgeous hair—typical Dean. The hair I was playing with the other night when we were watching a movie. The night he told me he's into women, not little girls.

"I've always been there, Fallon," he begins, almost lashes out like it's a bad thing.

"What?"

"I've always been there for you. With you. I've been there for every one of your scrapes and tantrums and achievements. Every single thing. I was there when you first got bullied in school. I was there when you kicked those bullies' asses. I was there when you failed math in third grade. I was the one who tutored you after that. Helped you with homework the rest of the year. I was there when you started high school. I drove you to school because you wouldn't go with anyone else. I've been there. Always. I've been the one you turn to for everything. So, what you feel for me, Fallon," he takes a deep breath and says slowly, like explaining it to a child, "is not love. It might be a strong affection. Infatuation. Which will probably go away when you meet the right guy. So yeah, there's the difference. You think you love me because you don't know what love is yet."

"I don't know what love is yet?"

His jaw clenches. "No. Because believe it or not, you're still young."

"So young people don't know what love is? Is that what you're saying?"

"What I'm saying is that it's ridiculous. The thought of you and me together."

I swallow. Once, twice, *thrice*. Four times.

"Ridiculous," I choke out the words. "Right. Thanks so much, Dean. Thanks for educating me. For telling me that the thought of us being together is *ridiculous*. And what I feel for you is not love. Thanks a lot." I nod and keep going against the expanding heart in my chest.

It's pressing on my throat, stealing away my voice but I don't care. Either I talk or I break down. And I refuse to break down in front of this . . . this heartless man who I thought was my friend.

"I'm so dumb, right? That I can't figure it out for myself. I can't figure my own feelings out. I can't understand why my heart races when you're close. Why I can't see anyone else but you. I can't understand why the hell I can't stop dreaming about you at night. I'm too dumb to figure out why I couldn't get out of bed for days when you left. Why everything lost its meaning when you weren't there. Why laughing was hard, harder than it usually is for me. And even now, after moving across the country for you, to be close to you, why it hurts when you hang up on me or when you refuse to see me. I'm too dumb to understand why, despite being mad at you for ignoring me, I can't stop myself from worrying about you. About how all you ever do is work, how you've distanced yourself from everyone. Of course, I can't understand any of that, can I? Because I'm just so fucking dumb."

"Language. Watch it," he grits his teeth, somehow angrier than before. Livid, even.

"I'm not a fucking kid," I almost shriek. "Do *you* understand that, Dean? I just told you I moved across the country for you. That I uprooted my life so I could be close to you, and this is what you say to me?" I shake my head and cross my arms, hugging myself, protecting myself against him. "Just because you're older doesn't mean you get to boss me around like you're my dad."

I take a step back when he closes the distance between us. All I can see is the wide expanse of his carved chest, his massive shoulders in the crisp white shirt. My breath hitches when he bends down to look me in the eyes. Like a pathetic fool, I admire his long, curled lashes. Instead of turning away from him, I breathe deep, so I can capture his citrusy smell, like I'll never get to do that again. I probably won't.

"And just because you wear dresses that barely cover your ass, doesn't mean you get to throw tantrums like a little girl."

God.

God. He makes me so mad.

"You know what? Get out of my room."

"Happily." He straightens up. "I want you out there, at the table. In five minutes. Don't keep me waiting."

CHAPTER FIVE

Dean

Fifteen years ago, a girl asked me to marry her.

I was seventeen and she was three. It was a joke. A story you tell over Christmas dinners or at family gatherings. A story you laugh over for some time and move on. I'm very well aware of that.

I've always been aware of that.

But for some strange reason, I haven't been able to forget it. I haven't been able to forget the hope shining in her eyes or the way her face crumpled when I told her she'd feel differently when she grew up. We bet on it, by hooking our pinkies together. And then, she ran away because someone called her name and waved a gift wrapped in pink glitter paper. It was her birthday and Fallon loves pink.

For some strange reason, I don't tell this story to anyone. I don't share it over a meal or laugh at it like I thought I would. Or I should.

I keep it close to my chest like it means something. Like, it was real. A three-year-old girl proposing to a seventeen-year-old boy.

I'm sick; I'm aware of that as well.

I call myself that every day. Every minute of every day, in fact. Especially when I hear her voice over the phone and heat grips every part of my body. It wraps itself around my limbs and doesn't let go. Thoughts—wrong thoughts—and longings surface in my brain, my gut. My fucking heart.

Avoidance and throwing myself into my work is the only key when it comes to Fallon and the things I feel for her.

It started as a strange protective instinct. I couldn't see her sad. I couldn't see her battle the bad days. It hurt something inside my chest when she'd come home crying from school. Saying she didn't want to go. Saying she had no friends because it was so hard to keep up with them.

As she grew up, that protective instinct grew with her. But

along the way, it took on an edgier turn. It became possessiveness. It became the need to hide her from the world and keep her for myself. Keep her smiles, her laughter, her heart for myself.

Nobody has made me feel even close to how Fallon does. Nobody has inspired my heart to beat or my soul to fucking sing, for lack of a better word.

She's the one. An eighteen-year-old, slip of a girl with silver hair and gray eyes.

And I can't stop staring at her.

We're in Ann Arbor, Michigan, and we've stopped for the night at a hotel. Tomorrow we'll reach New York and that's for the best. I can't take it anymore. I can't take us traveling together.

The moment she came up with the idea of a road trip, I knew it was going to be a disaster on my sanity. I imagined her in the seat beside me, the leather sticking to her soft, pale thighs. Her shifting, adjusting herself. Her sighs, her smell.

I imagined the long, torturous hours of her being close enough to touch but not being able to.

What I didn't imagine were her glares. Her silent treatment after what happened between us in Des Moines. I didn't imagine forgetting all the reasons I've accumulated over the years for us to not be together.

I didn't imagine her saying those words to me.

I love you, Dean. I'm in love with you. Don't you know that? I've been in love with you all my life.

Fallon's across the room, at a table different than the one I picked for us. She's too pissed to sit with me at dinner. I know I should apologize, but I think it's for the best.

Or it would've been if not for the douchebag talking to her.

Fury explodes in my gut when I see him leaning toward her. She arches her neck to listen to what he has to say. He looks like an asshole with low-slung jeans and spiked hair with too much gel.

I've got no idea why she's talking to this fuckface. Can't she tell he's an asshole?

Jesus. She always needs to be looked after, doesn't she?

But then I remind myself that technically, Fallon's an adult. She can do whatever she wants.

It's none of my business. Just as it's none of her business who I talk to. I know after my shitty response, I have no right to feel this absurd jealousy.

But I do feel it.

And when he leans in further and reaches out to touch her, I spring up from my seat. This isn't happening. Not on my watch. Not ever.

She loves me, you fucking asshole.

I stride across the room, grab hold of his collar and yank him away from her. Fallon gasps but I pay her no attention. Looking into the startled face of the guy, I grit out the words, "Take a hike."

He looks like he wants to protest but the look in my eyes—probably, something similar to murder—scares him away. As soon as I turn around to face Fallon, I'm met with a tiny firecracker, glaring and almost spitting out fire.

Sometimes I can't believe Fallon is all grown up. Fierce and beautiful. Fucking breathtaking.

"What the hell are you doing?" she snaps and the heat that blankets me every time I talk to her, look at her, even *think* of her, grabs hold of me now.

I hide it with anger. "Saving you."

"What?"

"He was talking to your chest."

She looks down at her chest and despite cursing myself in my head, my gaze follows hers. She's wearing a tank top with a quote from her favorite book series, Harry Potter. But like a pervert, I'm more interested in the soft-looking, smooth slope of her cleavage.

I grit my teeth angrily.

"Yes. Because I spilled something."

That's when I look at a mustard colored stain on her top. Even though it should calm my agitation, it doesn't.

"Well, it's none of his business if you spilled something," I grumble.

Frowning, she purses her lips. "Not everyone is a jerk like you, okay? Some people like to help."

"He was only helping you because he wanted something from you."

"Yes. A thank you. But how dare he, right?"

"Yeah, a thank you. But there's a lot of ways to get that," I growl, leaning toward her like that asshole was doing not a minute ago. Don't know what that says about me.

Actually, I do know what it says about me. I'm an asshole too. Because I can't stop staring at her lips. I can't stop thinking about how they'll taste, how soft they will be.

"You've lost your mind," she snaps again, breaking my thoughts.

"And you need to use yours. Because men only want one thing, Fallon. And it's not just a verbal thank you."

Men like me. Men who belong in prison for harboring such thoughts about someone so young. Men I've prosecuted myself.

How am I different from them?

So far, we've been standing at a respectable distance from each other. But Fallon moves closer. She looks up at me with a mutinous expression.

"Contrary to your belief, Dean, I do know what guys want. I'm not an idiot. And maybe I'll go give it to him. At least, he'll know how to treat me like a grown up."

She pushes me away, and I'm so startled, that she's successful in shoving me out of her way and storming out.

I take a couple of deep breaths, trying to calm myself. Calm the jealousy inside me that she's just flared to life. Once before I've felt this way, this out of control, and I hate it.

But as I watch her walk away, I realize there's no stopping it.

I leave the restaurant in her wake and catch up to her just as she's about to enter her room. Following her inside, I shut the door with a massive thud.

"What the fuck?"

"Language."

She shakes her head, sending her soft silver hair swaying

around her shoulders. "If you don't stop that, I'm gonna kill you. And I'm not kidding. Now, get the fuck out of my room."

"If you don't stop cursing, I'm going to wash your mouth out. And not with soap."

As soon as I say it, I pinch the bridge of my nose.

Fucking hell.

I did *not* mean to say that. Now, visions of things I could do to her pretty pink mouth won't stop bombarding me.

Fallon looks dumbstruck, as she should. I've never talked to her this way. I've always—even when it bordered on pain—tried to remember she's young. Far younger than me.

Not to mention, she's the daughter of the man who saved me when I needed it the most. I probably owe Fallon's father my entire life, my entire career. He took me in when my own dad didn't care about me and Mia.

"God, I never knew you were such an asshole, Dean," Fallon says.

Her face reflects heartbreak and despite all the promises I've made—I keep on making—I approach her. I try to find words to comfort her, to apologize for being such a jerk. I go so far as to circle her delicate wrist even though she protests.

But as soon as I touch her, all I can think about is touching her even more. Touching her in places where I'm not allowed to, and that only fans my aggression.

"Well, now you do," I growl, smelling her sweet strawberry smell.

Fallon loves strawberries. When she was little, she'd steal all my strawberries and give me oranges in return. I didn't mind her stealing, but she'd say, *my mommy says if I steal something from someone, I need to give them back something, too. It's only fair.*

Your mom teaches you about stealing, Tiny?

She'd grin, shaking her head and popping strawberries in her mouth. *Nah, I made that up. I just don't like oranges. You need to make them your favorite, okay? So I can steal from you.*

"Let go of me."

"No."

I tighten my grip and her fist connects with my chest, probably trying to push me away once again. But her effort is half-hearted.

When she glares at me for not budging, I wind my other arm around her waist, uncaring of the consequences. Uncaring of the fact that somehow, I'm betraying Simon, Fallon's dad. Uncaring that maybe I'm similar to those men who I put away for preying on the innocent. Uncaring that if a man like me, much older, jaded and more cynical, tried something like this with my sister, I'd kill him with my bare hands.

Uncaring of everything but her.

We've ended up in an embrace somehow, when that wasn't my intention at all. Fallon's glare has turned into a wide-eyed look and I know I won't be able to let her go.

"Stop looking at me like that," I rumble.

"Like what?" she whispers, panting, her chest almost touching mine, her eyes darken, clouded with desire.

Despite myself, I close that slice of a distance between us, until her soft body is touching mine. "I'm not going to kiss you, Fallon."

Her breaths escalate, and her eyes drop down to my mouth. "Good. Because I don't want you to."

I study the curve of her parted lips. "Liar."

She pushes against me, but again, it's half-hearted. "I don't want you or your mouth anywhere near me. Okay?"

My arm around her waist flexes. "I don't think you mean that."

"I can't stand you right now."

"I don't think you mean that either."

She growls, fisting my shirt, shaking me. "I hate you, Dean."

"Good," I grit out, still studying her lips before looking into her eyes. "Because you don't fucking know what love is."

"You're such an asshole. Just go away and leave me alone."

"I did."

"What?"

"You want to know what love is, Fallon?" I growl. "Let me tell you what love is. It's a burn. An explosion. It's like I'm exploding every second of every day. With the need, this fucking urge to see you. To touch you. To kiss you. Even though I know I can't. I can't do it because it's wrong. But it doesn't matter because that burn, that ache? It never goes away. In fact, instead of going away, it only grows bigger and bigger. And fucking bigger. To the point where all I can think about is you. All I can think about is destroying every single thing, every single reason, every single person who's trying to keep me apart from you. Love is watching you go to prom with your douchebag of a boyfriend and going so crazy, so fucking insane with jealousy, I cornered that sixteen-year-old boy and threatened him to stay away from you. That's what love is, Fallon."

I want to keep going but I don't think I can. I don't think I should even be touching her after confessing how petty, how small I've become in her love. But I can't seem to let her go, either.

Seconds pass as she studies me and then in a soft voice, she asks, "Y—You told Brad to stay away from me?"

"Yes."

"Is that why he backed out of our date just an hour into prom? Because you threatened him?"

Regret burns every inch of me. It was my lowest moment, threatening a sixteen-year-old boy because I was in love with his girlfriend. But I couldn't take it. I couldn't see Fallon wearing a girly, pink dress, all made-up and stunning, going on a date with someone who didn't deserve her. Not that I did, either. But I couldn't . . . stop. I didn't know how to stop.

"Yes," I repeat.

"I—I didn't know. I didn't know you threatened him . . ." She swallows, looking at me with new eyes.

She'll probably hate me now. Probably regret her confession from last night.

"I cried when he just left me there. I called you to come get me," she continues, as if remembering that night. "I kept crying in your arms. I thought there was something wrong with me."

I want to hang my head, drop down to my knees and ask for her forgiveness. But I pull up whatever strength I have and keep holding onto her.

"There's nothing wrong with you," I tell her with as much love as I can muster, as much anger as I can muster on her behalf. "He didn't deserve you."

No one deserves my Fallon, least of all me. When I said she inspires me, I wasn't lying. I've seen her at her lowest and I've seen her pull herself out of it, too. Her strength, her will to fight keeps me going, gives *me* the will to fight, to be better.

"What about you? Do you deserve me?"

A short laugh bursts out of me at her question. "Fuck, no. That's why I moved away. Because I'm so crazy in love with you I threatened a high school boy just because he was your prom date."

She grips my shirt harder. "Y-you are in love with me?"

My heart thuds loudly in my chest. "It doesn't matter. It's wrong."

So far I've been pushing my body over hers, trying to consume her like she consumes me. But now, she's pushing back. She's molding her body against mine. "What's so wrong about it?"

"I'm too old for you."

"So?"

"I don't have time for love. I have my job. My cases. I can't ignore them."

"I'm not asking you to."

"One day you're going to find someone your own age, someone who isn't jaded, a workaholic, control freak like me and you'll . . ."

"I'll what?"

A pressure forms in the vicinity of my heart as I say. "You won't love me anymore."

She lets go of my shirt and snakes her arms up and around my neck. Her fingers sink into my hair and I almost groan out loud. I don't know where she learned to do that, play with my hair like that and rake her nails up and down my scalp, but Jesus Christ, it relaxes me and makes me hard at the same time.

"Maybe," she whispers. "And maybe one day, I'll have a major depressive episode like my mom did. Maybe my meds won't work for me anymore. Maybe I'll try to . . . to end my life. And then, you'll leave me because I have epic issues."

I bow my head, taking up all her personal space. "I'll never leave you. Do you hear me, Fallon? Not a chance in this lifetime."

"That's what I'm asking for, Dean." She smiles slightly.

"What?"

"A chance. To be together. To love each other. There are a million things that could go wrong but I don't want them to stop us. I don't want anything to stop us from trying to be together. Maybe we're the exception, you know? Maybe we're the miracle, you and me."

"You and me, huh?"

Blinking her teary eyes, she nods. "Yes. Be my miracle, Dean. And let me be yours. Please?"

Nothing matters when Fallon is looking at me with wide, almost silver eyes. When I'm breathing the same air as her. When all I want to do is cover her with my body and protect her from everything bad out there, even her own mind.

It doesn't matter how many ways this can go wrong and how different we are from each other. I'm too old for her and her dad will probably never agree to us being together.

None of it matters because my love for her is stronger, unstoppable. I've tried purging it, but that hasn't worked.

Perhaps, I should try embracing it and see where it goes. Maybe I should try to be her miracle and let her be mine. Because the alternative—a life without her—hasn't worked me.

"Dean?"

Swallowing, I whisper, "I love you," before I cover her mouth with mine.

CHAPTER SIX

Fallon

Is this real?
Is this really happening? Is Dean really kissing me?
Oh God, please let this be real.
His mouth is warm and wet. And thorough. I feel it everywhere. In each and every part of my body. In my toes, even.

I've been kissed before. Brad, my high school boyfriend, kissed me a few times but that was nothing compared to this. This epic consuming of my mouth by another human being. It's like his kiss is my entire world.

If Dean stops kissing me, I'll die. I'll burn.

It's like he told me. Love is a burn. It's an explosion and with his mouth, his tongue, his teeth, his *taste*—citrusy and masculine—the way he's holding me, all tight and almost aggressively, he's showing me that.

I kiss him back with all the pent-up emotions of the past two years. I've been dreaming about this ever since he left me at the airport and said goodbye. I've pictured his lips over mine countless times.

But I didn't imagine this. I didn't even know how to imagine this.

His grip in my hair, my breasts flattened against his wildly breathing chest. His mouth slamming into mine as he groans like he's dying. His hot skin, soft hair and rough mouth.

When we break apart for air, my hands are tugging at the shirt at his shoulder and one of my legs is wrapped around his hips.

"I—I've wanted to kiss you for a long time," I admit to his glistening lips.

"Not as long as I have," he says.

I creep my hand up and tug at his hair. "I should be mad at you."

He swallows. "Yeah."

"I can't believe you scared away my date, Dean. And then, you just . . . left."

I should be angrier about this. Him threatening away my boyfriend—though, later I realized I didn't love him anyway—and up and leaving for California a month later. Not to mention, the things he said to me last night when I told him I loved him. But weirdly, anger is the last thing on my mind.

"I hated myself for doing what I did. I still do."

I raise my eyebrows. "For threatening a perfectly nice guy?"

He squeezes my waist, making me feel the sculpted slabs of his body. "For loving you a little too much."

I bite my lip to hide my smile. I can't stay mad at him for saying these things to me and looking so tortured about it. Maybe I'm a sucker, but, whatever.

I reach up and kiss the side of his pulsing jaw—something I've been dying to do ever since I saw him standing across from my dorm room four days ago. "How are you gonna make it up to me?"

He narrows his warm brown eyes at me. "What do you mean?"

My thigh clenches around his hip as I arch my back against him. "You ruined my prom, Dean. No fair."

"What did you want to do at your prom?"

"Dance, for one thing."

"I can put on some music."

I shake my head and kiss his jaw again. The bristles of his five-o-clock shadow taste so delicious on my tongue. "I was gonna lose my virginity, too."

"I'm glad I ruined it, then," he says with gritted teeth.

Smiling, I trace his harsh cheekbones and angled jaw with my hand. "Me too. Because I want you to take it." He goes to protest, if grabbing a fistful of my butt through my shorts is anything to go by, but I put a finger on his lips. "I know what your answer's gonna be. Because you think you know everything and I'm this innocent flower who has no idea what's going on in the world. But I do know things, Dean. I do know what I want, and I want you. I've been waiting for you forever. In fact, if you hadn't gone away, we'd be together right now. Instead of scaring away my date like an idiot, if you'd said something, we would've done it ages ago. So, it's only fair you make it up to me now."

Dean takes my hand off his mouth. "We wouldn't have done it ages ago. You weren't *legal* ages ago."

I wave my hand. "Minor detail. The point is . . ."

"What's the point?"

"The point is I love you, Dean. And you love me, and we've wasted enough time already. So, are you gonna give me my prom or not?"

"Fallon —"

"Besides I've heard it hurts, losing your virginity. And I know if you take it, it won't hurt."

I've never seen him look harsher than this. The room is flooded with light but strangely, Dean appears all dark and made of shadows. His eyes have turned black and his high, king-like cheekbones have a flush to them.

He's hard and barely breathing as he looks down at me. "And why's that?"

Maybe it's the way we're standing—my leg draped over his hip and our lower bodies intimately flushed together—but I feel his other hardness too. His dick at the juncture of my thighs.

"Because you'll take care of me."

"Is that right?"

I move against him, against *it*. "Yup. Because you always do."

He watches me for a few beats before looking up at the ceiling and shaking his head. Then, he grabs hold of my waist and halts my movements.

Pinning me with his eyes once again, he growls, "Stop tempting me, Tiny."

"I will, if you agree."

"I'll burn in hell for this."

I cock my head to the side and smirk, "I thought you were already burning. Exploding."

"Fallon," he warns.

His reluctance is weak, weaker than his desire to claim me; I can see it in his eyes. And it makes me bolder, shameless. "I'm burning too, Dean. I swear. It hurts, you know. I've been hurting ever since you went away and every night, I dream of you coming back and kissing me. Touching me where I hurt. In my—" I lower my voice and whisper the word I've only thought about in the dead of night "—p-pussy."

I don't even have time to catch my breath after that. Dean hauls me up, causing both my thighs to clench around his hips and he claims my mouth in a kiss. And then, we're moving. He's taking me somewhere, but I don't care about that. As earlier, his kiss becomes my entire world.

Until that world tilts on its axis and I'm lying flat on my back. I feel the softness of the mattress and the ceiling fills my vision, as Dean kneels before me, settling himself between my spread thighs.

From my position, Dean looks huge, larger than the sky. I should feel vulnerable or maybe even, shy. We're getting ready to have sex, aren't we? But I don't. Not even when he makes quick work of our clothes, and we're both naked in about three seconds.

I'm more interested in watching him. His broad, corded muscles. Grooves and dips of his body. Light scattering of dark hair on his chest.

Dean's eyes are scorching as he takes in my small body, and I writhe on the bed, willing him to do something . . . anything.

"Do you hurt, Tiny?" he whispers, his fingers trailing from the top of my chest, through the valley of my breasts to my trembling stomach.

"Yes."

"Where? Show me."

A flush overcomes me, but I'm determined to not let it deter me. I've waited long enough for this moment.

My hand shivers as I reach down and touch my most intimate part, making my hips jerk. It's not that I haven't touched myself. It's just I haven't done it in front of someone.

I touch my slick core. Gosh, it's so slick, so swollen. My fingers slip over the wetness. Under his intense stare, my pussy gushes. Again, I should feel shy but I don't. In fact, I can't stop touching myself. I can't stop watching for his reactions, either.

His chest is heaving. The muscles of his thighs and his stomach are flexing. Not to mention, his dick. His dick is throbbing. I've been avoiding looking at it because I don't wanna be afraid. On my stomach, through the layers of our clothes, his cock felt enormous. But I can't stop staring at it now.

It *is* enormous and dark, and the more I touch my pussy, the more I think it's never gonna fit. But then again, doesn't every girl think that? I mean, hello? It always fits.

A second later, I can't think about anything but Dean. Because growling, he falls onto me. Onto my pussy. His warm mouth envelops my entire core and even my fingers.

"Dean . . ." I moan, my hips going crazy, my legs shaking with sensations.

Dean splays his palms on my thighs and keeps them spread open. He sucks on my fingers, drinking down all my juices before focusing on my pussy. My hands go to his shoulders as I try to hold on against the waves of lust that rack my entire frame.

I've never felt this way, like, ever. This unmoored and this overcome. The pulses of lust fire from somewhere deep inside my stomach in all directions, making my heart race, making my toes curl.

But apparently, that's not enough. Dean lets go of my pussy and kisses and nips my thighs, my stomach. He keeps stimulating my clit with his fingers as he crawls up my body, sucking the flesh along the way. His mouth closes over my nipple and I lose it.

Arching my back and screwing my eyes shut, I scream out his name and come.

I come and come like never before, and it feels like it won't stop. My body won't stop coming or jerking or twisting. I won't ever stop feeling the rush of my orgasm.

My eyes fall open to find Dean hovering over my body. His hair's a mess and his lips are shiny with my juices. I'm so replete I don't have it in me to even blush.

"You know what you taste like, Tiny?" he whispers, settling himself between my legs.

The head of his dick touches my fluttering pussy and I dig my nails in his biceps. "What?"

Smirking, he tells me, "Horny."

"Shut up," I mutter.

"You were horny for me, weren't you, Tiny?"

"N—No."

He kisses me. "You were." He nudges my opening with his big cock, stretching me out slightly. "You are."

Without my volition, my back bows and he slides in a little deeper. We both hiss. There's a weird pressure in my pelvis. It makes me want him more even though I know it's gonna hurt.

"You are, too," I whisper.

He licks his lips, staying still inside me. "Yeah, I am."

I rub his shoulders with my palm, feeling his hot skin. "You're burning up."

"That too."

I open my mouth to say something but can't because I feel Dean playing with my clit once again. He bends down and sucks on the side of my neck, just under my ear. Who knew that was my sweet spot? I throw my head back and moan loudly, my legs going up and cinching around his waist.

He growls into my skin when my pussy flutters over the head of his dick. I can feel it shivering, juicing up.

I realize he's making it easier for me to accept him inside my body. The realization makes me fall in love with him even more.

"Y—you're taking care of me," I whisper, rubbing my cheek in his hair, feeling his thumb on my clit, his teeth on my neck.

Dean looks up, his eyes intense and full of what I feel for him in every corner of my heart. Love. "Always."

"I love you, Dean."

"I love you too, Fallon."

He kisses me then, and I lose all my words. I lose myself. In him, in his mouth, in his body that's moving in a slow, smooth rhythm inside me. I don't feel pressure or pain when he thrusts deep, taking away my virginity in one stroke.

All I feel is my love for him. My lust and hunger and this urge to make him mine forever and ever.

Dean feels the same, I think. He can't stop touching me, running his hands up and down my body. He can't stop kissing me, either. I give as good as I get. I touch him, play with his hair, rake my nails down his sweaty back.

It's the most wonderful feeling in the world, being connected to him like this. My best friend. My soulmate. The love of my life.

Dean's strokes become faster, more urgent. They shake my entire body, making me moan into his mouth. I feel my climax building and building, deep in my lower belly.

The moment Dean circles his arms around my back and hugs me to his chest like he needs me, needs my skin to breathe, it washes over me.

My second orgasm is even more intense, more charged up. I'm moaning, shaking constantly, massaging his dick with my pulsating channel. It triggers Dean's climax and he whips his cock out, spilling his cum over my stomach. It's hot and thick and smells like all my lustful dreams put together.

We breathe into each other's mouths, kissing lazily, trying to slow down our hearts. Although, I don't think that's happening any time soon. Our hearts are probably not going to relax for a long while, especially, if sex is going to be like this every time.

Dean stops kissing me and I open my eyes to find him watching me. "What?"

He traces a finger over the apple of my cheek. "You're fucking stunning."

I blush. "You are too."

He chuckles and presses a kiss on my nose. I smile at his tender gesture.

"Mom always knew," I tell him.

"What?"

"My mom. She always knew that I loved you and that you loved me."

Dean goes rigid over me. Rigid and frowny. It's like I'm hugging a mountain with my thighs and arms. "I'll handle your dad."

"Uh, no. We'll handle him. Together."

"Fallon, you're—"

I put my finger on his soft mouth and squeeze his waist with my legs. "Oh, were you going to say something like . . ." I deepen my voice to mimic his. "Fallon, you don't know how to do these things. Because you're just so young and naïve." Rolling my eyes, I say, "You know what, maybe you were right. Maybe I should've gone with a guy my age. At least, he wouldn't be so bossy."

Dean's eyes flare and he removes my finger from his mouth. "Maybe you shouldn't talk about other guys when my dick is this close to your pussy."

I feel him getting hard and grazing my still-wet core. "You're bad, Dean."

Smirking, Dean rubs our noses together. "You're no saint, Fallon. You seduced me."

"I did, didn't I?"

The look in his eyes changes, becomes grave as he declares, "I love you."

"I love you too."

As he enters me once again, I close my eyes and smile. I think of something my mom always said to me when I was a kid and didn't know why some days were sad for me. And why, on those days, I felt like crying or sleeping.

She always forced me to get up, to keep going. She told me I was a fighter. That if I didn't face the day, I'd miss out on so many things, so many possibilities. She told me I was born with more than blood in my veins. I was born with strength.

She was right.

But I was also born with something else. I was born with love.

Love for this man.

I was born with love for Dean and now that I have him in my arms, I'll never let him go.

♪

ABOUT THE AUTHOR

Saffron A. Kent is a Top 100 Amazon Bestselling author of Contemporary and New Adult romance. More often than not, her love stories are edgy, forbidden and passionate. Her work has been featured in *Huffington Post, New York Daily News* and *USA Today's* Happy Ever After.

She lives in New York City with her nerdy and supportive husband, and a million and one books.

More info available at: www.saffronkent.com

Say It First

NIKKI SLOANE

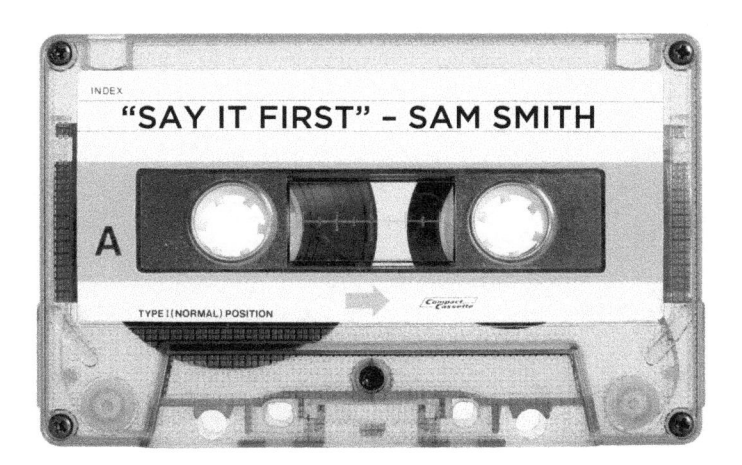

"SAY IT FIRST" – SAM SMITH

CHAPTER ONE

Anna

I left my agent's office with an assignment—choose my next role, so he could give both studios an answer tomorrow.

Anxiety poured into my stomach as I rode the elevator down to the lobby. My last movie had opened big, but I was still at a precarious stage in my career. If I didn't line up a good project, I'd risk fading into obscurity, and taking a wrong step wasn't an option.

A distracting Facebook notification leaped onto the lock screen of my phone. Someone had mentioned me, Annalise Shrader, in a comment. Which was strange. I'd been going by Anna Douglas ever since I moved to LA, and it was weird seeing my OG name.

My profile was set to private, and I didn't post—it was only to keep up with my relatives and stay connected. So who was this Samantha Hidenrite who'd tagged me?

I pulled the app open as I strolled off the elevator and headed for the exit, only to slow to a stop. Her profile picture, even as the small icon, was familiar, and the group where she'd posted her comment made it click into place.

Philpot High School - Class of '09, the banner across the top read.

Samantha Hidenrite—Sam Richards as I'd known her ten years ago—had added me to the Facebook group last week. She was organizing our high school reunion, which wasn't surprising. In school, she'd been homecoming queen, a cheerleader, and a classic overachiever. We weren't friends back then. Like the rest of my classmates, she'd looked down on me as a drama club freak.

Why the hell were we Facebook friends now? She must have requested me at some point, and I'd accepted. My mother would say it was because I was too nice, but it was entirely possible I'd done it out of pettiness. The industry was hardening me up.

I scrolled to the post and then her comment.

Samantha Hidenrite Still haven't heard from a few of

you. It'd be so awesome if we could get most of the class together! I'm sure **@Annalise** won't come.

Tim Washburn Did Anna say she couldn't?

Samantha Hidenrite I assume. Seems like once she got famous, she forgot we existed. Not like **@Jamie Campbell**.

My grip tightened on the phone. How ironic. She pretended I didn't exist in high school but didn't like it when the roles were reversed. I turned the screen off and pushed my way through the revolving door out into the Los Angeles sun.

I hustled across the sidewalk in a huff, down the street, and into the parking garage. I'd been home to Kentucky plenty of times since I'd started my acting career, but my visits had been less frequent recently. My schedule was a nightmare because I was always working, but that was a good problem to have, wasn't it? Plus, the press tour for my last movie had eaten away any desire to travel.

Right now, I needed to focus on my decision about *The Blindfold Club* project, not be thinking about my ten-year reunion. I hadn't enjoyed my four years at Philpot High School and had no plans to go back.

I climbed into my car, set my phone on the dash holder, and as I stuck my keys in the ignition, a new notification caught my attention.

Jamie Campbell mentioned you in a comment.

There was a strange flutter in my chest. Jamie had always been friendly, but we hadn't been friends. I'd probably spoken to him a handful of times. But everyone in Philpot knew him. Probably all of western Kentucky did. Until last year, he was easily the biggest thing to come out of our sleepy town.

Had I surpassed him in the fame department? It was tough to say. I didn't follow NASCAR, but a lot of people back home did. He was a professional race car driver, and that made him Philpot's favorite son.

Samantha Hidenrite mentioned you in a comment.

I tried to ignore the notifications as I turned my car key. The air conditioner blasted to life, blowing my brunette hair back over my shoulders. Was Jamie's hair still sandy colored? Or had it darkened as he'd gotten older?

Jamie Campbell mentioned you in a comment.

"Okay, what the hell?" I muttered. I snatched the phone up and went to the notifications.

> **Jamie Campbell** Not sure why I got dragged into this, but **@Annalise Vandevere** was in town over Christmas.
>
> **Samantha Hidenrite** I just meant you come back a lot and do stuff for the community. **@Annalise** doesn't. She acts like she's embarrassed by us. So I'm not going to hold my breath on her showing.
>
> **Jamie Campbell** I'm sure **@Annalise** really wants to come now. Good job, **@Sam**.

He knew I was home over the holidays? I typed out a snarky response to Sam but deleted it. Then I drew in a deep breath and thumbed out a new response.

> **Annalise Schrader** I'm not going to be able to make it work with my schedule, but thanks for thinking of me!

I wondered if she'd understand the passive-aggressive dig. What was her deal? I was by no means ashamed of my hometown. My parents and extended family still lived there.

Jamie Campbell wants to be friends on Facebook.

There it was again. That weird fluttering in my chest, which was ridiculous. He'd been pretty cute ten years ago, but I didn't get star-struck. I'd learned no matter how big a star seemed to shine, they were still just regular humans like the rest of us. If anything, meeting them caused the luster to fade.

I pushed the 'confirm' button without thinking about it.

We'd run in different circles, but I'd never heard anything bad about him. Just a rumor he'd gotten a speeding ticket for taking the Salem Drive challenge—where you drove on the rural road that ran alongside the bypass. The goal was to match the speed of the cars on the freeway.

They said he'd been going eighty and sweet-talked the female cop out of losing his license.

The chat icon lit up.

> **Jamie:** Is it cool I said you were home during Christmas? I realized after I posted you might not want people to know. I can delete.
>
> **Jamie:** Also, hello.
>
> **Me:** Hi! No worries, it's fine.

My trip had been low-key, so I was curious.

> **Me:** How did you know?
>
> **Jamie:** My mom. She does your mom's hair.
>
> **Me:** Oh, that's right!
>
> **Jamie:** Also, what's up with Sam? Was she always like this?
>
> **Me:** No idea. I wasn't cool enough to be friends with her.
>
> **Jamie:** Hey, me neither.

He was being humble. He'd been the epitome of cool.

> **Jamie:** She's messaged me a dozen times about coming. It doesn't rate real high on my priority list. I hated high school.

I tugged my eyebrows together in surprise. I didn't enjoy my time there, but hate was a strong word.

Me: Really?

Jamie: Yeah. Busywork to get ready for college. I wasn't going. I already had a car and sponsor lined up my senior year.

Jamie: I was counting down the days till graduation.

Me: Same.

Jamie: Did you always want to be an actor?

Me: Yup. You always wanted to be a driver?

Jamie: Yeah. I think we're the only ones out of our class who knew what they wanted to do. And neither of us will be at the reunion.

Me: You're not going?

Jamie: No. It's in the middle of race season. Even if I wanted to, the closest airport to home is two hours away.

Me: Yeah. It's not the easiest place to get to.

Jamie: Sam will be pissed when she finds out, but she has no clue what our lives are like. My schedule's bad. I bet yours is worse.

Me: I stay busy. Although right now I'm just sitting in my car.

Jamie: Hey, same for me. Which race track are you on?

Me: You're on the track right now?

Jamie: No, I'm kidding. I just finished training. Why are you just sitting in your car?

Me: I had a meeting with my agent.

Jamie: Was it . . . bad? Your car's not running in a closed garage, right?

Me: No, it was a good meeting, but I have to make a decision between two films for my next role.

Jamie: You picked the right place to work it out. I do my best thinking behind the wheel.

Jamie: Although my crew chief might disagree.

My short laugh punctuated the silence inside my car. This conversation was surreal, and I couldn't stop the smile that spread across my face.

Jamie: Can I help? Want to pro/con it with me?

Lord help me, I considered his offer. He was basically a stranger, but at the same time, not. He'd been a nice guy ten years ago. There wasn't risk in doing it. I wouldn't put anything in the chat I didn't feel comfortable getting out, and I had 'mom' insurance anyway. His mother was my mother's hairdresser, and in the South, that was the ultimate level of trust between women.

Jamie: I did a commercial for spark plugs last year, so I'm an expert at acting.

Jamie: Full disclosure, it was one line and I fucked it up, but still consider myself an expert.

Me: One role is a rom-com. The script is funny, but the director's last movie didn't do well. They haven't cast the male lead yet.

Jamie: OK. What about the other one?

Me: The script is amazing. Director has won two Oscars.

His message popped through while I was still typing.

Jamie: So maybe do that one.

Me: The problem is it's sexy.

Jamie: How sexy?

Me: The role calls for full-frontal nudity.

Jamie: Are you serious?

Me: Yup.

The Blindfold Club was based off an anonymous memoir written by a high-end escort, and the book was currently sitting on the *New York Times* bestseller list.

Speech bubbles danced across the screen, showing he was typing, but then they disappeared. Finally—

Jamie: OK.

I chewed on my lip at his plain response. In fairness, when he'd started this chat, he hadn't been expecting to help me decide if flashing my vajay was a good career move.

Me: I don't have a problem with nudity, but should I cross that line? This movie could be huge, but it's a gamble.

Jamie: So, rom-com = safe.

Me: Yes.

Jamie: Sexy movie is high-risk, but maybe high reward.

Me: Yeah.

Jamie: I'm probably the wrong guy to ask. I like risk.

Of course, he did. Every Sunday he drove in circles at two hundred miles an hour, knowing any second a crash could send him into the wall.

> **Jamie:** If you turn down the sexy one, how will you feel about it a year from now?

If I passed on *The Blindfold Club*, I was certain I'd spend the rest of my life wondering, *"What if?"* The role was an original. Not like the rom-com, where the chances of me being offered a part in some similar movie down the road were likely.

I was lost in my thoughts as I stared out the windshield, not seeing anything beyond the glass. Jamie had asked me a simple question, and it had given me my answer. Excitement skittered down my body, confirming I was making the right choice.

> **Me:** I'd have regret. OMG, thank you! I'm going to do it.

He sent me a thumbs-up emoji.

> **Jamie:** Cool. Don't forget to mention me in your acceptance speech.

CHAPTER TWO

Jamie

FOURTEEN MONTHS LATER

At the start of the season, no one else noticed the friction between me and Rob. My crew chief was conservative. Like, Old Testament conservative. The giant stick up his ass only got worse as the races went by. He stayed quiet when I did well, but the last two had been a shitshow, and he was all out of patience with me at today's practice.

As soon as I cut the engine, I yanked the earpiece out, happy to have Rob's voice out of my head. While I undid my gloves, movement caught my attention.

For fuck's sake.

Rob stormed toward the car, his face red. If I didn't know him, I'd say he looked irate, but it turned out he always looked that way.

"What's going on with you?" His tone was accusatory.

I did not want to talk to him right now. "Sorry. I slept like shit last night."

He frowned at my language. He legit *scowled* at the cussword like I'd uttered it while kneeling at church. Everyone else in the pit swore like they'd hit a hammer on their thumb, and Rob never batted an eye. Only when I cussed, did he get angry. I wasn't in the mood to deal with his puritanical ass.

Yeah, I'd had a slow, messy run, but it hadn't been entirely my fault. "The front's loose," I said.

"Well, it was too tight yesterday." He put his hands on his hips and stood too close to the window, blocking my exit.

It was hot inside the car, and even with the cooling system in my suit, I was melting. I grabbed the A-pillar and hoisted myself up out of the seat, not caring when I put a shoulder into Rob's chest. He needed to back off.

"Figure it out and get your head on right," he said, "or we're not gonna win a single race this year."

"Yeah, I got it." I gritted my teeth. "Thanks for the motivational speech."

Rob's statement was loaded with meaning. It was my second year driving for Randall Whitman, and the way things were shaping up, it might be my last. Rob had been with the crew for six years, and no one else seemed to have issues with him.

Maybe he just had it out for me.

Team chemistry was everything in this sport. If I couldn't make it work, no way was Whitman, the team owner, going to choose me over Rob.

I needed a top-five finish like I needed air to breathe.

I ignored my irritation with my crew chief and tried to focus on work. "Let's dial it halfway between yesterday and today."

Rob nodded and looked off into the distance. The conversation was over.

Yet he stayed rooted to the track. *Shit*. I braced for the incoming comment when he sighed loudly. "I can't wait till they put a new one up."

I knew exactly what he was talking about but glanced up at the billboard anyway.

The track we practiced on wasn't far from the freeway, and we could see one of the signs looming over it. Two months ago, it'd been advertising some new Frankenstein creation from Taco Bell.

Now the billboard was *her*.

Anna Douglas, photographed from her bare shoulders up, a blindfold clutched in her hand as she seductively bit down on the knuckle of her index finger. When the sign first went up, it took a moment to adjust to her blonde hair. She was really a brunette, but the lighter color looked natural on her. It looked good.

But I never got used to the billboard. Lap after lap, she stared at me with eyes full of hunger and sex. I couldn't stop staring at it.

"It shouldn't be there much longer," I said, my voice tight. "The movie came out today."

"It's porn." Rob shook his head in disgust. "Worse. That spanking crap? No woman should want to be treated like that. Little girls see that billboard and think, what? That a whore is a role model?"

I ripped at the neck closure on my suit, opening it, and unzipped the front. I'd do anything to keep my hands busy so I didn't tense them into fists. Rob would notice. And then he'd ask, and I wouldn't be able to keep my goddamn mouth shut. We were too close to race day for me to unload on the judgmental asshole.

Anna played an escort in the movie, but it wasn't porn—I knew because I went to a midnight showing last night.

By myself.

I'd put on a baseball cap and kept it slung low over my eyes, so no one would recognize me, and I probably looked like the biggest creep in the universe. I'd sat in the corner of the theater, wanting the movie to start before someone saw me, but also dreading the moment the lights went down. It was the point of no return—I wasn't going to be able to unsee a completely naked Anna.

I hadn't lied to Rob—I hadn't slept well last night. Hadn't really slept at all.

I wiped the line of sweat off my forehead with the back of my hand as I stalked to my RV, anxious for a shower. I climbed the steps inside, and as I stripped out of my suit, my phone in my bag chimed with a message.

Anna: How did your run go?

I sent back a GIF of a sloth trying to cross a road, its clawed arm reaching slowly across the asphalt.

Anna: Oh no! Was it the front again?

No, it's because I've seen you naked, and it's all I can think about.

Last year, I'd struck up a conversation with her and . . . it never ended. We chatted every day. Some nights we'd talk for hours. If she was filming or I was at the track, it would be a quick back-and-forth exchange. But I hadn't gone more than twenty-four hours without chatting with her in months.

One year and more than a thousand messages, and Anna Douglas had become my best friend.

> **Me:** This time it was the opposite. I was fighting the wheel the whole time.

> **Anna:** I'm sorry. Was Rob any help or did he just bitch about the billboard again?

I'd had too many beers two weeks ago and accidentally mentioned Rob's annoyance with the wall-to-wall promo for *The Blindfold Club*. She acted like it was funny, but it was hard to tell through text, and I wondered if it bothered her. I wasn't about to tell her what he'd said today.

> **Me:** He was the same. We'll figure it out.

> **Anna:** Are you going to be ready to watch in a few hours?

I grinned. When I found out she hadn't seen *Game of Thrones*, I talked her into watching. It only taken three episodes of her shooting me random commentary before I'd begun re-watching the show with her. We'd finished the Red Wedding episode on Wednesday while she was flying overseas, and naturally she was dying to see what happened next.

> **Me:** I think so. What time is it where you are?

Her movie came out today, but the Hollywood premiere had been last week. She was in the European phase of her press tour now, jetting all over the place, and I couldn't keep track. Was she still in Paris?

> **Anna:** It's 10pm. I'm in a cab on my way to a post-screening party. Side note: traffic in London is awful.

Side note: I've seen you naked, and you're even more gorgeous than I imagined.

Me: Never been. How is it otherwise? Good sights?

Anna: I only know what the hotels look like. :-(It's been one press junket to the next. Not to sound ungrateful, but I'm ready for this to be over.

Anna: I kind of want to go somewhere and just be a tourist, you know?

My ass hit the couch. The beginnings of an idea assembled in my head. I wasn't a patient guy. When I figured out what I wanted, I went after it, and the first step of my plan was being in the same room as her.

Me: You need a vacation. Me too. Let's do it.

The bubble appeared like she was typing, but it vanished. My chest tightened as I waited. What if she thought I was joking?

Anna: Go on vacation together?

Me: I've got two more races and I'm done. When's your tour over?

This could work. Hadn't she told me she wasn't slated to start her next shoot for a few weeks?

Anna: I think I'm back in LA by the end of the month.

Me: Awesome. Where do you want to go?

I set the phone down beside me and took off my shoes, dropping them to the floor with two soft thumps. Any second now, the phone would chime with a new message. She could pick any place; it didn't matter to me. Wherever she wanted to go, I was on board—as long as she was there.

I pulled my racing suit down around my waist and fought the chill of the air conditioning. My white undershirt was damp with sweat, and as the seconds of silence ticked by, I began to sweat all over again.

Had I put her on the spot? Maybe I needed to give a suggestion. The best bet was someplace sexy. I'd take every advantage I could get. Ideally, someplace tropical and romantic. What was close to LA?

Me: Hawaii?

The flight time wasn't too bad—easier than going to Europe. I was proud of myself for the quick thinking, and for a moment, my brain went fuzzy as I pictured us on the beach, her in a bikini.

But there was no response. Not even an attempt to type from her. I glanced up at the icon on my screen. I had a full signal, and she'd read the message.

Oh, shit.

I was so stupid. Anna had told me about a co-star a few months back. They'd become friends while filming, but he'd mistaken her friendliness for more. She hadn't said much about it, but I could read between the lines. The guy hadn't handled her rejection well and had made things really awkward.

I was fucking this up and making things weird between us. Suggesting a trip together was kind of strange, and it probably crossed a line. Nervous wasn't a feeling I got too often, and it freaked me out. I grabbed my phone and typed as fast as my thumbs could keep up.

Me: Or wherever. I think it would be fun to hang out as friends.

I grimaced as I sent the message to cover my ass. I didn't want to friend-zone myself, but better to be zoned than nothing at all.

I sighed with relief as a bubble popped up on the screen, filled with blinking dots. The anticipation of her reply was worse than waiting for a photo finish result.

Anna: Sorry, the driver wanted an autograph. This is crazy, but YES! And Hawaii! How do we make that happen?

CHAPTER THREE

Anna

Planes rolled by in the distance, taxiing toward the runway. I stood in the center of the luxury private suite with my arms crossed over my chest and my nervous gaze out the oversized window. As each plane lofted into the air, I had a similar feeling in my stomach.

Jamie should be here any minute.

He'd sent a text a little while ago that he'd landed. By now he'd gotten off the plane, been picked up by the suite escort, and was being driven across LAX. I shifted my weight from foot to foot, wanting to get the nervous excitement out before he arrived.

I knew him growing up. I'd watched his interviews and promo spots. We talked every day, meaning Jaime knew me better than my agent, my assistant Sato—really everyone. He was closer to me than any other friend.

And yet we hadn't *seen* each other in eleven years.

In that time, he'd become a devastatingly handsome man. A very attractive, very *single* man. Jamie hadn't always been. When we'd first started talking, he'd been with someone. He didn't talk about her much, and I didn't pry, but they'd called it quits not long after our daily conversations began. I suspected his long chats with me had something to do with it.

I uncrossed my arms and ran my palms down my skirt, smoothing out the non-existent wrinkles. I hadn't sat down since I'd entered the suite fifteen minutes ago. I hadn't turned on the TV or touched the snack bar, because balancing on pins and needles was taking all of my energy.

Friends.

I mouthed the word silently, reminding myself. That was how Jamie had pitched this trip to me. Would I be able to keep my desire for him stowed away so I didn't jeopardize our friendship? He'd never hinted he was interested me. Hadn't flirted, or even mentioned if he'd seen *The Blindfold Club*. The movie had been out for a month.

God, this week was going to be the hardest acting role I'd ever taken on. Pretending my feelings for him were platonic would demand an Oscar-caliber performance. I'd do my best.

There was a sharp knock on the suite door. I took in a deep breath to prepare myself, but the words came out in a rush anyway. "Come in."

The door swung open, and I dry swallowed.

His light brown hair was mostly hidden beneath a worn Carolina Panthers hat. The gorgeous blue eyes I knew he had were concealed behind a pair of aviator sunglasses. He had on a simple white t-shirt and blue jeans, and a bag slung back over one shoulder. My gaze landed first on his toned, muscular arm and its subtle flex, and then my focus drifted back to his enormous smile—all white and perfect teeth and incredibly infectious.

"Hey," he said. His grin was nonstop, and my knees softened.

"Hi," I breathed.

He twisted his arm, dropping the bag just inside the entry, and then pulled the door closed behind him. Off came the sunglasses, and with the full power of his gaze on me, the air in the suite went thin. It was no surprise why he'd landed so many endorsements even though his racing career hadn't taken off yet. He was "easy-on-the-eyes," as my mom would say, with his long nose, strong jawline, and lips that promised trouble.

I did what felt natural—I strode forward and held my arms open. A handshake wasn't going to cut it. It didn't occur to me until it was too late that this could potentially backfire. What if a hug made things weird? What if I put my arms around him and didn't let go?

I strangled back my eager groan as he squeezed me tight. He smelled incredible, like he'd just stepped out of the shower and not off a four-hour flight. Did he always smell like this, or had he ducked into a restroom and put on cologne? The idea he might have done it for me made my heart skip along.

"How was your flight?" My words were muffled against his shoulder.

"It was good, thanks." Rather than end the hug, he seemed to settle into it. "I can't believe we got this to work out. It's great to see you."

My already weak knees became less stable. *Damnit, Anna! Pull yourself together.* "Yeah, you too. I'm excited." It was the truth. I'd been looking forward to this trip from the moment he suggested it.

When we lapsed into silence, I slowly pulled back to end the hug but wondered if I should have lingered. I had the strange sensation he'd been as reluctant as I had been to step away.

Jamie's gaze slid from mine to scan the room. As he took in the couch and flatscreen TV, he hung his sunglasses in the neck of his shirt, probably knowing he'd need them again when it came time to leave. It was easier for guys to hide from their celebrity status. All they had to do was dress down, throw on a baseball hat and sunglasses, and they could blend in.

"Rough gig you've got here," he teased. He nodded to the sidebar, where a bottle sat in an ice bucket beside two glass flutes. "Is that champagne?"

"It is." I scurried to the bar, snatched up the bottle, and began to pour him a glass. "We're celebrating in person."

He looked confused. "Celebrating?"

Maybe driving in circles had given him temporary memory loss. "Your race? Your first NASCAR win." I passed him the glass and then poured my own. "That's huge. Congrats."

He gave me an "aw, shucks" look that was so cute, it was nearly fatal. He wasn't the type of guy to blush, but his voice softened. "Right. Thanks."

I clinked the rims of our glasses together. "Bet that shut Rob up."

As I took a sip, Jamie paused. He acted like his win hadn't made a difference.

"Really?" I asked. "You said a win meant he'd give you some breathing room."

He pressed his sexy lips together into a line for a moment

before speaking. "Breathing room, yeah. But I'm not safe. Rob's got a ton of pull with the owner, and—" Jamie straightened abruptly, and his expression brightened. "You know what? I'm on vacation, so none of that matters right now. All I want to do this week is finish watching *Game of Thrones* and hang out with you."

Inside, I was dying, but I gave him a controlled smile. "Sounds good to me."

CHAPTER FOUR

Jamie

I sat in my first-class chair, which was a private pod, and scanned the week's itinerary on my phone.

Even though I'd never been to Hawaii, I'd been the one to suggest the trip, so I offered to plan the weeklong vacation. I'd done it with Anna's assistant's help. Sato was fucking amazing at her job—I could message the woman any time of day, and she would respond instantly with whatever I needed. She was a human Google.

But because Sato was a professional and so on top of things, it meant she didn't have time for my bullshit. She either didn't get my sense of humor or didn't have the patience for it. I'd figured that out right quick after the first few email exchanges we'd had fell flat. I stuck to business after that.

The plans for the week were awesome, but it wasn't what I was most looking forward to. I sat up straighter in my seat and glanced over the divider that separated my pod from Anna's. We'd finished the final episode of *Game of Thrones* right as they served dinner, and she'd decided to grab a nap before we landed. She'd fallen asleep in two seconds after laying her seat flat. Maybe the engines had lulled her to sleep, but she'd probably become an expert at catching shuteye on planes.

She was a brunette again, like how I remembered her. Her maple-colored hair draped over the airline pillow, and since she was turned inward, the view of her peaceful, sleeping face was only for me.

Anna had been pretty in high school, but now? Fuck me, the girl was gorgeous. Her pale blue eyes were my favorite. I'd watched her, rather than my laptop screen, while we were finishing the final episode, and the way the range of emotions played through her eyes was fascinating. How they'd sparkle when she found something funny, or when they widened with surprise.

Or how the blue of her eyes deepened during a sex scene.

I was going to have to convince her to FaceTime me during the next show we decided to binge-watch. Now that I'd seen her reactions, I wasn't going to miss them again.

Her pink lips parted as she sighed in her sleep, and I had to rip my gaze away. I needed to stop thinking about how those lips would taste, or how she'd felt in my arms when we'd hugged earlier. It'd been hours ago, but my body didn't get the message. I was still buzzing like I did in the aftermath of a crash I was lucky enough to walk away from. Adrenaline coursed through me, amplifying everything.

I'd been existing in that heightened state since touching her. The longing I had—my desire—was it ever going to fade?

I finished the glass of water on my tray table and tried to figure out when and how to make my move. Was she interested in more? I needed to find out—but do it in a way that wouldn't make her uncomfortable or screw with our friendship.

"Jamie. Can I ask you something?"

I turned in surprise. Anna was awake? You'd never know she'd been asleep thirty seconds ago. She sat upright in her seat, the blanket pooled around her waist, and peered up at me with hesitant eyes. Her voice had been soft, barely loud enough to hear over the engines.

"Go for it," I said.

"Did you see my movie?"

Sure, I only saw it five times.

And the number would have been higher if there had been more theaters within reasonable driving distance. Showing up to see the movie alone was weird enough, I wasn't going to do it multiple times at the same location.

I dry-swallowed and wished I hadn't finished my water. "Yeah." I tried to look chill. "Didn't I tell you already?"

"No, I don't think so." She made a face as if she wasn't sure what to say next. "So . . . what did you think?"

Which time did she want me to answer for? Because the first

time, I didn't pay attention to a damn thing other than her. I'd had to go back and watch it the second time to follow the story. The third time? That had been for me.

I couldn't get her out of my head, but maybe my feelings were misplaced. Perhaps I was seeing her as the character she played, and my attraction was to that—not the real Anna.

Except when the show was over, I knew what I felt had nothing to do with the blonde escort from Chicago she played on-screen, and everything to do with the brunette actress from Kentucky.

The fourth and fifth time I'd gone because she was busy with her European tour and I was straight-up missing her. We didn't get much time to talk, thanks to her schedule and the time difference, so seeing her on the big screen was a consolation.

My long pause put fear in her eyes. "Oh, shit. You didn't like it."

No, I'd loved it. I'd seen her movie so many times . . . hell, I could probably quote the dialogue to her. But I wasn't about to. The last thing I wanted was to be weird and make her nervous. I had to play it safe.

"No, I did," I choked out. "It was good."

If I said anything more, I might start gushing like a fanboy.

Anna stared at me in disbelief, and why shouldn't she? My statement had been anything but convincing. I frowned at myself. *Try again, idiot.*

"It was really good," I continued. I leaned in, so she'd know I was serious. "You were incredible in it."

She blinked rapidly, and her eyes darted away, running from her blush. My compliment had surprised her? I wasn't the only one who'd said this; she'd gotten great reviews. But maybe the praise meant more coming from me? I liked that idea a whole lot.

"Thank you," she uttered. Slowly, her gaze drifted back, and her expression was warm. "How come you didn't tell me you saw it?"

I put a hand on the back of my neck and massaged the tension there. "I didn't know if it'd make you uncomfortable."

She flashed a small, knowing smile. "Because now you've seen me naked?"

Jesus, I had. Five viewings—and it'd nearly killed me each time. I cast my hand out as I shrugged. "We're friends. I didn't want to make things weird."

"That's sweet, but just so you know, if you'd told me you hadn't seen the movie? *That's* what would have made things weird." She grinned. "You played a big part in me taking the role. I mean, I can't tell you how glad I am you messaged me that day."

"Me too." It came from me instantly, and a spark ignited in my center. She softened in the seat, subtly leaning toward me. That was a good sign, right? Fuck, it had to be.

"Can I ask you something else?"

"Of course."

Mischief lit her eyes. "I heard a rumor about you in school."

"Yeah?" I chuckled. "Which one?"

"You got caught doing eighty on Salem Drive, but the female cop let you off with a warning."

"Was that before or after I had sex with her on the hood?"

Her eyes went wide. "Oh my God, did you?"

"There were, like, five different versions of the story going around. In some of them I was going a hundred, which isn't even possible. Salem has too many curves."

Anna, the girl who'd braved putting everything on-screen, for some reason seemed bashful to ask. "And the sex with the cop?"

"Also, not possible. An engine gets hot when it's going eighty—way too hot to put somebody on the hood."

The blue in her eyes darkened, which was another good sign.

I quirked my lips into a smile. "I don't think Officer Greer would have taken me up on the offer, anyway. He's married to my mom's friend." The Greers had basically been part of the family since before I was born. "The truth is I was only going sixty-five, and rather than give me a ticket, Officer Greer did something way worse. He called my dad." Who'd spent forty-five minutes at the dinner table that night putting the fear of God in me. "I wasn't allowed to drive anywhere but to school and back for the next month. Remember Jenny Hayes? She drove by while I was pulled over. I guess it started with her, but I dunno how the rumor got so big."

Anna's lips rounded into an 'oh.' "Yeah, I remember Pathological Liar Jenny. At least seventy-five percent of the stuff she said was made up."

"You mean she isn't cousins with Justin Timberlake? She told me that once."

Anna snorted. "Right, I'm sure she is."

The conversation shifted to the upcoming week. Sato had given the itinerary to Anna, but she'd barely been able to look at it between reading scripts and the wardrobe fittings for her next role. She seemed so excited about our plans, and I couldn't wait until we touched down on Kauai. Then, all it would be was a thirty-minute car ride and we'd be at the private villa Anna's assistant had helped me pick out.

The landing was smooth, and as soon as the seatbelt light was off, I was out of my seat, pulling down Anna's bag from the overhead.

"Hey," a male voice called to me. "Are you who I think you are?"

I slowed as I lowered the bag to the floor. Outside of racing, I didn't get recognized much, but it did occasionally happen. I turned to the passenger standing in the aisle behind me. He looked to be in his sixties, and the vacation had clearly started. He already had on the standard-issued Hawaiian shirt.

"Maybe," I said, giving him an easy smile.

"You drive the sixty-five car."

"Sure do. Jamie Campbell." After I pulled up the handle on Anna's bag, I offered my hand to the guy.

He took it and shook furiously, excited. "Mark Freeman. My wife and me, we're from Phoenix. We were there when you won the Cam-Am 500."

The wife ducked her head around her husband. "We were hoping Scott Kempen was going to win."

The guy hadn't let go of me, and his grip intensified while his face filled with embarrassment. "*Karen*," he uttered under his breath.

She shrugged. NASCAR fans—God didn't make a more loyal creature.

The driver she'd been rooting for was an asshole who could suck my dick, but I plastered on a smile. "Well, he made it a good race."

Anna stood from her seat and glanced at the couple, a thrilled smile curving on her lips. Was she getting a kick out of seeing me with a fan? Didn't seem like he was aware he was still shaking my hand.

His wife's mouth dropped wide open. "Oh my God, that's Anna Douglas!"

Why don't you shout it a little louder? I don't think the folks back in coach heard you.

Her gaze was laser focused, darting furiously between Anna and me.

"Who's that?" the guy asked.

"She was in that movie. I'm sure you remember, Mark. She was naked, and you couldn't stop talking about it."

"Oh." He turned beet red.

At this point, I decided I was okay with letting him continue to shake my hand all the way off the plane. I felt a little bad for him.

The wife's attention landed on the bag I'd pulled down and zeroed in on the floral scarf knotted through a zipper pull. "Are you two together?"

"No, no," I said quickly. "We're not together, we're just friends."

Wait. Shit!

In my attempt to make it clear we weren't '*together*' together, I'd overcompensated. I'd made it sound like the idea of Anna and I dating was silly. Like I didn't want that to happen, when it was *exactly* what I wanted.

Maybe I'd gotten lucky and Anna hadn't picked up the mixed signal I'd just sent—

A vacant smile was frozen on her pretty face.

Awesome.

I'd just friend-zoned myself.

CHAPTER FIVE

Jamie

Anna stood in the spacious living room, taking in the floor-to-ceiling windows at the back of the villa. If it was daylight outside, she'd be able to see beyond the deck and the amazing view of the ocean, but it was late, and the moon was hidden behind clouds. The beach was just down the grassy slope, and with the windows cracked, we could hear the waves crashing against the shore.

The villa was traditional Hawaii plantation style. The pitched ceiling in the open living room and kitchen had warm wood and exposed beams, reminding me of a sophisticated thatched roof. Some of the decor was beachy and tropical, but the couch was modern with oversized and squared off armrests.

The pictures online of this place were good but hadn't done it justice. The house was seductive and romantic. It was *perfect*.

The manager of the villa spent the last ten minutes giving us a tour, showing us where the snorkel gear was stored in the garage and how to work the outdoor shower to rinse off after coming back from the beach. She didn't get starstruck around Anna—maybe celebrities stayed here a lot, and the woman was used to it. The gated, luxury community meant we'd have privacy.

There'd been an awkward moment when the manager opened the master bedroom door and announced it was the better of the two rooms, so we should stay there. Anna didn't say anything, but I got the impression it was easier to stay quiet rather than correct the woman's assumption.

"Mahalo," the manager called out as a goodbye before she left.

As soon as she pulled the front door closed behind her, I grabbed Anna's bag and hauled it toward the master bedroom, the wheels clacking over the grout lines in the tile floor.

"Where are you going?" Anna hurried after me.

"You get the big room."

"No, that's fine. You can have it."

I ignored her and rolled the suitcase through the doorway, parking it beside the dresser. I turned and shot her a smile. "Too late. Your bag's already in here."

She frowned. "We're splitting this trip fifty-fifty. It's not fair if I get the nicer room."

The other room had a queen-sized bed instead of a king, a smaller bathroom, and no beach view, but I didn't mind. "It doesn't matter to me, but if bothers you, we can switch halfway through the week."

She gave me a look like I was driving a hard bargain. I loved how she was still polite and humble after she'd gotten a taste of fame. The Kentucky girl her parents had raised right was still there.

"Fine," she said, issuing a loud sigh. "I guess this will have to suffice." She faked disgust. "It's all just so huge and beautiful."

"I know, it'll be difficult." I glanced toward the doorway leading back to the living area. "You hungry? Want some wine?" The fridge and pantry had been stocked with everything on the list Sato sent over earlier this week.

Anna looked around the room, and I didn't miss the way she eyed the inviting bed. "Aren't you tired? You didn't sleep during the flight." She checked the screen of her phone and did the math in her head. "It's like three in the morning for you."

I was tired, but from the second we'd stepped off the plane, I felt a ticking clock. I only had so many days to convince her to give us a shot and wasn't going to waste time sleeping. I shrugged. "I can rally."

A shy smile on her? Jesus, it was hot. She tilted her head toward the bed. "Sorry, I think I need to crash. That way I'll be ready to go tomorrow. Is that okay?"

"Yeah, of course." Unlike her, I wasn't any good at acting, but I did my best not to look disappointed. "Well," I said, "see you tomorrow, then. Good night."

"Good night."

As I turned around and headed for the door, unease filled my gut. Was I imagining it, or had relief flashed through her expression?

She stole my focus as I took a beer from the fridge and rolled my suitcase into my room, only to discover I'd grabbed a soda instead. I was too lazy to go back to the kitchen and get what I wanted. Besides, what I *really* wanted was in the bedroom across the hall. Was I going to be able to dig myself out of whatever hole I'd put myself in?

I yanked off my shirt, kicked off my shoes, and undid my jeans, but each movement was slower than the last. Now that I was alone, exhaustion creeped in. I snapped off the lights and climbed into bed, desperate for sleep. Would I dream about her again? I did practically every time my head hit the pillow.

Last night I'd dreamt she was sitting in my lap, wearing only a bra and underwear and her mouth attached to mine. I'd undone the clasp at her back and pulled the bra straps down off her shoulders, but she didn't give me time to look at her perfect breasts. She'd slid down to the floor, kneeling between my legs.

As I thought about the part where she'd wrapped her lips around my dick, I reached under the covers and palmed myself. I was already half-hard. And, yeah, I was tired as hell, but the ache for her wasn't going away.

I'd have to be quiet. The villa was nice, but all the windows were open, and the walls seemed to be paper thin. Across the hall, I could hear Anna moving around in her enormous room, unzipping her suitcase and getting ready for bed.

I shoved my hand under the waistband of my boxers and closed my fist tight around my cock. Thinking about the dream with her so close by made it more vivid. I pictured her pink lips sliding up and down on me and matched the tempo with my own fist. My breathing picked up as I imagined the sensation of her wet tongue swirling over my skin.

Blood rushed loudly in my ears as I went faster. I was so fucking hard, it was unreal. Being around her all day intensified my desire, teasing me. I needed release. I pumped my hand harder, stroking down the length and twisting as I came back up.

As I got right to the edge, a faint hum drifted from her room. I stopped moving so I could focus on the sound better. Was she brushing her teeth with an electric toothbrush? I hadn't heard the water running. What was making that buzzing noise?

It became crystal clear when a faint sigh rang out.

Fuck me!

I'd know that sigh anywhere. It played on a continuous loop in my brain since the first time I'd seen her movie. Anna had given a similar breathy moan during the first sex scene where she was strapped to a table.

Only this sigh? It was real.

I froze in place, wanting to press my ear to my door so I could hear every detail better, but I was sure if I moved I'd come. So, I lay in the bed, my dick in my hand, listening to her soft moans that were pure torture. Her bed creaked, and I heard her shifting around, and I pictured her writhing on the sheets, the vibrator pressed between her gorgeous legs.

She came quickly, judging by the sharp gasp and how the buzzing ceased.

It took one pump of my hand, and I was done for. I slapped my free hand out and balled the pillow beside me in a fist, clenching my jaw. As the pleasure rocketed through me, I strangled back my groan through tight teeth.

Was there any chance she'd been thinking about me, like I'd been thinking about her?

CHAPTER SIX

Anna

I clasped my snorkel and mask in one hand, and my fins in the other, and leaned back until I was floating on the surface of the Pacific Ocean. The private beach was part of a bay, so during low tide it was relatively calm. The sun overhead was warm and made all the colors more vibrant. The lush volcanic mountains looming nearby were bright, beautiful green, and the water stretched around me was turquoise blue.

This place was paradise.

I circled my hands in the water and kicked my feet to keep me from drifting too far away. Jamie and I had spent most of the morning out here, watching fish dart around the coral that was only a few feet below us. We hadn't spotted any dolphins yet, but when Jamie discovered a sea turtle, he grabbed my hand to get my attention.

Except he always had my attention.

During the drive last night to the villa, I'd figured this week with my "friend" was going to be hard. Then, this morning he'd come out onto the balcony for breakfast in board shorts and no shirt. I knew he was in good shape. Driving a race car took stamina and strength. But seeing the results of his training and how he had those ridges of muscle along his ribs made me swallow hard.

This week was going to be torture.

Each minute around him felt dangerous. I was going to slip up and do something stupid, like flirt with him. Or find an excuse to run my fingers down his chest. Or tell him I'd had two sessions with my vibrator to take the edge off and it hadn't helped.

I came while I was thinking about you. That wasn't something friends told each other.

He was nearby, his face in the water with his yellow snorkel sticking up, and it gave me a moment to ogle him. But he must have sensed my look because his head popped up. He peeled off his mask and gave me a smile. God, he was cute even with the indentation line from his mask around his eyes.

Oh, crap. Did I have those marks? I got my feet under me, shifted my snorkel and mask into my other hand, and ran my fingers over my face.

"Taking a break?" he asked.

"I think I'm going to head in. One of my fins was pinching my foot."

He swam beside me until it was shallow enough to stand. Water coasted down his chest as we plodded up the sandy shore, dotted with black rocks. My head snapped forward, and my cheeks burned when he caught me looking at him.

I dropped my gear by our towels, but before I could bend down to grab one, Jamie scooped both up and held mine out. I hated how he was funny, and smart, and insanely hot . . . *and* he had manners. It was totally unfair.

There were other villas we shared this beach with, but we were the only guests out right now. A few yachts were moored at the end of the bay, bobbing in the gentle waves. "This place is amazing," I said as we began to towel off. "It's so beautiful."

"Yeah. It is." His voice was weird.

I glanced over at him and swallowed a breath. He wasn't looking at the ocean or the jungle-covered mountains. His gaze lingered on me, tracing the lines of my teal-colored halter top, over my bare stomach, and down to my matching bikini bottoms. He wasn't looking at me the way friends looked at each other. This stare was intense and sexual.

And then he blinked, and the expression drained away, as if he hadn't meant to do it.

A nervous, excited thrill shot through me. If seeing me in a bikini was what it took for him to have interest, I was cool with wearing it and nothing else the rest of the week. I smiled up at him as I bent over to dry my legs, and—

"Motherfucker," I hissed. Stinging pain snapped across the back of my heel.

His expression flooded with concern. "What's wrong?"

I tossed my towel onto the sand and sat so I could lift my leg and see the back of my ankle. The small blister was white, ringed with angry red. Jamie knelt beside me, and as I pointed to the spot, his fingers closed around my calf, holding me still so he could examine it better.

With his touch, the pain shifted and changed. It became a dull throb, centered deep between my legs.

"Damn," he said.

Yes, damn was right. His touch was electric.

He set my foot down on the sand, and his fingers slid slowly away. His blue eyes matched the color of the ocean we'd just come from, and I watched a water droplet skate down his neck and run through the valley between his pecs. His touch and proximity had disarmed me. It made everything hazy and confusing.

Jamie was staring at me, waiting for an answer. He'd said something, but I'd been too focused on the lucky water droplet to hear him.

"Sorry, what?" I asked.

"You need me to get you something?"

I shook my head. "Thanks, but I don't think there's anything that'll help. It's just a blister."

"I dunno, a beer might help."

I grinned. "Yeah, but it's not even lunchtime."

"Maybe not for you, but I'm starving." He wiped a hand over his mouth and sat back on his haunches. "Want me to make lunch?"

Our meals had been prepped for us, but it was nice he offered. Jamie had money and fame—which could easily go to a guy's head—yet it seemed like it hadn't touched him.

"Sure, if you don't mind," I said. "I was going to lay out for a bit and dry off, but I can come help."

He stood and wrapped his towel around his waist, which of course gave me the visual of him being naked beneath it, and my brain went fuzzy again.

"Stay as long as you like." He collected his snorkel gear. "It won't take both of us to turn on an oven."

"You sure?"

"Yeah, I got it." He shot me a boyish smile, and then he was off, trekking up the stairs over the rocks and onto the grassy lawn. I spread out my towel and lay down on my stomach, watching him as he rounded the stone wall and disappeared into the outdoor shower.

Birds chirped in the palm trees nearby, and the sun was warm on my skin. I was on a tropical vacation, lying on the beach, while my next project was already lined up, so I shouldn't have a care in the world. But all I could think about was surviving the rest of this trip without falling for a man who wasn't interested in more. It was probably already too late for me.

Was there a chance he was interested?

I groaned quietly in my frustration and rolled over onto my back, then lifted my hand to shield my eyes from the sun.

This was silly. I wasn't going to waste any more of our time together without finding out. I'd said yes to this trip as soon as he asked. We had great chemistry online, and I'd needed to know if the same was true in person—which it absolutely was.

I hadn't imagined the heat in his eyes just a few minutes ago. He'd cracked the door of opportunity for me, and I was going to nudge it open. I launched upright, gathered my gear and towel, and made my way up the slope to the house. I stacked my snorkel stuff beside his in the grass, then padded on my bare feet across the stone walkway that led to the secluded, open-air shower.

The walls were carved out of black lava rock, and since the balcony was overhead, it felt cave-like as I moved closer to the shower. I pulled up short at the sight of Jamie. He had his back turned and one arm out, his hand flat against the wall, and his head hung. Water from the rainfall showerhead drenched him, running in rivulets down his strong back, his powerful legs, and disappeared into the river rocks bordering the tile he stood on.

My heart wasn't beating in my chest, but my feet still worked. I took a silent step closer.

The mist coming off him was . . . cold? Now that I was closer, I could see the goosebumps dotting his skin.

He lifted his head, slicked back his hair with a hand, and froze when he saw me. I felt flushed under his gaze, and the longer he stared at me, the thicker the air became. Oh, I definitely hadn't imagined his heated look from before, because this one . . .

It was hotter than the sun.

My chest was tight as I inched forward, my toes in the cold water pooling on the tile. My voice nearly failed me. "Is the hot water not working?"

He broke our gaze, so he could grab the shower handle and crank it up. The water grew warm instantly. Or maybe it just felt that way because his blue eyes locked onto mine. My heart restarted, only it was in my throat now.

"Why were you taking a cold shower?" I asked.

His eyebrows tugged together, and he rested his hands on his hips. "Because."

"Because . . ." My tone was soft and hopeful. I had a theory but needed to hear him say it.

He stepped out of the water, bringing us chest to chest. My knees threatened to buckle as he set his hands on my elbows. His palms smoothed up my arms, glided over my shoulders and neck, and came to a stop cradling my face.

"Because," he whispered, tilting his head down and bringing his lips a breath away. "I was thinking about doing this."

He lowered his mouth the final inch and kissed me.

CHAPTER SEVEN

Anna

I gasped against Jamie's mouth and threw my arms around his neck, holding on like my life depended on it. His kiss was even more than I'd hoped it'd be. Urgent and greedy and dripping with desire.

His hands slipped down my body and settled on the small of my back, and as he stepped under the stream of water, he pulled me along with him, not letting up on our fiery kiss.

He adjusted the angle, and when my lips parted, his tongue dipped inside my mouth. *Yes*, every inch of me chanted. His tongue stroked against mine, and a bolt of heat shot down my legs. The water was warm, but I had goosebumps now too.

His kiss traveled down the length of my neck, and I heaved air into my lungs. "Do friends," I panted, "kiss in the shower like this?"

"I'm hoping to be more than a friend." He sucked gently on a spot below my ear, but whether my shiver was from his kiss or his words, I couldn't tell.

"Yeah?" I whispered as my eyes fell shut. What his mouth was doing was incredible. "Why'd you keep it a secret so long?"

His fingertips trailed up my spine, going slowly, one notch at a time. "I didn't want to fuck things up between us. Wanna hear another secret?"

"Yes." I threaded my fingers through his hair and clung to him. As his mouth moved to the other side of my neck, my head lolled back.

He mumbled it into my pulse point, his lips brushing against my skin. "I've wanted this for a while."

My heart galloped along. "Me too."

"I can't stop thinking about you. Anna . . . I saw your movie five times."

Oh my God. His confession melted my brain-to-mouth filter. Since we were talking about secrets, it spilled from me. "I had to use my vibrator last night because of you." He straightened, and I stared up into his stunning eyes. "And again this morning."

His expression went heavy with lust. "I heard, and it drove me fucking insane."

"You heard?"

The corner of his mouth quirked up into a smile. "I guess the walls are thin." He stroked his palm down my back until he could cup a handful of my ass. "I came while I was listening to you."

Well . . . that was fucking hot.

My mouth fell open, and he took advantage. He fused his lips over mine, and this time his kiss was erotic. It hinted what he'd like to do to me. His tongue slashed at mine as our lower bodies pressed together, and his dick was hard against my hip.

Rather than tell him what I wanted, I'd show him. I twisted an arm behind my back until I found the hook and undid the band holding my top in place. Our kiss broke, and his eyes widened with surprise, then flooded with heat as he realized what I was doing. He watched me lift the damp swimsuit over my head, and then he lurched for me, clasping one of my bare breasts in his hand. My top made a sopping noise as it fell to the ground.

Our tongues explored each other's mouths as our hands learned the shape of each other's bodies. He massaged and kneaded my breast, his fingertips circling over my nipple. I sighed and arched into his touch.

Eventually, he drifted lower. He ran his hand between my legs and gauged my reaction, testing the waters before going further. I tightened my grip on his shoulder and moaned eagerly. Was this race car driver worried about moving too fast? Fast worked for me. I felt like we'd been waiting for this moment for a long, long time.

When I palmed him through his shorts, he squeezed a hand on my hip. It came out in a rush from him. "You wanna go inside?"

Where there was a bed? Along with a stash of condoms in my suitcase? I nodded enthusiastically. Shower sex was difficult and overrated, anyway.

A split second later, I was stumbling along with him to the

stairs leading up the side of the house, my swimsuit top abandoned in the shower. I laughed at his determined expression and hurried pace. We came in through the side door, and I focused my gaze down the hallway. Would we go to my room, or his?

Surprise cut off a breath in my lungs as he wrapped his arms around my waist and carried me the five steps to the couch. He guided me to sit down on the edge of one of the flat, wide armrests, and I stared up at him. What was his plan? I wasn't convinced I wanted to fool around here, especially when we were still wet, but when his mouth latched onto my breast and he eased me back, I no longer cared.

All that mattered was he kept touching and kissing me. We'd spent so much time with this space between us, I was drunk off the physical connection. It looked like it was the same for him.

Jamie curled his fingers under the sides of my bikini bottom, his hooded gaze trapping mine as he peeled the wet fabric away. I lifted my legs up to help him along, and he stood, raising the swimsuit until it was past my ankles and he could toss it aside.

If he'd seen *The Blindfold Club* five times, he'd definitely seen me naked, but my heart swelled at the way he looked at me now. Like it was new and stunning. He parted my legs and dropped a kiss on the inside of my calf while he bent to take a knee.

Anticipation sizzled in my system as his mouth marched along, kissing up the inside of my thigh. Shit, how I wanted him to do what he was about to. My toes curled into points at the first sliver of his tongue on me. It was just a hint of pleasure, but acute.

The sight of his face between my thighs made a whimper leak from my mouth, and it was all the encouragement he needed. There was a flash of his pink tongue over my bare pussy, and then the edges of my vision began to blur as he caressed my clit.

"Oh my God," I groaned, clutching at the couch. I struggled to catch my breath, which was hopeless. I bowed up off the upholstery, gasping and panting. I clawed at the raised seams of the armrest and tangled a hand in Jamie's damp hair. My body didn't know how to react to how good he made me feel.

His hands were braced under my thighs, helping to hold my legs up in the air, and as his mouth increased intensity, I began to tremble. I planted the balls of my feet against his shoulders to brace myself. My moans swelled, echoing in the large room, bouncing off the tile.

I couldn't take much more of this. The need swirling inside me was overwhelming. I gently tugged a handful of his hair while gulping down breath, trying to slow my racing heart.

The smile on his face was wicked as he climbed to his feet. He ran his hands up my knees, down my thighs, over my hips. New goosebumps dotted my skin in the wake of his touch. Up his palms went while he leaned over me. He closed them around my breasts, pushing them together while his lips captured mine.

With our bodies pressed together, I could feel every inch of him beneath his shorts. Which—why the hell did he still have those on? I pushed a hand between us, trying to get at them.

He straightened, undid his shorts, and they slid down his legs. Now he was naked, and good lord, there wasn't anything more beautiful than Jamie Campbell in full-frontal. His gaze moved along the length of my body as he gripped just above my ankles, and he teased the naked tip of his cock through my seam.

His shoulders rose with his heavy breath. "You want it?"

I couldn't contain my eager moan, but he wasn't wearing anything. "God, yes. But—"

"Back in a second." He moved so fast, he was halfway down the hall before it registered. He ducked into his room as I lay back on the couch and listened to the rush of blood in my ears. The sound of his bare feet slapping against the floor grew louder as he hurried back to me.

"That was fast." I grinned as he tore open the condom wrapper in his hands.

His expression was pure seduction as he put it on and moved between my legs. He set a hand beside me on the edge of the armrest to support himself, and his lips hovered over mine. "I can go slow when it counts."

And he proved his point by sinking into me one fraction of an inch at a time. I arched up and wrapped my legs around his waist, trying to drive him deeper, but he moved in slow-motion. The sensation of him pressing inside me only got better as he went, stretching and filling me.

I let out half a groan and curled my hands around his biceps. "Oh," I gasped like I was cheering him on. "Oh, *oh*."

He straightened and cast his gaze down to where we were joined. The muscle along his jaw flexed, strangling what might have been a grunt. He drew back his hips, and I placed my feet flat against his shoulders. As he eased back inside a second time, he set his hands on the insides of my thighs, his fingertips right on the edges of my pussy. So he could peel me open and watch better.

I shoved my hands in my hair, using my arms to push my breasts together while he found his pace. I was going to burst. Each thrust gathered the intensity in my body, building toward release. He varied his tempo too, keeping me guessing. His quick, then slow movements caused my eyes to roll back in my head.

"Fuck, Anna," he whispered. "It feels so good."

I rose onto an elbow and reached for him. He was so far away when I needed his mouth on mine. My fingertips settled on his cheek as he came to my desperate kiss.

The padded armrest was surprisingly comfortable, but also precarious. I had to squeeze my core and hold my balance when he sped up his rhythm. The slap of bare skin meeting bare skin punctuated the air in the room, sometimes drowned out by my gasps and moans.

I was close to coming, and it felt like Jamie was too. He hauled me up so I was sitting, and I hooked an arm behind his neck to hold on, folding my legs around his hips. Our blistering rhythm made the couch inch along the floor.

The orgasm seemed near, but suddenly it was right on me. I jerked his head to mine and crushed my lips to his. The spike of ecstasy ripped through my center, sending waves of bliss along my legs and up my back. Jamie slowed as I cried out, but he didn't stop, and it made my orgasm last longer. Practically drew it out forever. I flinched and shuddered, fireworks of aftershock pleasure lighting me up.

"Fuck," he said through clenched teeth. His thrusts went wild and erratic, and the muscles in his chest tensed. He started his end just as I came down from mine.

Warmth rolled through my bloodstream as I felt the pulses deep inside me and listened to his long moan. He stilled, took in a recovering breath, and nestled his mouth against the side of my neck, delivering new shudders.

"That was fun," he said between two short pants. "Let's do that again."

"Okay." I was in total agreement with this plan. "Lunch first? You said you were hungry."

"Forget it. I can always eat tomorrow."

I pulled back so I could look at him. "Tomorrow?"

He feigned seriousness. "I'd like to fuck you all over this house, and we're on a timetable, here. We had breakfast. Do we really need food again today?"

I laughed and played along. "All right. Where—"

"The king-sized bed is next."

My grin had to be huge. "Well, let's get to it, then."

CHAPTER EIGHT

Jamie

Anna and I barely left the bed the rest of the day. After a second round, she thought I was out of commission—but I found her vibrator, and we had fun with that.

Eventually, we got up and ate a late lunch. We sat at the table eating our pasta with stupid grins on our faces. How the fuck did I get this lucky? I stared at her like a lovestruck teenager, and maybe it was true.

It was entirely possible I was in love with her, and had been for several months.

We did our best to make good on my promise of fucking all over the house. After dinner, I'd been doing the dishes when her hands slipped around my waist. She undid my shorts, turned me so my back was pressed against the sink, and went down on me. Her hot mouth made me so wild, the blow job ended with her bent over the island in the kitchen, my hands on her hips and hers squealing against the quartz counter top.

Her bed became our bed.

In the morning, it was still dark out when her phone chimed with a message.

And another.

On the third ding, Anna made a sound of frustration and hunted for the phone on the nightstand. I was half-asleep in a sex coma when she bolted upright, and it snapped me wide awake.

"What's wrong?" I asked. "Who's texting you?"

"My publicist." Her tone was hesitant. "She got a request for comment from TMZ."

It was still too early to process anything. "What?"

"They've already posted it and identified you." She turned her screen so I could see.

Pictures of me off the racetrack were always weird. I'd never understand why strangers would care about my personal life—I was barely famous. Anna had to deal with this shit way more than I did.

My first impression of the picture gave me a smile, but it froze. The invasion of privacy didn't usually bother me, but this one? It got under my skin. Most likely because it was with her.

The photographer had captured us on the beach yesterday. Anna, in her blue-green bikini, sitting on the sand, and me beside her, my hand on her leg. The perfect timing of the shot made that innocent moment between us look like a lot more. She was gazing up at me with a dazzling smile, and my body language read like I was leaning in to kiss her.

The picture was a lie, but also not. We'd made it true only minutes later.

"Whoever took it had to be on one of those boats," I said.

"Yeah, with a long fucking lens." She tossed the covers aside and climbed out of the bed, marching toward the bathroom.

I followed her, wincing as she snapped on the blinding overhead light. "This is bad?" I asked. "People knowing we're together?"

Anna skidded to a stop. She turned slowly to face me, her expression guarded. "Are we?"

I pinched the bridge of my nose. "Okay, it's early, so I'm not keeping up. Are we, what?"

"Together."

"Is this a thing you do? Talking crazy in the morning?" I teased. "Of course, we are."

She looked simultaneously relieved and nervous as she took a step in my direction, closing some of the space between us. "I mean, how does it work? We live on opposite sides of the country."

"We'll figure it out." I said it with all the confidence I possessed, because I wanted this and would do everything I could to make it happen. "And whatever you want to tell your publicist is fine with me."

"That's what I'm upset about. Couldn't we have had one day to ourselves? Just one freaking day?" She moved into my arms and set her warm hands on my chest. "People are going to find out, rather than hear it from us first. People like our parents."

Shit, she made a good point. I'd need to call my mom ASAP if I wanted to save myself an earful. I'd said Anna and I had become friends, but I hadn't mentioned I was going on vacation with her.

I hugged Anna tighter, running my hands up and down her back. "There's a silver lining though."

"Yeah?"

"Sam Richards is going to lose it when she finds out."

A tiny laugh shook her shoulders. "It's Hidenrite now. And honestly, it's hard to dislike her, because she's the one who got us talking."

"True."

She tilted her head so she could peer up at me. "Are you worried about what people will say?"

"Worried?"

"Not everyone liked the movie I was in."

I understood what she meant, how people judged her for the role. Like Rob did. "Well, those people are fucking idiots. It's nobody's business what we do, but whatever they say, I can handle the heat. I wear a fire suit at my day job, you know."

She lifted an eyebrow, silently mocking my lame joke.

"Yeah, not my best effort. As I mentioned, it's early." I kissed her deeply then dropped my voice low. "Come back to bed."

"Okay. I'll be there in a minute."

I strolled back to the bedroom, got under the sheet, and waited for her return. She was right. We needed to have a conversation about how our relationship was going to work, but I didn't see the rush. We'd spent a year talking—we'd earned one day of acting on our feelings before sorting it out.

The bathroom light flipped off, and the bed moved as she crawled onto it, her hand snaking across my chest. I covered it with my palm and cast my other arm around her, tucking her in at my side.

My phone rang. It didn't chime with a text—it *rang*.

I snatched it up, and as soon as I read the name, my stomach bottomed out. I sat up and tapped the screen. "Hello?"

"Are you seriously in Hawaii with that porn actress?" Rob demanded. His voice was loud enough, there was no way Anna hadn't heard him, and her flinch told me she had.

"She doesn't do porn," I snapped. "And it's none of your business where I am, or who I'm with."

"Listen, kid, I've been doing this since you were in diapers, so I know a thing or two. You can think it's nobody's business, but you're dreaming. Money makes that car go around the track. Not you."

A chill settled on my skin.

"Some of your 'fans,'" he said the word with disdain, "might not care who you're involved with, but our sponsors might. And *that* is very much Randall Whitman's business."

There was an inkling of truth in what he was saying. NASCAR was a conservative sport, and as a driver and the face of the team, I sometimes had to jump through sponsors' hoops. But I wasn't going to put up with this bullshit. "This is stupid."

"Yeah, I agree. Get yourself on the next flight home if you want to be here when I tell Randall."

Anna winced, and it banded a tight, uncomfortable feeling around my chest. She slid out of the bed and scurried toward the hall. *Fuck.*

"No, Rob, I meant what you're saying is stupid. You want to tell me what to do when I'm behind the wheel? Fine. But stay the fuck out of my personal life."

"You don't get a personal life, Campbell. That's the sacrifice you made when you got in the driver's seat of the sixty-five car. I'm ready to find a driver who can handle that."

This was it; he was making a move against me. I gnashed my teeth together. "Is that everyone talking, or just you?"

There was a pause. "I'm sure Randall feels the same way."

"Great. Let's schedule a call."

There was a long silence. He was expecting me to roll over or beg, but that wasn't my style.

"All right." He sounded smug. "If that's what you want to do."

He was sure when we went head-to-head, he'd come out on top—and he was probably right. But, fuck it. For two seasons, I'd put up with him, but this crossed a line. I was starting to realize losing my job wasn't so bad, because at least it meant I wouldn't have to work with him anymore.

Rob announced he'd get the meeting scheduled and hung up without another word.

I scrubbed a hand over my face, my fingers bristling on my stubble. It was the first time I'd gone more than two days without shaving since the start of the racing season. Whitman's PR company had it in my contract that I "always maintain a clean, All-American look."

I carried my phone out into the kitchen and set it on the counter. Anna stood nearby, staring out the back windows. The sun hadn't peeked out over the water, but there was an orange-blue glow on the horizon.

"Rob's an asshole," I said.

Anna turned and lobbed a sad smile in my direction, but her eyes didn't meet mine. "Do you need to head home and smooth things over?"

"No."

She gave me her full attention then, and worry etched her face. "Are you sure that's a good idea?"

"It's fine." I did my best to sound convincing, but I must have failed, because her concern grew.

"Jamie, all you've ever wanted to be was a driver. Don't let me put your job in jeopardy. If you need to go, I understand."

"No," I said with force this time. "The only way I'm leaving is if you tell me to. I want this. I want . . . *us*. Don't you?"

She softened. "Yes, but—"

"Okay, good." I was aware it might be too soon to talk about it, but I needed her to know I was serious. "Because, with you? It's different than how I've felt about anyone else."

Her eyes went as wide as tires.

"I'm not trying to scare you," I added quickly. "I know it's a lot, and . . . like, fast."

I'd come as close to telling her I loved her as I could without actually saying it. I liked risk, but putting those three words out there right now? It was a challenge.

Anna licked her lips as if her mouth had gone dry. "You're not scaring me." Her expression warmed, and she gave me that shy smile I loved. "I feel the same way about you."

I didn't get time to enjoy the way hearing her say that made me feel, because my phone dinged with a text message. It was from Rob with a link to the video chat and the start time of two p.m. Eastern.

It meant I probably had two hours left living my dream job as a NASCAR driver, but as I looked at Anna's smile, I was fine with whatever happened. I had her.

CHAPTER NINE

Jamie

Anna and I had a hike planned for the day. We were supposed to go on a waterfall tour, but my call with Randall Whitman forced us to cancel. Instead of climbing a volcano, I sat in the spare bedroom with my laptop open, watching the clock tick down until the most important meeting of my life started.

Rob's image came onscreen first. He sat in his home office, the background decorated with a shit-ton of awards and memorabilia he'd probably dug out of storage just to intimidate me. All I had was a blank wall behind me and my clean-shaven face.

"We need to make this quick," Rob said. "Randall squeezed us in, but just barely."

"This won't take long."

The asshole smirked. The window flickered, and Randall Whitman filled the screen. He was in his sixties, a stocky guy with white hair and bushy eyebrows. He could look friendly or formidable whenever he needed to. I liked that he was a cut-the-bullshit kind of guy—he'd inherited a struggling cereal company and turned it into a household name by the time he was forty.

"Campbell," he said. "Rob tells me there's a problem?"

I opened my mouth to speak, but Rob jumped in. "He's damaged the Whitman Racing image."

Whitman looked concerned. "What's happened?"

"He's dating a porn star."

If I could have reached through the screen and throat-punched Rob, I would have. "I'm not, and even if I was—"

"That movie is pure filth."

I clenched my hands into fists and took a deep breath. I had to ignore him. Nothing I said was going to change Rob's mind. "Mr. Whitman, I'm dating Anna Douglas. If that's a problem, I'd like to hear it from you."

Annoyance flashed through Whitman's eyes. "That's the issue? He's dating an actress?"

Rob blinked at this setback. "There are photos of them online."

Whitman's gaze narrowed. "What kind of photos?"

"One photo," I corrected. "And it's nothing." I tapped my phone and scrolled to the image, then held it up to the camera for Whitman to see.

He made a 'you gotta be kidding me' sound.

Rob's face turned an even brighter shade of red than it usually was. "Think about how this is going to look to our family-friendly sponsors." His tone said even he wasn't convinced.

"Rob, I don't have time for this. As long as it's within reason, sponsors aren't going to care about Campbell's personal life."

As Whitman shuffled the papers on his desk, the tension in my shoulders relaxed a fraction of a degree. If he'd gone the other way on this, I'd have given him a resignation speech, telling him I didn't want to work for someone who demanded that level of control over my life.

Rob's chest lifted as he took in a preparing breath. "Things aren't working between me and Campbell. They never have. He's not the right fit for this organization."

Whitman paused and lifted a thick eyebrow. "I'm not hearing that from anyone else."

"The kid doesn't listen, and I'm starting to wonder if there's even a brain in there."

I opened my mouth to defend myself, but Whitman sighed loudly. "I'm tired of hearing this. You should know, Rob, the only person I get complaints about is you." He ignored his employee's surprise. "You're right about it not working. I need guys who are on the same page. Campbell, you want to continue being part of the team?"

I straightened in my seat. "Yes, sir."

"Great." He looked satisfied. "Rob?"

Rob went cold as he laid it on the line. "No, not if Campbell's behind the wheel."

"All right, then. I guess we're doing this." Whitman stood from his chair and leaned over so he stayed in the frame. "We'll go forward with a different crew chief next season. Thanks for all your work with Whitman Racing."

"Wait—" Rob sputtered.

"Campbell," Whitman wasn't deterred, "I need to handle this, and I'll be in touch."

The screen jumped to black, and the message appeared announcing my call had ended.

Holy. Shit.

Did that just happen?

I padded out into the main room. Anna took one look at my dazed expression and launched to her feet from the couch. "What happened?"

"He fired Rob." Hearing it out loud was weird, but also, all kinds of awesome.

"Oh my God, really?" She looked relieved. "So, you're okay?"

It was like I'd crossed the finish line a million times over. I slipped an arm around her, putting my hand on her ass, and pulled her tight to me. "Are you kidding? I think I'm way better than okay."

I cut off her laugh when I kissed her. It started slow and sweet but didn't stay that way for long. Her tongue moved in my mouth and her hands were on my shoulders, sliding up into my hair.

"We can still make the hiking trip," I mumbled between her kisses.

"Too late," she said, undoing the button on my shorts and pushing them down over my hips. "Your pants are already off."

Jesus, she brought out the horny teenager in me. It was like no time had passed since high school. And with that thought came another. "Are you going home for Christmas?"

She was halfway out of her shirt and slowed her movement. "That's random, but yeah. Why?"

We'd been so busy planning this trip, I hadn't asked about her plans. The holidays were only a few weeks away. "That's when we can see each other again."

She beamed a smile as she undid her own shorts. "Awesome. Also, we need to get your schedule to Sato. She's a miracle worker."

The sight of a half-naked Anna made my heart rate jump. "See? I told you we'd figure this long-distance thing out."

She looked skeptical. "It kind of sounds like Sato's going to figure it out."

I shrugged. "Whatever. We've got this." I reached around her body and undid her bra. "Patio or jacuzzi?"

She laughed as if I were joking, and sobered when she realized I was serious. Her voice was low and sultry. "Jacuzzi."

"Yes, ma'am."

We took off like it was a race, only it was one where it didn't matter who got there first.

Just as long as we were together.

ABOUT THE AUTHOR

USA Today bestselling author Nikki Sloane landed in graphic design after her careers as a waitress, a screenwriter, and a ballroom dance instructor fell through. For eight years she worked for a design firm in that extremely tall, black, and tiered building in Chicago that went through an unfortunate name change during her time there.

Now she lives in Kentucky, is married and has two sons. She is a three-time Romance Writers of America RITA© Finalist, also writes romantic suspense under the name Karyn Lawrence, and couldn't be any happier that people enjoy reading her sexy words.

More info available at: www.nikkisloane.com

Broken Hallelujah

SIERRA SIMONE

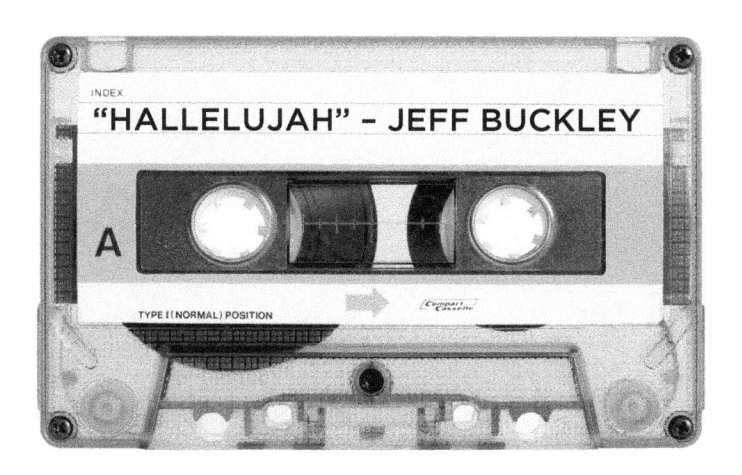

"HALLELUJAH" – JEFF BUCKLEY

NOW

There is life after death.

I know because I'm dead, and yet here I am, wet and miserable and very much alive.

My gravestone is a sharp, shiny black—so mirrored I can see the reflection of my booted calves and denim-clad thighs and the part of my long white coat around both. I heft the umbrella higher over my head so I can lean in to better examine the spray of flowers left at the base of the stone.

They aren't white or green or purple—the colors one usually sees in a cemetery—but bright, violent scarlet. Roses and poppies and dahlias, quickened and crimson against the rainy, silver world of the dead. They speak of sex and clenched, bloody longing.

Only one person would put those at my grave. But I don't touch them just yet, even though touching them is the closest I come to touching her. Instead, I take a deep breath and watch the rain gather in the cuts of my inscription.

Jenna "Jacey" Benjamin
1988-2016
"I have fought the good fight."
1LT
USMC

Nearly three years I've been dead, and still I can't get used to the sight of my name carved on this stone, any more than I'm used to seeing my father's name on the one next to it. I look over at his tombstone, larger and more imposing than mine, which is fair. He really *is* dead, after all. Somewhere under that wet green grass is a selfish, tortured man, and I don't miss him, I don't wish him alive—I wish only that all his fury and wrongdoing had also been contained by the platinum-inlaid urn along with his ashes. But alas, he still lives on in every decision Devon makes.

Devon.

I finally give in and touch her flowers, kneeling down atop my empty grave, not caring about the rain or the wet grass now, and just *touch*. Pretend I'm touching her face, her breasts, the sleek lines of her long thighs. Pretend she's touching my own body in that reverent, possessive way of hers, like I was a gift God left on an altar just for her.

I close my eyes and let my fingertips move over the wet, lush petals.

They're fresh. I wonder how often she puts them here. I wonder if she puts them here herself. I wonder if she misses me.

My fingers catch the edge of something that's neither petal nor thorn—pain slices bright on the inside of my first knuckle. I open my eyes to see fresh blood dropping onto the already blood-colored petals and disappearing into their silky depths. Tucked among them is a crisp white card, small and nearly imperceptible to all but the person who would run their fingers through the petals. And of course it would cut me. Nothing between me and her could ever be without pain.

I slide the card free, war clamoring in my ears, except this was a war I never even had a chance of winning.

I know, says the card in her spiky, aggressive script. And underneath that, it says, *I'm coming*.

I shoot to my feet, adrenaline pumping through me, scanning the silver-glass cemetery to make sure I'm unwatched. The rain makes veils and curtains of itself, hiding me from the rest of the world, but that doesn't mean I wasn't followed.

I crush the card in my palm and leave.

Devon knows I'm alive. Devon knows and she's coming for me.

♪

THEN

We were Marines in a war devised to mangle Marines.

We were marred, rent, disfigured. Carved into graven images of entropy.

Afghanistan.

2010.

The deadliest year of the war, and on record, women didn't go into combat, but the minute our plane touched down outside Kabul, the record meant shit. Everywhere was combat. Combat was underneath the streets ready to crumple your resupply truck with fire and force, combat was in the very stones, picking you off with *pings* and *cracks* the minute you left base walls.

The Bible says God is a man of war, and it was easy to believe there. No hammering into plowshares there, no wiping away tears, just torn flesh and burned flesh and whole flesh that nevertheless hid wounds that couldn't be seen. It was chaos.

But somehow, I managed.

I'd always been popular, charming, loved. I was strong and healthy and athletic—my broad-shouldered, curvy frame helped me thrive in activities like weight-lifting and archery—and with a father who'd been a Marine before he'd been in politics, my youth had been filled with push-ups and squat-thrusts (even if I insisted on doing calisthenics with fingernail polish and a full face of makeup). The male Marines liked me because I was funny and pretty and could sometimes beat them at arm-wrestling, and the women on my Female Engagement Team liked me because . . . well, because I was funny and pretty and sometimes beat the boys at arm-wrestling. And when we got to Musa Qala, my knack for Pashto and my boxes of free maxi pads for the local women made me pretty popular there too.

I wasn't a hero. I was just good.

I wasn't undamaged, but I was surviving.

I could have had a normal deployment. I could have came home fucked up from the shit in Marja, tired, broken, sleepless and haunted, but I still would have been Jacey. I still would have been myself.

But God is a man of war and his weapon was Devon.

♬

NOW

Maybe it was stupid to come back to Virginia, but I didn't know where else to go, and anyway, I steered as far clear from NoVa as possible. I found a nice little bungalow tucked into some nice, anonymous trees outside of Richmond, and I hid like my life depended on it. It probably did.

If you'd asked me ten years ago if I'd ever find a micron of solace living a life of near-monastic solitude, I would have laughed in your face. I've always thrived in groups and crowds, fed off the energy that came from being in the thick of things, loved meeting people and talking with them and laughing until my throat was sore.

A fake death puts a neat end to all of that, but what's more surprising is that I don't miss it. Maybe it's that I've needed three years of ascetic silence to move through the heartbreak, or maybe Devon's lessons actually paid off. Maybe I'd somehow transformed into a docile, patient submissive without even knowing it.

Well, *docile* might be a stretch.

I'm shaking from the rain and from Devon's note when I finally sit down in my living room. I put the note on the coffee table and stare at it. If Devon says she's coming, then she's coming. But why? And *how? How* does she goddamn know when the only other person who knows is my brother?

Because your brother is her husband, Jace. He must have told her.

I press my knuckles against my eyes, as if I can counter the pressure of the thought. The pressure of being betrayed by Michael. Again.

There's one other pressure though. The twisting, aching swell as my stomach climbs into my chest, as my heart climbs into my throat. Muscle memory collides with mental memory, and my cunt grows damp inside my panties, remembering. Her tongue. Her fingers. The feeling of her harness chafing against the inside of my thighs. Her teeth on my neck and the crack of her palm on my ass.

I press the knuckles in harder.

Be strong, Jacey, be strong, be strong bestrongbestrongbe—

No. I've been strong fucking long enough. So my body still belongs to her, so what? That doesn't mean she still has claim to my heart, although if I'm already being honest with myself, she was never interested in my heart anyway. She wanted a bigger prize—my soul, my essence. My everything.

I want to eat your light, she told me once right before she bit the skin over my heart. Rejecting the beating organ underneath in favor of something only she could see. *I want to eat up all your light for the rest of my life.*

I get to my feet, stripping off my wet coat and hopping out of my boots. A shower will help. A nice shower to clear my mind—

A key slides into the door.

I freeze, watching the dented doorknob rattle. Only Michael has an extra key, and he never leaves his Arlington cocoon long enough to come down here. Arguably, he made up for his betrayal by arranging and funding my fake death and anonymous resurrection after the roadside bomb that sent my father and I tumbling in a kettle of metal and flame. But neither of us feels at peace with the other; our very scant contact since my "death" was arranged and I was flown to a private Canadian hospital to recover has been strained and unpleasant. It's hard to fix something when no one did anything wrong. It's hard to fix something when I can barely muster the strength to speak his wife's name aloud.

It's just better we don't see one another, and Michael seems to agree.

So it's not my brother at the door. I stand there barefoot, in damp jeans and a thin sweater, wondering what to do. Where to go.

I know.

I'm coming.

It has to be her. It has to be Devon, and yet I can't make myself think past that to figure out what to do. How to feel. Do I stay? Do I run? Do I wrench open the door myself and strike her across the face? Scream until my screams pierce the gray veils of rain and reverberate through the woods?

I can't choose, can't decide. I've left her twice before, I've chosen pain after pain because they seemed like better choices than agreeing to still yet more pain, and I can't choose it a third time, I just can't. I don't have the strength, and I'm tired of being the only one who gives a shit about what happens to me, and I don't want to do it anymore, whatever *it* means. Living alone, crying tears into the dark, fucking my own hand like it's hers.

I'm not going to run. I'm not even going to scream.

Instead the door flies open, and I drop to my knees.

♫

THEN

There was stretch of road outside Lashkar Gah that chewed up soldiers and spat out bodies.

It wasn't a narrow pass or a bridge with vulnerable supports, nothing that obvious. Just a flat open road in flat open land, a path of compressed dirt and rock limned with fields of nodding poppies, green and pink and white and red. It seemed sleepy, like the middle of nowhere, a place where nothing should happen, where nothing ever would happen.

And yet.

IEDs were sown in the rutted track the way the poppies were sown in the fields next to it, and the harvest was sheared metal and blood. Sometimes the dogs would catch them, sometimes they'd detonate too early or too late and make for nothing more than an interesting show, but often enough they blowed us the fuck up.

The other FETs called the road Goliath. Big road, little Marines. And there we were, toddling up to death with our doggies and our grim prayers, and it was sometimes reassuring to think of us like David from the Old Testament, courageously approaching death with certain faith in God. But only sometimes.

Devon was driving a truck to Marja to drop off more FETs when it happened. *Boom.*

The bomb went off under the truck's back wheel, killing two female Marines and cracking Devon's head against the doorframe. She stumbled out, bleeding and disoriented, to a world of suspended moon dust and black smoke and bullets; death waited among the poppies, which were waist-high, thick, and perfect for hiding men with guns. They were far enough away from the other trucks in the convoy that Devon knew she was her own rescue, not that it probably fazed her in the least. She'd been born for this.

It didn't matter she was pinned down next to a truck of unconscious, injured Marines who needed saving, it didn't matter she couldn't see or hear, because heroes don't need those things. All she needed was breath in her lungs and God in her veins, and she would prevail. She did prevail. She saved everyone except for the two who died in the initial explosion, and she became a legend.

I finally met the David to our Goliath two days later when she moved into the flimsy tent-and-hut base we called home. She walked into the room I shared with four other women, set down her bag, and then looked down at me where I sat on my bed, trying to untangle my wet hair.

I looked up at her and suddenly couldn't breathe, because breathing felt almost heretical in the presence of someone so obviously loved by God.

I closed my eyes for a long beat, trying to etch the full mouth and the olive skin and the curling coffee-colored hair to memory. The tall frame with pert, high breasts that even her cammie shirt and her no-nonsense sports bra couldn't hide. She looked like an Artemis—war and untouchable sex—and she was so beautiful that I ached. Everywhere.

"Are you Jacey?" she asked, stepping closer. Her pants brushed against my blanket, and it felt so intimate, like she was touching me in all the places only my blanket touched me these days.

I opened my eyes. Yes, it still hurt to look at her, but I forced myself to look anyway. Forced myself to breathe, even though it felt as if she'd stolen my breath along with everything else.

I saw her, and I was taken by her. Not taken *with* her, you understand, I don't mean that I saw her and my heart fluttered and I felt some kind of emotional curiosity about this sultry, pout-mouthed newcomer.

No, I mean she *took* me. I looked at her and then she decided I was hers, and she took me. I belonged to her before I even said hello.

"Yes, I'm Jacey," I croaked out. I might as well have said, *please fuck me*, because those rosy lips curled up in a smirk that I presumed was usually given over cocktails or from the other side of a pillow.

"I'm Devon," she said, and I expected her to stick out her hand for a handshake, but she didn't. Rather, she put her hand on my shoulder in a way that could have been friendly . . . until she let her fingertips graze the back of my neck. "They told me you'd show me around."

I could. I would. I showed everyone around.

I was Jacey Benjamin, after all. Legacy girl. Fun girl. Popular girl.

I sucked in a breath and tried to pretend I hadn't just surrendered all that to a hero with a heart-shaped mouth. I would be fun and friendly and all the things I was best at.

"Sure. How'd you end up here, Devon?" I asked so I could have a way to introduce her—so I could say, *here's Devon fresh from the Kabubble*, or *Devon just finished in Nawzad, ladies, so she's used to the noise*. Friendly, cheerful shit like that.

But Devon just looked at me with those hero eyes and said, "God wants me to be here."

"He told you that, huh?"

She smiled at me then, a small, esoteric smile—the smile of someone who knows secrets as old as the dust currently filtering through the air around us.

"Maybe," she said.

And there was no way to tell if the shiver working its way down my spine was unease . . . or awe.

♬

NOW

She has the same mouth now. The same slender stretch of a body and the same dark eyes.

Her hair is no longer a lush cascade of curls—she's sliced it at the chin and styled it into a fall of sleek espresso. And there's the clothes, which are no longer the utility cammies and boots of our youth, but an impeccably tailored pair of black cigarette pants and a fitted white blouse that probably cost more than I made in a month as a Marine. Her feet are encased in delicately pointed heels—also black—and the thin ankle strap kisses places I used to kiss. The top of her foot. The inside of her ankle. The narrow ridge of tendon above her heel.

If I weren't already on my knees, I would have fallen there by now.

Devon stands at the threshold, her eyes glittering in the storm-soaked shadows of my living room, the rain itself behind her like a stage curtain. I should lower my eyes now, if I were really indulging in this facsimile of what we used to have, but I can't, I can't tear my gaze away from her, my warrior princess, my cruel queen.

"I still couldn't make myself believe it," she whispers. I can barely hear her over the rain. "Even when I saw you at the cemetery. I still thought it was a trick, or that I'd lost my mind . . ."

She stops, and I can see how hard she's breathing. That expensive shirt hugs the cups of her breasts and the narrow cage of her ribs, revealing her agitation, her anger, her . . . excitement?

She shuts the door behind her, as if only just now remembering it exists, and takes an uncertain step closer. "Why?" she asks. Begs. Her voice is throaty and balled full of hurt. "How could you leave me like that? Leave me to mourn? To *grieve* you?"

"I could ask you the same thing," I say, and I have a lot of pride in my tone for a woman who's on her knees, but I don't give a shit. I'm suddenly feeling every feeling it's possible to feel—angry and sad and horny and happy and just so, so fucking tired.

She hardens, soft emotion turning into sharp, cutting intensity. "Excuse me?"

"You left me first, Devon. For him."

Him leaves my mouth in a scalding, septic wave, a wave I can see break across her face like the ocean breaks on rocks. *Him* is an evil word between us, because it doesn't just mean *male* and *man*, but it also means *blood* and *brother*. It was a stab that I'd been left for a man, sure, but Devon had never pretended to be anything other than bisexual. But for that man to be my best friend and brother and heir apparent to my father's business and political legacy . . .

That was more than a stab. That was twisting the knife.

"I watched you put on a silk gown and walk down the aisle to him. I watched you put a ring on his finger and kiss—" I break off, unable to push the words off my tongue. Instead I say, "I *watched*, Devon. Every second of it. Because I naïvely thought there was still a chance, still a tiny chance, that you'd look into Michael's eyes and *know* it was supposed to be me."

"I didn't think I had a choice," she says, but she doesn't sound like she believes that.

I finally avert my eyes, not out of deference, but out of anger, and *that* launches her into action. She stalks toward me with five decisive clicks of those sexy heels, and grabs my chin, forcing my face back up to hers. She searches me.

"It hurt you so much you'd rather pretend to be dead?" she demands. "It hurt so much you needed to hurt me back? Nothing had to change, Jacey, nothing at all, we could have kept everything and gained so much!"

"Fuck you," I hiss. "I wasn't going to be your mistress. Not when I knew you'd go back home to *fuck my brother*."

Her eyes are pure fire now. "I never lied to you, Jacey."

It's true; she never did lie. She wanted what my father had—the defense contracting business coupled with a career in politics—hell, she wanted to be president someday, a queen in truth, with an empire of money spread around an empire of power. The moment she learned Jacey Benjamin was Saul Benjamin's daughter, she told me her plans. To be mentored by my father, to become my father. To become part of the family.

The only mistake I made was believing she wanted to become part of the family through *me*.

I see her run her tongue over her teeth, which only emphasizes that perfect cupid's bow mouth, currently painted a shade of red designed to make cunts wet and dicks hard. "Michael and I are getting divorced," she finally concedes. There's defeat and defiance in her tone. "I asked him even before I knew you were alive. I couldn't—dammit, Jacey, I couldn't pretend any more. You're it for me. You're the only one."

I've wanted those words for so long they're in my marrow. My bones ache as she says them.

"I'm sorry," she says. "I won't make excuses and I can't anyway, because I was wrong, so fucking wrong. I'm sorry for everything, Jacey. I shouldn't have—well, there's so many things I fucked up—but I never should have hurt you."

"It's too late," I say, and try to get to my feet.

Unsurprisingly, she doesn't let me rise, but what is surprising is she gets to her knees too, digging her hands into my hair and pressing her forehead to mine. "Let me stay," she begs, rolling her forehead against mine. I realize she's crying. "Let me atone."

"You can't," I tell her. Shit, I've waited three years to tell her that.

Tears sparkle in her eyes, and I nearly cave. She's too fucking beautiful.

But I make myself repeat it. "You can't. It's too late."

♪

THEN

Nothing happened, nothing happened, nothing happened.

For days. Weeks.

Nothing.

We'd walk to the tent that was our makeshift DFAC, and I could hardly think over the sound of the wind whipping around her deceptively delicate frame. We'd be on patrol, and I could barely concentrate on anything other than the sun dancing in the depths of her eyes. And at night? As we slept on cots not two feet apart?

I couldn't inhale, exhale, rustle or stretch for fear I'd miss the sound of her breathing.

She often looked at me like I'd signed a contract I'd forgotten about, like I was disappointing her in some subtle, unknowable way, but I didn't mind. Having her look at me at all was a gift. Privacy is a joke on a FOB and this was pre-DADT repeal, and anyway, it was still one of the worst years of the fucking war. We were busy, dirty, crowded, celibate. So God knew that Devon's stern looks were the closest thing to pussy I was getting those days.

I needed release. I needed it as bad as any man.

Salvation came when a handful of us were picked to head back to Bagram to report on the progress the FETs had made with the local female population. We'd be at a real base, staying in rooms with real walls and doors, and I couldn't fucking wait. The whole flight there, I kept thinking about what I'd do first, if I'd slowly tease my clit until it went hard and needy or if I'd simply ball up a pillow between my legs and grind one out, fast and hard. And there I'd be on my bench seat, wet and squirming with anticipation, and Devon would look up and meet my gaze, and I could have sworn she knew exactly what I was thinking about. And me, Jacey, the girl who'd gotten laid at least three times a week before deployment, blushed.

I *blushed*. And when I looked back at Devon, her expression had completely changed. Gone was the vague disapproval for some sin I didn't know I committed, gone was the disappointment. In its place was pure, ferocious hunger, the face of a starving woman whose only food was the blood-rich cheeks of a young woman.

I blushed even more.

We landed, we were introduced, given an efficient tour of Bagram's neatly ordered sprawl of barracks, mess halls, laundries and medical facilities, and then ordered to present ourselves at 0900 the next day to brief the brass. I was shown to a small room that was as flimsy and cheap as an interstate motel's, but it was brand new and after the dusty hovel that was our base back at Musa Qala, it felt like fucking paradise. It was no secret why we were given such comparatively nice rooms—my father, of course, and that far-reaching Benjamin name—but I didn't care about that either. If having a monster for a father was the price to pay for this unexpected luxury of a door and a real mattress, I'd take it.

I plopped my small bag of shit on the floor and went right to the showers, do not pass go, do not collect two hundred dollars. After the tented shower room with its weak dribbling bladders of lukewarm water, a real shower in a tiled space felt better than a day at a Swiss spa.

Clean and scrubbed and hornier than ever, I went back to my room.

I'd dressed after the shower for the walk back to my room, back in the good old olive drab T-shirt and a clean pair of cammie bottoms, so it took me a minute after I shut my door to unbuckle the woven belt and kick off the pants, leaving me only in boy shorts and the shirt. I had one knee on the bed and one hand in my boy shorts when the door opened.

Opened.

Leaving me exposed: bare legs, hair wet, nipples hard. Hand shaped to the swell of my long-denied cunt.

My head swiveled in panic as I tried to stand on both feet and pull my hand free at the same time, and ended up performing an awkward, jerky hop in front of my intruder.

It was Devon.

She was in a clean uniform, the chain of her dog tags gleaming around the slender column of her neck, and the way her booted feet filled the threshold of the doorway sent a long, slow squeeze down my spine.

She kicked the door shut behind her and then stalked towards me, her expression the same starving one from the plane, and I was frozen in place now, my fingertips still trapped under the waistband of my panties and my wet hair dripping onto my shoulders.

Her hand came up underneath my chin, lifting my face to hers, and she smiled. I'd noticed before when Devon Jesse smiled at anyone, she had the power to make them feel like the only person in the room, a combination of all that focused willpower and energy and conviction. And now, as she smiled at me with her fingers under my chin, I felt like the only person in all of creation.

"Sometimes you look at me like I'm the only one who can save you," she said.

I had a moment of real, true fear then, the sensation of being poised on a blade. My father was powerful, my superiors liked me, but there was no such thing as *safe* while being queer in the military. I wasn't flirting only with the usual regs about fraternization if I messed around with her, I was flirting with some real serious shit. Investigation. Discharge.

Fuck.

But when I looked into her eyes, dark and framed by impossibly long lashes, I couldn't doubt what I saw there. Desire, pure and simple, except maybe not so simple, because I had a feeling that Devon's desires were different than those of other lovers I've had.

"I can, you know," she added softly.

I sounded dazed and doubtful when I asked her to clarify. "Can what?"

"Save you."

I needed to be saved from celibacy, of course, but I felt like she was talking about something else, something I didn't even know about myself. I shivered, silently asked myself if I was willing to learn, decided I was, and then shivered again. "No one can know," I said on a swallow.

"Certainly."

"And why me? Why now?"

Her eyes ducked down, a becoming sweep of inky lashes on her perfect cheekbones. If I didn't know her, didn't know she was a hero and tough as nails, I would've thought she was feeling shy.

"Because you're the only one I even see any more. You're all I can think about, all I can fantasize about, and I can't stand having you so near, all warm and wet and waiting, without doing something about it."

She was raw and honest, her voice low and trembling and her fingers shaking ever so slightly around my chin.

"Okay," I whispered. "Okay."

I was rewarded with a hard kiss to the mouth, a kiss that tore the breath and uncertainty away from me, and then she pulled back, her mouth a little swollen and her pupils wide.

"There's a way it has to be between us," she told me. "And if you don't like it, at the beginning or at any point after, you tell me to stop and I'll stop, got it?"

"Got it. But what are you talking about?"

She gripped my chin harder and I whimpered.

Fuck, but I was innocent then. Sure, I'd screwed a healthy number of women in college and before deployment—being femme and a Marine put me at the center of a very fun Venn diagram and I never had to look hard for bedmates, provided I was looking in the right places. And yes, within that number, there'd been a smattering of playful bondage scenes and some interesting toys employed, but never what Devon needed. Never what Devon *was*.

I'd never looked someone in the eyes and known, gut-deep, that they would feed on me like a vampire if I let them.

It was exhilarating and terrifying, and suddenly I knew what she meant about saving me, because I realized I'd been waiting, possibly all my life, to be fed on.

"Show it to me," she said abruptly. "Your cunt. I want to see it."

Oh God, this was more than sex, she wanted more than a lush body to use. She wanted my dignity, my vulnerability, my doubt. That's what she would feed on, that was her blood.

And sure enough, when I swallowed and tugged the waistband of my boy shorts down past the pouting lips of my pussy, her nostrils flared and her pulse pounded at the side of her neck like she was running a race. She dropped my jaw, stepping back to look at what I'd exposed for her, her sides heaving with quick, rough breaths.

"Bad girl," she said, her eyes hot on the place where I ached. "Keeping that hidden from me all this time. You didn't think I needed it? All those cold nights, you didn't think I could use a nice, warm cunt to cheer me up?"

"I—"

"You don't speak unless I give you permission," she grated out. "And right now, you don't stand unless you have permission. On your fucking knees, Marine."

I went to my knees. Without hesitation, without argument or resistance, and I could easily have blamed it on my slick pussy, which was currently willing to beg, borrow or steal any possible means of getting attention, but it wasn't just lust. It was because I belonged there, at her will, at her beck and call.

It was because I already belonged to her, and I'd known it for weeks, I just hadn't realized *how* I belonged to her. But now I knew.

Now I knew.

It was harder to keep my pussy open to view like this—I had to spread my knees an uncomfortable amount—but Devon didn't seem to be particularly concerned with my comfort. Instead, she squatted in front of me, slid her hand past mine, and palmed my pussy with an authority that made me want to kneel down for her all over again.

"This is mine now," she informed me, two fingers breaching my entrance so there could be no doubt about what she spoke of.

And herself? Would I be the only one to kneel for her and pleasure her?

She seemed to read the question in my eyes. "Yes, Jace," she said, in a somewhat gentler tone. "I'm all yours too. I don't want—" She blinked, as if she were surprised to realize this. "It's only you, and it has been since the moment I met you."

I let out a long, breathy noise at that, my heart hammering with shock and pure joy.

"You have permission to stand, to undress and then back on your knees," she said matter-of-factly, standing and pulling at her belt. "You're going to eat me, and you're going to eat me good. Fuck knows I've waited long enough for it."

I was out of my clothes like Superman, back on the floor

and ready when she stepped within reach. I instinctively knew I shouldn't touch her, that touching her would be outside the rules of *the way it has to be*, but her naked body was like a revelation, like the landscape of heaven itself, and I had to touch her, I had to. Those bladed hipbones, and that taut stomach. Those small, pert breasts with their caramel tips. And that pussy, like a rich gift between her thighs.

I touched her.

Her ass pushed against my palms as I brought her to my mouth, and I reveled in the feel of it, of her, of the firm but plush curves so round and soft and strong all at once. And I held her as long as she let me—which wasn't long, because she gave my hair an eye-watering yank after only a few seconds.

"Only your mouth," she commanded.

"Or what?" I provoked, peering up at her with my lips still against her mound.

She arched a perfectly winged eyebrow at me. "Or I'll stripe your ass with my belt. Is that enough of a *what* for you?"

I had to say, it didn't sound so bad, not if it involved Devon and me with my pants off. But I obeyed for now, sliding my tongue over her erect clit and into the heart of her. She smelled of her own shower—soap-scented and clean and warm—but her *taste*, her taste was all her—a little tart, a little sweet, and all Devon. I could've stayed like that for the rest of my life, with my nose buried in those glossy curls and her core exposed to my mouth.

I shuddered. Again and again. I felt almost dizzy from her, light-headed with lust, about to pass out from the throb of my blood-swollen cunt and the raw desire twisting my stomach. Without realizing it, I'd started rocking my pussy against the empty air, seeking out friction or stimulation or *anything*, and that earned me another hair-pull, although when she spoke, she sounded amused.

"Poor Jacey," she taunted. "Needs to be fucked so bad she's trying to fuck the air. What would you be doing without me, hmm? Fucking your bedpost? Humping a pillow?"

I could only moan against her in response. Mapping out the

forbidden-until-now folds and wells of her female flesh with my tongue and lips had me mindless, panting, and despite her almost cruel teasing, she was now stroking my hair affectionately, as if I were pleasing her beyond simply tongue-fucking her.

It pleased her to have me humbled. Stripped of clothes and dignity. Desperate.

And who would have guessed?

It pleased me too.

I licked and sucked and swirled, until my face was covered in her and she had both hands cradling the back of my head, holding me tight to her while she took over and fucked my mouth like it was a spoil of war. The world disappeared, or rather, she became the world, my only world, her silk on my tongue, her arousal smeared all over my mouth and cheeks and chin, and the sinuous roll of her hips as she fucked my face, the only things I was sensible of.

She came like a queen.

She threw her head back, dark waterfalls of hair everywhere in a sinfully tempting display, her belly quivering and her hands still forcing me to her, forcing me to eat her orgasm and drink her pleasure in using my mouth. From below, my vision was a collage of regal sex—the long, delicate arch of her throat and glimpses of richly colored hair and the pebbled points of her nipples. I could feel the tantalizing contractions of her climax against my mouth, and I stabbed into her with my tongue over and over, ignoring every ache in my jaw and neck, because her satisfaction was the only thing that mattered. *She* was the only thing that mattered.

After a long minute of pleasure, she moved my face up a little higher to her clit. "That's right," she said. "Nurse on it."

I was squirming, aroused to the point of pain now, by her words and her body and the preemptory way she handled me—tugging down on my jaw when my mouth wasn't open enough for her or pressing my nose into her curls when it amused her to toy with my breathing.

And this time when she came, she murmured my name. *Jace, Jace, oh God, Jace, you wicked girl.*

When she finished, she made me suck her clit again and give her a third.

Then a fourth, this time with my fingers inside her and her hips rolling like mad.

Finally, finally, she took pity on me. I was nudged onto the bed and straddled, and she took my tits in hand, obviously pleased by their size. She'd hold one in a punishing squeeze and then slap the tip, free it and then slap it harder, she'd lean down and bite and nurse, and after my hands instinctively went to her head the first time my nipple was treated to the hot suck of her mouth, I was indeed striped by her belt. You'd think it hard to get a good sting out of a woven belt, but Devon managed. Oh, how she managed.

When she finished, she straddled me once more, and she was a queen again, and I was her steed or her throne, and then her fingers pressed against my clit and I was nothing at all. I was wet, screaming, the release so big and so pent up that it was agony to let it claim me, and it was only after it subsided and Devon removed the hand she'd clapped over my mouth to smother my screams that I realized I was sobbing.

I'd never had sex like this.

I only wanted to have sex like this for the rest of my life.

Devon had me stay in bed while she got me a bottle of water and some baby wipes. And after we were all clean and hydrated, she climbed into bed and curled her supple form against my back, stroking my arm as I still flew high on endorphins. It was unexpectedly tender after being used so thoroughly, and that's when I knew.

I was going to fall in love with her.

♫

NOW

It's too late.

But my thrumming pulse doesn't know that, nor the tightness

in my belly nor the aching points of my nipples. They all seem to say, would it really be so bad? Just once? Just one goodbye fuck?

"I know I'm supposed to back off now, I know I'm supposed to leave, and I swear to God I will," she says, and I believe her. Unlike most of us, when Devon swears to God, she means it. As much as He means what He swears to her, I suppose.

"But please, Jace, let me do something, let me do anything to show you how fucking sorry I am."

There's a part of me that thinks, this is still about her. Like her need to atone is bigger than my need to be away from her.

But with a crumpling, sinking feeling, I realize that's not entirely true.

It's never that I needed to get away from her—she was right about that. Everything that's happened since my ill-fated trip back to Helmand was because I wanted to hurt her, I wanted to hurt her like she hurt me. Recklessly and without pity. I wanted her heart clawed from her chest and torn to pieces by jackals.

The very thought deflates me. Who have I become? And why? What is the point of hurting her when hurting her means hurting myself?

I slump against her and she catches me, holding me against her.

"Please, Jace," she begs softly, her lips in my hair. My nervous system catches fire at the feeling of her mouth on me after all this time; my blood sings. "Please."

It will never matter how selfish she is or how cruel.

I still want her.

"Yes," I say, my mind defeated and my heart victorious. "Yes."

♪

THEN

We fucked constantly.

We fucked when it was dangerous and stupid, and when it

was safe and sedate. We fucked on leave and we fucked on base. We fucked slow and fast, quiet and loud, with toys and improvised bondage equipment and sometimes only with bare skin and imagination.

But all of our fucking was like the first time. Devon was my queen and I was her subject, and whatever pleased her to do, we did.

I loved it. I loved her.

She said it first though, my hero, my woman sent to war by God. We got back to Musa Qala after three days of furtive sex at Bagram, my ass beat raw and my stomach festooned with bite marks, and she threw her bag on her cot, turned to look at me and declared, "I love you."

"It's only been three days," I said. My chest felt like birds were trapped inside. I couldn't breathe, but in the best way.

Devon smiled that esoteric smile again. "It doesn't matter." And then she pushed me against the wall, shoved her hand down my pants, and made me come.

I didn't say it back to her for a whole year. I don't know why. Maybe it felt like it was cheap to offer it up in the face of her dauntless certainty, or maybe it felt like I was already vulnerable to her in every way and I couldn't bear to give up this one last vulnerability. Whatever the reason, I was only able to muster up the courage to say it after our deployment ended and we were back at Pendleton.

It was the day before she met my brother.

Looking back, I see the mistakes—and the mistakes were mostly mine. She made no secret of her awe of my father and my family, she often talked about wanting to know Saul, wanting to learn from him. And when I was candid about the fact that he'd never been more than coldly accepting of me, that he'd never accept giving power in the company to someone openly queer, she made only a small noise of rumination, as if it were a problem to be solved.

I should have asked her then, I should have pressed her, told her more, explained to her my hopes and wishes and needs. But she was so fearless in the face of bullets. Why wouldn't I have assumed she'd be fearless enough to marry me?

We had four good years after that. We were young and being stationed all over the place and so it wasn't until I'd done my four years of active duty and resigned my commission to work for my family's defense contracting company that I wanted to start making plans. I wanted to get married, I wanted to buy a house. I wanted children and backyard barbecues and Disney vacations and all the twee family shit I never had being raised by a cold, powerful man.

I told her on a cool, fall day, sitting outside my family's house in Virginia horse country. We were on the long verandah watching the wind toy restlessly with the almost-turned leaves, and I loved her and it was time.

"I want to marry you," I said. "So marry me. Please." I naively believed there were no excuses left to be had. She'd just resigned her commission too—also to work for the Benjamin empire—and the SCOTUS ruling meant all sorts of hurdles on the legal and bureaucratic ends would be sorting themselves out. My father adored her—was jealous of her, even—and while he still didn't like our relationship, he'd accept it eventually. After all, if parental objections really mattered, then hardly anyone would get married, right?

So I'd assumed I'd blurt it out, and maybe I'd earn a little hell in bed for not allowing her to propose first, but I liked hell in bed, and anyway, it was time, and so she'd say yes and we'd kiss and then disappear upstairs to fuck.

She didn't say yes.

She didn't say anything at all.

I eventually turned and looked at her. Looked at the wind caressing the soft brown silk of her hair.

She didn't look back at me. "I'm going to marry your brother."

She might as well have told me in Pashto for how long it took the words to sink in. "Excuse me?"

"I didn't—I don't—" For once my hero sounded uncertain. "I think it's what I'm supposed to do."

I didn't understand. I didn't understand. She and I were happy, we were in love, even five years in we were as frantic and horny and obsessed as we'd been when we first met. How long had she . . . had they . . .

"I haven't fucked him," she said, reading my thoughts. "But nevertheless, marrying him is what I need to do if I'm supposed to get where I need to go."

I still didn't understand. Nothing made sense, not her words, not her uncertainty, not her path, none of it.

She softened. "Jace," she said, "nothing has to change. I've already spoken with him and he understands that you and I will still be together. In fact, we'll be together even more this way. This is just a . . . formality . . . that keeps me in your father's good graces."

"Fuck you," was all I could manage at that. "Fuck you, 'nothing has to change.'"

She bit her lip, and I realized I'd become addicted to her surety and confidence over the years because seeing the absence of it was beyond disorienting. "I don't like it either," she whispered. "But I know there's this place, this thing, that I'm supposed to *be*, and this is the way to be it. Your father won't accept me marrying you, I won't be his right-hand man then. But if I marry his beloved son . . ."

"This is the stereotype, you know," I said bitterly. "This is why people say you can't trust bi girls."

I expected her to snap back, to defend herself because it was a shitty thing for me to say, but she didn't. Her shoulders rounded in unhappiness. "I hate this too. I hate it."

"Then *why?*" I demanded, my voice shaking and furious and choked with tears. "Just because you think God wants you to be some kind of king?"

"Yes," she said simply, and there it was. The certainty again, the wall around her tabernacle heart that I'd never be able to breach. She finally found a light she could eat and eat and never grow full of, and it wasn't mine. It was God's.

Tears and hysteria were strangling me, and any minute I'd succumb. I'd perish and dissolve, and I refused to let her see. Refused to let her have that indignity when I'd already given her so many. I stood up and she caught my hand, pressing it to her heart.

"I love you," she said earnestly, looking up at me. "I won't pretend this isn't a hurdle, but we'll figure it out, Jace, I promise."

"I'm leaving."

"I get it," she said, holding my hand even tighter. "I'll sleep in the guest room tonight. I know you need space while you digest this, and tomorrow we'll figure out how to make you happy too, okay?"

I just stared at her. She really thought a way could exist to make me happy while she married my brother? She thought I just needed time to *digest*?

I pulled my hand back. I said nothing. And I went and packed my bag and left her there with my family—which was now going to be just as much hers as it was mine.

She called and called. She texted. She wrote letters. She showed up on my doorstep for months afterward.

She loved me, she said. She needed me. Why was I holding her back?

"I'm not holding you back," I'd tell her. "Do whatever you want." I didn't mean that, though. I just hoped to be the only thing she wanted, but I wasn't, I would never be.

The trouble with heroes and kings, I guess.

I cried myself to sleep every night without her. For eight months. And then I went to her wedding.

I'd never responded to the invitation, had refused to discuss the matter with my brother and father, and had certainly refused to talk to Devon about it, no matter how much she tried to woo me into being her mistress. But I'd gone because I knew I had to see it myself, I had to extinguish that last part of me that pined for some kind of happy ending. The hope that she'd see me and change her mind and she'd spend the rest of the night fucking me while wearing her wedding dress.

None of that happened, of course. She married my brother. She kissed him, and it was a chaste enough kiss, but it didn't matter. She'd promised me once her body was mine and now it wasn't and why oh why had I ever thought I could have her? Keep her? Love her? I could claw and claw but never scratch her, I could reach and reach and never grab her. She would never be mine, she was never mine, she'd always been my father's, my brother's, God's.

And so I went with my father the very next week on a fairly dangerous trip back to Helmand, this time to check on our private defense installations and not as a Marine. When the bomb went off under our truck, there was a split second where I thought . . . *at last, at last,* at last God had answered my prayers for the pain to stop.

What a lie.

When I woke up, broken, stitched, drugged, Michael was there. "Dad's dead," he said.

"Okay."

"Devon's on her way."

"No."

"*Jace,*" he said, and his voice had trembled. His father was dead, his sister was nearly there, and his wife would be flying in to weep over the bed of the real person she loved. It must have been hell for him.

"No," I said. I didn't care about his hell. "Michael, please. Don't let her—tell her anything. Tell her I'm dead."

The moment the words bloomed on my tongue, I knew. It made sense. In every way except the obvious, it made sense. And Michael wasn't as hard to convince as he should have been; perhaps the idea of me being dead appealed to the parts of him that wanted Devon to be wholly his. Or perhaps he could hear the pain in my voice, the kind of weary misery that can only grow after heartbreak. Between the Benjamin name and the Benjamin money, it was shockingly easy to arrange in just a few short hours.

And so I died.

♫

NOW

Yes is all Devon needs to hear. I'm yanked to my feet and bent over the kitchen table faster than I can ask her what she's doing, and by the time I've caught my breath enough to ask, I don't need to anymore because my jeans are around my ankles and her tongue is in my cunt.

I pant against the table, my breath leaving clouds along the shiny surface, and she makes a sound of satisfaction, like a warrior running her finger along a sharpened blade. I'm hers once again, for however short a time, and we both fall headlong into the spell of that. She gives me a final lick that's more for her pleasure than mine, then stands up behind me. She palms my cunt, her middle finger pressing hard against my clit as she cups my heat, and I know I could come like this, just like this, because it's been so long and because it's her. *Her.* And no matter what she's done, it will always be her.

I'm spanked hard, although it's not punishment. I can't say *what* it is—something closer to worship maybe, an act of penitence and reverence, and the strikes are meant to heal me, to prove I'm the only thing she wants to touch and to own. With a long cry, I shudder out a climax just like that, grinding against her hand while my ass glows red from her attention.

"Stay here," she breathes, and then she walks out the front door while I bend bare-assed over the table, my sides heaving like a racehorse's and my pussy slowly wetting the insides of my thighs.

She comes back in with a black bag that's as familiar to me as the gold-flecked brown of her eyes, sets it on the table in front of my face. "You must have felt optimistic," I say, but I can't muster any real bitterness. Not when I want it as much as she does.

She gives an elegant sort of noise. "A good Marine is always prepared."

She strips me with care, lovingly, kissing and tasting all the skin her efforts reveal. I'm licked between the shoulder blades and down my spine. The soles of my feet are kissed too, my neck is sucked. By the time I'm completely naked, every single inch of my skin is tingling with want.

She pulls out a chair to the middle of the floor and sticks a thick cock to the wood, securing it with the sturdy suction cup at the end.

"On the chair," she says. "You know how."

I do know how. I am not new to what Devon likes to do with kitchen chairs.

I straddle the seat, as Devon leans down and takes my hip in one hand and grips the silicone dick in the other. She rubs the fat, cool head of it against my swollen pussy.

"It's big," I tell her.

"Where's the fun in small?"

I shiver. "It's been a long time since I've done this, Devon."

"Then I have to break my girl back in, don't it?" she says pleasantly and pushes me down.

The thickness spreads me open, parting me and tunneling through me, the pressure of it lighting up nerve endings that haven't been touched since before Devon told me she was going to marry my brother. Heat and tight desire radiate outward from the places where Devon's dick pierces me, and I moan at the sensation.

She sucks in a breath. "Dirty girl," she whispers.

I have to swivel to work myself down all the way, but finally I'm there, with my ass flat on the chair and my legs spread to straddle it. The cock is buried to the hilt, and every breath, every heartbeat, reminds me of its delicious invasion. Reminds me of her, and her will, and how much I love this. Being hers to play with and break.

After my ankles are secured to the legs of the chair, my wrists are tied to the back of the chair, and then the rope makes a wide X across my chest, doubles around my ribcage and fastens me even more completely to the wood. I can barely move.

"Oh Jace," Devon says, stepping back to look at me. I'm still wet, still squirming, my nipples bunched into tiny, tight points. I think the end of her cock is somewhere up in my chest. She groans as I squirm again. "I want to eat you alive."

"Yes, yes, yes," I chant, leaning my head back in a fruitless bid to try to move my hips forward to fuck the length inside me, but I can't move, I can't do anything but wait.

A vibrator emerges from the black bag, and I'm fascinated by the lewd contrast of it in her hand. Those expensive, delicate shoes and those designer pants—her slender hand with its impeccable manicure—it all frames the blunt, utilitarian shape of the wand. And soon this elegant woman is going to bend down to me and tease my clit with it while I'm impaled on a cock of her choosing and tied to a chair.

It's the kind of contrast only Devon could pull off.

The wand begins buzzing, and the minute she touches it to my swollen clitoris, she takes my mouth in a brutal kiss so she can eat up every gasp and grunt and sigh of mine. Her lips—soft and warm—part to allow her tongue to slide across mine, and she grips my jaw with her other hand to open my mouth even more to her claim. It's all silky tongues and deep, filthy pressure, and quivers of sensation chasing up and down my thighs and belly. It feels so good, so fucking good, and all those vibrations are shaking me apart, shaking my anger and my pain into pointless pieces and leaving nothing underneath but the girl I used to be. The girl who just wanted Devon all to herself.

I don't even realize I'm trying as hard as possible to fuck the chair until Devon says against my mouth, "Still that desperate little thing, aren't you? Needing it so bad?"

I answer with a climax that has me bucking against my restraints and crying out into her kiss—cries that she swallows hungrily. *Love me*, I want to beg. *Love me now.*

"I want another out of you," she says, and she does it. She presses the bulbous head of the wand even harder against me, coaxing a third orgasm out of me and then a fourth, until I'm crying and sweaty and pleading for her to stop in broken, agonized mumbles.

She stands up and takes me in with greedy eyes. "It killed me, missing this. Missing you."

I lick my lower lip, still trying to catch my breath, and her eyes go from greedy to downright vampiric. "*Fuck*, Jace," she breathes.

"What?"

"I fucking love you."

I'm shaken all the way apart now. "I love you too," I whisper.

She takes pity on me and unties me, helping me stand and supporting me when the slow drag of the cock out of my sensitive flesh is enough to make my knees buckle. Together, we go back to my room, where I lay naked and sweaty against her fashionable, still-clothed frame. I should be asking myself what I'm doing, letting her cuddle me and pet me, but I think maybe I don't care anymore.

I think maybe . . . I forgive her.

I shouldn't, she doesn't deserve it, and yet, there it is anyway. A shaft of light in a place that's been dark for three years.

"How are you?" she murmurs, running her fingers along my throat. "How are you feeling?"

"Like I just came three times on a giant-ass dildo."

"A *giant-ass* dildo or a giant *ass-dildo*?"

"Fuck you."

She just laughs.

The endorphins do their work, and I'm almost asleep when she says, "I left the company too, Jace. Along with divorcing Michael."

That wakes me up, and I roll onto an elbow so I can see her face. She simply keeps stroking my neck, her eyes clear and calm. "But that was your goal all along!" I protest. "To get to the top and follow in my father's footsteps."

She lifts a shoulder. "It was the wrong way. Hurting you never should have been an option, not ever, and that was the first sign I was doing everything wrong. I never should have wanted to *be* your father; he was afraid and jealous and angry all the time. I should have wanted to be my own kind of king."

"Why didn't you tell me all this before we fucked in my kitchen?"

Her hand moves to cradle my cheek and she gives me a smile with that perfect, heart-shaped mouth. "It's the right thing to do, and I didn't want to use the right thing to do as leverage in bed. I wanted to give you something without trying to manipulate you."

"Devon, everything you do is manipulation."

"Fine. I at least wanted to be transparent about the manipulation then."

We both laugh a little at that.

"And God?" I ask. "What does He want?"

She closes her eyes, regret and shame all over her beautiful face. "He wants me to be better, I think. I was so ready to be where I thought He wanted me that I forgot to truly listen, and I chased after power instead of honor."

She opens her eyes and says carefully, "It's a mistake I won't make again."

"You won't?"

She searches my face. "Do you understand what I'm saying?"

I shake my head, although I know what I hope she's saying, what I pray she means.

"I'll never hurt you again, Jace. I'll never put anything above loving you again, not power, not ambition, not anything, because I hate myself for what I've done and I love you more than anything. If you let me have you again, you'll be my entire world."

I want to be hers again. I want to forgive her, not because she deserves it, but because I love her and sometimes love means cold nights of howling into the dark and sometimes it means choosing to step back into the light instead. Love, like God, has to be merciful as often as it's terrifying, otherwise the terror of it all is for nothing.

"Yes," I say. "I'll let you."

She smiles, wide and happy and open, just like the youthful hero I met all those years ago. And I smile back.

"Really?" she asks.

"Really."

"I don't deserve it but fuck, I'm taking it anyway."

"That's the spirit," I laugh.

She yanks me into a searing kiss and rolls me onto my back, and within moments, she's naked and above me and together we move from sin and shame to ecstatic, carnal absolution. Together, our bodies make a kind of praise, a hymn and a worship.

A hallelujah that echoes through the night.
A prayer for eternity.
One in which I am very, very much alive.

ABOUT THE AUTHOR

Sierra is a voracious reader of all things including the smuttiest smut, young adult, piles of non-fiction for research, and everything Bill Bryson (especially on audio).

She loves writing the dirtiest things that she can think of, King Arthur, sparkling water, Tarot, coffee, leggings, and learning new words daily.

Her previous jobs have included firing ceramics, teaching living history lessons in one-room school house in full, 1908-approved school marm attire, and working as a librarian for several years—not in that order

She lives in the Kansas City area with her hot cop husband, two children, and two giant dogs. (And two cats, but they're so naughty we don't talk about them.)

More info available at: www.thesierrasimone.com

Say Yes

ELLE KENNEDY

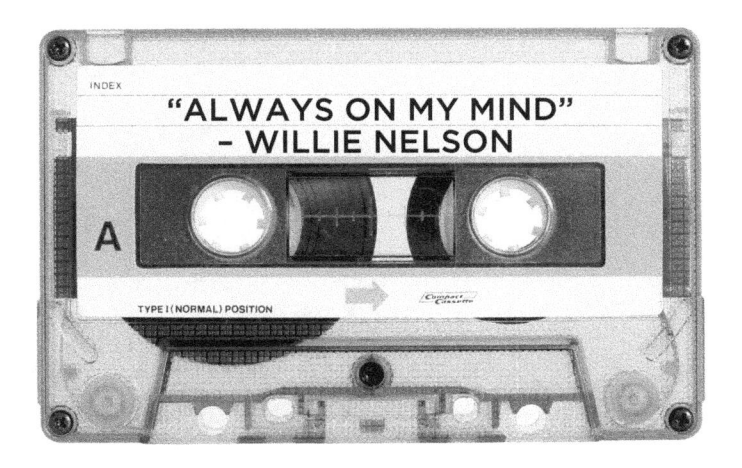

"ALWAYS ON MY MIND"
– WILLIE NELSON

PROLOGUE

Marcy & Devon

SAVE THE DATE

JANUARY 4, 2019

CHAPTER ONE

Emilia

Tom, 29
Interests: the gym, hiking, basketball, beers with the boys

Fine, so any man who lists "beers with the boys" as an "interest" probably isn't a viable long-term partner.

But who says I'm looking for one of those?

Tom's online profile might lean toward the douche side, but it doesn't stop me from swiping through his pictures. He likes the gym, all right—I find three gym-mirror selfies, one in which he's holding a dumbbell to show off his very defined biceps. Then we have the token shirtless shots, two on the beach, one at a swim-up pool bar with a bunch of guys who I'm assuming are "the boys." But where's the shirtless, bathroom-mirror selfie? There's always at least one of—there it is. Right on cue.

Tom has a pretty-boy face and an honest-to-God twelve-pack. Seriously, I can't even count the number of horizontal ripples slashing his tight abdomen.

The only problem is, he's *glistening*. I don't know if it's sweat or tanning oil, but his skin looks wet in every photograph.

As much as I'm hoping to score a fun hook-up for the night, I don't know if I would enjoy Tom dripping all over me.

I swipe left.

Bradley, 25

Ugh, I should probably change my age settings. Twenty-five is too young for me. But even if I had been able to ignore the age difference, there's no way I can overlook Bradley's teeny-tiny doll hands. In my experience, that old saying about a man's hands is one-hundred-percent true, and I have no desire to find myself in another awkward micropenis situation.

I swipe left.

And keep swiping left.

One left after the other.

Dammit. Where are all the hot men who are DTF? I swear, it's getting harder and harder to find an actual hook-up partner on this app. It's like all the men on here actually want to . . . shudder . . . date.

Don't get me wrong, being part of a couple can be awesome. I've done it a few times. Cuddling and farmers' markets? Sign me up. I was with my college boyfriend for three and a half years, my longest relationship. My most recent was a six-month fling with a firefighter named John, but the spark fizzled out—no pun intended—about seven months ago.

I enjoy being single, though. It means I can starfish in my bed every night without worrying about some snoring jackass hogging the blanket. I can watch whatever I want on Netflix, listen to my music in the car. It's nice.

But I'm still a red-blooded woman who needs to get laid sometimes. And this is the perfect opportunity for a no-strings, anonymous hook-up. I checked into the Blue Valley Lodge a day early for this precise reason, since I knew that once all the wedding chaos began, I wouldn't have time to indulge. I'm the maid of honor, so I anticipate the next three days will involve doting hand and foot on Marcy, the bride.

Confession: I'm still a bit shocked she even asked me to be the maid of honor. I haven't exactly been the most available friend lately. New apartment, huge promotion at work, more hours and responsibilities . . . I could probably list more excuses, but they'd be just that—excuses. It takes zero effort to send a quick text, even if you're the busiest person on the planet.

Marcy and I were inseparable in middle school. Her mom called us Siamese twins because we were glued at the hip. In high school, our paths began to veer; I attended a private arts academy and she went to public school. We still spoke, but it wasn't the same as seeing each other every single day, and eventually even our weekend plans became few and far between. After college we'd reached the point of a phone call once a month, and when she asked me to be her maid of honor a few months ago, we hadn't spoken in nearly two years. There've been some social media likes and brief texts, but nothing substantial.

Hence the confusion. But I guess Marcy still considers me her friend despite my absence of late, and there was no way I could say no when she asked. This was Marcy, my Siamese twin. Of course I said yes, and now here I am in Colorado, staying at this gorgeous chalet-style hotel in the mountains—and not an eligible bachelor to be found.

"Another drink?" the young, dark-haired waiter asks.

My head lifts abruptly. I'm holed up in the corner of the lounge, with its wood-burning fireplaces and mahogany-paneled walls. It's so cozy I keep forgetting I'm in public. I feel like I'm in a log cabin.

I glance at my empty Cosmo. "Yes, one more, please. But make sure to cut me off after that." I'm a two-drinks kind of girl. Anything more and I get a bit . . . wobbly.

"No problem." He grins before wandering off.

I return my attention to the app, rapidly swiping left on three guys who look like actual lumberjacks, flannel and all.

But the man that comes next . . .

Oh my.

Vivid gray eyes and a strong jaw peer up at me from his profile photo. A snug black T-shirt hugs a very defined chest. It's not a Tom twelve-pack, but equally appealing, and at least it doesn't look like he bathes in a vat of oil.

Dirk, 32

Okay, not the most attractive of names, but he's age-appropriate. I just turned thirty-one last week. His interests aren't filled out, but his mini bio definitely sparks my attention.

Only in town for a few days. Looking for someone to have a good time with.

I respect the honesty. But in the end, it's not even our perfectly aligned motives that win me over—it's his top song on Spotify.

"Always On My Mind." The Willie Nelson version.

AKA my all-time favorite song.

Everybody I know prefers the Elvis version. *Everyone.* But not Dirk. Dirk likes Willie.

Clearly we're soul mates.

My heartbeat speeds up. This is the nerve-wracking part. The moment that could potentially suck: when you actually like somebody, so you swipe right . . . and nothing happens.

I want the "*It's a Match!*" screen to pop up and confirm that Dirk—he really doesn't look like a Dirk—likes me, too. I want to meet him and find out if we have any chemistry. I mean, he's hot, looking for a good time, and only here for a few days? He's perfect.

It occurs to me that maybe he's here for Marcy's wedding, too, but that's fine, I suppose. If the chemistry's there, maybe a weekend fling is in store for us. I'm even willing to overlook the fact that his name is *Dirk*.

So I swipe right.

I hold my breath and bite my lip and then my heart skips a beat because there it is.

It's a Match!

CHAPTER TWO

Him: Hello gorgeous . . .

It's not the most original opening message, but it's about the level of originality I'd expect from someone named Dirk.

I snicker to myself, just as the waiter returns with my second Cosmo. "Funny meme?" he prompts, gesturing to my phone.

"Sort of." I pick up the glass and take a dainty sip. "Ooh, this is great. Thank you."

"Glad to hear it. Let me know if you need anything else."

"Will do." Once he's gone, I focus on the message thread on my phone, deciding to play along.

Me: Hi handsome . . .

Three dots appear to indicate that he's typing.

Him: Are you a Colorado native?

Me: Nope, just here for the weekend visiting some friends.

My instincts tell me not to mention the wedding. The W-word tends to freak some guys out, the ones who operate under the assumption that me watching a couple swear their undying love to each other means I'm desperate for the same thing.

Me: How about you? You're from Blue Valley?

His current location is the same as mine—this gorgeous little mountain town that apparently has a population of eight hundred or so.

Him: No, here for a work thing.

Okay. Vague. But I just lied about my reason for being here, so I can't exactly judge.

Him: Where are you from originally, then?

Me: D.C. Our nation's capital.

We make some more chitchat for a few minutes. To be honest, it starts to drag, and boredom slowly creeps over me. Mutual Willie Nelson love or not, I'm about to declare this an unsuccessful match when Dirk throws me a curveball that makes me smile.

> Him: What are we doing here, gorgeous?
>
> Me: What do you mean?
>
> Him: I mean, this isn't eHarmony or Match.com. We both know what this particular app is for, and we're both on it at . . . hmmm, 11:18 pm, which is well into booty call territory. So what do you say we cut the small talk and tell each other what we really want?

His forthrightness triggers a tingle between my legs. Yes, he still comes off as kind of douchey, but he writes in full sentences with perfect grammar, his pictures are hot, and he's right—we're both on here for the same reason.

> Me: Okay. Tell me what you want.
>
> Him: I want to put my mouth all over you. In real life. I'm not into sexting.
>
> Me: Me neither.
>
> Him: So let's meet up. I'm staying at the Blue Valley Lodge.

A surprised squeak flies out of my mouth. We're at the same hotel?

> Him: But I suppose you won't want to go to a strange man's hotel, so how about I come to wherever you are?

I find myself hurriedly scanning the lounge. I thought it was occupied mostly by older couples, but a sweep of the dimly lit room reveals a sole patron in a shadowy corner of the room. His back is turned to me, so all I glimpse is dark hair and the hint of wide shoulders.

Is that him?

My pulse takes off. On a whim, I type out a quick message.

Me: Describe what you're looking at right now.

The brief delay tells me I've confused him.

Him: A roaring fireplace. Wood-paneled walls. A leather chair beneath my ass, a tumbler of scotch in my hand.

Holy. Shit.

Me: Turn around.

The stranger swivels his head. Our eyes lock from across the room. I hold my phone up, a bit sheepishly, and husky laughter wafts in my direction.

Him: You've gotta be kidding me.

I don't bother responding, because Dirk, in all his real-life glory, is already striding toward my nook. As he walks, he tucks his phone in the pocket of his jeans. They're dark blue, and he's paired them with a gray sweater that stretches across impossibly broad shoulders. He's even better looking in person, and I wish I knew what he did for a living. Is he an athlete? Because he sure as hell is built like one. I swear I see his muscles flexing beneath his sweater every time he moves.

"Emilia," he drawls.

"Dirk," I drawl back.

"What are the chances? One would think the universe wants us to get together tonight."

"One would think."

"May I join you?" He gestures to the empty armchair

"Of course."

He sits down and sets his tumbler on his left knee. His gaze wastes no time studying me. Thoroughly.

I'm caught off-guard, because I hadn't anticipated meeting him right this second. I thought I would have time to go upstairs, freshen up. I feel less than sexy in my bulky cable-knit sweater, leggings, and my hair thrown up in a messy bun.

"Anyone ever tell you you're incredibly sexy?"

Huh. I guess he likes the disheveled look. "Thank you." I can't help but narrow my eyes. "Are you really staying at this hotel?"

He grins. "Well, I don't make a habit of hanging out in hotel bars for no reason."

"Hey, you never know. This could be your hook-up hunting ground."

"Could be yours," he counters.

"True." I point to the keycard sitting on the table. "I'm a guest here, too."

We observe each other over the rims of our respective drinks. Aw man, he's got a dimple that I just want to *lick*. And the stubble sweeping his jaw begs for my fingers to stroke it. Heat unfurls in my body. It's been a long time since I've experienced such an instant attraction to somebody, and I don't think I can blame it entirely on my seven-month sexual drought. That thing he said about putting his mouth all over me? I want to do the same thing to him.

"You're looking at me like you want to eat me alive," he remarks.

"That's because I do."

He looks amused. "That's honest."

"Honesty's my middle name."

"Is that so?"

"Yup. Well, no, my middle name's Natasha. But I think honesty is my best trait. My dad thinks it's my biggest flaw." I roll my eyes. "But that's probably because he doesn't like my brand of honesty. He's got five divorces under his belt and doesn't enjoy hearing that he's a marital fuck-up." Ugh, and dammit, why am I talking about my father with the guy I'm potentially going to have sex with?

He doesn't seem to mind, though. "Yeah, I can see how he might not like the reminder."

"Then he should really stop getting married every other day."

Dirk laughs.

I hate that his name is Dirk. It's such a terrible, terrible name.

"So . . ." He of the unfortunate name takes the last sip of his scotch and puts the glass down. "We're doing the small-talk thing again, Emilia."

A smile tickles my lips. "Yes. We are."

He raises a dark-brown eyebrow. "Are you nervous about going upstairs with me?"

"Who says I'm going upstairs with you?"

His lips curve in response. "Oh, I see. We're playing hard to get now."

"Nope, I'm still sussing out the situation. Deciding if you're worthy of going upstairs with me."

"Worthy, huh?" He smiles wider, flashing me a set of perfect white teeth.

Maybe he's not an athlete but a male model. Because he's so insanely sexy. The smile, the body, the silver eyes gleaming with heat. This man is sex on a stick.

"I feel like we're in negotiations," I admit with a sigh. "Like we're setting up rules for potentially banging each other's brains out."

"Rules?" Dirk winks. "I don't play by the rules, gorgeous. If you want to lay some down, though, I'm all ears."

"I only have one." My tone becomes firm. "This is only going to be a one-night thing, so you're not allowed to fall in love with me."

He chuckles. "I think I already am."

"Funny." I stick my hand in my purse, fish out a twenty-dollar bill, and drop it on the table to cover my two cosmos, plus five extra for the waiter. Then I rise to my feet. "Come on, handsome. Let's go."

With another blindingly sexy smile, Dirk follows me out of the lounge.

CHAPTER THREE

His tongue is between my legs. Greedy, wet, demanding.

He knows exactly what he's doing, and holy hell it's fantastic. He makes out with my pussy instead of resorting to the trademark move I've gotten from other men—when they flick their tongue super fast over my clit like a tiny little jackhammer. It's really not pleasant, especially when they lead with that move. My pussy needs to be seduced. I want soft kisses and long licks from a man. I want husky moans from him. I want to look down, like I'm looking down now, and see his dick straining against the front of his pants. I want to know that he loves what he's doing and that it's making him hard.

And this guy, Dirk, he of the unfortunate name, does not disappoint. He had me on the bed, flat on my back with my leggings off, before I could even blink. He hasn't even kissed me yet; he's too busy creating the most delicious sensations in my body. Shivers of pleasure dance through me, and my clit is throbbing beneath his lips. Release isn't far away and he's only been doing this for a couple of minutes.

Somebody give Dirk a gold star.

"Oh, fuck," I whisper.

This is no joke. My knees are wobbly, and my body feels as if it's sinking into the mattress. This jelly stage usually means orgasm is imminent.

"Don't tell me you're close," he teases, then kisses his way toward my inner thigh and gives it a light nibble.

"I am," I confess. "I'm *so* close. I don't even know how this is happening right now."

"I do," he says smugly. The tip of his finger teases my opening. "I'm good at what I do."

Damn right he is. I add "gigolo" to the list of potential professions I'm compiling for him.

I reach down and grab a hunk of his messy hair, tugging his head back toward my core. "Please don't stop," I order.

"Never," he vows.

His mouth covers me at the same time his finger—his long, talented finger—slides inside me, triggering a body-numbing release. He lightly kisses my clit as I come, rubbing his lips over me while I shudder on the bed, and it's the hottest thing ever.

"Oh my God," I moan. "What the hell was that?"

His chuckle tickles my thigh. "Feel good?" he murmurs.

"So good."

When the mattress shifts, my eyes flutter open to watch him rise and kneel at the edge of the bed. Sweeping his tongue over his bottom lip, he takes his sweater off, then yanks his leather belt from its loops. The buckle clangs when his pants hit the floor.

Almost instantly, my mouth waters. He's wearing nothing but black boxer-briefs now. His thighs are rock-hard, and so is his cock. I can see the outline of it underneath the cotton, and it's impressive.

"Come here." I crook a finger at him.

He smiles devilishly as he lowers himself over me. His bare chest crushes my sweater, alerting me to the fact that although I'm naked from the waist down, I'm dressed like a ski bunny from the waist up.

His lips find mine in a fleeting kiss before he groans in displeasure. "This sweater is like a foot thick. It needs to fucking go." He wastes no time shoving the material upward.

I shift my position to help him rid me of the bulky sweater. I'm wearing a tank top underneath, but no bra. When the tank comes off and Dirk lays eyes on my bare boobs, he makes a sexy, dirty sound that sends a sizzle of lust to my clit, which comes to life again.

"Your tits are amazing," he says before bending his head to suck one nipple deep in his mouth.

This is the best hook-up I've had in a long, long time. We roll around on the bed, making out while he grinds his briefs-covered dick against my soaking wet core. His chest is incredible. Hard planes and sinewy ridges strain beneath my fingertips as my palms glide over his flesh.

"You're so delicious," I whisper in his ear before biting the lobe.

With a groan, he captures my mouth again, his tongue hungrily sliding inside. I can taste myself on him and it makes me even wetter. I hook a leg around his hip and let out a frustrated sound when I once again encounter the cotton barrier.

"Why are these still on?" I growl.

"Because you haven't taken them off me. Bad girl." His eyes gleam.

Bad girl, indeed. What am I thinking, allowing this glorious cock to remain covered? I grip the elastic waistband and shove the briefs down his hips, and there it is, Dirk's dick. Dirk's big, hard, wonderful dick. I almost weep with pure joy. I want it inside me so badly I can barely breathe.

He must read my mind, because something akin to desperation flashes in his eyes. "I wanted to see your mouth wrapped around my cock, but I need to be inside you even more and I think you agree."

"I *so* agree."

Without delay, he leans over the edge of the bed and fumbles for his jeans. "Probably should've had this handy before we started," he mutters, returning with a condom.

I sit up and wrap my arms around him from behind. I stroke his chest, my thumb grazing one flat nipple. "Hurry," I plead.

His laughter tickles my cheek. "Has anyone ever told you that patience is a virtue?"

"Has anyone ever told you that your dick is so fucking hot?"

He twists to grin at me, even as he rolls the condom on. "Are you always this outspoken?"

"I told you, honesty is my thing."

He shifts around and brushes his lips over mine, then whispers, "I fucking love it."

The next thing I know, his hands are under my ass and he's lifting me onto his lap, impaling me with his erection. There's no preamble, no teasing. He fills me to the hilt, and I grab his shoulders to hold on for dear life. Holy shit, this is amazing. I feel so full. My inner muscles clench, eliciting a croak from him.

"Jesus, you feel good." He brings his hand between our bodies, circles my clit with his thumb, and my eyes damn near roll to the top of my head.

"We're good at this," I tell him. Even I don't miss the slight awe in my voice.

"Yeah," he says huskily. "We are."

And then we start moving and it's as if we've fucked hundreds and thousands of times before. I ride him, and when the position isn't giving me everything I need, I shove his chest and he falls onto his back, laughing. Then he grips my hips and pounds into me with sharp upward thrusts.

One hand slides up to cup my left breast, his voice an encouraging rumble that fills the bedroom. "That's it, baby. Ride my dick. Make yourself come again."

"On it," I mumble.

He chokes out another laugh. "Yeah, you are."

I laugh, too. But not because of the lame joke. I'm in the midst of the best sex of my life and it's happening with a stranger named *Dirk*. Who would've thunk it. Tension coils tight between my legs again, but just before I'm about to fall apart, Dirk sits up and flips us over so that I'm on my back. He's on top of me now, fucking me hard, powerful hips thrusting, hitting a spot so deep that he wrenches the orgasm out of me. It's so intense, all I can do is lie there, my legs hooked around him, my heels digging into the tightest ass I've ever encountered as I come and come and don't stop coming.

"That's it, Emilia. Yes," he growls, burying his face in my neck. He makes a strangled sound as he shakes from his own release.

We lie there for several heart-stopping moments, breathing heavily. "That was ridiculous," he mumbles.

"Yeah."

He finally rolls over and stares up at the ceiling. His chest is still heaving. So is mine. I can scarcely catch my breath.

"Emilia," he says.

"Hmmm?" I glance over.

He flashes me that dimpled grin, which I need to memorize, pronto, because I won't be seeing him again after tonight.

His tone is thick with urgency. "We need to do that again. At least ten more times tonight."

"Agreed." I roll toward him. "So let's stop wasting time by talking."

♪

It's nearly four o'clock in the morning when I pry myself out of Dirk's arms. I chose to hook up in his room for this reason—so that I could leave whenever I wanted and wouldn't have to deal with the awkward morning after.

I quietly slip out of bed, and there's a delicious soreness between my legs. I can't even remember how many times we had sex tonight. I don't think we made it to ten, but the array of empty condom wrappers on the carpeted floor tell me it was at least—I squint—five times. I'm pretty sure that's about the number of orgasms I had. I don't know if Dirk even came the last time. He'd been hard as granite, but I don't think anything actually came out. He was drained. I drained Dirk.

Dammit, why does his name have to be Dirk?

Sighing, I gather up my clothes. It's time to say goodbye to this magical creature and go back to my own room. I quickly slide into my underwear and leggings. I can't find the tank top, but I throw my sweater on anyway. Whatever. Dirk gets a souvenir.

"You're leaving?" His sleepy voice stops me before I can turn the doorknob.

"Yeah," I whisper. "Sorry, I didn't mean to wake you. I have trouble sleeping if I'm not in my own bed."

"It's not your bed," he says drowsily. "It's a hotel bed."

"You know what I mean. I just . . . I prefer to sleep alone."

"All right."

I can't make out if his tone holds disappointment or relief.

"Leave me your number," he adds.

No, it's not relief. He *is* disappointed.

I look over my shoulder, but I can't quite see him. He's just a shadowy lump on the bed. "Dirk . . ." His name sounds awkward on my lips. "I told you, this was a one-time thing."

"You said you're here for the weekend. Let me take you to dinner one night."

"That's probably not a good idea. I'm going to be busy with my friends."

"You're really not going to give me your number?" When I hesitate for a beat, he goes on and says, "It's fine. I'll message you on the app." The bed sheets rustle. "Good night, Emilia."

"Good night," I murmur as I walk out the door.

It's not until I reach the elevator bank that I pull out my phone and open the hook-up app.

I experience only the briefest moment of regret before I click on Dirk's name and press *unmatch*.

CHAPTER FOUR

"You're here!" Marcy's happy shriek causes me and everyone else in our vicinity to visibly wince. She's not allowed to be shrieking, because she has a naturally high voice to begin with. It's one of those cute baby voices that, unfortunately, leads many people to assume she's an airhead. In reality, she's a rocket scientist.

I'm not even joking—Marcy is an aerospace engineer at NASA. Or something like that. To be honest, I'm not entirely sure what she does in D.C. It sounds very complicated.

And then there's me, the lowly graphic designer, or at least I was up until last year. Now I run the design department at my advertising firm, though we're not exactly building spaceships over there. The project I'm currently heading is an ad campaign for men's underwear.

"Of course I'm here," I tell my oldest friend. "I'm the maid of honor."

She throws her arms around me in a hug tight enough to cut the air supply to my lungs. "You look amazing," she says when she pulls back.

Clearly she's lying, because I saw my reflection this morning and I looked exhausted. It took several coats of concealer to cover the bags under my eyes. And I can't even bask in the *reason* I'm tired: Dirk and his fabulous dick. Because they're in my past now, my orgasm-laden past. Now that the rest of the wedding party has arrived, for the next two days I'm here for Marcy and only Marcy.

"You're the one who looks amazing," I correct. "I swear, you're glowing." She really is. Her cheeks are rosy and she's beaming from ear to ear. "Sure you're not knocked up?"

"Fairly certain," she answers with a snort.

She links her arm through mine and leads me across the hotel lobby. It's bustling with new arrivals. I think Marcy said there were about a hundred guests attending the wedding. Which is small compared to other weddings, but that's still a lot of people to be staying at one hotel.

"My mom is so excited to see you," she says as we find a small seating area away from the crowd.

"I'm excited to see her too."

Marcy's mom Joanna was my surrogate mother growing up. My actual mom died in a car accident when I was five, and her death completely shattered my dad. She was the love of his life. Losing her made him desperate to find a replacement, which resulted in a slew of stepmothers over the years. We're on number six now, though she doesn't like to be referred to as my stepmother.

Belinda is twenty-six, which makes her thirty years younger than my dad and five years younger than me. And I hate to say it, but she's dumb as a bag of flour. It makes me sad, because Dad is super intellectual and holds a PhD in Philosophy. But I think after wife number three (not counting my mother) he gave up on trying to find that perfect replacement and started letting his male needs drive the bus, because his wives get younger and their boobs get bigger.

Joanna, however, was the mother that my stepmoms weren't. She'd pick me up from school every day and I'd go to their house until my dad came to pick me up. I'd have dinner every weeknight with Marcy and her parents. When I got my first period, Joanna was the first person I told. She took me to the drugstore and showed me what I needed to tell my dad to buy. I'm not sure I would have survived puberty and adolescence without her.

"Where is she?" I ask, searching the lobby for Joanna's familiar auburn curls.

"She's getting my dad settled upstairs. He has a migraine."

"Oh no. Is he going to be okay for the rehearsal dinner?"

Marcy nods. "He should be. He took his meds. I think it was the flight, and the altitude here. We probably should've gotten married in D.C., but my grandparents are too old to travel." Marcy's family is originally from Blue Valley. They lived here until she was six, before moving to Virginia, where I met her in the first grade.

"It really is beautiful here, though," I assure her. "This chalet is such an amazing location for a wedding."

"Right? Devon actually picked it. Originally, I wanted to do it in the church where my grandparents got married, but it's so tiny. It wouldn't have been able to accommodate everyone."

"So, Devon picked the venue. Good job, Devon." I grin. "And when do I finally get to meet this mysterious man?" They've been together for a year and a half, but since Marcy and I hadn't really been in contact for the last two, I haven't even met her soon-to-be hubby.

"Hey," she chides gently, "I send you Facebook invites for everything, Em."

Guilt pricks my stomach. She's right. She does. Trivia nights at the pub, board games at their apartment, the engagement party I was out of town for. "I'm sorry I haven't been around much the last couple years," I say quietly.

A shadow falls over her eyes. "It's okay. I've missed you, though."

"I missed you, too. I've been so caught up in this new job. For the first time ever I'm not answering to some jackass boss. I'm in charge of the whole department now. But it is a lot of hours," I admit.

"You work too much. You always have."

"Look who's talking, Ms. Astronaut."

"You know I'm not actually an astronaut, right? I design and test hardware for spacecraft flight systems."

"That sounds like an astronaut to me, dude."

"I don't actually go up into space, *dude*." She rolls her eyes. "Anyway, Mom wants to take us out for brunch, so let's look up a couple of restaurant options on Yelp."

I pull my phone out of my purse. "Just us, or with the rest of the bridal party?"

"Just us. It'll be a nice intimate catch-up, just the three of us, before all the wedding chaos hits. Tonight's the rehearsal dinner, so the bridesmaids and groomsmen and immediate family will be there, and I guess you won't meet Devon until tonight because he's planning on—actually, wait, there he is now!" Marcy whips up her arm and waves to someone across the lobby. "Babe!" She points happily to me. "It's my BFF!" she calls to her fiancé.

I turn, armed with a smile and a wave.

But in a heartbeat, the smile freezes on my face, and my hand drops limply to my lap.

The man by the elevator banks is more than just familiar to me. I memorized every inch of his tall, muscular body last night.

I had his dick in my mouth.

His lips were all over me.

We fucked through half a box of condoms.

Nausea bubbles in my stomach and then barrels up my throat. I gulp hard to stop myself from throwing up.

On the other side of the cavernous room, Dirk gives a half-hearted wave in our direction, then makes a harried gesture to indicate he's got to keep moving. He quickly ushers a white-haired lady into the elevator. His hand is splayed over her bony shoulders, that big hand with the long fingers that were buried inside me when he made me come.

Holy shit, I'm going to hurl. I'm actually going to vomit right here on Marcy's pretty red ballet flats.

I can't even believe this is happening.

I slept with the groom.

CHAPTER FIVE

It's a miracle I manage to make it through brunch without throwing up. Seriously, it requires superhuman effort to keep my lobster bisque down, all the while pretending to listen to everything Marcy and Joanna are saying.

The moment we return to the hotel, however, my luck threatens to run out. Bile coats my throat as Joanna and I step out of the elevator. The wedding party and guests are all staying on the third and fourth floors of the lodge. Marcy is in the penthouse, sharing the honeymoon suite with—my stomach lurches violently. With her fiancé. Dirk.

No, not Dirk. *Devon*. That bastard was on a hook-up app using a fake name. I should've known nobody would ever be named *Dirk*. It's a porn star name. A fake, dirty cheater name.

My God, I have to tell Marcy.

Right?

"You're looking a little green, Em," Joanna says in concern.

"I think the lobster isn't sitting well with me," I mumble. I'm already fumbling in my purse for my keycard. "I'm sorry, Mama Jo, I need to, um, take care of this. I'll see you at the rehearsal dinner."

I frantically tap the card until the keypad flashes green and then dive into the hotel room. But once I'm kneeling in front of the toilet, I don't actually lose my lunch. Now that I'm alone and able to sit with my own thoughts, my stomach begins to settle.

Okay. I need to figure this out.

Marcy's fiancé, the man she's going to marry tomorrow, had sex with the maid of honor.

In the maid of honor's defense, she didn't know he was the groom. And chances are the groom didn't know he was boning the maid of honor. In fact, I don't think the groom cared who he was boning as long as it wasn't his soon-to-be wife.

I have to tell Marcy. I just . . . have to.

My throat closes up. This time with overwhelming guilt. I slept with Marcy's fiancé. Unknowingly, yes, but she's still going to be devastated. And she's *never* going to forget this. Even though I didn't go out of my way to seduce her no-good, lying fiancé, his penis was still inside my vagina last night. No friendship could come back from that kind of biological betrayal.

Maybe it wasn't him?

My brain makes a last-ditch effort to defuse this horrible bomb that will blow Marcy's life to smithereens. Her comment about those Facebook invites suddenly comes to mind. Of course. I can easily verify who this guy is.

I hurry to the bedroom, grab my phone, and log on to Facebook. A billion notifications await me, but I ignore them all. I hardly ever go on this damn thing, mostly because it seems everyone uses it to whine about their problems or pick online fights.

When I go on Marcy's page, I don't need to look in a mirror to know that my face is green again. Yup, that's Dirk. Right there in her profile pic. He and Marcy are smiling at the camera, and his perfect teeth taunt me. He looks more wholesome in this picture, his gray eyes missing the sensual gleam, but I guess he saves that for his anonymous hook-ups, when he's cheating on my best friend.

I scroll through her feed. There aren't as many pictures of the happy couple as I expect, but there is a status update that says she and Devon got engaged.

Fuck you, Dirk. I'm going to rip your fucking balls off.

I tamp down the bloodlust and close the app. I have no idea how I'm going to handle this awful situation. The rehearsal dinner is in a couple of hours. I need to shower and get my hair done, then pick up all the bridesmaid dresses for tomorrow from the dry cleaner downstairs. Deliver them to each room, make sure they fit.

Being a maid of honor is stressful, and that's before you factor in the fact that I slept with the goddamn groom.

♫

By the time I'm done zipping up the little black dress I brought for the rehearsal dinner, I've come up with a plan.

First, I'm going to confront Devon/Dirk. Alone, in order to give him a chance to offer his side of the story. Yes, the idea that he could have a "side" makes me want to laugh hysterically, because what alternative explanation could he possibly have? He cheated on the woman he's going to marry. Not once, either. We fucked all night long. Oh, and then—and then! He tried to ask me on a *date*. He wanted to have *dinner* with me. He's actually a monster.

Nevertheless, I'll be the bigger person and give him the benefit of the doubt first.

Then, once he confirms that he is indeed a monster, I'll take Marcy aside and tell her everything before the rehearsal dinner gets underway. There's no way I'm letting everybody shower the happy couple with well-wishes and make speeches.

I slip into my stilettos. They're bright red, matching my crimson lipstick. My reflection in the mirror looks a tad wild-eyed, probably because I'm about to blow my best friend's life apart and I don't want to do it.

As I leave the room and tuck the keycard in my clutch, I wonder, if the situations were reversed, whether I would want to know.

The answer to that is *hell yes*. I'd never want to marry someone who had sex with somebody else the night before. Marcy will be crushed, but I hope she'll eventually come to thank me for this. At the end of the day, she'll know I have her best interests at heart.

The dinner is taking place in the chalet's restaurant, a grand room with crisscross wooden beams spanning a soaring ceiling. I hear silverware clinking and chatter as I approach the arched doorway. Catering staff waltzes by with trays of champagne flutes. Round tables fill the massive room, and then there's a long rectangular one, the head table where the bridal party will sit.

Marcy's already here, chatting with her dad, who looks well rested. I scan the room looking for Dirk—I mean, Devon. It isn't until I hear a familiar voice behind me that I realize he found me instead.

"Emilia?" There's a note of shock in his voice.

I whirl around, and sure enough, there he is, the lying, cheating snake. He looks amazing in a black suit that's perfectly tailored to his broad body. His dark hair isn't tousled like it was last night, but swept away from his forehead, and he's clean-shaven now. The gray eyes are exactly the same, though. I remember them peering at me when he was moving inside me, and a wave of fury crashes over me.

"What you doing here?" He looks startled.

"Are you fucking kidding me right now? How could you do this?" I hiss.

His brow furrows. "Do what?"

"You slept with me last night," I say accusingly.

The bastard has the gall to quirk up the corner of his mouth in a smug smile. "Yeah. I did."

"Are you . . . is that pride . . . are you *bragging* about the conquest? Are you actually proud of yourself for what you've done? I'm the *maid of honor*," I spit out, and it's miraculous I don't raise my voice.

"Really? I'm in the wedding, too."

Incredulous laughter lodges in my throat. Oh, is that how he's going to phrase it? "Yeah, I figured," I snap, disgust dripping from my tone. "What the hell is wrong with you? How can you just stand there and—"

"Is everything okay?"

Marcy.

Oh my God. This isn't going according to plan. I was supposed to get Dirk alone first. But now Marcy appears in front of us, looking so perfect in a short pink dress with a sweetheart neckline. She's wearing white pumps and pearl earrings, and her strawberry-blonde hair is arranged in a fat braid hanging over one shoulder. She's just the cutest, sweetest person in the whole world, and I—

"I slept with Devon," I blurt out.

All the color drains from her face. "W-what?" Her bottom lip starts trembling, confusion clouding her expression as she stares at me.

Nearly choking on a lump of misery, I force myself to speak again. "I slept with your fiancé last night."

CHAPTER SIX

Marcy's always had the most expressive eyes. They make it impossible to hide what she's thinking or feeling, and right now they're pleading at me. They're saying, *please say you're joking and take back this insanity because this is my wedding and you're ruining my life.*

But I can't take it back. The truth is out.

"I'm so sorry," I whisper. "I had no idea that he . . ." I trail off shamefully.

The man whose dick was in my pussy glowers at me. "You slept with Devon?" His lips set in a tight line. "Was this before or after you hooked up with me?"

I shoot him an irritated look. "What the hell are you babbling about? You know it happened last night."

"You slept with my brother last night?"

"What?"

"What?"

"What?" Marcy says.

I have no idea what's happening right now. The three of us are engaged in some weird three-way duel, except instead of guns it's baffled stares.

I take a deep breath and focus only on my friend. "Last night I matched with someone named Dirk on a hook-up app. It was *him*." I point at the man beside me like a witness accusing her attacker in open court.

"Evan," Marcy says.

"Devon," I confirm.

"No, that's Evan."

"What?"

"What?"

"What?" Dirk says.

Another eye-duel commences.

"Okay." Dirk/Devon chuckles softly. "I think that, one, we really need to expand our vocabularies—maybe a book club? And two, I know exactly what's going on here, and trust me when I say it's a misunderstanding I can very easily clear up."

"Oh, really?" I challenge.

"Then please clear it up before I have a panic attack," Marcy orders.

He slings his hands in the pockets of his suit coat and grins at Marcy. "Dirk is my online alias."

Her laughter comes out in a high-pitched squeak. "Are you serious, Evan? *Dirk*?"

"Hey, the ladies don't seem to mind." He winks at me.

"Don't wink at me," I order. "And I *did* mind. I slept with you *in spite* of your name, not because of it."

Marcy breaks out in a huge grin, her now excited gaze moving from me to him. "You two slept together?"

"This is what I've been trying to tell you. I slept with the groom."

"He's not the groom, Em. This is Devon's twin. Evan."

I shake my head a few times, because it feels like it's filled with cotton balls. Thoughts are having a hard time penetrating. "You're marrying Devon," I say slowly.

"Yes," she replies.

"And this is his brother. His twin brother. Evan."

"Yes."

"Devon and Evan." I flick a brow at him. "Were your parents on drugs the day you were born?"

"They thought it was cute." He smirks for a second, before a contrite look enters his eyes. "I'm sorry I lied about my name. It's just that with my job, I don't like putting my real information out there."

"So, you picked *Dirk*?" I growl.

"Again, it's worked for me in the past."

"I can't believe you two hooked up." Marcy looks like she's fighting back laughter.

"It was a one-time thing," I grumble.

"Well, not necessarily," Evan hedges.

"Yes, necessarily. I don't do encores."

He winks again. "We'll see about that. Anyway, now that we've cleared this up, I should probably go find the groom. The actual groom. He's running a bit late."

I unwittingly admire his perfect butt as he saunters off.

Okay. I need to digest this.

So, I didn't bang the groom. Thank God, because that means I'm not destroying Marcy's life.

But I did bang the groom's twin brother.

Whose name is Evan.

Which rhymes with Devon.

Because apparently their parents wanted to raise Dr. Seuss characters.

Beside me, Marcy is practically bouncing up and down on her white heels. "You and Evan?" she exclaims happily. "Oh my God, Emilia. I *love* this! Imagine if you two fall in love and get married? We'd be married to *twins*! And you could have your wedding on Valentine's Day! I wanted a Valentine's Day wedding, but the fourteenth is Dad's birthday and I didn't want my anniversary to be on the same—"

"Marcy," I interrupt. "How about we rein in the crazy a bit? I'm not marrying the guy. And I'd never, ever do something as cheesy as a Valentine's Day wedding." I make a frustrated, grumbly noise. "It was just a stupid hook-up, and now it's time to forget about it."

"No way. This is the best thing ever. Like, *ever*!"

I scowl at her. "Agree to disagree."

♫

The rehearsal dinner goes smoothly, though I'm not sure why the word "rehearsal" is even in there, since there's no actual rehearsing. The evening consists of a dozen heartfelt speeches, tears from the parents, and Marcy blushing every time someone forces her and Devon to kiss by tapping a utensil against a wineglass.

And talk about jarring—Devon and Evan are *identical*. Not fraternal twins, but completely indistinguishable from each other, features-wise. The only reason I can tell them apart is because Evan is wearing a black suit and Devon is in navy-blue. Oh, and also because every time Evan's sultry gaze lands on me, I know without a doubt he's imagining me naked.

The jerk is downright *smoldering*, the heat he's generating actually causing beads of sweat to break out at the nape of my neck. By the time dessert is over, I'm eager to get out of there. But Marcy won't let me leave. She wants me to get to know the other two bridesmaids, whom I've never met. Natalie and Robin seem nice enough, but it's hard to concentrate on getting to know them when Evan is getting to know me with his eyes.

"Excuse me," I blurt out when Robin pauses to take a breath. She'd just spent the past ten minutes describing her work at NASA to me. Yup, another fucking astronaut, but she works at a facility in Florida, not Washington.

"The best man is waving me over," I say, injecting an apologetic note into my tone. "Hopefully it's not some last-minute hiccup about tomorrow."

"Oh, go ahead," she says instantly, shooing me away. "We don't want a single hiccup to ruin Marcy's big day."

"I agree."

Without delay, I march toward Evan, who's leaning against one of the huge exposed beams in the restaurant. Several of the tables in the center of the room have been cleared away to create a dance floor, and he's watching the band set up. But his gaze immediately shifts to me as I approach.

I cross my arms. "Can you please stop?" I order through gritted teeth.

He smiles innocently. "Stop what?"

"Looking at me."

"Oh, now I'm not allowed to look at you?"

"No, you're not. It's making me uncomfortable."

He narrows his eyes "Really."

"Really. I told you, last night was a one-time thing. I don't need to be constantly reminded of it with you looking at me like a horny hyena."

"Encountered many horny hyenas in your day, have you?"

"Shut up. You know what I mean."

"Fine. I'll stop looking at you. That is, if you agree to go to dinner with me."

"We just had dinner," I mutter. "And tomorrow's the wedding, where we'll eat another dinner, and then the day after that I'm going home."

"I know. I want you to have dinner with me when we get back. We both live in D.C., remember?"

"Pass."

He rolls his eyes. "You're honestly going to stand there and tell me that you didn't have the best sex of your life with me last night?"

"I'm not saying the sex wasn't good. I'm saying I don't want to go out with you. There's a difference." I arch a brow. "Now, if you were asking me to fuck again, that's a whole other story."

"Yeah?" He gives a husky laugh. "So, if I asked you to fuck, you would say yes?"

"Nah, I'd still say no. You seem high maintenance, to be honest."

"Uh-huh. *I'm* high-maintenance." That sexy dimple appears as he grins broadly at me. Then he takes my hand, and a bolt of heat shoots from his fingers to the tips of my breasts. His touch is just . . . ugh. It brings back the memory of everything we did last night, and I try hard not to shiver.

He doesn't miss the response. "C'mere." He tugs me toward him, close enough so that our bodies collide. "Feel that?" he rasps.

Oh, I feel it. There's absolutely no mistaking the erection pressed up against me.

"I woke up with that this morning. And it was more than just morning wood. It was Emilia wood."

I snort. "Lame, Dirk." I say it mockingly now that I know it's not his actual name.

"It's the truth. Every time I've thought about you and your sassy mouth today, I've gotten rock-hard." He brings his lips close to my ear. "I want to fuck you again. Hell, I'd fuck you right now if you said yes. In front of everyone, I don't care."

Holy hell, I'm temped. To just wrap my legs around him, push my panties to the side and let him do me right here in the middle of the restaurant. That's how badly I want this guy again. But tonight isn't about me. This weekend isn't about me. The whole point of last night's hook-up was to get my jollies out of the way so that I could then focus on dedicating all my time to Marcy.

Reluctantly, I step away from the heat of his body. "Look, I'm not saying I'm not tempted, but I'm here for Marcy, not the best man. I can't sleep with you again."

"Fine, then at least dance with me. The band's about to start."

As if on cue, the lanky lead singer of the flannel-wearing foursome addresses the crowd gathering near the stage. "Evening, everyone. We're The Whiskey Wagon Band, and we're gonna start you folks off with a slow one, at the request of the bride."

I glower when the familiar opening notes of a very familiar song fill the room.

"Always On My Mind."

Fuckin' Marcy. Sometimes it really sucks having friends who know everything about you.

I twist around and glare at the head table where Marcy is seated. She's watching me and Evan with unmistakable delight. When our eyes lock, she gives me an enthusiastic wave.

I hate her.

"Normally I'd say yes to a dance," I tell Evan in a sweet voice, "but I actually really hate this song. Sorry about that. Good night, Dirk."

It's hard to walk away gracefully when my panties are soaked, but somehow I manage.

CHAPTER SEVEN

As someone who's been to many a wedding (six alone were courtesy of my father), I can honestly say that Marcy and Devon put on a beautiful one. Her dress is miles and miles of white lace and tulle, and everyone gasps when she appears at the end of the long, flower-petal-strewn aisle. She looks like a princess. When Devon lifts the veil and sees her face, tears actually fill his eyes. Now that's a man in love.

His twin brother? Well, that's a man in *lust*.

During the entire ceremony, I feel Evan's hot gaze on me. But I refuse to meet his eyes because I'm wearing a formfitting dress and no underwear, which means I can't afford any wet spots. It pisses me off, how much he turns me on.

After the "I Do's" and the minister's triumphant, "You may kiss the bride," Marcy and Devon practically float down the aisle. Then it's my turn to walk with Evan. As he takes my arm, he looks at the newlyweds and murmurs, "Look how happy they are. Isn't it nice to see?"

"I guess," I say grudgingly.

"What? You have something against romance?"

"Not at all."

"Marriage, then?"

"I'm not saying that, either."

We reach the lobby of the chalet. The newlyweds duck through a pair of French doors that lead into the ballroom, where the wedding photos are being taken. For the moment, only the bride and groom are needed, so Evan and I linger near the entryway.

"But . . . if I'm being honest, it doesn't seem like marriage is what it used to be," I tell him. "Like those couples that used to be married for twenty, thirty, forty years? You don't see that anymore."

"No," he agrees. "A lot of marriages these days seem short-lived. People don't want to work on the relationship. They'd rather throw in the towel because it's easier."

"But your parents are still together, right? That's cool."

"Maybe that's why I'm not as cynical as you. You said your dad keeps getting remarried?"

"Yeah, he's up to number six with Belinda. She's five years younger than me."

"Age is nothing but a number."

"So are IQs and hers doesn't even crack triple digits."

He snickers. "Your dad must see something in her if he married the girl."

"Oh, he does. Not a number, though—letters. As in, double Ds. He's gotten superficial in his old age."

"Hey, as long as he's happy, right?"

"True," I say, "but I don't think he actually is. He's never gotten over my mom's death. He spent the last twenty-six years trying to find someone he loves as much as he loved her, and it just doesn't happen for him. He always ends up disappointed."

"I see. Is that why you're still single?"

I roll my eyes. "Because my dad keeps getting married and divorced? Are you a therapist? If so, you might need to study up on a new diagnosis or two. Daddy issues is too easy."

"It's usually the right one. And no, I'm not a therapist."

"What is it you do, anyway?"

He surprises me by revealing, "I'm a criminal lawyer. So's Devon. We work at our father's firm."

"Keeping it in the family."

"Yup. And we represent a lot of D.C. bigwigs, so that's why I don't use my real name on the dating apps."

"Do you like criminal law? It seems like it'd be stressful."

"It is, and I do. I thrive under stress, and the courtroom is like my own personal battleground. It feeds into all my caveman instincts." He chuckles. "My brother doesn't like it as much, though. He's far more wholesome than I am, in case you couldn't tell."

I glance over to see Devon nuzzling Marcy's neck during their photo shoot. Yeah, he does seem like a puppy dog compared to his brother. Evan's a wolf.

"But, see, I don't think you're like your friend Marcy," he goes on. "I don't think you want the teddy bear."

"Oh really, and you know me so well?"

"Mmm-hmm. I got to know you at least five times last night."

"Sex doesn't mean you know me. Just means you know what I look like when I have an orgasm."

His voice turns growly. "You look hot when you have an orgasm. And I'm dying to give you another one." Then he clears his throat and gestures to Devon and Marcy. "But you're right, this weekend isn't about you and me. That's why I want to take you out when we're back in D.C., so it can be all about us."

"Why do you want this date so bad?" I ask curiously.

"Because I find you fascinating. You make me laugh. You turn me on. All of the above." He shrugs. "Say yes, Emilia."

Luckily, the photographer chooses that moment to call out, "We're ready for the rest of the bridal party!"

"We'd better go in." Swallowing my relief, I walk away from Evan. Again.

It's becoming a habit.

♬

I skip out early on the reception. Normally I'd feel guilty, but I don't think Marcy even notices when I leave the ballroom. She and Devon are wrapped up in each other's arms on the dance floor. They've been dancing and cuddling and kissing all night, with eyes only for each other. Which is how it should be. So many other weddings turn into this terrible tightrope walk of pleasing family members and placating egos, when it should be about the bride and groom.

I'm happy Marcy got her happily-ever-after, but I'm too exhausted to stick around and witness it. I didn't get any sleep the night I spent with Evan, and today I woke up at the crack of dawn so I could be available to Marcy. We ran a million last-minute errands during the day, spent hours getting ready, then came the ceremony, followed by a seven-course dinner, an hour of speeches, and now people are dancing and I have no idea how they're even on their feet.

It's only nine-thirty and I've officially turned into a pumpkin.

The moment I enter my room, I trust-fall onto the king-sized bed, and the mattress welcomes me with its heavenly softness. When I kick off my heels, it feels so good I actually moan out loud. God. There's no better feeling than ridding your sore feet of a pair of heels.

A knock sounds on the door.

I ignore it. Nope. I'm not frickin' moving.

A second knock. "Room service," someone says.

"I didn't order anything," I inform the door.

"Room service," the muffled voice repeats.

Arghhh. Goddammit.

I wearily climb off the bed and throw open the door, only it's not a hotel employee on the other side. It's stupid Evan.

"Seriously?" I balk. "The room service ploy?"

His answering grin is smug. "It worked, didn't it?"

"Nope," I say cheerfully, and start to close the door.

Chuckling, he sticks a hand out to stop me. "Nuh-uh, baby. You're not getting rid of me that easily."

CHAPTER EIGHT

I grumble in annoyance as he muscles his way into my room. "Go away, Dirk. I'm tired and sore."

"Let me make you feel better." He slides one hand down the silky material of my pink bridesmaid dress and lightly cups my ass.

It's such a sleazy move, but for some reason it makes me laugh. "Go away." I swat his hand off and flop back on the bed.

To my irritation, he flops right down beside me, toeing off his black dress shoes and loosening the top two buttons of his crisp white shirt.

I sigh. "What are you doing, Evan?"

"Isn't it obvious? I'm lying next to the sexiest woman in this hotel."

"Flattery won't get you a dinner date. Or into my panties. Actually, wait, I'm not wearing any."

His sex-drenched groan echoes between us. "You had to say that, eh?"

Dammit, why did I? I'm an idiot. Now I'm feeling all tingly downstairs. But I wasn't lying before—I really am too tired for this.

"Emilia," he says.

"Evan."

"I've never met anybody like you."

"I'm sure you say that to all the women."

"Oh, I've used the line before," he admits. He props up on his elbow and gazes down at me, a rogue grin playing on his lips. "But I would never, ever use a line on you. You'd see through it in a heartbeat."

"Of course I would. We live in the world of online dating. I know all the lines, babe."

"Well, I'm being truthful. You keep me on my toes. You're brutally honest. Sexy as fuck." He gently rests his free hand on my hip.

I shiver when his thumb moves in a light caress. "I told you, I'm exhausted. Stop fondling me."

"Really? This?" He caresses me again. "You consider this

fondling?"

"Well, it's turning me on, so . . ."

He pounces. "Ha, it's turning you on!"

"Oh, shut up."

He shifts closer and lays his head on my shoulder, his stubble-covered cheek abrading my skin. At first, I stiffen, resisting the close contact, but my muscles are too weary to remain coiled. I loosen up and accept the cuddling.

"I asked Marcy earlier why she never introduced us," he says, his hand traveling aimlessly up and down my arm.

"Yeah?" I'm still staring at the ceiling. "What did she say?"

"She said you guys had lost touch these past couple years."

"We did," I confirm regretfully. "I got a promotion at the ad agency where I work, and . . . it's on me. She kept inviting me to board game nights, the housewarming party when she moved in with Devon, and . . . yeah . . . I chose work, like an asshole." I bite my lip. "I was actually surprised when she asked me to be her maid of honor."

"I'm not. She's only had amazing things to say about you all weekend. She adores you."

"I don't deserve that," I murmur. "I could have been a better friend."

"Hey, you're here now and that's all that matters."

We fall silent for a moment, and then I feel his lips brush my jawline. "So about that dinner . . ."

I fight a smile. "Do you ever give up?"

"No." His lips hover over mine. "What are you so scared of?"

My eyelids flutter shut. "I'm not scared of anything."

"If you say so, Emilia." Then he kisses me, and I'm relieved because it means we're not talking anymore. My tongue is in his mouth and his hands are tangled in my hair. He smells so fucking good. Spicy, with a hint of lemon. I breathe him in and moan against his lips.

"I thought you were tired," he teases.

"I am," I mumble, and I'm not lying.

"How about you just lie back, then."

I like the sound of that.

He slowly undoes the side zipper of my dress and proceeds to peel the silky material down my body. My strapless bra comes off, too, and now I'm completely naked and on display for him.

I sigh in anticipation. I expect him to prop my legs apart, maybe spatter kisses on my thighs before going down on me like he did before. But the bastard has other ideas.

He ditches his suit, shucks his briefs, and the next thing I know he's kneeling beside me and fisting that big cock that made me scream yesterday. Damned if my mouth doesn't water. Um yeah, forget going down on me. I want this more.

"I want you in my mouth," I whisper.

"Good, because you're about to get it." He straddles me, tucks a pillow behind my head, and slides his dick between my parted lips with one smooth glide.

I suck him eagerly. God, he tastes good. And he feels amazing. Velvety smooth beneath my tongue.

"Oh Christ," Evan chokes out. His fingers are in my hair, stroking gently, guiding me, urging me on. "Feels good, baby."

I take him in deeper, bringing one hand around his body to squeeze his ass. He's in phenomenal shape. I wonder if he hits the gym when he's not in court, or if he plays a sport, maybe on some men's league. Questions bite at my tongue, so it's probably a good thing my tongue is otherwise occupied with his dick. I don't want to ask him those questions, because I don't want to get to know him. I think I would like him a lot if I got to know him. And . . . maybe he's right. Maybe I am scared of dating and relationships and love. I've never been very good at any of it.

This, though, I'm good at. Sex. Physical connections. Bodies and orgasms are so much simpler than love.

"Fuck, I want to come in your mouth. Are you gonna let me, Emilia?"

Even with my lips wrapped around him, I manage a smile. I peer up and nod at him.

He thrusts harder, and the head of his cock nudges the back of my throat. When I swallow, he goes off like a rocket.

"Holy *fuck*," he groans as he comes in my mouth. I'm breathless by the time he pulls out and collapses beside me. "You're incredible," he croaks.

"I know." I demurely wipe my mouth and curl up beside him. I'm naked and turned on, but far too tired to move. Luckily, Evan knows what I need. His hand drifts between my legs, and his fingers play with my clit until I'm gasping.

"You're so wet," he mumbles.

"All thanks to you, Dirk."

His laughter heats my shoulder. He slides two fingers inside of me, and I ride them shamelessly. "Can you come from me fingering you?"

I manage to find my breath. "Probably not." I'm always honest about this stuff. I don't see the point of faking orgasms to protect a man's ego. He should be secure enough to know that a woman doesn't come every time and from every position.

"What do you need?" he asks.

"Your tongue on my clit, or your dick inside me with a finger on my clit. Common denominator is the clit."

"The elusive clit." Evan laughs again. "Let's see what I can do." He disappears for a minute and I hear crinkling from the vicinity of his pants. He's putting on a condom.

He's hard again and I love it. It's rare to meet a man whose libido matches mine. John, the fireman I dated last year, was a one-and-done fella. But I know from experience that Evan can go all night long.

While he's up, he flicks off the lights, bathing the room in shadows, and then finally he's inside me again. Fucking me nice and slow, propped up on one arm so he can reach between us and gently stroke my clit. It's the most beautiful feeling in the whole world, and when the orgasm surfaces, it washes over me in languid waves instead of one huge crash.

"Oh, that was sweet," I say dreamily.

His hot mouth latches onto my neck, sucking softly even as he continues to move inside me. "So sweet," he agrees. There's a beat. "Have dinner with me in D.C."

My eyes pop open. "You're incorrigible."

"Is that a yes?"

"No. It's a 'you're incorrigible.' Now come for me again, Dirk. I love seeing your face when you lose control."

His nostrils flare slightly, arousal stretching his features taut. "Fuck. I can't get enough of you," he growls, and then he's up on his knees, my ankles are on his shoulders, and he's pumping into me furiously until he comes.

And yes, that wild, hazy look in his eyes is exactly what I wanted to see.

I could get addicted to this. I could really, *really* get addicted to this man.

"Evan?" I mumble a while later, as we lay there spooning.

"Mmmm?"

"What do you think of the Elvis version of 'Always On My Mind'?"

"Don't like it. Too fast and upbeat. You?"

I smile in the darkness. "Hate it."

"Willie's acoustic version is so raw and beautiful," he adds.

"It is," I agree.

He wraps his arm tighter around me, holding me close. Silence falls between us again. I feel myself drifting off when I hear his sleepy voice say, "Dinner?"

I laugh into my pillow.

"Come on, say yes. Willie would want you to."

"We'll talk about it in the morning," I lie, and then I snuggle closer to his warm body and fall into a deep sleep.

CHAPTER NINE

"I knew it!" The hushed accusation greets me the moment I roll my carry-on into the carpeted hallway.

I'm totally busted.

Marcy stands in front of me, fully dressed in jeans and a sweater. She looks well rested despite the fact that it's six in the morning, and there's no reason why she should be outside my room right now and not tangled up in Devon's arms, basking in newlywed bliss.

"What are you doing up?" I demand.

"Thwarting your escape."

I roll my eyes. "I'm not escaping. My flight got changed. It leaves at nine now."

"Really? Flights typically get delayed, not moved up from five o'clock in the afternoon to nine in the morning."

I jut out my chin. "Well, this one did." Because I purposely changed it. I even paid the hundred-and-fifty-dollar penalty to get the earlier seat.

"Liar," she says.

"This is ridiculous." I throw a quick glance over my shoulder before stepping forward and closing the door. "Quiet. You'll wake . . . everyone," I amend with a vague gesture to the other doors lining the hall.

"I'll wake Evan, you mean?" she says knowingly. "I saw him leave the reception last night about two minutes after you did, Em. It doesn't take a 'me' to figure out what you two were up to."

I can't stop the laugh that pops out at Marcy's trademark joke. After she snagged her position at NASA, she went from saying 'It doesn't take a rocket scientist' to 'It doesn't take a me', and damned if I still don't find it hilarious, even years later. Anyone else might come off as pompous making that joke, but Marcy is just so damn cute with her rosy cheeks and baby voice that nobody could ever view her as pretentious.

My laugh dissolves into a weary sigh. "If you're determined to interrogate me, at least come downstairs and do it over a cup of coffee so we're not lurking in the hall."

She gives another look at my closed door. "Emilia."

"Marcy."

"Fine."

We quietly make our way down the hall and take the elevator to the lobby. The breakfast buffet is just being set up in the restaurant, and, despite the early hour, we're not the only ones up. A few couples are already down there, waiting for breakfast. A waiter comes over to our table and I gulp down the coffee he pours for me. It nearly sears my tongue off, but I need a clear head right now. AKA a lot of caffeine.

"Last night Evan told me you keep turning him down for a date." Marcy gets right to the point.

"So?"

"So, I think you're making a mistake. He's a really good guy."

"I know he is." I take another sip of the scalding liquid. "Great in bed, too."

She heaves a sigh. "There's more to life than sex, Em. Although I guess keeping everything about just sex has been your MO for a while now. Since senior year of college, when your dad got engaged for . . . the fourth time, I think?" She flicks both eyebrows up. "That's when I realized you're a scaredy-cat."

"I'm not a scaredy-cat."

"Yes, you are. You dumped Bryce like three weeks after that for no good reason. He was *such* a great guy. He adored you, and I know you loved him, too."

She's not wrong. I loved my college boyfriend deeply, but we both moved on. "Bryce is married with four kids now," I tell her. "I'm happy for him. And I'm happy being single."

"You're only single because you're scared of falling in love and then losing it, like your dad did."

"It's too early in the morning for a therapy session, Marce."

"Come on, you know I'm right. Your dad's love life is a mess."

"Doesn't mean I have commitment issues because of it."

"Sure, you do. You've been closed off to the idea of love since Bryce. You use sex as a way to keep a distance."

"Um, the way I see it, sex kind of brings people closer together. No?"

"Not when there's no intimacy involved. Look at what you're doing, Em. You had sex with Evan and now you're running away like a thief in the night."

"I have an early flight," I protest.

"Bullshit. I saw the way you were looking at him at the rehearsal dinner, and then again at the reception." She softens her tone. "I've known Evan for almost two years. He's a good guy. And I think you'll regret it if you don't give him a chance."

"I have to go home, Marce. There's this huge project at work I need to finish. I don't have time to date."

"Sure, keep telling yourself that." She shakes her head in disappointment.

Ugh. I much prefer when people are pissed at me. I don't handle disappointment well.

"Look, you lucked out with Devon," I say. "He clearly worships the ground you walk on. And yes, I like Evan. We get along." I put down my cup. "I'm glad I met him, and I'm glad I finally got to meet Devon. I'm so happy that you found your forever person. And when we're back in the city, I promise I won't let another two years go by without seeing you."

She nods. "Me neither. It's unacceptable."

"Unacceptable," I echo. "But just because you're a wifey now doesn't mean I want the same thing."

"He's not asking you to be a wifey," she sputters. "He wants a *date*."

"Sure, and one date leads to another, and then another, and the next thing you know . . ." I lean in and gently tap the gold band on her ring finger. "I don't want that right now."

"Sounds like more excuses to my ears. But I can see I'm not going to win here, so . . . fine. Don't go out with him."

Both our spirits are a bit low as we finish our coffee and head back to the lobby, where I line up an Uber. I feel guilty that I didn't say goodbye to Evan in person, but I did leave a note on the hotel stationery for him. Pretty much saying I had a good time, it was awesome meeting him, and good luck on his next trial or some bullshit.

Fuck, I really am a coward.

"Are you sure about this?" Marcy asks when we step out into the early-morning chill. She's not wearing a jacket, so she wraps her arms around her chest to ward off the cold.

"Positive." I glance over to see my Uber pulling up. "I should go—I don't want to miss my flight. And you need to get back inside before you catch a cold."

We exchange a long hug. "I love you, Em," she says. "But I think you're an idiot."

"I love you, too, and I think you're wonderful."

I give her one last squeeze before sliding into the car.

♫

The GPS on my phone says we're ten minutes from the airport. We've already been driving for about thirty, and I chose to sit in the back so I wouldn't have to make conversation. It's way too early for small talk.

The driver's choice of radio stations only makes matters worse—it's a country/country pop music station, which means a lot of Luke Bryan and Carrie Underwood and Garth Brooks. Not exactly my cup of tea, but I lean back and close my eyes and try not to think too hard about why I'm on my way to the airport.

It's not until a familiar crooner wafts out of the car speakers that my eyes snap open.

"Dammit, Willie," I mutter under my breath.

The driver twists around. "What was that?"

"Nothing. I was just . . . talking to the song. It's one of my favorites." My tone is grudging.

"I prefer the Elvis version," she reveals.

Of course she does.

"Do you want me to turn it up?" She does it, anyway, despite my lack of response, and Willie's voice gets louder.

I sit back and listen as he sings about his regrets, wishing he'd acted differently, lamenting about all the wasted time, and a lump of emotion fills my throat. I don't know if Marcy's right and I'll regret not giving Evan a chance. I don't know if Evan is my happily ever after. I don't know if happy endings even exist. I mean, my dad sure didn't get one. But that's my dad, not me.

So no, while I can't be sure that Evan is my forever person, I'm pretty damn positive that Willie Nelson would kick my fucking ass if I didn't at least try to find out.

CHAPTER TEN

What a difference one hour makes. The Blue Valley Lodge is humming with activity when I return to the hotel. At six a.m., it was dead. At seven a.m., there's a throng of people milling in the lobby. I spot a tousled-haired Robin at the front desk, looking sleepy. I remember her saying she had an early flight to Florida today. An actual early flight, and not the one I paid extra to get on. By the way? Having to pay *another* hundred and fifty dollars to make *another* change to get back on my *original* flight? Marcy is right—I am an idiot.

"Morning," I murmur as I pass one of Marcy's uncles on my way to the front counter. I greet the available clerk with a half-hearted smile. "Hi. I checked out online already, but did anyone come downstairs to bring the keycard back? Room three-oh-nine."

He types something on the computer and checks the screen. "Yes, actually. A gentleman dropped it off about ten minutes ago."

Shit, I was hoping he might still be in my room. More so, I was hoping he hadn't read my stupid note. "Okay, thank you. Did you happen to see where he went?"

"Sorry, I'm afraid I didn't."

"Okay. Thanks, anyway."

I give the lobby another scan. No Evan. So I wander into the restaurant, and this time I see him. Standing in front of a table of croissants, loading a plate. His hair is messy, and I think I spot a hickey on his neck, which brings a flush to my cheeks. I was sucking pretty hard on every part of him last night.

Without hesitation, I race over to him and blurt out, "Yes!"

His eyes widen at the sight of me. "Wha—"

I cut him off. "Yes, I'll go out with you. I'm saying yes, okay? I want to have dinner with you in D.C. Like, actual dinner, it's not code for me wanting to fuck you again. Well, I want that, too, because you know how much I love your dick, but—"

His cheeks turn bright red, and that's when I stop.

Because the Evan I know would never blush at the mention of sex.

"Devon," I say with a sigh.

"Yup." He gives me a jovial salute, and once again I can't fathom how these two are twins. One exudes buckets of sexual charisma, and the other does things like *salute*.

"So. I'm guessing all that was meant for my brother . . .?" He lets the question hang.

"Um, yes." I shove a strand of hair out of my eyes. "Have you seen him this morning? I heard he already came downstairs."

"He's right over there." Devon nods to the left, and I follow his gaze all the way to the floor-to-ceiling windows across the room. The windowpanes are covered with white frost and snowflakes. It started snowing around the time I got back, but it looks like it's picking up.

Evan is alone at a table, gripping a mug with both hands. His expression is stormy, signaling he's pissed. It doesn't take a Marcy to figure out why.

"Thanks," I tell Devon.

He smiles wryly. "Good luck."

I touch his arm gratefully, then straighten my shoulders and leave the buffet area. Suspicious gray eyes pierce into me as I approach Evan's table.

"Hey," I say sheepishly.

He just cocks one eyebrow and takes a sip of his coffee.

"Yes, I'm an asshole," I inform him. "I'm well aware of this."

Finally, he speaks. A low, bitter drawl. "That's the second time you've snuck out and left me in bed alone."

"I know." I bite my lip. "I guess it doesn't help that I left a note?"

"Nope."

"Okay. Well. Does it make you feel better to know that I just told your twin brother I would go on a date with him and that I love his dick?"

Evan makes a strangled sound, as if he's trying to choke down a laugh. "I bet he loved that."

"I think I scare him."

"You scare me."

I eye him in challenge. "No, I don't. You're a courtroom shark, remember? You wouldn't let a little thing like me scare you."

"Well, I've put myself out there a dozen times these past two days and you've rejected me every single time, so yeah, you're a bit terrifying, Emilia."

I pull out the chair next to him and sink down on it. I lean forward, rest one hand on his knee, and use the other to gently pry the mug out of his hand. When I lace my fingers through his, he resists at first, but then his grip slowly loosens.

"Look. Evan. I'm not good with relationships or the idea of falling in love," I confess. "I'm not open to it, and apparently I use work as an excuse to not get serious with anyone and sex as an excuse to avoid intimacy, which is stupid because sex *is* intimacy, but Marcy says it's not and she's my new therapist."

His laughter finally slips out.

"But I do like you and I'd like to go on a date with you," I finish.

"Only one?"

"Seriously?" I say in frustration. "That's all I can commit to right now, Evan! We literally met *two* days ago. I just told you I'm open to the idea of falling in *love* with you." I scrub both hands over my eyes. "I came back this morning because I was in an Uber and Willie Nelson came on, our *song* came on." I groan into my hands. "We already have a *song*! What more do you want?"

I blink when he tugs my hands away from my face. His dimpled grin greets me. "I'm just fucking with you. Let's start with one date and see what happens." He chuckles to himself. "What time is your flight today?"

"Four-thirty."

"To Reagan or Dulles?"

"Dulles."

"Sweet. We're on the same flight. I'll try to switch seats so we're sitting together." He flashes his pearly whites again. "We can discuss our date on the plane, maybe pay for some of that obscenely priced wi-fi and look up restaurant reviews. I've got some ideas already."

My lips twitch in humor. "Are you always this involved in the planning of a dinner date?"

"When it's the first and potentially last date we'll ever have? Fuck yeah, I'm going all out for this. I need to impress you if I want date number two, and then three, four, five—"

"You're getting ahead of yourself again. AKA scaring me."

He brings his lips to mine, giving me a fleeting kiss before saying, "Relax, Emilia. It's just dinner."

EPILOGUE

Emilia & Evan

SAVE THE DATE

FEBRUARY 14, 2020

ABOUT THE AUTHOR

A *New York Times, USA Today* and *Wall Street Journal* bestselling author, Elle Kennedy grew up in the suburbs of Toronto, Ontario, and holds a B.A. in English from York University. From an early age, she knew she wanted to be a writer, and actively began pursuing that dream when she was a teenager.

Elle writes romantic suspense and erotic contemporary romance for various publishers. She loves strong heroines and sexy alpha heroes, and just enough heat and danger to keep things interesting!

More info available at: www.ellekennedy.com

All I Want

MARA WHITE

"ALL I WANNA DO IS MAKE LOVE TO YOU" – HEART

♪

The Sailor's Ruin was usually a sure thing. Seedy, but not disgusting. Dark enough for some anonymity but with surprisingly not-too-revolting bathrooms that were well-lit enough for her to check her temperature. Certainly, Ove would never step foot in this place and that was the secret ingredient of her well-baked plan.

Marilyn didn't need to drink to loosen up for this. She didn't have to count days or even bring her thermometer, because the truth was, she had the routine down like breathing. Those first months, she'd chant under her breath, *a means to an end, a means to an end*. But there was no longer any need to soften the impact. She was fully aware, as well as committed to the necessary betrayal in order to obtain the desired outcome.

Marilyn loved Ove, and he in return, adored her. The nearly twenty-year age difference, seventeen to be precise, had never made her flinch. The fact that, once upon a time, long ago, she had been his graduate student, no longer mattered at all. He was divorced when she met him, and they immediately clicked. For him, she gave up the mainland and agreed to embrace his love of living on the island.

The most pressing-devastating-catastrophic incursion on their union, wasn't the cheating—it was Ove's apparent sterility. Never mind the man had fathered four children with his first wife, that for all other intents and purposes, he was fit as a fiddle, in the words of his physician and close friend, Dr. Bonner. But his sperm count was low and seemingly inadequate to get her pregnant after many years of trying.

Marilyn wanted a child. She longed after infants, envied her friends who pushed them around in the latest prams, salivated over their onerous complaints about the cost of preschool and cloth diaper services.

She and Ove gardened. They grew things. Made homemade pasta and agonized over sauces prepared from scratch with ingredients plucked from their own flower boxes. Ove did scrimshaw with ethically and legally sourced materials he acquired from antiquing and online estate auctions. Marilyn preferred needlepoint over knitting and always had a project in her hands, for she was a creator at heart. Ove read nonfiction and she loved thrillers with her feet in his lap or on the back of their slumbering Labrador, Pete.

What she ached for was the slapping of tiny toddler feet against the kitchen tile, the slamming of the side screen door after years of being told to close it softly, the shoes and socks discarded on the floor that she'd have to stoop to retrieve. Marilyn wanted it all. Cheerios and squashed bananas on the floor. Fingerprints to wipe from the stainless steel in the kitchen. Ove had done it four times already nearly a lifetime ago—and he was ambivalent about the idea. Marilyn suspected that his indifference came from wanting to see her happy, to please her in any way he could.

Her hand slipped down to her belly where the excitement began to brew. She loved Ove, but through her indiscretions, had also discovered a surprising truth about herself—that she loved sex—with strangers too.

"Mar, I'm getting ready to do last call. You want a last spritzer or should we settle up?"

Larry, the barkeep, knew her, what she drank, her not-so-subtle reason for sitting alone in a bar on a rainy Wednesday evening. Although he most likely believed her to be cruising for hook-ups and hadn't yet devised the deeper, and purposeful secret.

She loved Ove. She also loved the rush that came from touching live flesh for the very first time, the crash of a new lover's foreign lips against her own. Greedy hands, hard bodies, the sting of a slap, the rawness from rubbing, the musk of sweat, the feel of a heartbeat vibrating under her fingertips. The black silence of orgasm. When a scream of ecstasy could be violently ripped from her chest.

Needlepoint and reading under the lamp while sipping hot tea were for Fridays. Marilyn used her Wednesdays and Thursdays for something else entirely.

"I'm finished. Just the bill please," she whispered to Larry. He quickly dumped her ice and glass into his slosh sink and tore the top paper carbon bill off of his pad.

"No luck tonight, huh?" Larry said triumphantly as he laid down the check.

Marilyn could read the glee in his somber mask of indifference. She also gloated because she would never stoop so low as to ask Larry for assistance in her project. She reached for her card and placed it on top of the check. She didn't want to reward him with an answer.

She loved Ove, that was what she had to keep telling herself.

Larry eyed the white band of skin around her left ring finger—the scar of commitment, she had to use lard or olive oil to get the damn thing off. There was a porcelain swan by the dish soap upon whose neck it hung every Wednesday and Thursday night.

Her temper was firing. Her body, so used to adamant attention by this time of night, was staging a protest. Nipples aroused, silken panties rubbing innocently against freshly waxed tender folds.

Marilyn grabbed her card and exchanged it for a crisp twenty-dollar bill. No need to leave a paper trail. Why invite inquiry when she had no need to do so. It was uncomfortable enough explaining the cigar smoke that lingered in her cashmere sweaters or her short mohair skirts.

"See you tomorrow?" Larry had the nerve to wink at her.

Marilyn scoffed and nearly rolled her eyes at him, but she'd been overly educated and trained in manners since childhood not to engage in such things.

"Thank you. Good night." She almost fell off the stool. It had been a mistake not to eat dinner.

There were a few lingering couples who she eyed jealously as she took concentrated, steady steps toward the door. She could already picture them in bed, caressing, sucking, crying out in ardor. The knot in her stomach tightened to an almost unbearable proportion.

She loved Ove.

"Mar!" Larry jogged up behind her as she pulled the heavy front door open laboriously into a gale-force wind. She turned on her sturdy, sensible high heels and the gust caught her skirt whisking it upwards to display her stockings, garters, and barely existent black lace underwear. A woman on the prowl had certain tools and lingerie was one of them. "Umbrella," Larry told her winded. He was portly and smoked, snuck scotch behind the bar—more than was healthy for anyone. "We've got a whole slew of them in the lost and found. Customers leave them all the time. No sense in getting soaked."

Her panties were soaked in arousal just from Larry's chubby fingers resting on her shoulder. Lust was addictive, a habit-forming substance like any other. Marilyn licked her lips slowly and smiled at the barkeep.

"Thank you. See you tomorrow."

Head down, she raced to her car. Perhaps some lone man in the bar had seen the display of her underthings thanks to the timely wind and was dodging giant raindrops through the parking lot and making his way over to proposition her. Accordingly, she turned on the car slowly. Set the radio to an old rock station, taking her time. She lit a cigarette and tested her own sobriety by counting backwards by sevens. It was way off, she gave up after two tries.

Marilyn loved Ove, but she also hungered for bottomless passion, rowdy sex, and the impossibly hard cocks that youth bequeathed on men.

A failure. That was the conclusion to this Wednesday. Her life. Her inability to reproduce and the subsequent barren backyard space where a swing could hang perfectly from the old apple tree. A treehouse even in the elm by the driveway.

A useless back mudroom with no mud. A rooster shaped cookie jar with no cookies inside. An empty uterus so ravenous it was sinful. *Fuck it*. She lowered the window and tossed her butt into the blinding rain. She was sick and tired of feeling so empty.

Marilyn wasn't nervous as she could do this drive in her sleep. Knowing, for example, that there were exactly seven landmarks she'd pass before she reached the turn-off for their cozy and quiet neighborhood. First, came an exit that took you down to the harbor, where sleepy boats rocked in the quaint marina and seagulls hovered awaiting dawn and the first fishermen to venture out on the glassy waters. Next, there was a small cross next to an oak tree, a memorial to a victim of some terrible traffic accident. Then, the on-ramp to the highway. A row of three hotels that she was intimately acquainted with. Knew the smell of the musty pillows and the tang of the iron heavy water that leaked from the bathroom faucets. A gas station. A hitchhiker—

A hitchhiker?

Marilyn slammed on the brakes as her car veered onto the shoulder. The man leaped out of the way and down into the ravine off the side of the road, disappearing from view.

A hitchhiker? But it was pouring, and hardly summertime anymore—the Halloween decorations were already on display at the drug store.

She put the car in park and stepped out into the rain, forgetting the umbrella Larry had so kindly loaned her. The heels of her shoes sank in the saturated peat and her headlights lit up the sideways angle of the squally onslaught of cold rain.

"Help!" Marilyn squawked into the noisy deluge. *Help?* She wasn't the one who needed help. She'd pulled over *to* help, yet some part of her was frightened that she'd hit the man and knocked him clear into the muddy ravine, necessitating another sad little cross. "Hello?" she corrected herself, leaning pathetically into the dark. Her skirt and sweater were now soddened and heavy against her heaving chest. "Hello? Is someone there? Are you all right?"

The man crawled out of the ditch like a Darwinian creature emerging to rectify her night.

"It's true what they say about your life flashing before your eyes," he told her almost cheerily.

"I'm sorry. You startled me. I've never seen hitchhikers on the island before. Ray's Cab Service runs all night. If it rings for awhile, he's sleeping, but he'll get up eventually. Where are you headed?"

"My truck broke down back yonder and I don't carry a phone." The man shielded his eyes from the torrential downpour, as if his hand were any match for the deluge that pounded down around them.

"I'm sorry," she said again. "We can speak in my car." Marilyn gestured to her car and put her hand out to steady herself on the familiar chrome of her vehicle she'd driven ever since they moved to the island.

They hopped in the car speedily and the man shook water from his hair not unlike Pete did after fetching sticks from the foamy ocean.

"Woohoo, what a monsoon!"

"It's hurricane season," Marilyn said, shaking her head. "You must not be from around here." He obviously wasn't from around here. He smiled at her and shrugged. The man was easy-going and light, unheard of qualities in the men from these parts. His emerald eyes stopped her from reaching for the key. They were unlike any color she'd ever seen before in any other iris, bright and jewel-toned, faceted and sparkling like a diamond. She pressed her lips together and swallowed, lifted her skirt so her milky thighs were exposed right up to the line of the garter. Because they were wet and so was she. Drenched. Dripping. Her muscles quivered in anticipation.

She wanted to spout off baby names from the tip of her tongue. Her obsession was perverse. She wanted to suck him dry and leave as full as possible. Maybe the night wasn't a total washout after all.

"Wow, you're really beautiful," the man said quizzically and then quickly covered his mouth. "Sorry, that just slipped out. And totally inappropriate considering the circumstances. You just caught me off guard."

"No matter," she dismissed his apology. Her eyes voraciously sized him up, lingered suggestively on the bulge between his legs, his lips, and then returned to look deeply into his gaze. "Where do you want to go?" Marilyn enunciated every syllable and laced her words with temptation.

"Oh, a hotel, if there's one close by? If not, I suppose a gas station or a twenty-four-hour diner would do me right."

"There's a hotel up ahead." She stepped on the gas and pulled back on the road with purpose.

The orange blinking sign of the motel blurred double through the windshield and falling rain. She turned into the lot and savored the familiar crunch of gravel under the car's tires; a sound she'd come to associate with acute anticipation and welcome nervousness.

"I really can't thank you enough. I know stopping for a stranger this day in age really—"

"Shut up," Marilyn replied curtly. She opened the car door and stepped out into the parking lot. She peeled the wet cardigan off and dropped it on the ground behind her as she marched toward the yellow-lighted reception where Josephine lorded over the peg board of keys like pirates' gold. Marilyn hated her priggish insistence on inspecting the rooms upon checkout while she stood humiliated under the florescent light, love bruises blossoming on her chest, swollen lipped, and reeking of sex. Josephine wasn't dumb, she knew exactly what Marilyn was up to and made her pay simply by adhering to puritanical policies in the face of her guests' messy discomposure—or in Marilyn's case—her loose whoring and insatiable flesh.

"Sinful," she heard Josephine sniff as the bell chimed and the door bumped her backside.

"I need a room," Marilyn told her robotically.

"Hey, I can take it from here," the John said as he ran in from the rain, he held a local paper over his head that he must have grabbed from the metal newspaper machine by the door.

His eyes lit up a room. Marilyn grinned slyly as she watched Josephine try to mask her reaction to the stranger's beautiful face. Marilyn appraised his backside as he made his way to the desk.

"The usual? 107, Mrs. French?"

It was a bogus name. Josephine got her kicks out of using Mrs. every time she ducked in the woman's blasted, chiming door. The hotel was stifled at least four decades behind. Campy and over-compensatory, apologetic for its hideousness. Marilyn stuck her tongue out like a snake tasting the stale air.

"Oh, we have her credit card on file here, dear," Josephine

delightedly told the John. It didn't seem to faze him.

"This way," Marilyn yelled at him. Josephine threw the keys with the sad green plastic fob at her and she snatched them out of the air. "Fucking cunty old bag," Marilyn muttered under her breath.

"Listen, I'm not sure what's going on here, but you didn't have to pay for my room . . ." The John jogged behind to catch up with her as she marched with purpose toward 107. She didn't bother to move her car, she wouldn't be too long and the rain was already waning. "Do you have a name? I really do appreciate you picking me up."

Insert key. Pull shitty plywood door toward you first, then push in as you turn hard to the right.

"Marilyn," she said. "What's yours?"

"Decker," he replied. Decker chased behind her innocently, probably still befuddled over what the hell had transpired in the last fifteen minutes to get him to this moment.

She shoved open the door and breathed in deep, the must, the mold, the cheap air freshener they used to cover the unpleasantness. Marilyn knew to turn on the lamp and not the glaring overhead light. She marched through the dark toward the bedside table and clicked the dial on the wire illuminating the orange and gold décor of Cliff Side Motel.

"It's not beautiful, but it works." She shrugged dismissively, kicked off her heels, unzipped the back of her skirt and let it puddle around her feet. She shrugged off her camisole to reveal the black lace of her bra, panty, and garter against her pale cream skin.

"God, you look familiar, like an actress or something. Do I know you?" Decker asked her. He seemed desperate to keep his jaw up as realization of her intentions was finally dawning on him.

"No. I'm not." She pulled her bra down and slipped the lace underneath her breasts, essentially pushing them together and forward so they tipped up succulently as if on a platter offered to her new friend. It was D day, time for her succinct soliloquy to explain what she wanted.

"I paid for this room tonight, because I want to fuck. For as long as you can and as hard as you can. I want you to make me come as many times as you are capable. I, in turn, will make you come as many times as is physically possible. My only caveat is that you come inside me without protection."

At that she reached inside her purse and extracted the paper that she'd unfolded and re-folded so many times it had become delicate like a crunchy fall leaf.

"I'm clean. Here's my lab results. I trust you to tell me right now if you suffer from any STDs or otherwise contagious diseases."

He backed up to the wall until his boots hit the baseboard.

"Holy fuck," he whispered. His bright green eyes, so full of wonderment, lowered from hers to her breasts.

Marilyn dipped her own head and tongued her lifted nipple. She couldn't quite suck it, but her agile tongue grazed it long enough to make it pucker and tingle.

"So, are you clean, Deck-er?" she divided his name into two competing syllables. Marilyn sauntered over to him nearly naked, with a sense of urgency brewing between her legs. With one hand she grasped the bulge in his jeans and raked the denim with her long red-painted fingernails. "Up to the task?"

"I can't believe this is actually happening," he said, running a distraught hand through his boyish hair.

"Only if you want to," she quickly assured him, removing her hand discretely. "You can just sleep too and I'll be on my merry way. I don't mean to scare you."

"Oh, hell no, I'm down. So down. Just let me get my bearings." He licked his lips, looked toward the ceiling and seemed to utter a little prayer to the shitty fiber tiles above him. "My grandfather always told me I was a *lucky sonofabitch*, but this might take the cake." He reached for her breasts, and thumbed her nipples instantaneously making them harden again.

Marilyn stepped up on her tiptoes and brought her mouth to his. "Remember, come inside me as many times as you possibly can," she whispered into his mouth.

"Yes, ma'am," he said as he swept her up in his arms.

♪

She loved Ove, but this was . . . better.

Decker wasn't shy about using his tongue, he kissed her hard and opened-mouthed, sucking her tongue into his own warm mouth. His kiss was immature bordering on brutal, like coitus in how he fucked her mouth, thrusting and groaning as if his eager tongue were an extension of his swollen dick. She loved it and moaned.

"Jesusfuckingchrist," he said in response to her sounds.

His thumbs worked her nipples as he cupped the swells in his palms. When he ducked his head to suckle the two aroused stones, he first bit the rounded mounds shoved up by her bra. His teeth scraped her flesh and her abdominal muscles clenched down in a rush of desire so fierce it felt like a fever break.

"How hard can you fuck me? How hard is this cock?" she asked him as he devoured her breasts, nursing one nipple and then the next, swirling his tongue over the tip roughly. She was turned on to the brink of insanity. Her fingers found their way into his jeans and she cupped and tugged his balls. "Give it to me. Empty yourself inside me," she taunted him as he suckled her ripe breasts. He licked the hardened nubs in retaliation, until her head fell back and she hissed at the ceiling.

Marilyn was so wet she felt herself drip in anticipation. Decker continued eating her tits like a starved man who couldn't sate himself. She wrapped her fingers around his erection and smiled at the size and girth of tonight's catch.

"Oh my God," she said. "You're going to fuck me so good," she told him running her loosely clenched fist up and down the long shaft.

"Holyfuckingshit," Decker said before he thirstily took her mouth again.

"You want to be on top?" Marilyn asked him kindly as she helped him out of his jeans and light flannel.

"I want to eat your pussy," Decker told her. He caught her

nipple and latched on again sucking voraciously. Marilyn was afraid she'd come just from the friction her two thighs made together. She struggled to take a deep breath and calm her pounding heart and her need-to-get-pounded nether regions. *Calm down,* she told herself.

He could eat her out, but she wanted him inside her when she came—get the muscles moving in the right direction to take in his precious seed.

"You can if you'd like, but I want to come from your dick, with you inside me." She felt the release of precum from his tip that burst forth with her words. "And you can fuck my face too, if you want, but the same goes. I want you inside me when you come," she said looking sincerely into his eyes.

"Ohmyfuckinggod, this can't be real." He pushed her back onto the bed.

She scooted up the length, bent her knees, and then spread conservatively before him to reveal her glistening, nearly pulsating slit.

"What's the most you've ever come in one night?" she asked. He crawled up toward her, a cocky smile displayed on her lips.

"Just twice, but I'm willing to try anything," he told her. He pinched the inside of her thigh hard enough to make her squirm and squeal. Then lowered his head and licked up her crack from hole to hole.

"Good boy," she told him and lowered her hips to the mattress.

♫

When he penetrated her with his tongue to the hilt, the stubble of his chin grazed her asshole. She screamed out in sheer frustration from holding back the powerful orgasm that was completely overtaking her anatomy.

"Fuck me, fuck me. Give me your cock, now!" she hollered.

"Shhh!" he shushed her, putting a finger to his lips. "You'll wake the neighbors." He smiled at her mischievously, his bright green eyes sparkling in the lamp light. Wrapping a hand through her long hair, he yanked her toward his straining erection that was pushing against his belly.

She swallowed his cock deeply, craving every ridge and every bulging vein against her lips and tongue. Decker had no problem pushing deep and fucking her mouth as if it were a bottomless hole. His balls slapped under her chin while ropes of saliva strung down her face. She liked that he was unencumbered, that he fucked her hard realizing he should take advantage of the opportunity.

"You feel so fucking good," he told her. He pulled her hair to control her head, his grip soft, but the size of his raging erection and the thrust of his hips nearly took her to the limit. She gagged on his cock and he didn't back away. Instead, he caressed her cheek as if she were precious, mouth stuffed with his dick. "Suck my balls," he ordered her as he finally pulled back, slowly, taking his time to extract every millimeter of pleasure.

Marilyn obliged him, tugging the heavy sacs softly with her full lips. He massaged her breasts in circles until his thick fingers skidded across her stomach to find her clit. He slapped at her pussy with a cupped hand and the sensation sent shock waves resounding through her muscles. She was so afraid to come, with his cock too far from her cunt.

He slapped her again and Marilyn yelped, holding in the orgasm to save her life. She licked up his tightened shaft and rolled the hard edge of his cut tip across her lips, in and out of her mouth. She pulled herself up higher, clinging to his biceps until she was standing on her knees just like him. She rubbed the tip of his dripping cock with her belly button.

"You want me to put it in?" he asked coyly. He knew what she wanted. "Ask me, nicely, Marilyn and maybe I'll let you ride me. How bad do you want this dick?"

Decker slapped his erection to the side and fisted his dick with a fluency that translated as beauty to her eyes. He handled himself so well, obviously knew how to get himself off. He could just jerk a few times right now and spill the precious fluid Marilyn coveted so much.

"Decker, I want it so badly. Please let me ride your dick, please fuck me. I'll do anything you want if you put it inside me!" She didn't even know she was capable of spouting such nonsense, begging for a cock like a hungry little whore with zero self-respect. But alas, that's what she'd become. His semen was gold to her, life essence, that she'd pay for however he wanted her to, drop for every last drop.

"You ever been fucked in the ass before?"

"Nope." Marilyn shook her head. She popped a finger into her mouth thoughtlessly.

"You look like a little baby when you do that," he told her.

She smiled.

"Here, suck on your grown-up pacifier." He stuck his furious cock in her face and she took him again into her mouth. "I just want to get it in your ass. You're so tight and I'm so big. Just a little warm-up through the back door. Okay, Marilyn?"

She pulled back from the mouthful he'd given her.

"Whatever you want, Decker, I'm yours all night long." She resumed licking the head and running her tongue up and down the shaft.

"Turn over and stick your ass up. No crying. Don't be a baby."

He jerked her back by the hips abruptly shaking the answer from her mouth. His tongue landed hot and heavy on her little hole and he swirled around twice before breaking the barrier and shoving forward with his mouth.

"Ohhh!" Marilyn squealed at the unfamiliar feeling and in response he slapped her ass with a stinging smack. He spit on her asshole and gently pushed his thumb past the ringed sphincter all the way to his knuckle.

Marilyn squirmed and felt a tugging fire that ran from her mouth to her nipples, her clit all the way to her back door. She pushed back hesitantly and Decker spit again. Once she accommodated his finger fucking she pushed back tentatively in surprised enjoyment.

"I'm in your ass, Marilyn. I think you like it," he told her devilishly.

"Decker—" His name barely fell from her lips and he was lifting to stand on his knees, withdrawing his thumb, and smacking her backdoor playfully with his dick.

"Marilyn, do you have lube in that bag of tricks of yours?"

"Aquaphor," she told him. She couldn't speak straight with the impending prospect of getting fucked in the ass.

"That will work." Decker promptly got to work lubricating himself with the ointment in her purse. She squeezed her eyes shut tightly and grimaced at the thought of what was about to happen to her. But she was willing to endure it for the pearly prize she needed so badly.

"If you don't relax, it's going to hurt."

She feigned a relaxed face without leaving her ass-in-the-air pose. He laughed at her antics as he coated his cock. When he climbed back on the bed, Marilyn crossed her ankles and it was her turn to say a prayer.

"I'll be gentle," he whispered as he began to massage her clit with the tips of his fingers. His pace and pressure were surprisingly accurate for a man his age and Marilyn's body gripped and readied as if it were about to climax against her solid and stubborn will, which at this point, was grasping at straws—grasping and panting.

When he started to slide in, every muscle fiber in her clenched. Marilyn forced her body to calm down, reminding herself that mind over matter accomplished incredible feats.

"Try to let the muscles in your lower abdomen relax, it will trigger the whole chain to respond—"

"Like that?"

"There we go," he told her. The head of his cock was inside and the burn made her want to cry and then punch him in the face. But, alas, she'd asked for it. *Goddamned ass-expert.* The more she slackened her lower belly—the more he slid home. And, inadvertently on her part, the more the burn turned into alarming pulses of decadent pleasure. When his balls knocked into her clit, she shuddered and bore down on his dick trying to expel him.

"So tight, Marilyn, so freaking good," he told her rubbing soft circles on her behind.

"Please don't come in my ass," she begged him.

"Don't say *'come in my ass,'* or I'm going to fucking come in your ass," he admonished her.

She could tell from the tone of his voice that he was holding back a laugh.

"So, what do you think? You like my cock in your ass?" He fucked her with trained strokes full of compassion that inexplicably made her tear up. She sniffled and he patted her rump with affection. "You love it," he whispered into her ear after he leaned forward. With a handful of her hair, he pulled her head back. "You love getting your ass fucked."

"Ohfuck, ohgod, sofuckingtight," he said as he increased his pace.

"Please," she reminded. Her answer came in the form of a hand to her clit that also picked up the pace. Marilyn screamed as the orgasm tore through her, shredding her dignity and splitting apart her soul. The center of her climax was a raging firestorm with rings that resounded outward, rattling her very bones. She shrieked as she began to come down and lose touch with the bright light. Her body oozed into a pile on the bed, she was liquefied, her mind obliterated into nebulous vapors that drifted around her head.

Decker pulled out, then yanked her down on the bed by her feet. He walked on his knees to her body and spread her legs. She couldn't move, nor could she speak.

Lowering himself down on his strong biceps, he ran his impressively virulent and resilient cock through her folds. She quaked in response and dragged her eyes to his face.

"Come inside you, still the name of the game?"

She nodded once and closed her eyes. He rammed forward to the hilt and tremors wracked her body, spiking her nerve endings into action. He stroked once, twice, and on the third stroke, he spilled what she wanted inside of her.

"Happy?" he asked her.

Marilyn nodded.

♪

Marilyn awoke with a start in the middle of the night. Decker was beside her, his arm extended under her neck, his hand casually touching her hip. He was naked except for the sheet that draped around him like an Italian Renaissance sculpture. He snored lightly, more of a rasp than a full-on honk like the one Ove did.

Ove.

He'd probably fallen asleep in his chair with his glasses still on. She could never figure out how his neck didn't fall forward. He'd stumble to bed without even realizing she was gone—or if he did, he'd guess she missed the last ferry back and had spent the night at her parent's place—as she often told him.

Ove was a good, good man. Fascinating, so smart, still curious and positively engaged in life. He was kind, generous, and noble, a decent man if ever there were one. She knew that even at his age and on his fifth run on the course, he'd be an exceptional father.

She loved Ove. And the guilt from the betrayal curdled her stomach. So, she pushed it out of her mind and focused on the task at hand. Despite feeling existentially exhausted, her statistical chances would surge if she could get the sleeping male angel beside her to go again.

Marilyn decided to wake him with a blow job. All men liked to be woken up that way and if they said otherwise, it was a case of petulant denial.

Decker was still semi-hard and wore the scent of their two mingled bodies. She started slow at the tip and worked him into a raging hard-on by sucking him deep and slow. He rolled on his back and opened his shockingly green eyes. The smile that spread across his face was decadent, like a cloud of whipped cream atop an already indulgent dessert.

He touched her face and let her long hair run through his

fingers, with an affectionate look on his face that made Marilyn sad she couldn't take his feelings into consideration.

"I'd think you were a succubus or some kind of apparition, if you didn't feel so real." His voice was husky, gravelly after waking. She imagined getting him coffee and bringing him the paper like she did for Ove every morning. Decker wouldn't need slippers or a robe, he'd walk into the kitchen barefoot and wearing nothing more than boxers.

Marilyn admonished herself for having domestic fantasies, forced herself to focus on the present. Take the semen and run. Nobody gets hurt. Desperation can make anyone lie to themselves.

"You know today started out totally fucking terrible and then got even worse when my truck broke down. Felt like I was being tested, put to the limit. And then this happened."

"They don't call you a lucky sonofabitch for nothing," she said. He laughed openly, and the sound struck her as melodic and joyous.

She crawled up his fit but slender form, admiring not only his pulsing cock, but the way his abdomen tapered, the strawberry-blond color of the fine hairs that covered his body, the warm scent of his flesh—like summer rain. That's what he was, a sun-shower.

She lowered herself onto his straining erection while he took her sore breasts in his hands and began once again, the sweet torture of her nipples. She was raw, dead-tired, and feeling delirious, but her anatomy responded to his touch like a soldier standing at attention. Eager, committed, ready to go—they had chemistry, the two of them, and she couldn't deny the glint of connection that was brewing between them. It wasn't a good thing.

♫

She rode his body with pure hedonistic lust. As his cock dragged leisurely through her channel, she thrust harder so that his tip rammed into her G-spot.

The third orgasm that rocked Marilyn that night was

painstakingly slow to rouse and usher forth. But when it finally arrived, it was worth the effort and her noises of pleasure were so erotic and uninhibited that it pulled Decker's climax into the race, and they detonated together. She collapsed down on top of him as her muscles continued to suck the precious potential toward her womb. She smiled into his chest hair, while he scribbled invisible sonnets down her back with the tip of his pointer finger.

When at last her knight of pleasure had returned to his gentle rumble of sleep, she separated her torso from his cautiously and crept from the bed. She took the risk of showering because even a sleepy, absentminded professor would be able to detect the heady scent of sex on her flesh. Her clothes, still wet from the rain, were a bother to shrug into and felt like a prison to her extra sensitized and over-stimulated skin.

She pulled her hair into a knot and peered into the dreary bathroom mirror. There were cigarette stains on the porcelain sink and she smirked thinking about how much they must weigh on the proprietress Josephine's prude and judgmental conscience. After looking just once at her reflection, her eyes flashed back, for she saw a touch of change that registered immediately. Marilyn laughed out loud and slapped her hand over her mouth. Her eyes pricked with tears and her shoulders wracked with silent sobs.

For in the echo of herself she saw what she'd always wanted to see, and it didn't take a pee strip, or an ultrasound, or a blood test for her to confirm that her life, at that moment, had changed on a fundamental level. Her woman's intuition had never failed her. She was pregnant. There was a new life growing inside of her. It was the one wish she desired more than anything else.

♪

At this stage of the game, she'd grab her purse and march to the car. Sometimes suffer the wrath of Josephine who'd come sniff the room in disgust and look at her as if she were a whore. But today was different in so many ways. Marilyn spotted a pad of paper by the phone. She grabbed the pen supplied beside it and began to draft Decker a note. Since he was *the one*, it seemed only fair. And there was a trace of innocence to the man that had her feeling obligated to some accountability—not an explanation—but a token of gratitude to help soften the blow.

He lay there looking like a Greek god, so beautifully chiseled and still semi-hard. *Bless his heart,* she thought to herself. A man like that you could fuck every day for the rest of your life and always find a new attribute to appreciate.

To eat and run was terribly rude and she knew it. She also knew all too well what getting fucked and ditched felt like, and even though they were men, she didn't wish upon anyone the sense of worthlessness those few nights in college had made her suffer. Decker was special, so she'd leave him a note and then hightail it the hell out of there.

♪

Dearest Decker,

I'll forever be indebted to you for the joy you've brought me. I hope that an ounce of what I experienced was mutual and that you will look back upon this night with utmost fondness. But I do ask now for protection, when last night I likely appeared adamant to forgo it altogether. I implore you not to speak of this encounter, to allow it to live in your memory alone and never seek me out. I am in love with another man, and any further communication on our part would inflict damage and heartache. I wish you well. Success. Happiness. Deep love. Gratifying adventures. And last but not least, a lifetime full of exceptional sex. Thank you from the bottom of my heart. Tonight could not possibly have been any better.

-M

♪

SIX YEARS LATER

Mr. and Mrs. Nilsson, although it's apparent that your son is very, very bright, I'm just afraid he's not a fit for our school at this time.

Marilyn's eyes blurred with tears and she crumpled the offensive letter and tossed it clear across the kitchen. In the cabinet above the plates was her secret stash of cigarettes, which she'd convinced Ove had been given up completely, over a year ago. She lit one on the stove and sucked in the welcome blast of nicotine.

Another day, another rejection letter. Maybe private kindergarten just wasn't for them. She wouldn't mind getting out of the commute on the ferry to the mainland every morning. The local public option wasn't terrible and it was conveniently close. She hid the smoke behind her back and opened the glass sliding door into the fenced-in backyard.

Ove Dexter chased the dog, and they ran back and forth through the sprinkler, making a muddy mess of the grass.

"Do you want lunch, darling?"

Ove Dexter stopped and handed her his undivided attention.

"Where's Dad?"

"He's taking the last ferry in. He had errands to run and a meeting at the university."

"I thought he was retired," Ove Dexter said, tilting his head to the side. The child was articulate—on another level in comparison to neighborhood children his age—or maybe every parent believed the same about their kid.

"Emeritus doesn't always mean completely retired. Or like Dad says, he has to *show up a couple times a year or they'll stop sending his paychecks.*"

"What would happen if Daddy didn't get paychecks?" Ove Dexter inquired.

"Then we'd eat fish for dinner every night and we'd have to catch it ourselves."

Ove Dexter smiled at her answer, revealing the gap where his two bottom teeth used to be. His bright green eyes made her heart surge like the roar of a jet engine. The child was the greatest gift, and the center of her whole universe.

"Would we live on a boat?"

"Yes, and you would wear your pirate costume for real."

Ove Dexter looked thrilled.

"Okay, Mommy!" He lunged at the dog and they both slid in the wet grass.

At least he'd already ditched his clothing and wouldn't stain his last decent pair of pants. The cigarette singed her fingers. She'd forgotten she was holding it. She flicked it haphazardly in the direction of the sink.

"I'm going to heat up the chowder from last night and we can have that with grilled cheese. How does that sound?"

"And crackers!" Ove Dexter hollered as he waterskied in the grass, holding the dog by the tail. His underpants were sopping wet and covered in mud. She'd have to sic the hose on them or wrangle them into the bathtub.

She closed the door to preserve the air conditioning and picked up the crumpled letter, tossing it in the trash. She'd save Ove from the disappointment of reading it himself.

In truth, their son was peculiar. He didn't show any interest in the amusements that other children lost their minds over. He didn't like sweets, or birthday parties, and Marilyn would be hard pressed to get him to watch an episode of Sesame Street, or any television at all for that matter.

He liked doing activities alone and would express only high stress, or sometimes terror, at playdates. Ove Dexter was oddly devout when both she and Ove Sr. had no tolerance for religion. Now Marilyn found herself in service every Sunday, holding his little hand and filling the collection plate with his weekly allowance.

He loved the ocean like she loved him—without pretense, endlessly, and at times, so much it hurt. He'd learned to swim at the tender age of three and braved the ocean waves on days the sun didn't shine, and it was too cold for her to even stick her toes in.

The two of them began every day with a walk along the shore and Ove Dexter wore his swim trunks—rain, shine, or delirious with fever from chicken pox. She wore baggy jeans rolled up to mid-calf and was always prepared to jump in after him for rescue if the occasion arose.

The boy had an ecological and environmental concern that bordered on obsession. In fact, she'd consulted a psychiatrist about how to protect his developing brain from reading catastrophic reports about the state of the climate, and the fate of the world's water.

"How does he know in the first place?" the doctor had asked with an air of incredulousness.

"He reads anything he can get his hands on."

She'd cancelled the National Geographic subscription and refused to take him to the Marine Museum. But he'd seen the fishing nets come in and Marilyn had no way to erase that, or to console his broken heart over how hateful humanity could be to the great mother who had created it.

So, he cried and prayed and worried himself sick. Spent days picking up garbage on the beach and in the parks. And Marilyn walked dutifully behind the child, steadily picking up the scattered pieces of his heavy heart.

It didn't mean that Ove Sr. wasn't present—he was, by all standards, a devoted and loving father. Ove Dexter was whip smart due to their investigative interactions. The child knew more about pirates and shipwrecks and marine navigation than most adults who dabbled in those subjects. He could rattle off oceanic currents, and depth charts, wonderful and weird facts about obscure flora and fauna. The child was a walking sponge and nothing got past him. When he slid open the patio door after finally tiring of his antics with the dog, she wiped him down with a bowl of soapy water and a tea towel.

"Mama, were you smoking your cigarettes?"

She smiled at him and put her finger to her lips. "Can that be a secret between you and me and not your father?"

He nodded, wide-eyed, and Marilyn trusted that nod about as

much as she trusted the current political administration.

Ove Dexter was incapable of telling lies. She herself was a reformed liar. She hadn't cheated, or even so much as looked at another man since the night of her son's conception. She loved Ove, and this life was perfection.

♪

After lunch, they changed and made their way to the garage that was now converted into her painting studio. The minute her body was cultivating new life, the urge to create was upon her like an all-consuming maelstrom—to call it a compulsion would have been a gross understatement. She'd suffered through her first trimester gagging and puking at the scent of turpentine, yet it didn't deter her from producing six new works in the months leading up to Ove Dexter's birth.

"Mama, what are you working on?" the boy asked her as he chewed thoughtfully on a celery stalk.

"Just a landscape. Turbulent sea in a storm." She pulled the drape back from her easel and showed him the ominous scene.

"Is that a warm front or a cold front? Or maybe a nor'easter?" he asked her, tilting his head to evaluate the chop of the waves and the height of the clouds.

"Hmmm," she replied. "Maybe last October when we got that storm that took out the weather vane and over-turned boats down at the marina?" She took a wild guess.

"Warm front. Tropical depression from Hurricane Maria," he said. Ove Dexter filled her recycled stewed-tomatoes tin can with fresh turpentine, celery stalk fitted securely in the gap provided by his missing lower teeth.

"Right," Marilyn told him. "Did Dad tell you the carnival is in town? I was thinking maybe we could go this weekend?"

"Okay," he shrugged, looking less than thrilled. "Mr. Bridgeport once told Dad that carnies were all sex offenders who couldn't find any other jobs. He said, 'caaah-nies are all forma' convicts and sex offenda's.'" The child reproduced a near perfect old timer New Englander accent on demand.

Marilyn tried not to smile and brought the back of her hand to her lips.

Ove Dexter tied the strings of her waist apron around her back. Her painter's smock consisted of one of Ove Sr.'s giant flannel shirts worn with the buttons toward the back. She was always covered in paint and she wore it like a gold star, in her hair, on her fingers, and sometimes on her face.

"Maybe we could hold your hand the whole time and not let you go?" she suggested.

"All right," the child agreed. "I'd be interested to know how the mechanisms in all those rides work."

♫

She painted until the sun began to set with the boy perched next to her on a stool. He, in turn, read until natural light faded and looked up at her, blinking expectantly. The dog barked signaling Ove Sr.'s arrival from the ferry.

"I guess we'd better go in," she lamented, setting down her paintbrush. "You're going to need glasses soon at the rate you're going, kiddo," she said, mussing up his sandy blond hair.

"Did you make a plan for dinner?" he asked.

"Leftovers?" she said, and scraped her pallet clean of the greys and dusky blues.

"We already ate them for lunch," the boy told her matter-of-factly. He was right. The kid was always right, despite being raised by two absentminded parents.

"What do you think we should do?"

"Spaghetti is easy. Even Dad can make that."

She straightened his hair with her fingers and sighed at his beauty. Before Ove had gone from salt and pepper grey to shocking white, he'd had dark hair and brown eyes to match. Hers was a rich chocolate—the same shade as her eyes. Her son was towheaded, warm golden skin and astonishing emerald eyes. He didn't burn, but freckled instead, abundantly until the freckles began to connect into a patchy pattern that took over his summertime shoulders and the bridge of his nose.

"Spaghetti it is then," she kissed his forehead and covered up her work.

"That one will sell for a million dollars and they'll put it in the Met," Ove Dexter told her, smiling from ear to ear.

"If you alone like it, I'm satisfied," she said.

"I love it," he told her. They walked slowly back to the house, hand in hand while a chorus of peepers sang and opened their eyes to the dusk.

♪

Marilyn didn't have a lot of friends, but her neighbor Paula was a confidant. They were around the same age, both married, but Paula didn't have children—she had dogs. Dogs, which were treated better than most humans. Paula was a cynic, a straight-talker, and loather of bullshit.

Paula was married to Scott, but they were the same age, unlike her and Ove. The couple struck her as being stuck in the decade that was cool when they were teenagers and never stepping into the modern age. Their clothing was out-of-date, as was their hair, and the music they listened to. Marilyn found their denial of the progression of time comforting in an age where the world was saturated in upheaval and violence.

One evening, while sitting at Paula's kitchen table, drinking Captain Morgan with Coke, smoking, and listening to the Counting Crows, Marilyn found herself in the midst of a streak of jealously. She watched Paula and Scott make their way around steaks on the grill and chopped salad, and opening a bottle of wine, while it dawned on her that in their bubble, there was no 9/11.

There wasn't continuous war in the Middle East, a refugee crisis, worsening natural disasters due to a disastrous climate. They'd given up paying attention some time after a president and a blow job. Paula once confided in her that their move to the island was an attempt to escape reality and retire at thirty.

She was envious of their certainty that they could just keep on thriving, ignorant of the perilous balance of a world sometimes teetering on the edge of ruin.

"Do you want dessert, Mar? I made banana pudding," Paula asked. Their house was coated in dog hair, even though all of the outdated furniture was covered in yard-sale blankets. It was a patchwork house, haphazard additions had been added on throughout the years without so much as a nod given to the original design or style of the entire structure.

Marilyn worked some of the dog's fur off her skirt and let it sail to the floor. Her belly was heavy with red meat and red wine, her eyelids drooping, mind and body ready to shut down.

"Sure. We never have dessert. Ove and Ove Dexter don't like it," she told her friend, pushing Bailey, the golden retriever's nose out of her crotch for the twentieth time that evening. The boys had gone to see a play in town and she'd opted to stay home.

"Maybe he wants to emulate his Dad. It happens," Paula clucked. She got up to take the orange bowl full of pudding out of the freezer.

Marilyn went to respond, but the comment tripped her up.

"Well, what do you mean? It could be an inherited trait?" She bristled on the defensive, ready to defend the secret with her life if she had to.

"Oh, I'm sorry," Paula said. She looked ready to drop the dessert. "I guess I just assumed you Murphy Brown-ed it and used a donor because Ove was too old."

Scott handed her a look that told Marilyn they'd clearly discussed it. He grabbed a beer and his cigarettes and excused himself to the backyard, avoiding the topic.

"You gotta admit, they look nothing alike," Paula said, driving the coffin nail in farther.

Marilyn was dumbstruck and moved her mouth like a fish out of water. It wasn't so much that her friendly, early-nineties-stuck neighbors had her all figured out, it was the idea that if her child's paternity was so glaringly obvious, then who else assumed, or felt they knew conclusively, that Ove Dexter's father was not the old professor with whom he ambled about.

Was it the real reason why the schools on the mainland wouldn't accept her child? Did everyone look at their family with suspicion and doubt?

"I guess I did, I mean, I did use a donor of sorts," Marilyn stumbled over her words.

"Ove doesn't know?" Paula intuited, refilling Marilyn's lowball with fresh rum. "It goes great with the bananas," she told her in explanation. Paula extinguished her cigarette in the ashtray and lit up another one in anticipation of a good story.

Marilyn took a swig of the strong concoction she hadn't had since parties in high school. The glass was bottom heavy, the ice cubes cooled the sides, and the drink sweated against her fingertips. She shook her head and extracted a tiny piece of tobacco from the tip of her tongue with her pinky and thumb, lit cigarette in hand.

"Or maybe if you know, then everyone knows, including him. It is a small community with lots of rampant gossip." Her conjecture wasn't accusatory toward her friend, it was merely an observation as she realized what she thought was so well-hidden, could in fact be, abundantly clear to even the casual observer.

"Not even a peep of any theory has ever left this kitchen," Paula said. She placed her hand over Marilyn's in either solidarity or reassurance. Marilyn balked at her own stupidity. It was a tiny, isolated community. A hair out of place was discussed at the grocery and over-the-counter in the local diner as coffee was poured and money exchanged. She'd believed her truth was shrouded in secrecy, when in reality, it was on full display.

"I've been wearing blinders," she said absently. "It's a deliberate screen that I've placed there myself."

"People probably don't even notice. I mean, same race—ethnicity. Some genes are recessive and—"

"It's all right. You don't have to sugarcoat. I've done enough of that myself."

"He looks Irish, and you're what again?"

"Mostly Hungarian. Ove is Swedish and Italian."

"It's his eyes. That color is supernatural—it's extra-terrestrial!"

Marilyn thought of Decker's eyes and then pushed the memory out of her mind. She looked down at the dog, who was still insisting on a head scratch even though she'd been steadily going at it for the last fifteen minutes.

"Mar, I didn't mean a thing, honestly. I've got nothing but respect for you and your family. God, the art you make alone is . . . The kid is a fricking genius, everybody knows that, and Ove is wonderful. It doesn't matter how you got there—am I right?"

"You got there," Marilyn finished. She squashed out her cigarette in the ashtray and downed the rest of her drink.

Maybe the time warp neighbors weren't so quaint after all, maybe they were actually terrifying. Or perhaps it was the whole world was a hostile and unfriendly place.

"Thanks for dinner, Paula. I think I'll head out. The boys should be back soon and I've got to let the dog out anyway."

"Listen," Paula said as she stood. "I hope this doesn't change things. I love you guys, and I don't judge."

She kissed her neighbor on the cheek and ran home to change her dog hair blanketed clothes. If Paula and Scott knew, then more likely than not, Ove was well-aware of her manipulation of fate, and the sins she committed along the way.

♪

The carnival stayed only a week in one place, bookended by two weekends, one on each end. All the residents made a visit whether they liked the damn thing or not, because the local politicians had warned that the fair would scratch the island right off the map if attendance didn't improve. It was a massive effort to transport the trucks over by barge, and not an easy feat to run, set up, or take down in an environment prone to temperamental weather and quick moving storms.

It was then, their civic duty to attend the run-down, nearly macabre, nostalgia-filled fest. Eat funnel cake and hotdogs and scramble themselves silly on dangerous rides run by traveling hillbillies with suspiciously low intelligence. They swung Ove Dexter between them every three counts as they perused the games and yellow lightbulb-lit food stands. The air was perfumed with spun sugar and wailed the demented polka calliope of circus tunes on repeat.

"Ove Dexter, what would you like to eat?" Ove Sr. asked.

"Is there someplace to get a salad?" he looked up at his father in wonder. A carnival obviously wasn't their kid's jam.

"How about you and I go ride the bumper cars?"

Ove Dexter jumped at the idea and Marilyn waved as she watched them go. She strolled through the gauntlet of games, while the vendors called out the stakes into microphones with auctioneer speed, but classic carnival cadence.

"Step right up, Ma'am, try your luck on this one here tonight! You look like a lucky lady, step right up and spin the wheel. Going once, going twice."

She took in their faces and their painted-on enthusiasm that registered as sinister under the garish lights. The humid breeze tasted of salt, and Marilyn licked her lips. She squinted up at the top of the Ferris wheel and marveled at the fact they transported it here. A wheel of wonder and lights turning against a night sky and surrounded by ocean. It was worthy of a picture—maybe even a painting—if she painted those kinds of things.

Her attention spiraled back down to ground level when she heard a laugh that felt quite familiar, but the sound made her start, nonetheless. Her eyes ran up the end of the gauntlet to the source. The culprit was a man with a young, pretty woman on his arm, both of them loaded down with stuffed animals, LED light toys, and inflatable team spirit sticks. They marched happily down the aisle, both enchanted by something funny he'd said.

"*Lucky sonofabitch*," she thought to herself.

She would recognize the boy's father in the poor visibility of inclement weather, or camouflaged with new facial hair, or even disguised in full costume. His energy was vibrant and it spoke to her as it had since the moment she'd met him. She stood bone still in their path like there was no way to avoid the encounter, when she had plenty of time to whip around, or even make a total run for it—if that was what she truly wanted.

But his malachite eyes flashed forward as if driven by the same force. When their gaze met, she gasped and he dropped some of his hard-won prizes. Then she heard the boy's voice, telling his father he needed to use the bathroom. She caught their figures in her peripheral vision, and it was too late to stop the last chime on the clock from sounding. Her time was up and she froze.

Decker's verdant eyes merely scanned the smaller, but equally vibrant jade of the boys', then flashed back to her face, again to the boy, this time taking in Ove Sr. as well. He looked the boy over once more and then directed a furious glare her direction.

"Mar, I'll take the boy to the lavatory," Ove Sr. called to her.

"Okay, I'm going to ride the Ferris wheel!" The spontaneous decision came at her fast. She pivoted on a dime and took off running to the base of the giant rotating death trap at a thief's velocity. And a thief she was, because she'd stolen something precious that didn't belong to her.

Decker took off after her and his pursuit made her run faster than she knew she was capable of running. She hated heights, and also knew you couldn't run from the truth, but said, *to hell with this*, as her body moved on adrenaline and pure cowardice.

She swept through the crowd and deftly cut the line. He pursued her with a predator's precision and possibly a father's determination, but that was still only for her to know—she'd be zip-lipped to the grave and refuse to tell him anything.

Her heart finally stopped pounding when she was escorted into the metal seat and the bar lowered over her heaving chest. She checked his position in line and figured she'd be, at least, a few cars away from him. It would give her ten minutes to form a two-bit-catch-penny plan. Claptrap excuses? Explanations? Half-truths, or maybe play the dumb innocent card?

She placed her hand over her heart and praised the cosmos as the wheel jerked and began to wind her backwards and away from him.

Then Decker did the unthinkable, and stage-dived off the safety railing straight into her shoddy, chipped, pink-painted buggy. Marilyn screamed as he tumbled into the dolly head-first. He sat at the bottom across from her so she had no choice but to look him in the eye.

"Of all the low stunts, I've ever seen, yours takes the grand prize," he told her, jumping right to the kill.

"Speaking of stunts, how the hell did you do that?"

"Mosh pit practice in college, I guess. I hit my head though."

"I think it's bleeding," she told him. She produced a meagre tissue that promptly got snatched by a warm gust of wind.

"That my kid?" he asked her, scratching his chin.

"Biologically speaking, he is your offspring."

He laughed, and looked out the footwell to the miniaturized crowd below.

"You've got a way with words. It's Marilyn, right? You could have asked, you know."

But she didn't ask. And she couldn't have asked in the moment, because she was hell-bent on the outcome and took no prisoners in the process. Maybe he would have said yes, but none of that mattered now.

"Don't plead innocence. You know what happens when you ejaculate inside a woman without using protection."

"I honestly thought it was some kind of fetish."

"Please don't ruin my life," she whispered to the stranger she knew so intimately, a man whose blood ran through the veins of the beloved boy she'd adored since the moment one single cell separated into two.

"What's his name?" Decker asked. He seemed drunk to her if she didn't know better.

"Ove. Ove Dexter," she added hesitantly.

"In homage to me or after the television show?"

"Neither, well both, I mean. My husband doesn't know." She struggled with words that appeared inadequate to encompass all she needed to communicate to him.

"Decker is my last name. My name is Dallas. I'm guessing you're not Marilyn French either."

"Dallas Decker," she blurted. "It sounds like a porn star." She abandoned her filter completely.

"Says the lady who fucks like one," Decker clapped back, raising his chin at her.

Marilyn blushed a deep crimson, bit her knuckle, and tried to suppress all the funny feelings that jumped to attention with those words. She wanted to tell him to go away and leave her alone, to never come looking for them, but thought better of rashness, realizing one wrong move could take her down—permanently.

"What do you do?" he asked, catching her off guard.

"I'm a painter. Landscapes. A researcher by trade until I started making money off of my work. What about you?"

She wondered if he lived on the island and how it was possible a run-in hadn't happened before.

"I'm an oceanographer. I teach at the University of Toronto. Came down here on a sea-level project to measure the topographical changes effected by global warming. Then I met you and forget about numbers. You made my whole world go topsy-turvy for a while."

Oceanographer. Well, that explained a lot.

"And this time? Is she your wife?"

"Hannah? No. My girlfriend. I was impressed with this place and always wanted to come back."

"It's beautiful, isn't it?" Marilyn looked wistfully toward the sea and felt the gravity of her own selfishness.

"You're beautiful. And so is our child. Does your father know?"

"Ove? Ove is my husband." She'd gotten the comment before, and didn't take it to heart. It was his white beard and the tweed jackets with elbow patches, the pipe of tobacco he insisted on chewing while they strolled in the evening.

"I see," Dallas told her.

She'd been bracing for his ire, his *see you in court*, paternity tests, and visitation rights—the works. The man could irrevocably destroy her life if he were inclined to. But maybe Dallas was so kindhearted that he was, once again, about to bestow upon her the most sacred gift.

He pulled a small moleskin notebook from his back pocket that appeared to contain lists of double digit numbers. Sea levels perhaps, or maybe he was a spendthrift and diligently balanced his checkbook. He scribbled some notes down, tore the paper, and handed it to her.

"Write yours down, Marilyn, and no lying this time. Your lies are criminal."

She scanned the scrap of paper and it appeared to contain his full name and email, his phone number and address in Toronto. His blood type, his ethnic heritage, and the briefest of family health history. She squinted to read his scrawl and made out: *Father, heart attack 63, mother, breast cancer, 69.*

"I'm so sorry," she said as she frantically wrote out the same.

She tore it off and handed it to him, but when he went to grab it they missed, and it lifted off into the air. They watched it glide back and forth slowly as it descended to the funland below.

"It's okay," he dismissed the mishap. "I don't really need it. But keep yours, god forbid he need a kidney or marrow transplant someday."

"I can't . . . I don't know how to thank you." Tears freely streamed down her face.

"I'm not letting you off that easy. I want you to tell him, tell both of them—in fact, the sooner the better. And I'd like to see him when he turns eighteen, but the choice is his. You don't even have to come. I'll pay for the plane ticket and he can stay the summer or whatever he wants."

"I owe you so much," she whispered, the tears still flowed forth, making her nose run.

"Are you happy, Marilyn?" he asked.

She was a liar and a traitor, the worst kind of thief, a lowly manipulator to boot, and she should never be forgiven for her hurtful mistakes. She hated herself, but she loved Ove Dexter more. He was not a mistake.

"He is all of the good and all of the love in this great world wrapped up into a tiny, curious, and wondrous package. I couldn't be happier, Dallas," she whispered gratefully. She liked saying his true name and the crystalline way it fell from her lips. "Thank you. So much."

He smiled at her then, that exuberant, thrilling grin. She smiled back through the tears as her anxiety and greatest fears were somehow laid to rest at the top of the ride. She came back down to earth a new woman, fearless, forgiven, and rectified.

Ove and Ove Dexter were waiting for her hand-in-hand down below. Ove Dexter looked curiously at the man who leapt out of the carriage, waved, and then looked back fondly at his mother.

"Just one question before I go," Dallas lingered with his hand on the hinged door.

"Anything. Ask me." He wanted to know little Ove's favorite food, color, or sport. If he slept well and what scared him in the night.

"You fuck him like we did?" he asked, eyeing Marilyn's mature, but sweet husband.

"That would be a no," she said, blushing as Dallas helped her out of the pink chipped chariot.

"Put him in an early grave, I'd suspect. I've never been able to achieve, or um, well, replicate should we say—"

"Me either. It was a singular experience. Thank you again."

"Take care. Of the boy and yourself." He went to shake hands and then doubt shadowed across his face. Marilyn thought he was possibly coming in for a hug. But instead, he saluted, first Marilyn and then her family.

Ove Dexter saluted back, and Marilyn began to cry again.

Dallas jogged off in the opposite direction and quickly disappeared into the crowd.

The twinkling lights began to fade in the distance as they made their way back to the car. Ove looked at her with curiosity burning brightly in his gaze. Marilyn shook her head and wiped her nose with the back of her hand.

The soothing rhythm of the drive put the boy to sleep. Ove pulled him from the car seat and lay him sweetly over his shoulder as he carefully picked his way over the flagstones that led to their front door.

Marilyn flicked on the light in the entryway of their cozy Cape Cod home and Ove passed the slumbering boy into her waiting arms.

"Was he the father?" Ove whispered as he handed over the child. The look on his face was free of rancor, and Marilyn felt great love bloom anew in the crimson depths of her heart.

"You are his father, Ove."

"You know what I mean."

She searched his eyes for any sign of hurt. Betrayal cut like a scalpel—effortless in slicing through, but difficult to understand exactly how deep the wound reached.

"Yes," she said carefully. She didn't know what the admission would do to her family—her entire life.

In the end, it turned out truth was a potent elixir that only served to set her free from her lies.

♪

Twelve years would come to pass before she'd see Dallas Decker again. Five years after Ove Sr. had passed from congestive heart failure asleep in their bed. The loss was devastating to both her and the child. But she was still happy, albeit sometimes lonely. She found great joy in her painting and in raising Ove Dexter, who was rapidly sprinting his way to manhood.

Adolescence hadn't yet marred his soul with irony, or indifference. The young man remained passionate about the environment, and still dreamed of sunken shipwrecks. He read his father's dusty journals and had early acceptance to Yale. He knew by heart the story of how his mother had seduced a stranded and unsuspecting hitchhiker to conceive him. He found it troublesome, and at the same time, extraordinary. It was an epic origin story he sometimes shared with close friends when they were sneaking beers, or the hard-to-come-by joint.

His mother was herself epic too and did nothing without flare. She'd worked her way to becoming one of the foremost American landscape painters of her generation. She sold works that could easily put him through college.

The two of them were anomalistic in their closeness, preferring the quiet company of one another over that of strangers, acquaintances, or even friends. He still perched on a stool by her easel and studied while she painted.

Ove Dexter had chosen, after careful deliberation, to spend the last summer before college with his biological father in Canada. But when Marilyn called him to come up with a plan, they'd mutually decided that it would convenience them all for Dallas to travel to the island for the summer instead. That way the boy could still see friends and his mother wouldn't miss out on what could possibly be their very last summer together.

Marilyn and Ove Dexter, both plagued by overwrought nerves, met Dallas at the ferry. He stepped off the boat, pulling a small suitcase, his hair blowing in the wind. Hair which had greyed nicely and his face had acquired a few deep lines with time, that if anything, only served to make him more ruggedly handsome. He was fit and agile and strode toward them with confidence.

"Holy shit, I look exactly like him," Ove Dexter said to his mother. They exchanged an exuberant smile and squeezed one another's hand.

He approached with a sunny happiness lighting up his face, his emerald eyes shining and looking at the two of them expectantly.

"Hugs or handshakes?" he asked them warmly.

Ove Dexter threw his arms around Dallas who bear-hugged him back, tightly clapping him on the back with genuine affection. When they pulled back, both men were crying. Marilyn lifted her hand to her face and swiped at the spill of tears.

Dallas squeezed Ove Dexter's shoulders. "I can't wait to finally get to know you," he told the young man earnestly.

He looked at Marilyn, who held both hands to her mouth, trying to hold back an onslaught of emotion. She couldn't help but scan his finger for a ring. She felt absurdly possessive, like Dallas belonged to her—to them both—like he was part of their family.

Seagulls cried overhead and the deep fog horn of the ferry sounded announcing its departure.

He pulled her hands from her face and held them in his, still standing apart and taking her in.

"As stunning as the day I met you," he said. "But the real question is, are you happy?"

Marilyn nodded and experienced the gratification of being wrapped up in Dallas' arms once again. She had no idea what would come, although she was positive she both adored and fully trusted this man.

Please, Decker, I'll do anything you want me to.

They walked away, the three of them automatically a tight unit, Dallas with an arm flung over each one of their shoulders.

The two men were already discussing a boating excursion to see the local sights. Their voices similar, and their feisty laughs, nearly indistinguishable from the other.

She'd loved Ove, she had, with all of her heart. And Ove Dexter was the very best part of her life. But this reunion, was one she had dreamed of.

The gift of a stranger had given her a lifetime of incalculable happiness.

♪

Epilogue

They often spent the morning lying in bed until the sun traveled its way across the room and wrapped them in sharp golden light, heating up their limbs to the point of escape and voluntary expulsion from the nest.

She liked to stare into his handsome face and contemplate fate, and think about the ever-changing ocean surface and what next to paint.

Ove Dexter left for college and Dallas had stayed.

"Remember how I told you I was married for four years?" Dallas asked her. He took her paint spotted hand and held it in his. "We tried to conceive the entire time, until it took its toll and drove us apart."

"I'm sorry," Marilyn told him. She'd been there before, could remember exactly what that kind of cavernous emptiness felt like. The hunger it bred and the resulting drive that could propel one into near madness.

"Here's the strange part. When we finally gave in and went to see a specialist, they told me it was my count that was low and Hannah was perfectly fertile."

He smiled at Marilyn, lit up with both the invading sunshine and the high of sharing his secret.

"Are you saying you and I make miracles together?"

"Well, let's just say I think that night was supposed to happen. The rain, the car, you striking out at the bar. I never forgot you. And I was always grateful to you for stopping."

Marilyn remembered the first moment she saw him standing in the rain, and pondered the possibility that the universe had conspired to bring them together—that the fateful encounter from one night could set the supernal course to navigate them into each other's arms—or maybe Dallas, her fated lover, was just one lucky sonofabitch.

ABOUT THE AUTHOR

Mara White is a contemporary romance and erotica writer who laces forbidden love stories with hard issues, such as race, gender and inequality. She holds an Ivy League degree but has also worked in more strip clubs than even she can remember. She is not a former Mexican telenovela star contrary to what the tabloids might say, but she is a former ballerina and will always remain one in her heart. She lives in NYC with her husband and two children and yes, when she's not writing you can find her on the playground.

More info available at: www.marawhite.com

Toothpaste Kisses

XIO AXELROD

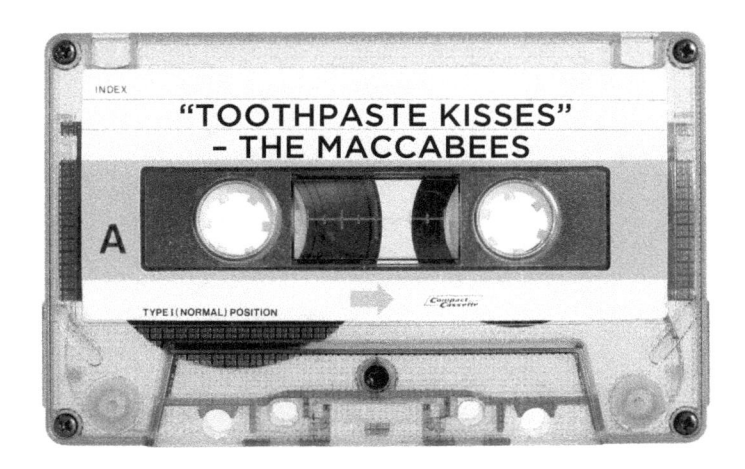

"TOOTHPASTE KISSES"
- THE MACCABEES

CHAPTER ONE

For Malcolm Zaha, the worst part about starting over was the silence. Sitting in his brand-new office, behind his brand-new desk, in his brand-new Herman Miller office chair, Mal had never felt more alone.

At the Law Offices of Cohn and Zaha, solitude had been a rarity, regardless of the hour. During the day, the practice had bustled with junior attorneys, paralegals, and interns, plus the administrative staff. Mal and his partner – former partner – Joshua Cohn, had built the firm up from nothing.

Rather than line someone else's pockets, they'd gone against all sense and reason and started their own practice. Just two twenty-something, know-nothings and, God, they'd been so naïve. Maybe their naïveté had worked in their favor because it wasn't all that difficult for them to find clients and build Cohn and Zaha into something respectable and respected.

They carved out a niche, representing start-up and mid-sized businesses. Everything from construction and local furniture chains, to food suppliers and pizza franchises. It had been good business, but Mal had always felt he and Josh could do more.

Mal wanted to work with Philadelphia's creatives, and there were so many. Artists, musicians, and craftspeople, as expected, but also theaters, recording studios, dance companies, and the like. He believed, had Cohn and Zaha opened their doors to the community, the community would have treated them well. Philadelphia may have had a reputation for unruly sports fans and gastronomically challenging fast food, but there was so much more to the city, and Mal longed to shine a light on its creative brilliance.

At least he had.

Now he wondered if he should leave the area and start fresh somewhere new. A clean slate in a new city, where no one knew him, was an almost irresistible siren song. Cohn and Zaha had built their reputation as the firm who'd scored Philly's brightest rising businesses. Now, Mal was left with a bare bones staff and only a handful of smallish clients from their partnership.

Partnership.

That word encompassed so much for Mal. Late night debates with Josh over strategies for their clients, and all-night marathons full of sex, booze, and more sex, sometimes until they were both too sore to walk the next day. Whatever else went wrong with their relationship, the chemistry between them had always been spectacular. It was one reason Mal had hung on for so long. Josh used sex to solve their problems, and it had worked until it didn't work anymore.

"Knock, knock."

Mal looked up to find Evelyn Magill, in all her five-foot-five-inch, redheaded glory, standing in his doorway. Mal tried to smile for her but failed. Change sucked.

"Hey, Ev."

Evelyn's brows drew together as she stepped into the room. This time, the silence also held the weight of her pity, and pity was the last thing Mal wanted from any-fucking-body, particularly from his right hand. He wanted to scream at her to get the hell out and leave him to stew in his own juices. But Mal couldn't lash out at Evelyn. She was all he had left.

To Mal's surprise, she didn't launch into a monologue of empathy. Instead, she cleared her throat and tossed a thick folder onto his desk.

"Choose."

Her tone was sharp, her eyes assessing him. When Mal dared to glance up at her lovely, heart-shaped face, the pity he thought he'd seen in her expression was gone.

Mal spun the folder around and opened it. Dozens of color copies fanned out with the movement, photo after photo of paintings, vases, lamps, and various other *objets d'art*. Mal rolled his eyes.

"I told you, I don't give a fuck." He glared at Evelyn but, as usual, she merely waited for his temper to cool. "Do we really need to fill the place with junk? I fucking hated how Josh felt the need to cover every available surface with knickknacks."

"Junk?" Evelyn raised one dark eyebrow. "The Mal I know would never call his precious Van Der Rohe tables *junk*. Moreover, I don't expect you to pick out every vase and lamp, I know your taste well enough, but there are a few key pieces you will need to choose. We need to furnish this place, and I'm not going to do it all for you just because you're too busy sulking."

Mal ignored the jab. Malcolm Zaha never sulked, goddammit.

"Why the fuck not?" Mal was aware of his petulant tone but wasn't in the mood to care. And he knew Evelyn wouldn't put up with it. She never indulged him for long. "What am I paying you for?"

"You're not." She stated, reminding Mal he had won no new clients for his new solo practice.

Josh had kept nearly all their old accounts, leaving Mal not only without a partner and a place to live, but also without an adequate source of income, for him or for his beloved Evelyn. Anyone would think Mal had been the one who'd fucked up their relationship. If he hadn't been notoriously anal about squirreling away money in a separate account, he would have been in dire straits after the breakup. As it stood, he'd dipped into his nest egg to get this new practice up and running, or at least secure a decent office for it.

An office that was cavernously empty. Maybe Evelyn had a point.

Sufficiently chastised, Mal offered Evelyn a sheepish grin. "Have I told you how much I appreciate you sticking by my side through all of this?"

"Words are empty, Zaha." Evelyn stood over the folder and shifted through the images. She stopped when she got to the ones at the bottom of the pile. "I need you to choose a piece for the foyer. Whatever you pick will set the tone. It'll be the first thing clients see when they come through the door. Well, that and Quentin's smiling face."

Mal's head snapped up. "Who the hell is Quentin?"

Evelyn shook her head, mumbling to herself as she formulated her response.

Mal wondered at the patience the woman had when dealing with him. He knew he'd been an asshole, especially over the last month.

"Quentin Cook is the new receptionist you signed off on last week." Evelyn met Mal's confused stare with another shake of her head. "The business student from Temple?"

"Oh. Right." Mal had a vague recollection of a discussion they'd had regarding hiring for that position. Evelyn had seemed pleased with the guy's résumé, and that had been enough for Mal. As long as the kid could answer the phones, handle the random walk-ins, and manage not to fuck anything up, he'd do fine.

"Anyway, as I was saying, I'm not going to pick that piece for you. It's your business. It will represent you. It has to scream Malcolm Zaha when people walk in."

Leaning back in his chair, Mal eyed her for a moment. "And what exactly does *Malcolm Zaha* say to you?"

She grinned. "Stop fishing for compliments."

"I'm really not," Mal assured her, genuinely curious.

Evelyn squared her shoulders and leveled her gaze on him. "Malcolm Zaha is tough, fearless, resourceful, charming-as-hell, and he knows how to cut through bullshit like no one I've ever known."

Her smile was fierce, then it fell. She sat in the chair across from Mal and clasped her hands on the edge of the desk between them. Meeting his eyes, she continued, her voice soft.

"He's also the best boss anyone could hope for, the best friend anyone could want, and the best man I know. Except for Pete."

Mal held her earnest gaze and swallowed past the lump forming in his throat. "No one's better than Pete."

Evelyn's smile returned, brighter than before. "My husband is a gem."

"So are you, Ev." They shared a quiet moment before the silence veered too close to sentimentality for Mal's taste. He sat forward and thumbed through the prints again. "So, don't let him forget it or I'll have to remind him."

Just about every style of modern art was represented in the

selections, from Cubism to Impressionism to Pop. He recognized the Klimt and the Chagall, but there were also some contemporary pieces.

"Anything jumping out at you?" Mal couldn't seem to organize his thoughts enough to really see anything.

Evelyn leaned closer. She reached for the pile and sifted through it, sliding out a few printouts for him to see.

"I knew you liked Modern, so I asked them to include some prints and repros. We can scale those to any size we want, but really—it would be a copy of a copy."

Mal nodded. "You're thinking original."

"Yes," Evelyn agreed, sliding out some papers from the bottom of the group. "More specifically, local artists. It is, after all, your brand."

She handed Mal a few pieces to consider. They weren't bad. The first one that grabbed him was by a man named Tim McFarlane. Mal thought he'd heard the name spoken in his dealings with the art crowd. The piece itself was abstract and nonrepresentational, yet it had an energy and focus that appealed to Mal. It wasn't what he wanted for the office, but it would look great in his apartment. He set it aside.

"For Cherry Street?"

Mal looked up at Evelyn and nodded. "Yeah. I like it, but not for here."

"I thought you might."

Mal wondered at that, how this woman could know him so well. Better than anyone, probably. Before, he would have said anyone but Josh.

He continued to look through the pages when a pop of color caught his eye. Broad, sweeping lines of swirling motion were layered upon a pool of crimson and deep purple suggesting chaos. But the lines themselves were in soft blues and creams, and the colors lightened as the viewer's eye traveled north. It was the suggestion of emotion. The suggestion of discovery or of just . . . surrender. Of giving in to something.

Mal didn't know what the fuck it was, but the work called to him.

Aroused something in him. He couldn't drag his gaze away from it.

"Really?" Evelyn reached down and spun the print to face her. "Hmm. It's . . . different, that's for sure."

"That's the one." Mal's own certainty surprised him. "Get it."

"What if it's too small for the space?"

"If it is, I'll choose something else, but I want that painting regardless."

Evelyn stood and gathered up the prints, all but the one Mal couldn't seem to tear his eyes from.

"On it." She rose and turned for the door but hesitated. "By the way, Cohn called. He said he has a box of your things. You want to have them delivered here or at the penthouse?"

Mal's mood, which had lifted a fraction, darkened immediately. "Tell him he can burn it for all I fucking care."

Evelyn gave the barest roll of her eyes. "The penthouse it is."

His attention fell back onto the print of the painting he'd chosen. It was damn compelling.

"Ev?" Mal called out just as she disappeared from view.

She poked her head around the doorframe. "Something else?"

"If you find other pieces by this artist, I want to see those too."

Evelyn raised her eyebrow but nodded. "Yes, boss."

CHAPTER TWO

There was inky, midnight blue paint under Pell's fingernails. That was the only thing stopping him from clawing the eyes out of the woman who stood in the middle of the broom closet she'd rented to him. Too much evidence. That and his desire not to get blood on his still-drying canvases.

"Mr. Lindt," the woman started with a tone so polite it couldn't possibly be sincere. "You assured me that this month's rent would be on time."

Mrs. Thorn looked around at Pell's various works in progress. Her face was pinched and narrow, like a bird's, and her expression filled with distaste. If Pell were still drawing caricatures at Cherry Street Pier, it would have been a challenge to depict her as any less of one than she already was. The word hawkish came to mind.

Pell stifled a laugh at the thought. He hadn't hidden it completely because her withering glare returned to him.

Her lips thinned into nothingness, and the look on her face would have wilted him if Pell hadn't just made the sale of his career.

"I promise, I'll have your money for you first thing Monday morning."

The shrew smiled, and it was all teeth. "I'm afraid it's a little late for that. I need you to move out immediately."

Pell tilted his head. He wanted to shake it, clear his ears or something. He couldn't have heard her correctly.

"You want me to what?"

Mrs. Thorn reached into her purse and pulled out a piece of paper. "You've violated the terms of your lease on multiple occasions, Mr. Lindt, leaving me no choice but to insist that you vacate the premises."

A smile tugged at the corners of her thin mouth. The old witch was actually enjoying this.

"But I'm only a few days behind this month, and I can pay you for the next three months up front as soon as the money clears my account."

Surprised, she seemed to consider Pell's offer. Then she shook her head, placed the paper with the words EVICTION NOTICE emblazoned in red across the top on one of the few clean spaces he had on his work table, and turned for the door.

"Aside from your delinquencies and this . . . mess, you've been a model tenant. I'll give you until the close of business today to vacate. After that, I'll be forced to return with the Sheriff."

"The Sheriff? Are you fu- . . .? You can't be serious."

"Quite, Mr. Lindt. I am not running a charity here. I'm not going to give you a pass on timeliness just because you fancy yourself the next Franz Kline or whatever famous German artist you aspire to be."

"I'm Belgian."

Thorn shrugged. "Six P.M., Mr. Lindt, and I'm being very generous. You have eight hours to gather all your pots and brushes and whatnot. Oh, and I will be keeping your security deposit."

She looked around the small room, no doubt noting the blotches of color splashed all around the work sink. Pell had covered the hardwood floors with canvas tarps, but the place was still a kaleidoscopic mess.

"Goodbye, Mr. Lindt."

Thorn didn't bother to close the door behind her, and Pell didn't bother to right the pot of cadmium red he kicked over after she left.

♫

"Can she do that?"

"Unfortunately, yes."

"Bitch!"

Pell sat in the back corner of Sassafras Coffee and stared down into his chai latte. Across the table from him, Amelia Frazer fumed on his behalf.

"I knew there was something off about that woman." As best

friends went, Amelia was the cream of the crop.

Pell eyed her curiously, though. "In what way?"

"In that nineteen-fifties, Stepford matron kind of way." She groaned at Pell's confusion. "Christ, I sometimes forget you weren't born here. You have no accent to speak of, and you're just so . . . *normal.*"

Pell laughed, used to her ridiculousness. "Uh, thanks I guess? Are we foreigners not usually normal?"

Under the table, Amelia kicked him. "You know what I mean. You usually get all of my pop culture references, but then we'll run into one you don't get, and I'm reminded all over again you're not one of us."

Pell's jaw dropped.

Amelia's light brown skin paled. "I-I-I didn't mean it the way it sounded, shit. I'm so sorry. I know that's a sore spot for you."

She reached across the table and covered one of Pell's hands with her own. It was warm and a little damp from being curled around her own latte.

"Shit, babe. Just ignore me today. I can't seem to keep my foot out of my mouth."

"It's fine," Pell assured her. "Really. It's been a weird sort of day. First, I sell a bunch of work—"

"Wait," Amelia interrupted. "You did?"

Pell smiled. "Yeah, enough that Brianne offered me a spot in the next show. She had someone drop out last minute. And then the buyer agreed to let her display the pieces they plan to buy. Well, except for one."

"Oh my God, Pell!" Amelia jumped out of her seat and launched herself at him. Settling her petite frame onto his lap, she wrapped her arms around his neck, and they hugged tightly. Then she sat back and punched Pell in the shoulder.

"Ouch! Fuck." Pell rubbed the sore spot, never prepared for her violent ways. "What was that for?"

"Way to bury the lead." She grinned, clearly proud of him.

Pell returned her grin and wrapped one arm around her waist.

From the outside, Pell and Amelia's relationship probably looked very different than it actually was. Their casual affection often bled into romantic territory, or at least the appearance of it. And though Pell was bisexual, and the thought might have occasionally crossed his mind, two things prevented their relationship from ever taking another path. One, Amelia was very much a lesbian. And two, Pell was loathed to do anything that would jeopardize what they already had.

He had never known anyone like Amelia-never-Amy Frazer. She loved big, laughed hard, and took no shit from anyone, either on her own behalf or on behalf of the people she cared about. Which were few.

Pell considered himself lucky to be counted among them. He didn't know how he would have coped without her. Amelia had been there for him when he'd lost his parents. She'd been there for him when he'd lost his first real home. She was his biggest advocate.

If it weren't for Amelia and the endless network of contacts she'd made from managing the hottest coffee spot in Old City, Pell wouldn't have met Brianne Mayer. He wouldn't have a painting hanging in the Emerging Artist section of her gallery. And he certainly wouldn't be preparing for his first real exhibit. Pell owed everything to Amelia. She kept him fed, kept a roof over his head, and kept him sane. More or less.

"I would have called you as soon as I found out, but I knew you'd want to hear it in person."

Amelia smiled. "Damn right."

She kissed him on the forehead and stood.

Pell watched as she grabbed a handful of raw sugar packets from the counter and sat back in her chair. She ripped open one pack and poured a little on her tongue. It was bizarre, but then so were most of Amelia's food habits. Always drank her coffee black, no sweetener or cream, but give her sugar on the side and she was a happy girl.

"So, tell me about this big sale. Who bought the stuff?"

Pell shrugged, his excitement and curiosity returning in tandem.

"I have no idea. All I know is that the buyer saw a print of *Closer* and requested to see more. Brianne sent over photos of five of my smaller canvases, and they put three of them on hold."

"That's fucking amazing, Pell. And I so love that piece." Amelia's voice vibrated with all the awe and respect Pell would ever need.

He'd given up on the pipe dream of becoming an important artist years ago, while he was still a student at the Fine Art Institute of Philadelphia. Back then, he'd harbored thoughts of being a diamond just waiting to be polished and discovered. But he hadn't fit in at FAIP. Pell didn't fit in anywhere, so it made sense that his art would suffer the same fate. Only now, he had validation in the sale and the show. He had to admit, it felt damned good.

"I am curious, though," Amelia mused. "Maybe you've landed a mysterious benefactor. Or a patron! Do artists still get patrons?"

"*Je ne sais*," Pell responded, exaggerating his accent. As expected, Amelia melted. He grinned. "But I don't care, as long as they show the work to all their friends, and all their friends come looking for Pellam Lindt originals of their own."

"Oh, I have no doubt." Amelia dumped another packet of sugar onto her pink tongue. "And then I can say I knew you when. That is if you don't dump me once you're rich and famous."

Pell balked at that. "Never, *mon ami*. Not for all the money and fame in the world. Besides, it looks like I'll need to borrow your couch for a while."

"Of course! You know you're always welcome. I told you before you didn't need to sleep in that rat trap you called a studio." She picked up another packet but seemed to think better of it and dropped it just as quickly, scowling at the sugar as if it had forced itself into her mouth. "This is a nasty habit."

"It is."

"Why don't you make me stop?"

Pell laughed. "I've tried."

Amelia stuck her tongue out at him, and Pell laughed again. Someone might think they were both twelve instead of twenty-five.

"I've got to get back to work." Amelia stood and scooped up

the remaining pile of sugar packets. "You need something to eat? A sandwich?"

"No, I'm all right. I'd better finish packing. Brianne said I could store my shit in the back room of the gallery until I find a new space."

"Good, I didn't want to say anything, but I was worried about having it in my place." Amelia smiled with relief.

"I'd never do that to you." Pell placed his hand over his heart. "Sketchbooks and pencils only."

"Oh!" Amelia exclaimed, batting her eyelashes at him. "Will you draw me like one of your Belgian girls?"

CHAPTER THREE

The box had been waiting on his doorstep when Mal returned from the office on Tuesday. For two days, he'd walked by it without the slightest desire to examine its contents. Now, on Friday morning, he found himself frozen outside his front door staring down at the fucking thing as if it were about to sprout tentacles and snatch him up.

Josh's name glared up at him from above a goddamned PO box address, as if Josh didn't want Mal to know where he was living now.

"This is fucking ridiculous," he growled. "Man up, Zaha. Shit."

Mal opened the door and pushed the box inside with his foot. It was heavier than he'd anticipated, and he checked the front of his Prada boot to make sure he hadn't scuffed it. He stalked into his galley kitchen and grabbed one of the Shun steak knives he rarely used. He should have cared about desecrating such a precision instrument on a cardboard box, but anger clouded his ability to give a fuck.

The damned box had been taunting him.

Mal flipped open the flaps and peered inside. Two sweaters sat folded on top, soft cashmere blends he and Josh had picked up on a ski trip in Switzerland. One mocha brown and the other cornflower blue. His and his. Mal took a surprisingly difficult breath, shoved the garments aside and froze. The box was filled with memories, their memories. A framed photo of them on the beach in Maui. The pewter cup Josh had won in grad school from their circle of friends for having the highest GPA among them. The leather jacket Mal had given Josh on his thirtieth birthday. At the bottom lay a small burgundy box that contained what would have been their wedding rings.

He glared at it, anger, hurt and disbelief warring inside him, and stormed out of the apartment, shutting the door with a satisfying bang.

During his commute, Mal's tolerance for shitty drivers was at an all-time low. On a less drama-filled day, he would have hopped on the train but stuffing himself into an overcrowded subway car would have been a recipe for disaster. He'd nearly popped a blood vessel yelling at every asshole that got in his way on the road.

Stopped at a red light, Mal read a text message inviting him to yet another dinner party he had no desire to attend. He quickly and politely declined. Mal knew he needed to quell his natural tendency toward solitude or he'd lose what few friends and colleagues he had left. His only other option was to withdraw emotionally from everything and everyone and, unfortunately, he was exceptionally good at saying 'Fuck the world.' Something Evelyn had tried to help him unlearn.

Stepping off the elevator onto the 17th floor of the Liberty Building, Mal spotted his new receptionist. He stood in front of . . . Mal didn't know what it was.

"Kevin!" Mal's volume hurt his own ears, but that only stoked his bad mood. "What the fuck is that?"

Mal pointed at the enormous, ugly brown package leaning against the wall. It was flat, square, and at least six feet across. Even before the sputtering young man could explain it had been delivered from the gallery, Mal realized what it was.

"It's, uh, Quentin."

Mal's gaze snapped to the boy. "What?"

"My name. It's Quentin, not Kevin." He swallowed hard. "Sir."

Mal reassessed the young man.

He was short but slim and lean, with dark hair and eyes, and fair skin. He seemed a little too demure for a high-pressure law office. But despite the fear etched in his expression, he held his head high as he corrected Mal about his name. That earned him some points.

Mal gave him a short nod. "Quentin suits you better anyway. When did this arrive, and why hasn't it been installed?"

"I, uh, I think Ms. Magill wanted your final approval on it first."

Mal stepped up to the parcel. Finding a seam in the paper, he tore a strip away, revealing a shade of red so deep it bordered on violence. Mal kept ripping, and enlisted Quentin to help him. Between the two, they uncovered most of the artwork.

It was stunning.

"Wow." Quentin's awed reaction mirrored Mal's.

The photocopy hadn't done justice to the work itself. Scaled up, the painting threatened to swallow you. Drown you in its possibility.

Mal could make out the individual brushstrokes and realized now why he'd sensed so much movement in the print. The painter, whoever they were, had suffused motion into the piece with every stroke.

Suddenly, Mal needed to see the whole thing, unmarred by the remnants of paper and twine.

"I want this mounted within the hour."

Beside him, Quentin jumped as if he'd been electrocuted. He scurried to the front desk and picked up the phone.

"This is Mr. Zaha's office. The painting in the foyer needs to be installed right away." He frowned, shaking his head. "No, that won't do. Have someone here in thirty minutes, or we'll find someone else to take over the contract."

The corner of Mal's mouth lifted to form the beginning of a smile. He should have trusted Evelyn to find the right person for the job. Clearly, there was more to Quentin than met the eye.

When Mal got to his desk, he was surprised to find a piping hot double-espresso waiting for him. There was also an email from Pazzo Shoes in his inbox.

Pazzo had been an early client of Josh and Mal's, but they'd lost the account several years ago. Mal never got a straight answer out of Josh when he asked him why.

According to the email, which was congratulatory, Pazzo was interested in meeting with Mal about possible representation. Securing an account that large would effectively be a seal of approval for Mal's new practice.

As he formulated his response, inviting the CEO of Pazzo Shoes, Lydia Hahn, to meet with him, Mal got Evelyn on the phone.

"Boss?"

"My office. Now."

"On my way." Thirty seconds later, Evelyn appeared in the doorway. "What's up?"

Mal stopped typing and sat back in his chair. "Pazzo just emailed me."

Evelyn's eyes widened. She moved into the room and crossed her arms, thinking. "Interesting."

"I thought so too."

Mal studied her for a moment, watching the squirrels run around in her brilliant mind.

When he and Josh had split up and dissolved their business, Mal had been more upset at the thought of losing Evelyn than he had been about Josh and everything else. Though he would never admit to such a thing out loud.

Still, Evelyn got him as few others did. Maybe no one. Shame he wasn't even a little bit straight, or he probably would have snatched her up long ago. Married or not.

"What does the email say?"

Mal brought it up on his screen and read aloud. "Intrigued to hear that I've parted ways with Josh, curious about the new practice, always respected me, blah blah blah."

"Hmm." Evelyn stood behind the chair opposite him. "Pazzo would be a great get."

"It would," Mal agreed, eyeing her and waiting for the 'but' he thought he heard in her voice.

Evelyn nodded, but her eyes were unfocused, as they often got when she was deep in thought. She would have made a shrewd business attorney, having graduated top of her class at Wharton and paid her dues at top corporate firms up and down the mid-Atlantic coast. Evelyn absorbed corporate law like the proverbial sponge and knew almost as much about it as any lawyer Mal knew. It was one reason Mal had breathed a sigh of relief when she chose to stay with him. Evelyn was one hell of an employee.

She was also his friend, maybe the only one left standing in the aftermath of Josh and Mal.

"Obviously, she wants to meet. But she wants me to make the first move."

Evelyn smiled. "Of course, she does. Lydia wants you to woo her."

Mal grinned. "That I can do. Question is, should I?"

Evelyn stepped around the chair and sat down. She crossed her legs, smoothing her steel gray pencil skirt down over her shapely thighs.

Yep. Damn shame Mal wasn't bi.

Pursing her lips, Evelyn nodded. "I think you'd be crazy not to at least invite her for a meet. Keep it casual, though."

"I was thinking drinks."

"That works. It's less formal, and there's a built-in expiration date if things get weird." Evelyn nodded to herself. "What am I saying? It will get weird. Just tell her you have a dinner meeting, but you have some time before."

Mal frowned. "Why is weird a given?"

"Because Josh may have lost her account, but she has no idea how much you were involved in what happened with the Flavian case."

The Flavian case. Pazzo's chief U.S. competitor in the mid-range, fashion shoe market had allegedly stolen designs from Pazzo's development team. Lydia had suspected espionage and Josh had dismissed the thought as ludicrous. Never to Lydia's face, not exactly, but his position on the matter was hard to miss. After all, "they were only shoes." But Cohn and Zaha had taken the case, or rather Josh had. Mal had been neck-deep in another client's mess.

When the suit was settled out of court, Mal had thought the matter resolved. But then Pazzo abruptly fired the firm, and Josh chalked it up to greed, saying Lydia had wanted more from Flavian than was fair or even plausible. Mal had taken him at his word. He really shouldn't have. With anything.

The settlement had effectively put Flavian out of business, so there was no more blood to squeeze out of that stone.

"You're saying I need to woo her without it seeming like I'm wooing her."

"Exactly," Evelyn agreed, standing. "Think on it a while."

Mal nodded to himself. The phone rang, and he put it on speaker.

"Mr. Zaha? The installation is done."

"Thanks, Quentin." Mal killed the call and met Evelyn's eyes. They shared a smile. "He's all right, that kid."

"He is."

Mal rose, and together they walked to the foyer. They found Quentin standing in front of the canvas, which took up most of the wall next to the reception area.

A worker was putting the finishing touches on the small nameplate next to the piece. He stepped back and looked up at the canvas.

"All done."

"Thank you." Mal walked up beside the man, but he couldn't take his eyes off of the painting. Something in that mélange of color and movement called to him on a bone-deep level. Mal didn't understand it. He liked art, sure, but he'd never had a piece speak to him like this one.

He didn't need to turn his head to know that Evelyn and Quentin were equally enthralled.

"It's perfect," he heard himself say. Mal moved over to the nameplate. Reading the title of the piece for the first time struck him like a bolt of lightning.

'Closer' by Pellam Lindt, 2018
Oil on Canvas

It was as if the artist had reached down to the bottom of Mal's soul and not only dredged up every want and need he had but was showing him that each and every one of them mattered. Bringing to light desires Mal had locked away in a very old, very dark place.

He needed to know more about Pellam Lindt, whoever they were. He needed to look into their eyes and see himself reflected in them.

"Ev, does Lydia like art?" Mal turned to meet her coffee-brown eyes.

"I believe she is one of the main supporting patrons at the Barnes, so I'd say so."

Mal stepped back and looked up at the painting again. "Didn't you say the other pieces I requested are still on display at the gallery?"

"Yes, the Mayer gallery on Race Street." Mal could almost hear her put the pieces together. "And I believe the reception for the new exhibit is next Friday. It only makes sense you would want to go take a look at them in person."

Mal turned to Quentin. "Contact the Mayer gallery and let them know I'll be there."

"Yes, Mr. Zaha." Quentin made a bee-line for his desk.

"Oh, and Quentin?" Mal waited for the young man to meet his gaze. "My father was Mr. Zaha. You can call me Malcolm."

CHAPTER FOUR

Pell would have been lying if he'd said he had given no more thought to the mysterious person who had bought his most personal, most revealing work to date. So, when Brianne Mayer told him that the man himself, someone named Malcolm Zaha, was coming to the opening reception, Pell got honest-to-goodness chills.

Malcolm Zaha. Just the name conjured images of power, wealth, and mystery.

That is, until Brianne informed him Zaha was an attorney, and that the six-foot canvas that Pell had poured his blood, sweat, and tears into now hung behind the front desk of a fucking law firm. It would take everything in him for Pell not to march right up to the guy and demand to buy the painting back from him.

Only, he'd voiced that thought to Brianne and Amelia both, and both women had shot him down. Hard.

"Don't be an idiot." Amelia had said to him as they lounged on her plush, comfy sectional early Friday morning.

Pell had been pouting, and he knew it. This should have been the most exciting day of his life. His own corner in an exhibit at a major gallery in a big city like Philadelphia? He should have been over the moon. Instead, Pell kept glancing at the door during the reception and taking guesses at which attendee could be Malcolm Zaha.

"You should have just looked him up online." Amelia was lovely in her royal blue maxi dress. It flowed over her curves like water. She popped a shrimp ball into her mouth and washed it down with a few sips of red wine.

Pell was too wound up to eat. "I did search for him. I couldn't find any photos, well none that showed me definitively what he looked like."

"Ohhhh," she sighed. "I do love a good mystery."

"Not much of a mystery. He's a lawyer who thinks fine art is something to hang behind the potted plant in his office."

Amelia laughed. "Geez, Pell. Generalize much? He could be

an environmental lawyer or an entertainment lawyer, or he could-"

Pell didn't hear whatever else came out of Amelia's mouth because his focus had snagged on the tall, impossibly handsome man who had just stepped through the door.

He was well over six feet with warm brown skin, bright hazel eyes, and a body that made his suit look like an extension of his aura. One hand in his pocket, the other dangling casually at his side as he took in the room, he was the very picture of grace and command.

The fingers on Pell's right hand twitched, something they did when he needed to paint. And he needed to paint this man.

"*Merde.*"

"Do you think that's him?" Amelia had moved in close. Her breath tickled Pell's ear as she spoke.

"God, no." The very thought made Pell queasy.

The guy had such a regal air about him. Pell thought perhaps he was an actor, or maybe a conductor for the Philharmonic. Or an opera singer, he had the presence. Or he could have been the CEO of some major foundation or – gasp! – the curator at a New York museum. No, London.

Pell rolled his eyes at his own flights of fancy. Still, something about the guy piqued Pell's interest in a way that no ambulance-chasing lawyer ever could.

But as the man made his way across the room, his gaze never landing on any one piece of art for more than a second or three, Pell's conviction wavered. Particularly when he stopped to talk to a woman Pell knew from his volunteer work at the Barnes.

Lydia Hahn was the CEO of a clothing company—or shoes, or something—and her interest in the arts revolved solely around the fact that she could buy recognition. Something she clearly craved, as did many arts supporters. If they didn't have the talent, they'd find another way to memorialize their names.

Pell knew his thoughts were harsh, and that many patrons were genuinely interested in supporting the community and helping where they could. Lydia Hahn just wasn't one of them.

He had once heard that she'd had the manager of Ruby

Prime—the fanciest, costliest steakhouse in Philly—fired because her photo wasn't on their wall of fame. Apparently, she'd sent them a framed headshot and was incensed to learn they hadn't seen fit to mount it in a prominent place.

"Looks like your Romeo has a girlfriend."

Pell turned to glare at Amelia, who merely grinned at him. "Why are you like this?"

"Like what?" She popped a grape into her mouth. Always eating, his girl. "You were totally eyeballing the man candy. I'm allowed to give you shit about it."

"If I didn't love you so much, I'd kill you in your sleep and memorialize it on canvas."

Amelia laughed, but she needed to take him seriously. Artists were a temperamental lot.

Pell shook himself. It was time to get his head in the game. Spotting Brianne across the room, he grabbed Amelia's hand and dragged her toward his corner of the exhibit.

"I should at least stand by in case anyone wants to chat with the artist. Right?"

"Now you're thinking clearly." Amelia squeezed his fingers. "This is your moment. Enjoy it."

If she didn't catch Pell glancing over his shoulder at Mr. Dark and Delicious, well, that was his secret to keep.

♪

Mal had forgotten how dry Lydia's personality was. If the discussion wasn't about her bottom line, it was hell to maintain any sort of flow in the conversation. If she could have appeared less interested in the art on display, Mal would have been impressed. How she could be so disinterested, he did not understand. Some works were truly inspired.

"These little galleries make such an effort, I feel obligated to at least show my support." Lydia held a glass of white wine in her slim fingers.

She was a tall woman, nearly eye-to-eye with Mal in her four-inch heels. Her thin frame showed not even a hint of a curve, save for her small breasts which appeared to have been harnessed inside something too severe to be called a bra and not structured enough to be called a corset.

Rigid. That was the word that came to mind when Mal thought of Lydia Hahn. Rigid and difficult to please.

"I don't know much about art," Mal lied. "But I'm impressed with the exhibit so far. I had no idea Philadelphia harbored such diverse talent."

She tittered as if he'd compared the Mayer to the Louvre. "Really, Malcolm. I thought you had more discerning taste. Or perhaps that too fell to your former partner. Whatever the firm's shortcomings, the offices at Cohn and Zaha were somewhat tastefully appointed."

Mal grit his teeth. Maybe this meeting wasn't such a great idea.

The gallery, though smaller than he'd imagined, was a treasure trove. Brianne Mayer had an eye for talent. There were works in every medium including mixed media sculptures, and watercolors, but the exhibit was dominated by oil paintings. The unifying theme, *From Many, One*, was well-represented in the offerings.

Mal had already spied a glass vase that would look fantastic on his mantel at the new apartment, but he had seen no more work from Pellam Lindt. As his chat with Lydia kept getting interrupted by people stopping to greet her, Mal found his gaze traveling around the room in search of the Lindt pieces.

"My dear Ms. Hahn, so lovely of you to join us this evening."

Brianne Mayer offered Lydia one of those barely-there hugs Mal despised. By the look on her face, Ms. Mayer didn't seem to enjoy them either. Her narrowed gray eyes hovered over a tentative smile as Lydia assessed her.

"Brianne." Lydia mouthed the name as if it were a chore. "I wasn't planning to attend, really, but Mr. Zaha here persuaded me."

Brianne's flinch was barely noticeable. This was a woman used to dealing with the likes of Lydia Hahn.

Mal dialed up the volume on his considerable charm. "It's a pleasure to meet you, Ms. Mayer."

He watched as recognition filled her eyes. Her smile for him was warmer than the one she'd offered Lydia.

"Mr. Zaha, it's such a pleasure to finally meet you."

"Please, call me Malcolm."

"Of course, Malcolm. I'm Brianne." She extended her hand to shake, and Mal accepted it. Her skin was smooth and warm to the touch, her handshake firm but inviting.

She was a lovely woman, with olive skin and gleaming chestnut hair that fell in waves just past her shoulders. Her makeup was minimal, especially in contrast to Lydia's.

Mal returned her smile, holding her gaze a little longer than necessary, and watched as the color rose in her cheeks.

Brianne extracted her hand from his and cleared her throat. "Your assistant said you would be stopping by tonight. I assume it's to see the other pieces we've held for you?"

"Did you actually buy something from the gallery, Malcolm?" Lydia's voice held more than a note of incredulity.

Mal chose to ignore it, and he could see that Brianne hadn't been fazed by it either. She was probably used to such comments. And again, Mal wondered why he thought meeting Lydia there, or even meeting with her at all, had been a good idea.

Ah, right. The legitimacy. Pazzo would be an enormous coup for Zaha & Associates and having Lydia as a client could open the door to others. Still, Mal wondered if it was worth it.

"Malcolm, have you had a chance to see Pell's other work?"

"No, I haven't."

"What sort of name is Pell?" Lydia scoffed.

"It's short for Pellam. Pellam Lindt," Brianne supplied. "Mr. Za . . . er, Malcolm acquired one of Pell's most important paintings last week."

"Really, Brianne. I hope you didn't trick Malcolm into buying some monstrosity on the pretense that this *Pell* had produced some sort of masterpiece." Lydia shook her head disapprovingly as her gaze drifted around the room. With no more than a few words and a look, she had made it clear how little regard she had for the works on display, leaving Mal to wonder just why the hell she frequented these events.

He also bristled at Lydia's commentary about the Lindt painting. Mal had a direct view of the piece from the window in his office and had lost minutes staring at the thing. The more he'd studied it, the more details had emerged.

There were hidden symbols within Lindt's brushstrokes, things one could only see from certain angles and only from very close-up, where the paint was the thickest. Mal had found a mouth in one spot, open and waiting for something to fill it, with the barest hint of a tongue resting on the surprisingly inviting bottom lip.

In another area, he'd detected the unmistakable shape of someone's ass, rounded and pert. And, unless his eyes had deceived him, the distinct outline of a handprint on one cheek.

On the bottom left corner, near Lindt's signature, Mal thought he could make out the fat head of an erect cock.

These weren't things someone could have seen on a digital print, or even from more than a foot away. But Mal had studied the painting for what seemed like hours. And it had lit a fire inside him he'd long thought dormant, making him even more determined to meet Pellam Lindt.

Brianne seemed to take Lydia's comments in stride.

"Well, Lydia darling, Van Gogh was widely regarded as a hack by his peers which shows that having an eye for true talent isn't something that everyone can possess."

At that moment, Mal fell a little in love with Brianne Mayer. He was about to compliment her eye for beauty when his eyes were suddenly filled with a vision his brain couldn't quite comprehend. Everything inside him went still. Just stopped. His breath, his thoughts, his pulse. It all ceased.

The man's blond hair wasn't a trait that usually appealed to Mal, and his skin was so pale it practically glowed under the gallery lights. Well under six feet, with a slight build and delicate features, he shouldn't have captured Mal's attention. But captured it he had.

The vintage jacket he wore was velvet, a deep burgundy that looked incredible against his complexion. Beneath it lay what looked like a simple black t-shirt, and he'd finished the outfit with a pair of jeans. They were well-worn, and Mal knew that the fading and small tears in the denim resulted from frequent use and not overpriced fashion.

The woman next to him, a lovely concoction of brown curls, russet skin, dimples, and curves, whispered into the man's ear. His answering smile lit the whole of Mal's universe.

Mal felt lightheaded.

It was ridiculous.

A hand on his elbow brought Mal's attention back to the women at his side, but his thoughts were scattered in the general direction of the man across the room.

"Come, let me show you Pell's collection." Brianne dropped her hand from his arm and smiled, a note of pleading in her eyes.

Mal didn't need her to tell him she was done playing hostess to Lydia.

"Please, lead the way." He turned to find Lydia already engaged in another conversation. "I'll touch base with you later. Enjoy yourself."

She offered him a brief nod and went back to her new companion without missing a beat.

Mal took a quick glance across the room, but the object of his interest was gone. The disappointment was a living thing, but Mal knew—well, hoped—he was still there somewhere. The universe couldn't be so cruel as to reveal a creature like that to Mal and then snatch him away before Mal could engage and assess his chances.

When they were out of earshot of Lydia, Brianne slipped her arm through Mal's and leaned in close. "I'm sorry if I was rude to your friend, but she hasn't been my biggest fan since I opened this place."

Mal tucked her hand into the crook of his arm as they strolled.

He fought to keep his focus on her when what he really wanted was to find the young man he'd seen.

"Oh? Why is that?"

"Ms. Hahn is on the board of the committee that wants to tear this block of Race Street down to build a new mega-museum."

That didn't surprise Mal. Lydia was of the ilk that believed in preservation only as far as it went toward securing prestige. And nothing bestowed prestige in the city like a big, shiny new building with your name on it.

"Well, I for one am glad you and the community are resisting," Mal assured her. He took in several offerings as they passed. "I love how vibrant and eclectic the area has become. It's a point of interest for residents and a destination for tourists. I call that a win."

Brianne's face brightened, and she brought her other hand up to squeeze Mal's bicep, leaning into him a little more.

"Yes! Thank you. I love what we've created here, and I'm so glad you can see the value in it."

"I do," he agreed, enjoying her passion.

"Unfortunately, the preservation effort is down to its last appeal. If we don't win this one, it won't matter how many tourist dollars and magazine write-ups we garner. The non-resident property owners in this district only care about the spike in property values that a project like that would likely cause. They'll sell, leaving people like me no choice but to sell."

They stopped in a back corner of the gallery and Brianne didn't need to tell Mal that they'd reached Lindt's section. After staring at his own Pellam Lindt masterpiece for more hours than he cared to admit, he recognized the same energy and genius in the pieces on display.

Letting go of Brianne, he stepped forward to get a better look.

"Remarkable, isn't it? His vision?" Brianne's voice held more than a hint of reverence.

"Quite."

It was Lindt's use of color that captivated Mal the most. Unlike the painting that hung in his office, this work was more muted in tone. It still conveyed a longing that betrayed an unspoken desire. This time, not for carnal pleasure, but for something else. Peace, perhaps. Maybe even love.

"He's here somewhere, the artist." Mal turned to look at Brianne, and she smiled. "Would you like to meet the man behind the canvas?"

The image of the man Mal had seen minutes before burned behind his eyes. How likely would it be that the unearthly creature he'd spotted amidst the crowd and his enigmatic artist were the same?

"Yes, very much," he finally replied, barely able to disguise his interest as anything other than what it was.

CHAPTER FIVE

Pell couldn't hide his relief when Brianne appeared at his side. He'd been caught in conversation with one of the other exhibiting artists, a man so full of his own self-importance Pell had barely gotten a word in. Worst, his best friend had abandoned him to that fate, claiming she'd spotted some famous athlete or another. Pell didn't believe her for a second.

Traitor.

"Hello, Lucas." Brianne accepted the other man's lukewarm, half-hug and then turned her attention to Pell. "My love, I'm so sorry to tear your away, but there's someone I'd like you to meet."

Pell gave Lucas what he hoped was a look of contrition. "Sorry, duty calls."

"It always does, doesn't it?" Lucas sighed loudly. "Oh well, don't let me keep you. Go peddle your wares."

Brianne guided Pell away, leaving Lucas to admire his own work.

"Thank you, thank you," Pell whispered, grateful.

"My pleasure." Brianne grinned, wrapping an arm around Pell's waist. She was taller than him, and he nestled against her side. "It wasn't a lie, though. There is someone I need you to meet."

"A potential buyer?"

"Yes and no," she teased. "It's the man who bought *Closer* and placed those other three on hold."

Pell's pulse quickened. The elusive Mr. Zaha, at last. No small part of him hoped it was the man he'd spotted earlier. He turned wide eyes to Brianne, only to find her grinning at him.

"What?"

"I think you're as intrigued by him as I am."

"I'm curious, that's all," Pell insisted. "I haven't even met the man."

"I know," Brianne said, patting his cheek. "But he is well worth meeting. Trust me."

They turned the corner, and Pell stumbled to a stop. Standing in front of *Du Ma Vie*, a favorite of his pastels, was the gorgeous specimen he'd spotted earlier.

His back was to them, but it was definitely one and the same.

Pell ached to hear the voice those remarkable lips could produce. He was about to tell Brianne to give him a few minutes to gather himself, before she took him to meet his benefactor, when she released him and stepped forward to address the man himself.

"Malcolm Zaha, this is Pellam Lindt."

Mr. Zaha turned around, and Pell nearly gasped aloud.

Dear God, he was gorgeous.

Up close, he was almost too much to take in, and Pell stepped back before he could catch himself.

Impeccably dressed in a tailored suit that probably cost more than Pell's entire wardrobe, Malcolm Zaha was half-a-foot taller than Pell's five-foot-seven, and nearly twice as broad. He was a wall of a man but somehow compact, like a nuclear bomb contained inside a lithium battery. Pell had no doubt of Zaha's power.

The man's whiskey-colored eyes assessed him from head to toe as if he were savoring the view, and Pell felt that look in every molecule of his being.

After a moment, Mr. Zaha extended his hand. "It's a pleasure to finally meet you, Pellam. I'm Malcolm."

Finding it hard to breathe, let alone look into Malcolm's hypnotic eyes, Pell took the hand. It engulfed his fingers in a grip that was both gentle and firm. Malcolm's skin was softer than Pell had expected because nothing about Malcolm Zaha seemed soft.

Except for the smile he gave Pellam at their first contact.

Pell cleared his throat and forced himself to meet Malcolm's gaze. "It's nice to meet you too . . . Malcolm."

He watched as the man's pupils dilated, which answered the question Pell had been too nervous to ask himself when he'd spied Malcolm across a crowded room. Malcolm Zaha was attracted to men, or at least to him.

As if to confirm his conclusion, Malcolm brushed his thumb across the back of Pell's hand.

He drew in a quick breath and shuddered when Malcolm

tightened his grip ever-so-slightly before letting him go.

"I'll leave you two to chat." Brianne slipped away, leaving them alone in the quiet corner.

Pell had forgotten she was there.

Malcolm turned back to the pastel. "What inspired this one?"

His voice was rich and buttery, crafted to pour into an unwitting ear and command any soul to do his bidding. Of this, Pell had zero doubt because he wanted to obey a command he hadn't been given.

Pell stepped forward to stand beside Malcolm. He clasped his hands behind his back to prevent himself from reaching out and running his hands over Malcolm's dark, velvety hair.

It was cut short, close to Malcolm's scalp but with enough length that Pell could make out gleaming waves. His skin was flawless too. Everything about the man screamed perfection.

"I'm not sure if I can explain it in a way that someone else would understand."

"Try."

Pell glanced over at Malcolm, but he was engrossed in the painting, studying the canvas closely as if he could divine its secrets. And maybe he could.

Clearing his throat, Pell returned his attention to the piece. It was another favorite, though it had been done at a moment when he thought he'd found love. A moment that had died unfulfilled.

He'd bathed the very top of the canvas in midnight blue, dark as a night sky, and then capped some peaks in light gray. The blue bled down into lighter gradients until it gave way altogether to oranges and pinks. By the time he reached the bottom of the canvas, he'd dipped into creams and golds.

Funny, he couldn't even remember his ex-girlfriend Molly's voice now, only the feeling he'd captured in this painting, the feeling of being cherished by someone. If just for a moment.

How was he to explain all of that to a man like Malcolm Zaha?

"It's called *Toothpaste Kisses*. It's about capturing that feeling you have the first time you wake up next to your lover. I'd originally titled it *Cherish* because, when I painted it, I felt cherished."

Malcolm nodded. "There's a sense of peace in your strokes here. Very different from the one I bought, a different energy entirely. I believe, rather than oils, emotions might be your true medium. You paint with your whole heart on display."

And . . . wow. Pell didn't know how to respond to that.

"My painting, your *Closer*," Malcolm continued. "I'll just say it spoke to me in a language I hadn't learned yet. There are so many layers to that piece. It's brilliant."

"Well . . . Thank you for saying that." Pell struggled to convey his thoughts, overwhelmed by Malcolm's presence and insights. "The aftermath of what inspired *Closer* wasn't a good time for me, but I managed to somehow survive the . . . the madness that had overtaken me. I suppose I could have titled it *Eros*, but I was in my song-title phase. This one is a song title too."

It was strange. These were the first words they'd ever exchanged but, with each one, Pell found it easier and easier to open up. The tightness that had been in his chest since the doors to the exhibit opened had all but disappeared. Even the nervous energy he'd felt when Brianne introduced them had subsided and been replaced with a soothing warmth.

Malcolm turned his head, and Pell found himself once again caught by that penetrating gaze.

"It's beautiful." Malcolm licked his bottom lip, drawing it into his mouth before he bit down on the plump flesh.

Pell's throat went dry.

"Both paintings are incredible, really, but *Closer* – which is hanging in my office, by the way—is the work of a genius."

Pell felt the heat rising to his cheeks. How could he survive this man? Having Malcolm Zaha's full attention was like standing in front of a roaring fire.

Malcolm's gaze shifted to the next framed work. "And this one?"

It was one of Pell's earliest pieces. He hadn't wanted to display it, but it was one of Brianne's favorites, and she had insisted.

Concentric circles of white, ivory, and soft yellows cradled a small, red heart at the center of the canvas, the paint so thick in places it was almost three-dimensional. The heart itself was as close to photorealism as Pell had ever come in his work. Brick red, crimson, vermillion, and black made it appear to pulse with life.

"Is this from the same period as my piece?"

Pell smiled. "How could you tell?"

Malcolm met his eyes. "I sense the same drive here, and the same fear."

"Fear?"

"What you referred to as madness, I suppose. The artist was afraid he'd drown in his own needs."

Pell drew a quick breath. "How . . .? How did you . . .?"

"I know true desire when I see it."

One corner of Malcolm's full mouth lifted. He blinked slowly before his eyes mapped every inch of Pell's face. There was a question there. If pressed, Pell could only describe Malcolm's expression as one of invitation.

The silence stretched between them until Pell thought he might spontaneously combust. This was too intimate a moment for two men who had only known each other for five minutes.

"I'd love to see more."

"More?"

Malcolm pulled his full lips into his mouth as if he were literally biting back words.

"More of your work."

"Oh!" Pell knew his face was bright red. He cursed his skin for showing his every emotion. "My studio is actually in the back if you . . . If . . ."

Malcolm's smile was predatory. "Show me."

♫

Mal couldn't seem to help himself. He hadn't meant to exert such control over his interaction with Pellam, but the man had responded so beautifully. It was a relief to know that the intense attraction he felt toward the young artist wasn't entirely one-sided.

Pellam had practically vibrated as they stood side-by-side discussing his work. It was all Mal could do not to back the kid up against the nearest flat surface and claim his pretty, cotton-candy-pink mouth. Fuck.

They walked to the back of the exhibit room, and Pellam opened a door that led into the administrative area of the gallery. As Pellam led him further down the darkened hall, Mal noted several small offices and a storage room. The smell of paint and sawdust drifted in the air, and Mal took a deep breath. It was somehow soothing.

"It's just through here."

Pellam brushed up against a plank of wood propped against the wall. He didn't notice the thing tilting toward him.

Mal stopped the plank from crashing over Pellam's head, grabbing the young man by the waist and using his other arm to push the offending object back into a less precarious position.

Pellam gasped. His body was stiff in Mal's embrace, and Mal quickly let him go. He tried not to think about how good it felt to have Pellam's lean frame flush against his bulkier one. Didn't want to dwell on how much fun it would be to play with that dynamic.

Pellam straightened and turned to look at Mal.

"*Mon Dieu*," he breathed, revealing an accent Mal hadn't detected before. "Thank you, I didn't even know it was falling. Are you all right?"

His gaze quickly darted over Mal's body, checking him for injury. Delicate fingers brushed small bits of dust from Mal's lapels.

"I'm so sorry."

Mal waved off the concern. "I'm fine, but it might be better if this hallway were clear of that sort of debris. If an inspector were to come through here, he would undoubtedly deem it a fire hazard."

Pellam's eyebrows lifted.

"Not that I intend to report it," Mal felt compelled to add. "Just an observation."

"Right," Pellam said, finally smiling. "You're right, of course. I'll talk to Brianne about clearing it."

Pellam turned and continued, stopping when they reached the final door. It was splattered with paint and what looked like oil stains. Larger by far than the doors they'd passed, Mal had no doubt the room beyond it had once served as a garage or carriage house. Pellam needed both hands to slide the door open.

"She's letting me use this space temporarily until I can find something else," he said, struggling a little with the ancient hinges.

Mal thought about assisting but refrained. He needed to give Pellam some space, both for his own sanity and to maintain any sense of propriety. His pull toward the man unnerved him, but not enough to walk away just yet.

Having his hands on Pellam Lindt, for even that brief second, had stoked the flame Mal had lit for him long before he knew what Pellam looked like or how he felt against his body. Now that he knew, Mal found it difficult not to make a move. But he held a position of power, and Mal refused to take advantage. If anything happened between them, Mal would make sure the attraction he'd sensed from the young artist was genuine and the desire to act upon it mutual.

At the flick of the switch next to the door, light flooded the room. Mal had been right in his initial assessment. The area had served as a garage at some point, but it had been converted into a workspace. The back wall consisted of a broad, rolling door made up of wood and glass panels. The panels were dingy, but Mal imagined the room would flood with sunlight during the day. He had no trouble picturing Pellam in the space, covered in paint and lost in his own world.

He wanted to bear witness to that, to Pellam's creative spells. He wanted to know the man, and not just Biblically.

"Here we are." Pellam stepped aside and let Mal walk past him.

There was so much to see, Mal scarcely knew where to look. Colorful canvases leaned against the right wall, six or seven deep in places. Others, in various stages of completion, sat on easels.

"Is this all your work?"

"Most of it, yeah."

"You're quite prolific," Mal observed as he made his way through the space.

Pellam remained by the door.

Mal could almost feel the other man holding his breath. The thought that Mal's opinion meant so much to him already, swelled his chest with something close to pride.

"Sometimes I wish I weren't," Pellam lamented as he walked over to where Mal stood. "Sometimes, it's too much. I don't know if that will make sense to someone like you."

"Someone like me?"

Pellam shrugged one shoulder. "Someone who thrives on pressure."

"What makes you think I do?"

His laugh was musical. Shaking his head, Pellam dropped his chin to his chest. "Call it artistic instinct. If I could paint you, it would be a blur of color on an otherwise bleak landscape. Purple for your magnetism, gold for your integrity, brown and cream and . . ."

He trailed off, seemingly lost in the vision.

Mal stepped closer, and Pellam lifted his eyes to meet his gaze. They were an unusual shade of green, like a pale jade, and his lashes were sinfully long. Mal had to stop himself from lifting a hand to trace the man's high cheekbone or from running it through his silky hair.

"Is that how you see me?"

Pellam opened his mouth. Closed it. Bit his lip.

Mal groaned, and he watched Pellam's breath catch. Literally catch.

"I . . . I'm just babbling." Pellam swallowed hard, his throat working in a way that made Mal want to do unspeakably dirty things to him.

"Pellam."

The young man blinked up at him, his eyes dark with desire. Mal found it hard to breathe around his own arousal. He took a tentative step closer, encouraged when Pellam made no move to retreat.

"Please tell me if I'm misreading the situation."

Pellam released a heavy sigh, his breath coming in stutters. "No, I don't think you are."

"You don't think?"

"You're not." Pellam took a deep breath. "I . . . Please, just . . ."

Mal stopped short of touching him. "Please, just what?"

He was almost afraid to hear the end of that sentence. *Please just be quick? Please tell no one about this? Please be gentle? Please take me, now?*

"Please . . . just . . . ?" Mal prompted again.

Pellam closed his eyes. His next words came in a rush. "Fucking kiss me before I go insane."

It was all the assurance Mal needed. He closed the distance between them, finally cupping Pellam's cheeks in his hands. As he'd suspected, Pellam's skin was supple to the touch. He trembled a little, which brought Mal's protective instincts roaring to the surface to battle with his baser needs.

He settled for a chaste kiss, just a brush of their lips, but it was enough to send his libido into overdrive. For his sake, and Pellam's, Mal released the young man and stepped back. Closing his eyes, he took a deep, cleansing breath, the effects of which were erased when Pellam launched himself into Mal's arms.

Mal groaned under the weight of the other man and then groaned again as Pellam swept his tongue across Mal's bottom lip. All of Mal's good intentions went out the window. He'd been transformed into a tight ball of *Want. Need. Now.*

Pellam moaned into the kiss, and Mal coiled his arms around the man's narrow waist. He'd thought the blond would feel dainty in his embrace, but there was power in his small frame. A strength that should have come as a surprise but somehow made sense. For all of his shy glances and nervous stuttering, Pellam Lindt's true self had been revealed to Mal through his art. He'd poured so much of himself into the work that Mal briefly wondered if there was anything left.

The answer to that question was in Pellam's undulating body, in his greedy hands, and in his demanding mouth. It was in the hard cock Mal felt pressed against his thigh, and in the pleading whimpers Pellam spilled into Mal's mouth.

God.

Mal needed to make a choice, stop this now or drag Pellam into the nearest dark corner and feed the driving hunger he'd excavated from the depths of his soul.

"Here you are!" At the sound of the woman's voice, Pellam jumped back.

He made brief eye contact with Mal before he turned to the newcomer and smiled.

"I've been looking everywhere for you."

"You found me." Only a slight tremor in Pellam's voice indicated his state of mind.

Reorienting himself to the here and now, Mal turned as Pellam's friend – *or, fuck, girlfriend?* – approached them. She was, in a word, adorable. Her evident affection for Pellam tugged at Mal's brotherly instincts.

Pellam opened his arms to her, and she engulfed him in a hug. The smile on his face matched hers.

"Amelia," he said, still a little out of breath. "This is Malcolm. Malcolm, this is my best friend and sometimes roommate, Amelia. She also makes a great latte over at Sassafras."

"Mal," he heard himself say.

Funny. Only the people Mal considered close to him were allowed to call him that, but he'd put it out there, so . . .

Pellam raised one pale eyebrow.

"Nice to meet you, Mal." Amelia extended her hand, and he shook it. "Has Pell convinced you to sit for him yet?"

Mal returned Pellam's raised eyebrow with one of his own. "No, *Pell* has not, though he has strongly hinted at the idea."

Pellam grinned, but the nickname reminded Mal how little he knew of the man. Reminded him how much he wanted to know. Which was, perhaps, everything.

"I'm sorry if I came on too strong," Pellam said, sounding not very sorry at all.

"You didn't." Mal returned his grin, holding the blond's gaze until he blushed.

"Then you're open to the idea?" Amelia prodded, hopeful.

Mal unleashed the full wattage of his smile upon her, pleased with the twinkle in her eye.

"I'm very open to the possibility, yes."

CHAPTER SIX

"You haven't stopped smiling all day." Evelyn strolled into Mal's office, closed the door behind her, and dropped into the chair across from him. "Did someone have a good weekend?"

"Didn't do much, actually," Mal replied. "I still had some unpacking to do. And some stuff to toss."

Evelyn didn't dare ask Mal if he was referring to Josh's box, she knew him too well. He loved that about her.

"Did you decide to hit the clubs then? Find a little distraction?"

Mal looked over her shoulder toward the lobby. He'd gotten into the habit of leaving the glass in his office window unfrosted when he wasn't with a client. It offered a perfect view of Pellam's painting, conjuring up the memory of the man's pliant mouth every time he looked at it. He'd already had to lock himself in his bathroom once that morning to satisfy his needy prick.

And all they'd shared was a kiss. Christ.

All weekend, he'd kicked himself for not taking Pellam to bed. Not that he was in a rush, but he also didn't see the need to wait. The attraction was mutual, that much was certain. And yet Mal had gone home alone. Not only alone but without so much as the guy's cell phone number.

Fucking amateur.

"Nope," Mal answered. "Didn't feel like going out."

"Bummer. I miss hearing about your extracurriculars. So, what has you in such a good mood? I haven't seen you grin like this since . . . " Evelyn seemed to catch herself. "Well, in a long time. Care to share?"

Mal thought about it for a moment. His moment with Pellam felt intensely personal, but this was Ev.

"Come on, Mal. I can tell you're holding out on me. And I know the one-eighty in your attitude isn't because of Lydia Hahn. She's left a thousand messages, by the way. I assume the gallery thing went over well?"

"Fuck, I totally forgot about Lydia." Mal rubbed a hand over his face. He needed to stop mooning about like a teenager and get a handle on his business. "I think she enjoyed it, yeah, but I'm not going to pursue the Pazzo account."

"Oh, thank God," Evelyn exhaled, slouching back into the seat. She shrugged at Mal's amused expression. "Sorry, but I wasn't looking forward to working with her staff. They're just as intolerable as she is."

"Well, you don't have to worry about it now, though there is something I'd like you to look into for me."

Evelyn sat up, attentive as always. "Name it."

"Do you know much about the initiative to tear down the Race Street galleries to build a giant tourist trap?"

"You mean Lydia's pet project for the shiny, new museum of something or other?"

"Brianne Mayer mentioned it to me on Friday."

Evelyn's expression soured. "It's a horrible idea and would drastically change the neighborhood. I don't think it would be for the better either. I love how quirky it is down there."

Mal nodded in agreement. "Brianne mentioned her group has one last chance to stop the zoning approval."

"Brianne, eh?" Evelyn eyed him. "Is that who's brought out your dimples?"

Mal rolled his eyes. "No, and knock it off. I need the team to find out what they can about the case, why the appeals were denied, et cetera. Oh, and set up a time when I can meet with Brianne and the other hold-outs."

"Are you thinking of representing them?" Her smile was hopeful.

"If they're amenable, yes. They need someone in their corner who isn't in the pocket of Lydia and her cronies. Plus, I know how people like Lydia think and how low they're willing to go."

"Can't argue with you," Evelyn replied. "It would be more in-line with your vision for the old firm. I'm curious, though. Why the sudden interest? Was Brianne's argument that convincing, or was it something else? Or should I say, someone?"

Mal bit his lip.

"You met him, didn't you? Pellam Lindt." Her question was a statement.

"Wait, have you?"

She nodded. "I have. Last week."

Mal blinked at her. "And you didn't tell me because . . .?"

Evelyn smiled. "Because I wanted you to meet him without any input from me."

Mal contemplated that for a moment. Then he hit a button on his desk that frosted the glass in the window that faced the foyer. He needed privacy for this conversation.

Folding his arms, Mal tested her. "He's not my type."

She nodded. "I admit, he's different from the people you usually go for."

"Indeed." Mal leaned forward to brace his elbows on the desk. "But you knew I'd like him. Why?"

"Because . . ." Evelyn drummed the fingernails of one manicured hand on the desk as she formulated her response. "Well, for one, you haven't stopped staring at that painting since you first saw a photo of it."

Mal snorted.

"And, two . . . I'm not sure. There was just something about him. I only met him briefly, and he didn't know who I was, of course, but . . ." She shrugged again, then eyed him closely. "Did you seduce him?"

Mal laughed and sat back. "No."

"But something happened," she said, the hope returning to her eyes.

He didn't bother to hide his smirk from her. "Something happened."

Evelyn all but bounced in her seat, something Mal had never seen her do.

"And? Don't leave me hanging."

Mal shrugged one shoulder, trying desperately to keep a lid on how affected he'd been by such a brief encounter. He didn't want

Evelyn to know he couldn't get Pellam out of his head, or that he'd jerked off so much in the last two days, he was surprised his dick hadn't fallen off. He didn't want to reveal that he'd been trying to figure out a way to contact Pellam over the weekend without coming off as a stalker.

"Spill it, Mal." Evelyn's impatience was endearing. "When are you going to see him again? Are you going to see him again?"

Mal's desk phone chimed. He picked up the receiver, and Evelyn rolled her eyes at him.

"There's a guy named Pell here to see you, sir."

For a moment, Mal's mind went blank. "Uh, send him in."

"Actually," Quentin squeaked as if he expected Mal to fire him on the spot. "He asked you meet him in the foyer."

"Tell him I'll be there in one minute." Mal hung up the phone and let the grin he'd been suppressing take over his entire face. "The answer to your question, my darling Evelyn, just walked in the front door."

♪

Pell hadn't known what to expect when he visited Malcolm's office. He wasn't even sure why he'd decided to come, except he'd been chastising himself for not at least exchanging contact info with him at the reception. Then again, Malcolm – he refused to call him Mal – hadn't asked for his number either, nor had he offered his own.

This was a bad idea.

But, before he could slip back onto the elevator, a charming young man asked him if he needed help with anything. The next thing Pell knew, he had invited Malcolm to meet him in front of his painting.

Pell certainly hadn't expected to find *Closer* staring at him as soon as the elevator doors opened onto Malcolm's floor. It was jarring but also kind of humbling. He had thought the painting would be behind the front desk, framed by potted Ficus trees, or maybe tucked away in the corridor that led to the restrooms.

Malcolm's office, or maybe even Malcolm himself, had apparently taken great care to have the painting properly installed. The lighting was gallery-worthy, and it also had its proper nameplate.

Pell couldn't stop staring at it. Of course, this is where he and Malcolm would meet again. It had to be here in front of the painting that had brought them together.

He knew Malcolm had arrived before he opened his mouth to speak. Not only because the receptionist sat up straighter in his chair, but because the air seemed to change whenever Malcolm came close to him.

Pell suppressed a shiver.

"I almost changed my mind," Malcolm said. His voice was close, but not close enough for Pell.

"About?"

Pell turned to look at Malcolm and, oh my. He was even better looking than Pell remembered. He wore another suit, this one as expensive as the one he'd worn Friday night and just as exquisitely tailored.

Malcolm's eyes drank him in, and Pell returned the favor.

"I thought about hanging it in my home, but then I would be robbing others of its beauty and power."

"Beauty and power, eh?" Pell smiled as Malcolm approached him. "You sure know how to stroke an artist's ego."

Stopping when they were toe-to-toe, Malcolm leaned in and spoke into Pell's ear.

"You have no idea." Malcolm stepped back and offered him a wink.

Pell wanted to know. He desperately wanted to know, and he recognized the moment when Malcolm realized it.

His gaze darkened. "Come to my office?"

I'll come anywhere you want, Pell wanted to say. Instead, he nodded and let Malcolm lead the way.

A hand on Pell's elbow, Malcolm steered him into an enormous office decorated in a sleek contemporary style. A large glass desk sat on the left. On the right, a white leather couch lined the wall. Another door sat off in the corner, probably a bathroom. The giant window across from the door had a clear view of the Philadelphia skyline. They were on the seventeenth floor, and the view was spectacular, but Pell was too aroused to appreciate it.

Malcolm closed the door just as Pell's patience ran out.

"You never asked for my number." Pell had meant to tease, but he couldn't keep the whimper out of his voice. He was so damn thirsty for this guy.

All weekend, he'd listened to Amelia drone on and on about how he'd blown it by not slipping his phone number into Malcolm's pocket. As if Pell needed any more reminders of how colossally stupid he'd been. So addlebrained by that incredible kiss he hadn't had the presence of mind to do something as simple as asking the guy for his number. *Merde.*

"A mistake I won't make twice," Malcolm responded. He held out his palm. "Give me your phone."

"My . . . ?"

"Phone."

That smirk was so fucking sexy, it took a moment for Pell's brain to catch up with the demand.

"Oh!" He unlocked his cell and handed it over.

Pell watched as Malcolm programmed several numbers into his contacts. He then dialed his own phone to capture Pell's information. Malcolm handed it back and held Pell's gaze until the rest of the world melted away.

"I'm going to kiss you now, Pellam."

Just like that, his spine went butter soft. "*D'accord*"

Malcolm traced the seam between Pell's lips with the tip of his tongue, teasing and tasting. Daring him.

Pell groaned, opening to accept the kiss. He slid his hands behind Malcolm's nape as heat flared between them, inhaling the scent of the man and committing it to memory.

One of Malcolm's hands found its way up into Pell's longish

hair, his nails raking Pell's scalp in the most delicious way. The other hand pressed against the small of Pell's back, pulling him closer.

Malcolm's arms felt incredible around him, strong and sure, and Pell deepened the kiss, languidly sweeping his tongue against the other man's. God, how he had craved this, the chance to be vulnerable with someone so powerful and yet so gentle.

Malcolm broke the kiss and trailed his lips across Pell's cheek and down to his neck, teasing the tender spot he found there. Just as Pell tilted his head to give Malcolm better access, the phone on his desk crackled to life.

"You've got to be kidding," he laughed.

Pell smiled, blushing as he stepped back and ran a shaky hand through his hair. This was insane.

Crossing over to the desk, Malcolm hit the intercom. "Yes?"

"Sir, your five o'clock with UOI was canceled."

"Okay. Thanks, Quentin." Staring into Pell's eyes, Malcolm bit his lower lip and rolled it between his teeth.

Pell's cock, already half-hard, sprang to full attention.

Malcolm held Pell frozen with just a look. He hit the intercom on his phone. "Quentin?"

"Sir?"

"Has Evelyn left for the day?"

"She left right after your, uh, guest arrived. You want me to call her for you?"

"No," Malcolm answered, removing his tie. "That's not necessary. You can leave too. I'll lock up."

"As you wish. Thank you. Have a good evening, sir."

Pell could have sworn he heard Quentin chuckle before he signed off, but Malcolm didn't seem to care, so neither did he.

Feeling bold, Pell walked over and locked the door, earning a slow smile from the man on the other side of the room.

"Why didn't you ask for my number Friday night? Or, even better, just ask me to go home with you?" Pell shrugged out of his jacket and let it drop to the floor as he went to work on his button-down.

"It wasn't a lack of desire." Malcolm all but ripped his suit jacket off his shoulders. Apparently, he'd reached the end of his tether. "Couldn't stop thinking about you."

His jacket landed on the desk.

"Every day, since I first laid eyes on that fucking painting."

Next came the tie.

"Every minute since Friday night."

Pell unbuttoned his jeans, taking his time because, fuck, if his hands weren't shaking. "And now we're here."

Malcolm's eyes were dark and unfocused as he stepped out of his trousers. His body was a living, breathing work of art and Pellam stilled for a moment, needing to drink it in.

His skin, unmarred by any blemish Pell could see, was smooth in places and covered with a dusting of black hair in others. The tone of it was so luminous, he looked like he'd been set to canvas already. And though they had been joking about it Friday night, Pell knew that someday, somehow, he would commit this man's lean, taut body to oils.

They were both practically naked now, standing only a few feet apart from each other, and Pell thought he might go out of his mind if Malcolm didn't make a move soon.

For a moment, the man merely stared at him. No, that's not right. Malcolm's eyes devoured him, every inch of his body until Pell felt consumed.

Malcolm's advance was slow. When he finally wrapped an arm around Pell's hips and pulled him in close, he used one hand to cradle Pell's neck and the other to cup the curve of his ass.

"Fuck, Pellam," Malcolm exhaled, his voice a low rumble against Pell's cheek. "You are so goddamned beautiful."

Pell grabbed Malcolm's head and smashed their mouths together. He was frantic, so hungry he thought he might combust. He stretched to press his body flush against Malcolm's and was rewarded with the feel of the man's rigid erection grinding against his own.

Pell turned his head to gulp some much-needed air. "Fuck, you're so hard."

"It's what you do to me." Malcolm backed Pell into the

leather couch.

Pell stretched along the length of it and stretched his arms up in invitation.

"I couldn't stop thinking about you either," he whispered.

"God, baby. You have no idea." Malcolm knelt between Pell's knees, his eyes dropping to the outline of Pell's throbbing cock. He was leaking already, and Malcolm used his thumb to tease the wet spot on the front of Pell's boxer-briefs. "I've wanted to touch you since the first moment I saw you."

Malcolm lowered himself to suck at the ridge of Pell's prick through the cotton of his underwear.

Pell couldn't help it. He bucked underneath him, his breath caught in his lungs while Malcolm's soft chuckles floated in the air.

"I hope this room is soundproof." Pell didn't think he could keep quiet, not with this man. This floor was empty, but the building had twenty-three more.

"It is," Malcolm mumbled into the flesh of Pell's belly. He worried the waistband of Pell's briefs over the sensitive tip of his dick. "Scream all you want."

"You've thought of everything. Oh! That's . . ." Pell glanced up to watch Malcolm swipe his tongue, again and again, over Pell's weeping crown.

"It's what, Pellam?" Malcolm's smile was cocky, but his lips were kiss-swollen, his eyes were wild, and he was the most beautiful thing Pell had ever seen. He wanted to commit the sight to memory so he could paint it later, but Pell's thoughts scattered as undiluted pleasure poured over him.

"Ah, fuck," Pell gasped. "So good."

"How about this?" Malcolm slid his hands beneath Pell's ass and, in one swift motion, swallowed him down to the back of his throat.

"Shit!" Pell tensed, cupping his hand over Malcolm's soft waves as he worked Pell over relentlessly. Pell didn't want it to end so soon, but it was out of his hands. His back arched off the sofa, and he came after only a few strokes from Malcolm's talented lips and tongue.

♪

Mal couldn't get to his wallet fast enough. After sheathing his demanding dick in a condom, he pulled Pellam's hips forward and ripped open the packet of lube. His hunger screamed at him to take the man with one long thrust, but his common sense prevailed.

After such an intense orgasm, Pellam would be sensitive and Mal wasn't an asshole.

He toyed with Pellam's entrance and watched as he floated down from his orgasmic high. It was a sight to behold.

Pellam was delightfully uninhibited, and his breathy sighs had threatened to undo Mal before they'd even begun. The blond opened his eyes and met Mal's, a small smile on his cupid's bow lips.

Mal stroked and teased his hole.

Sooner than he expected, Pellam's cock hardened.

Mal arched an eyebrow. "Impressive."

"Not usually," Pellam managed, his voice husky and sexy as fuck. "I guess that's what you do to me."

Mal kissed him. Couldn't get enough of kissing him. Didn't think he ever would. And the man's miles and miles of creamy skin were too much of a temptation to resist.

"Need you." Pellam lifted his knees to his sides and shook his head, as if ashamed of the admission. "I don't even know you, but-"

"You will." Mal locked his gaze with Pellam's, showing him the seed of his true desire. "Something tells me you'll probably come to know everything about me."

Mal lifted up to settle his hips between Pellam's parted thighs. Dragging his cockhead across Pellam's hole, he smeared the lube, making himself even more slick with it, and then positioned himself to enter. He pushed in slowly and watched Pellam's face for any sign of discomfort.

"I won't break," Pellam begged, rocking his hips.

But Malcolm was thick, and he didn't want to hurt him. He pulled out and then pushed in again, just as slowly but deeper this time.

Pellam spasmed around him.

Malcolm wasn't going to last long. "Fuck, you're so tight."

"I haven't-" Pellam inhaled a shaky breath. "It's been a while."

Malcolm went still, stunned by the confession.

"How long?" He asked softly, pushing a few strands of hair out of Pellam's eyes.

"Over a year." Pellam shrugged, and Mal's heart twisted with a feeling he couldn't name. "Dare I ask?"

"Three months."

Pellam's eyes widened. "Really? Why?"

It wasn't the ideal time for this conversation, but Mal didn't want to keep anything from this man. Everything about the moment told him they were at the beginning of something.

"I was with someone, my ex, for five years. We split up six months ago."

Pellam wrapped his legs around Mal's hips and cupped his face with his slender fingers. The tenderness Mal saw in the other man's eyes cracked any barrier he'd left up between them in two. He recognized the same surrender in Pellam's eyes. Then Pellam moved his hips, and all of Mal's focus went to one place.

"Make me come again." The corner of Pellam's mouth lifted.

Mal thrust deep and pulled out before circling and repeating the movement with steadily increasing speed.

Pellam yanked him down into a kiss that was feral. Needy. Soon they were rocking together, racing toward the finish line.

Pellam came first, his cock trapped between their bellies, and thank God because Mal couldn't hold on any longer. Sun flares burst to life behind his eyes as he dropped his head to Pellam's shoulder and emptied himself inside the condom, sending Mal hurtling into a new realm of possibilities.

They stayed locked together, unmoving and breathing heavily, for what seemed like an eternity before Mal gently pulled out and disposed of the condom.

He crawled back into Pellam's arms and drifted for long

moments on a cloud of bliss while Pellam ran gentle fingers up and down his spine. When he'd reclaimed a few of his brain cells, Mal lifted his head and looked down at Pellam. His brilliant, little artist.

Mal smiled to himself.

"What?" Pellam grinned as he drew circles on Mal's hips.

"I was thinking about the pastel from the exhibit."

Pellam frowned in thought, stilling his hands. "*Du Ma Vie?*"

"No, the one you were going to call *Cherish*."

"Ah." Pellam resumed his soothing touches. "*Toothpaste Kisses*."

Mal nodded. "That's the one."

"You liked it?"

"Very much, and I understand its meaning, now."

Pellam's eyes were suddenly sad. "Oh, I wish I had known, someone bought it."

Mal kissed his forehead and smoothed away the damp tendrils that clung there, taking a moment to savor Pellam's quiet beauty.

"I know," he said against Pellam's lips. "It was me."

Pellam laughed. "You are something else, Malcolm Zaha."

"I know."

Pellam pinched his side, and Mal retaliated. He hadn't laughed so much in years.

"I hope you have it lit properly," the blond said when they quieted down again.

"Why don't you come home with me and make sure that I do?"

Pellam's smile was radiant. "Only if you promise to sit for me."

To bring Pellam Lindt home with him? It was the easiest promise Mal had ever made.

ABOUT THE AUTHOR

Xio Axelrod is a *USA Today* best-selling author of contemporary romance, romantic fiction, and what she likes to call, strange, twisted tales.

Xio grew up in the music industry and began recording at a young age. When she isn't writing stories, she can be found in the studio, writing songs, or performing on international stages (under a different, no-so-secret name).

She lives in Philadelphia with one full-time husband and several part-time cats. She occasionally writes erotica under the name Xio Nin.

More info is available at: www.xioaxelrod.com

Wild Pitch

REBECCA SHEA

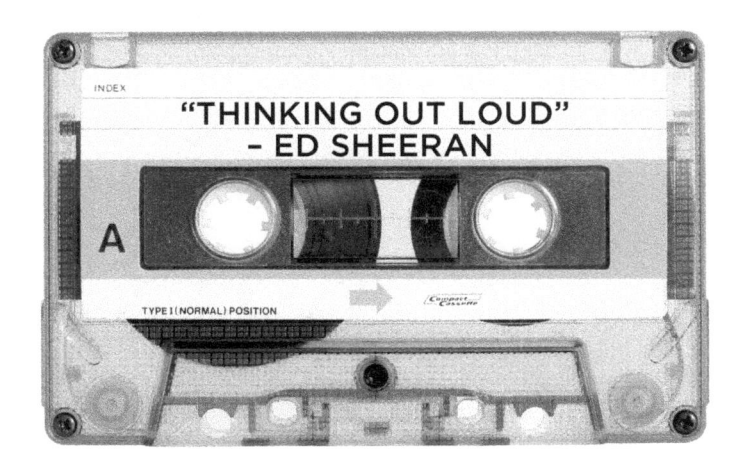

"THINKING OUT LOUD"
– ED SHEERAN

CHAPTER ONE

"Ladies and gentlemen, we have started our descent into Reno. Please make sure your seat backs and tray tables are in their full, upright, and locked position . . ."

I tune out the flight attendant and press my forehead against the small oval window, taking in the beauty of the snow-covered mountains in the not so far distance. It's been four years since I've visited my parents' cabin outside of Lake Tahoe, and I'm anxious to spend Christmas at my favorite place, with my favorite people.

My parents bought the cabin right before I graduated from high school. With my older brother Jensen off at college in Texas and myself heading to New York, my parents wanted a cabin to retreat to on the weekends, away from the hustle and bustle of Orange County, California. I've only been here a handful of times, but it quickly became the one place I feel most comfortable.

I use the term "cabin" loosely, as it's really a luxury home built in the middle of nowhere. *Literally.* The closest town is almost twenty miles from the house, and consists of a small market, a gas station, and the tiniest post office I've ever seen. Even though my father could have done satellite television and internet, he chose not to. He wanted to feel "off the grid" from technology, yet, he didn't spare any expense when it came to the actual cabin itself. What I used to think was a nuisance is now welcomed, as I relish the break from my phone, texts, and email.

I deplane, use the restroom, and collect my bags from baggage claim before heading over to the car rental counter. The older gentleman working looks up at me over his small, wire-framed eyeglasses, and smiles.

"Reservation for McNeil. Mia McNeil."

He punches the keyboard with both of his forefingers, slowly. "Young lady, may I please have your driver's license and credit card that you booked your reservation with?" I pull both cards from my wallet and slide them across the counter. "For ten dollars more, I can upgrade you to a four-wheel drive. You're going to need it with this weather." He glances over his shoulder at the large window behind him, and I can see the snow flurries swirling around.

"It wasn't snowing when we landed," I remark, and he nods, acknowledging me.

"Just started." His voice is hoarse, as if it's the first time he's spoken today, and he clears his throat. "News said we're supposed to get fourteen to eighteen inches in the next twenty-four hours—"

"I'll take the four-wheel drive," I say, cutting him off and glance at my watch. It's four o'clock. I need to stop by a grocery store and get to the cabin as quickly as possible if the snow is going to continue like this. Five minutes later, I'm dragging two giant suitcases across the airport and out the doors to a black Jeep Cherokee. I must look helpless because two nice men from the rental car company rush to help me lift my suitcases into the back of the waiting Jeep.

I program the address to my parents' cabin into the GPS, plug in my phone to charge, sync the Bluetooth, and carefully edge out of the airport and onto the road that is now accumulating the falling snow. It takes me nearly forty-five minutes to get twenty miles, but I finally find a grocery store on my way out of town.

I purchase more than I probably need, but I know my parents have nothing at the cabin. Hell, they don't even know I'm in town yet. I wasn't expected to arrive for almost another week, but I changed my mind—and my plane ticket—last-minute, to spend some alone time relaxing before the craziness of the holidays begins. I have plans to sleep in, read an endless number of books, and soak for hours in the outdoor hot tub under the stars. In between all that, I intend to do some yoga, bake, snowshoe, and simply enjoy the peace and solitude that being in the middle of the woods brings.

Since the weather is supposed to turn worse, I decide to shoot my mom a text, letting her know of my change in plans, and that I'm headed to the cabin earlier than they were expecting. With a car packed full of groceries and suitcases, I head toward the cabin.

The drive takes much longer than anticipated, not including

my pit stop at the store. The sun has now set, and the quiet, rural roads are getting progressively worse as the snow falls harder. With the car in four-wheel drive, and driving no faster than twenty miles per hour, it takes me an hour before I finally spot the wooden sign that reads, "McNeil," and I turn onto the secluded drive that leads to my parents' cabin.

"One more mile," I mutter under my breath as I take the narrow, winding drive that is already covered in close to six inches of snow. As I round the last turn, the large house comes into view and the headlights illuminate its sprawling expanse. I forgot just how beautiful this place is.

I pull up to the garage, jump out, and quickly punch in the code to open the garage. The large door doesn't move.

"Shit," I mumble, then remember the side service door where my dad has a key hidden. I move quickly, the wind and snow whipping against me. I locate the key and open the door, rushing into the cold garage. It's dark and empty, and I move my hands around in front of me, searching for the pull that will unlatch the garage door so I can open it. Finding the rope, I give it a firm yank and hear the latch release. With a little effort, I'm able to lift the garage door and pull the Jeep into the garage, killing the engine.

I finally allow myself to take a deep breath now that I've safely arrived and am off the treacherous mountain roads. I quickly unload the car, dropping suitcases and grocery bags just inside the door of the dark house. I'll sort everything once I get inside. Right now, I just want to get the car unloaded and close the garage door before the snow starts blowing all over the place.

I remember the house is run on a combination of solar power for electricity and propane for heating. I pray my parents already had propane delivered as I turn on the heater and wait for it to start. The temperature inside the house reads a very chilly fifty-five degrees on the thermostat, and I rub my hands together quickly, to keep my fingers warm and from going numb.

With no power, I get to work grabbing grocery bags and hauling them back to the garage to unload into the outside fridge. With the garage as cold as it is, the food won't spoil in there until I can figure out how to get the power on in the house. With the help of the headlights from my rental car, I unload boxes of pasta and jars of sauce. Since I plan on doing a bunch of baking, I made sure to pick up some eggs, milk, and other supplies. In case the storm gets so bad I'm not able to make it out of the house for a while, I also stocked up on peanut butter, bread, and lunch meat, as well as a few cases of water. All those things, together with pizza rolls, veggies, bacon, and other snacks, and I should be set. I figure what I don't eat, Jensen will finish off when he arrives with my parents next weekend.

In the dark, with only the light from my worthless cell phone, I drag my suitcases to the bedroom I claimed as mine years ago, shoving them in the corner and shivering at the frigid temperature of the room. The space is exactly as I remember it, with a queen-size bed, fireplace, and a private bathroom, making it the best of the spare bedrooms. The other room has twin beds, where Jensen and his friends always stayed.

Anxiety settles in my belly when I realize I don't know where the solar power box is, and that without power, the heater won't start, leaving me with no lights or heat.

"Think, Mia," I talk to myself as I debate my next move. Stay—and tough out the cold tonight—or get back in the Jeep, brave the storm, and search for a motel in the middle of nowhere.

Then I remember the woodpile. Every spring, my dad would have wood delivered to get us through the summer bonfires, as well as the winter, with the two fireplaces in the cabin. Mom always used to poke fun at him, saying he'd bought enough to kill a forest, but every last piece of wood would be gone by the next spring.

I retrieve my snow boots from my luggage and pull on my gloves. Wrapping my scarf high up around my face, covering just below my eyes, I pull a flashlight from the hall closet. Without power, the outside floodlights won't work, leaving me only the flashlight to work with. Making my way through the main living room, I can already see the snow drift building up against the glass patio door. I'm going to have to work quickly if I plan on having any heat tonight. Flipping the deadbolt and the slide lock, I turn the handle and the heavy door swings open with a gust of brisk air.

Stepping out onto the wood patio, my boots sink nearly up to mid-calf in the snowdrift. Propping the flashlight on the deck railing, I make my way down the steps and across the backyard to the covered structure that holds enough wood logs to almost make me cry with relief. I work fast, carrying four to five logs at a time across the snow-covered backyard and up the four steps of the patio. I leave a pile beside the door, knowing I'll move them inside next. I make a good eight or nine trips before I determine this last trip should be enough wood to get me through the night. If I have to get more in the morning, I'll deal with it then.

I take the patio steps slowly, dropping the last armful of wood on top of the pile as the wind picks up and the snow beats against my back. I know I have to work faster to transfer this pile into the house, but just as I'm about to open the door, I spot a tall, dark figure standing in the living room of the cabin.

CHAPTER TWO

"Holy fuck!" I stumble backward, tripping over the pile of wood at my feet. I land hard on my ass, breaking my fall with my arm. A shooting pain sears through my wrist, and I yelp in agony. Through the glass, I see the large figure ambling closer and my heart rate skyrockets. I do my best to get on my feet, but I slip and slide on the slick snow, almost falling again.

Tears sting my eyes and my heart pounds against the walls of my chest as the door opens. I sense the towering figure getting closer and know I should grab a piece of wood to use as a weapon, but my feet are locked in place, fear incapacitating me. Then, a deep, familiar voice paralyzes me and my heart leaps.

"Mia! Is that you?"

Even though his voice is deeper now—more like a man, and *so much less* of a boy—it's a voice I'd recognize anywhere. Mateo Rojas. Jensen's best friend, and the boy who grew up three houses down from us. The first boy I kissed, and the only boy I've loved. The one boy who broke my heart when he up and left to chase his dreams of playing professional baseball. I never saw him again after he left, sealing our goodbye with a kiss I'd never forget. Four years later, I can still feel his mouth pressed to mine, his soft lips showing me what we were both too shy to say out loud.

Mateo was a baseball prodigy, drafted right out of high school. He played two years with a minor league team before being called up to play in the Majors almost three years ago. He's now one of the most popular and highest paid baseball players on the roster, and also one of the most eligible bachelors, according to *People* magazine.

I hold my throbbing wrist in the palm of my opposite hand and slowly face him. My cheeks fill with warmth at the sound of his voice saying my name, and I pull the scarf from my face, stuffing it under my chin. Our eyes meet and I catch my breath. With the light of the moon reflecting off the snow, I can't help but notice how different—more grown up—he looks, yet he's the same Mateo that still comes to me in my dreams. Gone are his soft, round cheeks, now hollowed out by high cheekbones and a muscular, chiseled jawline. His hazel eyes are still outlined by long, dark lashes, his signature dimple ever present when his lips twist into a smile that can still melt my heart.

"Mia." He says my name again, this time softer, more concerned, as he steps over the pile of wood and closer to me. "You scared me."

"Mateo." I mutter his name like I do so often when I think of him. "I think it's *you* that scared *me*," I whisper under my breath and wince when I try to move my wrist.

"Come inside." He wraps his hand around my uninjured arm, guiding me over the pile of wood. His large hand easily circles my upper arm, and he's gentle as he steers me into the house. Just inside the door, I kick off my boots, leaving my jacket on, and I sink into the corner of the large, plush couch.

Mateo stands over me, his eyes taking me in. I can see his breath in the air with each exhale. He sits down on the couch next to me, the side of his body pressed to mine. Just like he would do when we were kids. Mateo would squeeze in between Jenson and me, but he always had to be touching me. It was innocent, but I always wanted it to be so much more.

"Jensen said no one would be here. So, you can imagine my surprise when I walked in and saw you on the patio."

"No one knows I'm here," I admit, sounding guilty, and hiss when I try to move my wrist. "I tried texting my mom, but the text wouldn't go through."

"No shit," he answers with a muffled laugh. "Here." He pulls a large blanket from a basket my mom keeps at the other end of the couch and covers me with it.

"God, it's good to see you." Those words fall on a whispered breath, causing mine to hitch. He places his warm hand over mine, giving it a little squeeze. "We have so much to catch up on, but let me get this wood inside and get a fire started. It's freezing in here. Then, I want to have a look at your wrist."

We do have a lot to talk about. Like why he left without saying goodbye. Why he hasn't reached out in the four years since he's been gone. And did he feel what I felt that night he kissed me, the night before he left? My heart rate picks up, and I simultaneously feel a little nauseous.

Mateo moves quickly, bringing in the wood I had gathered on the porch. He starts a fire with ease before turning his attention back to me.

"How is it?" He nods at my wrist while rubbing his hands together to create warmth. The room is freezing, and I'm afraid the small fire isn't going to make a dent in this cold. The room is too large for a fire to adequately warm it.

"Fine, just a little sore." I rotate my wrist in a circular motion slowly, showing him I can move it.

"Probably just a little sprain, let me see it." He throws himself down onto the couch next to me and carefully takes my wrist in his hand. His long fingers brush against my cold skin as he gently pushes and rolls it, looking at me for any sign of pain. "Does this hurt?"

I shake my head no in response, and continue watching him examine me. Everything he does is methodical and with precision.

"What about this?" He turns it the opposite way.

"No," I answer him quietly. "I don't think it's a sprain. Probably just a little bruised. I'll be okay." I shift on the couch, pulling the blanket up a little higher as I suddenly feel just how cold the house really is.

"The fire isn't putting out much heat, is it?" he asks, pushing himself up and grabbing another couple of logs.

"This fireplace won't," I tell him. "This room is too big. The fireplace in my bedroom can keep it pretty warm, but that's because the room is small."

He squats down in front of the fire, pulling the screen away and tossing three more big logs on the already burning wood. "Well, it's a good thing there's a heater in this house—"

"It doesn't work," I cut him off.

He turns his head to look at me, his face twisted in confusion. "What do you mean, it doesn't work?"

"It doesn't work without power. I can't get the power on. Remember, my dad has this entire place on solar. I assumed everything would just work, but he must have the power off. I'm sure there's a switch somewhere, but I don't know where."

"Shit," Mateo hisses as he comes back over to me. "Do you know if the solar box is outside?" I raise my shoulders in a shrug. "You're still useless," he says with a small laugh, nudging my shoulder playfully with his.

He used to joke that I was useless as a kid. I'd sit for hours watching him and Jensen play, not participating—just studying every move of his. I was a fly on the wall, but I always wanted to be there, and Mateo always made sure I was included, even when I didn't join in their shenanigans.

Even now, a playful touch sends warmth spreading through my body. Mateo has always had that effect on me.

"What are we going to do?" I ask him, concern beginning to grow in the pit of my belly. He turns to look out the glass patio doors at the heavy snow that continues to fall.

"I'm going to go get more wood. You said there's a fireplace in your room, right?"

I nod and answer him. "Yeah."

"Okay, while I'm getting wood, take the flashlight and collect some extra blankets, and go to your room. I'm going to try and get enough wood in here to get us through the night, so we don't freeze to death. I'll get more wood tomorrow and hopefully find that power box."

I carefully get up and begin collecting blankets, tossing them on the bed in my room. Does this mean he's staying in my room with me tonight? My stomach does a little flip at the thought of sharing my bed with Mateo. Isn't this what I've always wanted? Except, this is forced, a means of survival. This isn't romantic. Hell, we haven't seen each other in nearly four years.

I layer more blankets on top of the bed and collect a few pieces of wood from the living room, carrying the logs to my bedroom. I stack five logs in the fireplace and use some paper to get the fire started. I baby my sore wrist, but I'm thankful I can still move it. The flames are slow to get going, crackling against the cold air. Once the wood finally catches, the room glows in the amber light.

"Here," Mateo says, shouldering his way through the door, his arms full of more wood. I jump up and reach for the logs, stacking them in a pile on the small log holder next to the stone fireplace.

"There's too much wood for that," Mateo says, nodding at the metal holder. "Start stacking them on the floor. Once we get power, I'll help you clean up any mess they make."

I start a new pile along the floorboard, and Mateo disappears, returning at least five more times, until we have a giant stack of wood in the room. "That should get us through the night," he says, dropping the last bunch of wood on top of the pile and then shrugging out of his jacket. Even in the cold room, sweat beads along his hairline and on his forehead.

He looks around the room before suddenly holding up a finger. "I'll be right back. Forgot one more thing." A few minutes later, I hear him shuffling around in the kitchen, drawers opening and closing, before he reappears, his arms full of something else this time.

"Couldn't spend the night locked in a room without some necessities." His arms are overflowing with a bottle of wine and two glasses, some bottles of water, crackers, and a package of pre-sliced gourmet cheese slices.

I reach for the large glasses, taking them from him, and carefully set them down. He manages to set everything else on the small wardrobe while I close the bedroom door, hoping to contain what little heat the fire is putting out in the room.

My heart thunders in my chest when I think of us spending the night together in this room. My mind takes me back to the million sleepovers we had as little kids, innocent and pure. Laughing and making fun of each other, and staying up way too late.

Shoving that memory aside, I move away from the door and

stand in front of the fire, a blanket draped over my shoulders, as Mateo opens the bottle of wine. I can see the muscles of his arms flex under his thin t-shirt as he twists the wine opener.

With a loud *pop*, Mateo uncorks the bottle and fills the two glasses nearly half full of wine before turning to me, his hand outstretched with a glass. His beautiful eyes find mine and butterflies dance around my stomach.

"So, where should we start?" he asks, as I take the glass of white wine. His lips pull into a full smile and he winks at me. "We have a lot to talk about, don't we, babe?"

CHAPTER THREE

Babe?

Did he just call me babe? After kissing me, confiding in me, and then disappearing four years ago, never to be heard from again, he has the audacity to call me *babe*?

I roll my eyes at him. "Don't *babe* me, Mateo." Forcing a hearty chug of the crisp white wine down my throat, I revel in the burn from the alcohol as it pools in my belly. I'm going to need a lot of wine to get through this conversation.

He releases a long sigh. "Mia." My name falls off his tongue with a low growl. "Sit down."

He drops down to the floor in front of the fireplace. Pulling a blanket onto his lap, he pats the plush carpet next to him. I slowly fall into place beside him, and he drapes half of his blanket over my legs. Our shoulders brush against each other as we both face the fire, the warmth finally hitting me.

Mateo leans forward, and with his long arms, pulls another two logs off the pile, tossing them into the fireplace. I watch the flames crawl around the cold log, doing its best to penetrate the bark and ignite the large pieces of wood.

I keep my eyes fixed on the flames dancing inside the brick fireplace, but I can feel Mateo's gaze on me. I always could. He can bore holes into my head with the weight and power of his stare. He nudges me gently with his shoulder. "Talk to me, Mia."

"About what?" I don't mean for those words to come out as short and bitter as they do, but he takes notice, and I feel him sit up a little straighter.

"You're mad at me." It's not a question.

I clear my throat and take a deep breath, finally looking at him. "You disappeared, Mateo. You just left and I never heard from you again. We were . . . we were . . ." I pause, swallowing down the growing lump in my throat, a flood of anger and hurt I buried so long ago making its presence known. We were more than just friends. We had a bond that was indescribable.

Mateo's eyes hold mine, and I will myself to blink back the tears I feel forming behind my eyes.

"I had to," he whispers.

"Why?" I snap at him.

"It's complicated, Mia."

I choke out, "You were my best friend—"

"And you were . . ." He pauses. "And you *are* mine. After all these years, you're still my best friend." His eyes hold the same sadness mine do.

"A best friend doesn't abandon their friend, Teo."

Teo. That's a name I haven't called him in years. I was the only person allowed to call him that. He huffs out a small laugh at the nickname.

"Mia—"

"Let me finish," I snap at him, but he cuts me off with his lips. Warm, soft lips take mine, just as I remember and longed for all these years. I try to pull back, but he moves with me, anticipating my retreat. Tangled in the blanket, he gently pushes me down, my back meeting the soft carpet.

"That's why," he mumbles against my lips before continuing. I can feel his heart beating against my chest and warmth pools between my legs. He slows, finally pulling his lips from mine. "You felt that, right? The feeling that happens when I touch you?"

I swallow hard and nod.

"I felt it too, Mia. I felt it before I ever kissed you. Back when we were kids." He pushes himself up and helps me back into a sitting position. "The night we kissed was the best night of my life, but I knew I had to leave. We both had dreams, Mia. I knew you'd abandon yours for mine, and I would have abandoned mine for yours. We needed to grow up. We needed to live our dreams without sacrificing them for one another."

There's no hiding the tears anymore. They pool in my eyes and a single tear falls, rolling down my cheek as he continues. "I needed you to go to New York City, and I needed to go to San Francisco."

I don't know what comes over me, but I reach out and place my palm to his cheek. I need to touch him as he shares his heart. He cradles his head in my hand and I choke back a sob.

"I needed you," I manage to get out, and he shakes his head slowly in disagreement.

"You needed to grow into the woman you are now, without me. I knew we'd find our way back to each other, Mia. I always believed it here." He places his hand over his heart. "And look at you." He pauses. "I could not have imagined you'd be as beautiful as you are."

My heart physically aches as I think of all the birthdays and holidays we've missed. All the missed goodnight texts, or the simple check-ins that friends do with each other. But he's right. There's something different about us now. Something more mature, more honest and real.

"Tell me this." He pulls my hand from his face and places it between both of his. "If you and I had tried to make a long-distance relationship work, we would have failed miserably. You know it's true, right, Mia? You were in design school, and I was working my ass off in the Minors. Do you really think we could have made it work? Through all of your classes and my traveling, there would have been little time left for us."

His eyes were honest.

"Your dream was always New York, and I wasn't going to take that away from you. And my dream was the Majors. If I knew you were hurting, I would have packed up and moved to New York City to be with you, and vice versa. One of us would have sacrificed their dream for the other."

He looks at me and holds my face with both of his hands now. "Would there have been miscommunications and hurt that we couldn't fix because we were twenty-nine hundred miles apart?" His eyes search mine for answers, ones I'm unable to vocalize. "The answer is yes. I *had* to create this distance for us. So we could grow into each other and not away from each other."

My heart pounds in my chest. *Grow into each other and not away from each other.* I've never heard such beautiful words that hurt so much at the same time.

"Did you get the emails I sent you?" I choke out.

His jaw clenches and he nods. "I did."

Another tear falls from the corner of my eye. "You never responded."

He shakes his head slowly before shamefully dropping it. "I'm sorry, Mia."

I poured my heart and soul into those emails. I told him how much I cared for him and how much I missed him, only to have him never respond.

I swat at my cheek, wiping the tears. I must look like an idiot, crying over the past. Except Mateo was so much more to me than just my past. From the very depths of my soul, I've loved Mateo, starting the day I met him, and I know I'll love him until the day I die.

"Please don't cry." His voice is soft and comforting, and his large hand cups my cheek. I shake off his touch and sit up straight, doing my best to swallow down my emotions.

His voice is caring yet firm. "I'm here now, and I'm never letting you go again."

CHAPTER FOUR

I'm never letting you go again. His words play on repeat, over and over through my brain. What does that even mean? I still live in New York and he's still in California. We're literally an entire country apart.

"Mateo—"

"Shhh . . ." He presses a finger to my lips before moving it slowly across my cheek. The fire crackles and the room begins to warm, or maybe it's the effect of Mateo's touch. I can see the flicker of the flames in Mateo's deep, hazel eyes as he hovers over me and my pulse quickens.

"What are we doing?" I ask, as he leans down and brushes his nose against mine, his lips barely grazing the side of my mouth, teasing me.

"Making up for lost time." Then his lips crash against mine and the weight of his body settles on me. I can feel his erection through his jeans, long and hard, pressed against my stomach.

I pinch my eyes closed and inhale sharply as he rocks gently against me—allowing me to feel him. Slowly and methodically, he moves, my legs falling farther apart with each unhurried movement he makes. Suddenly, Mateo pushes himself up and yanks the blanket out from between us. Shrugging off his jacket, his eyes never leave mine. He's wearing a navy-blue t-shirt and fitted blue jeans. His jeans are just tight enough I can see the outline of his muscular thighs and his erection, and he smiles deviously when he catches me looking.

Leaning down, he tugs each of my boots off while I pull my arms out of my parka, tossing it aside. The room is still cold, but my body is on fire. The weight of Mateo's gaze causes a shiver to roll through me.

Lowering himself, he sidles up next to me then pulls the blanket over us and tucks my head under his chin. His long arm wraps around my waist and he pulls me even closer to him. So close, I can feel his heartbeat and his warm breath against the top of my head.

We lie, watching the fire, all wrapped up in each other. Content and quiet, comforted in each other's arms. The silence should be uncomfortable but it's not. It never was with us. Mateo and I could read each other's mood and emotions with a simple glance.

His fingers make small circles though my shirt onto my stomach, and the soft pattern of his breaths lull me to sleep, in the arms of the boy I thought I'd never see again. Somewhere in this moment, all the years of hurt I've been carrying around, disappear.

♪

I'm not sure what time it is, but the sound of Mateo piling more wood onto the fire wakes me. The room is now comfortable. Not hot, and not cold, but having been wrapped in Mateo's arms under the blanket actually has me feeling warm.

"Didn't mean to wake you," he says, his voice rough.

"You didn't." I wiggle on the floor as I stretch my arms above my head, and a little groan escapes me.

"This isn't very comfortable, is it?" He also stretches before standing up. "Let's move to the bed and get off the floor."

He pulls back the comforter and top sheet on the bed as I push myself up, wobbling on my tired legs.

"How's the wrist?" he asks when he sees me favor it, having accidentally used it to steady myself against the wall.

"It's sore, but not terrible. Hopefully, it won't even bother me tomorrow."

"Good." He smiles at me, his eyes heavy and tired. "Let's get you in bed."

I nod toward the attached bathroom. "I'm going to change first." I gesture toward my jeans that aren't at all comfortable to sleep in, and I'm dying to get this bra off. Sleeping in an underwire is my version of hell.

Mateo grabs my suitcase from the corner and lays it across a chair my mom must have added to my room because I don't remember it being here before. I pull out an oversized t-shirt, along with my toiletry case. Using the flashlight from my phone to illuminate the bathroom, I quickly change. The space isn't warm, and goose bumps prick my skin. I turn on the sink to let the water run for a minute before I wet my toothbrush. I want any old water or dirt in the pipe to clear.

The water is frigid. So cold, my teeth actually chatter when I run my hand through the slow but steady stream.

I brush my teeth quickly and rinse my mouth before hurrying back to the bedroom, damn near diving into the bed and under the covers. Mateo has already taken his side of the bed and pulled the comforter over him, up to his mid-chest. Mid-*bare*-chest, I should add. The tan skin of his shoulders peeks out from the top of the comforter, and my eyes take in the defined muscles that travel from his chest, over his shoulders, and I'm sure onto his back.

My stomach flips when he reaches for me under the covers and pulls me to him, much like he did when we were on the floor. Only this time, I face him. Our faces are mere inches apart, our noses almost touching. His warm breath dances across my face, and his full lips are so close, I'd only have to tilt my head to feel them on mine again.

"I'm glad you're here," he says quietly. "I'm glad we get some time alone before everyone else gets here."

"*If* they get here," I remark, hearing the wind blow wildly outside. I can't even imagine what it looks like or how much snow has accumulated. He chuckles. "But I'm glad we get this time too," I answer him.

His hand rests on my hip where he wiggled it underneath my t-shirt, his fingers skimming the outline of my panties. The gentle movement causes a heat to rush through me, pooling between my legs.

How I've dreamt of his fingers touching me, stroking me, plunging inside me. I've longed for his touch all these years.

His hand slides to my lower back and he pulls me closer. Chest to chest, hips to hips. I gasp when I feel him, *all* of him, naked and pressed against me. His bare leg nudges its way between mine, and his firm erection is pressed against my stomach, only my thin t-shirt between us. My nipples are hard little peaks rubbing against his chest and with every movement, a jolt shoots down from them to my core. I moan as his leg moves higher, brushing against my center.

He can feel my heat, my want, and his eyes grow darker when he sees my need. A need matching his own.

"I won't do anything you don't want to do, Mia, but I'm not going to lie. It's fucking hard laying here next to you and not being inside you."

I swallow thickly at his admission and close my eyes.

"I've always wanted you." He leans in, pressing a kiss to the side of my mouth. "Your body." He runs his hand up from my back, over the side of my chest, and to my breast where he cups it, giving my sensitive nipple a little pinch. "Your mouth." He drags his lips over mine and gently sucks on my lower lip. "Your heart." He gently moves his warm hand from my breast to my chest, where he rests it against my wildly beating heart. "All of you."

And that's when I lose all self-control.

"Touch me," I barely muster, as I pull him on top of me. I roll to my back and Mateo hovers above me, caging me with his arms.

My hips fall open and he rests himself between my legs, my wet panties pressed against his thick and throbbing bare cock.

"You're so wet, Mia," he remarks, pushing himself into a sitting position. His fingers tug at the hem of my t-shirt, and he pushes it up my chest and over my head before tossing it to the floor. "And we won't need these either." He pulls at the black lace panties I have on. "Although, black lace is my favorite." He wads the lacy material into a ball and throws it to the floor, where my t-shirt sits, discarded in a pile on the plush carpet.

His strong hands grip my thighs and he leans in, pressing a kiss to the inside of each one. His soft lips lightly pepper kisses up to my center, where he slides his tongue over my bare slit. He looks up at me with a devilish smile on his lips before lowering again and pulling my clit between his lips.

"Mmmm," he rumbles, his warm tongue circling my clit. Mateo draws himself back, sitting on his knees. His eyes are dark and needy, and I writhe underneath him, desperate for him, his touch. He lowers himself between my legs, our warm skin touching. His chest is dusted with a small amount of dark hair, just enough to make him a man, and no longer the boy with the smooth chest I fell in love with as a child.

My fingers trace the muscles of his shoulders down to his chest and over his hips, finally coming to a rest on the hard muscles of his ass. His tongue laps at my nipple, gently sucking and biting, as his hands slide underneath me, resting under my own ass. He lifts me, tilting my hips, where's he aligned himself at my center.

"I'm clean," he says, between sucks. "But I have a condom if you want me to wear one."

My head rolls from side-to-side. "I'm clean too, and on the pill." I can't imagine not feeling him bare. He's the one man I've saved that for. No one else has been allowed to touch me without protection.

He pauses, pressing the tip of his nose to mine. His hazel eyes hold mine as he drags his hard cock through my wetness, positioning himself again at my entrance.

"Look at me," he says. "Don't close your eyes." I groan as his head pushes through my folds. "I've always wanted to know what your face would look like when I was inside you."

My fingers dig into the flesh of his hard ass as he slowly pushes into me, our bodies joining for the first time. My entire body jolts as he enters me, long, firm, and wide. I gasp at how large he is, and my body finally relaxes as he fills me.

"God, Mia!" he groans as he begins to move. One long, slow thrust after another. Skin-to-skin. He pulls completely out, and fills me again. Every movement deliberate and methodical. His pubic bone presses against my clit and my entire body tingles as he works me over.

"So tight," he mumbles against my lips, between ragged breaths. "So warm." His movements quicken, and I can feel him grow harder inside me. "Come for me, Mia." He grinds into me, harder and faster. My entire body shudders and my back arches off the bed as I cry out his name.

"That's my girl," he grunts. With three more heady thrusts, he stiffens, spilling his release inside of me.

As he collapses on top of me, his lips press against the curve of my neck, and I breathe in the clean scent of his warm skin. Our breaths are shallow as our bodies shake and slowly come down from the high. He stays seated inside me, and I can feel him soften. I want him to stay like this, but he finally pulls himself from me, and I can feel his warm release slide out of me.

"Let me clean you up." He jumps up from the bed and walks to the bathroom, his back on full display, filled with rippling muscles.

When he returns with a wet washcloth, he winces. "It's going to be cold," he says, nudging my knees apart. I startle when the ice-cold cloth hits my most sensitive skin, and he gives me an apologetic look. "Sorry."

He gently cleans all of me, his touch delicate, careful, and comforting. When he's finished, Mateo tosses the washcloth into the bathroom and slides back into bed next to me, pulling me against him.

"Sleep, sweet girl," he whispers against my ear. "There's a lot more of that to come."

I can feel the smile tug at my lips as I close my eyes, sinking my back into his warm chest, and fall asleep in his arms.

CHAPTER FIVE

The smell of burning wood wakes me, and my body hums with a delicious soreness. "Good morning, beautiful." Mateo's voice is quiet and raspy, and the only sound I ever want to wake up to again.

"Morning." I open one of my eyes to find him sitting on the edge of the bed next to me. The fire still roars in the fireplace, a sign Mateo has been up tending to it. "What time is it?" I roll to my side, pulling the comforter up under my armpits. My bare shoulders are chilly, but Mateo runs his finger over one of them and I don't want him to stop.

He glances at his wrist. "Six-thirty, and it's still snowing," he remarks. "It's coming down really heavy. The drifts are insane but I was able to get us more firewood from outside, and I think I located the solar power box. I just have to get to it through the snow."

"Where is it?" I ask, and push myself up, resting my back against the fabric headboard.

"Side of the house"—he points—"but there are literally six-foot snow drifts."

"Shit," I mumble.

"But if I can get over there, we'll have heat, hot water, and power."

"Do you want me to help you?"

"No. It's freezing outside of this room. Stay in here while I go try to get to it. With the snow continuing to fall, the sooner I try, the better." He pushes himself up from the side of the bed and pulls on a hooded sweatshirt, then layers a large ski jacket over the top of it before sliding his large hands into some gloves. "Wait for me here." He winks at me and strolls out of the bedroom.

While Mateo is outside, I brush my teeth with ice-cold water and twist my hair into a messy bun on top of my head. I put on an oversized, cable-knit sweater and a pair of leggings, both of them comfortable and warm, and perfect for the chilly situation we're in right now.

Busying myself, I unpack my suitcase, then throw a couple

more logs into the flames to keep the fire blazing. I put on my parka and collect all the candles from throughout the house, setting about ten of them on my dresser to use tonight, if needed.

After making the bed, I finish tidying up the room just as I hear Mateo return inside. His cheeks and nose are bright pink against his tan skin and his jawline is showing the first signs of a five o'clock shadow.

"Any luck?"

He shakes his head and shrugs out of his jacket, hanging it on the door handle. "Looks like another night in here . . . not that I mind." His eyes find mine and he smirks. "I've been waiting a long time for last night, Mia."

He takes three short steps and rests his hands on my shoulders. My heart thrums wildly in my chest.

"Me too," I answer, almost shyly. I've never been timid, especially around Mateo, but he has me tongue-tied. His hands fall from my shoulders and slide down my arms to take my hands in his. I look up into his hazel eyes and my world stands still, déjà vu slicing through this moment.

"Remember the night before you left, when we danced in my bedroom?" I ask, and his lips twist into a giant smile at the memory.

"I'd never forget it." Mateo's right hand slides behind me, finding that spot on my lower back, like it did so many years ago.

I rest my forehead against his neck and breathe in his clean scent. Everything about this man is perfect. I clear my throat and stand up straighter before looking up into his eyes. "Every time I hear an Ed Sheeran song, I always think of you," I admit reluctantly.

He pulls me closer to him and begins to hum the tune of "Thinking Out Loud," causing goose bumps to prick my skin. This was the song we danced to when he first kissed me, which was also the same night he left me. I'll never forget the way Mateo felt in my arms that night. The way I could feel how much he wanted what I did, and how devastated I was when he pulled away and left. I swallow down those emotions and bring myself back to the present. To where we are now.

We dance slowly, wrapped in each other's arms, his warm body pressed to mine and, for a fraction of a second, I allow myself to feel scared and vulnerable again. Like I did the night he left me. Is this how we'll end a second time? The same way we did four years ago? Mateo's arms adjust, pulling me even closer to him, so tight against his chest, like he'll never let me go. An unspoken promise.

"Let's make this work, Mia," he whispers in my ear. "I don't want to live another day without you as mine." My heart thrums wildly in my chest as he speaks those words. "I love you. I've always loved you."

Those words, so honest and true, melt me. They are the words I've dreamt of him saying to me.

"I love you too, Teo. I always have."

"Then tell me we'll make this work, Mia. Give us a chance."

I wiggle out of his arms, taking a step back, simply to catch my breath. These last twenty-four hours have been a whirlwind of emotions for me and while this is what I've always wanted, it has definitely caught me off guard.

"Are you being serious?"

He nods. "Dead serious. We've accomplished what I felt we both needed to do on our own. Now let's conquer the world together."

My eyes well with tears and I nod excitedly. Mateo picks me up and twirls me around at the foot of the bed. With a *thud*, we land in the middle of my newly made bed.

"Don't know why you bothered making the bed." He winks at me and presses his lips to mine. "I'm not done with you."

Heat floods my body and my core throbs with want. Mateo slides off the bed, taking my leggings with him. I lift my bottom to help him and he tosses them to the floor. I shiver, and he notices. "Cold?"

I'm not sure if it's the cool air or the way he looks at me that sends another jolt through me.

"Come here." He smirks as he reaches out and pulls me up from the bed, then grabs a chenille blanket and lays it on the floor in front of the fire. "You won't be needing this either."

He reaches for the hem of my sweater and lifts it over my head. I stand naked, on full display for him. His eyes smolder as he takes me in.

"Fuck, Mia," he hisses. Reaching out, he cups my breast in his palm, rolling my nipple between his forefinger and thumb. "You're perfect."

Mateo leans down and pulls that nipple into his mouth, sucking it. He releases it with a *pop*, just as he reaches down and unbuttons his jeans.

I help him with his shirt and before I know it, he's lowering me to the floor on top of the blanket. The warm fire roars next to us and he settles between my legs. "I'll never get enough of you." He sucks on my other breast, and I feel his cock rub against my wet center. I lift my hips in invitation and Mateo growls as he's seated at my entrance.

"Last night was amazing, Mia, but today . . . today, I want to fuck you."

I gasp as he plunges into me. Hard and needy. My fingernails claw into the soft flesh of his back, and I hitch my legs up and over his ass. He's deep. So fucking deep. He stretches me with each thrust, almost to the point of pain . . . that pleasure-filled pain that has me begging him for more.

"Harder," I bite out and arch my back.

He pulls out of me completely before sinking back in and doing it all over again. "You like it rough, Mia?"

I can't find it within myself to use my words, so I show him instead. I press against his chest and roll him over in one swift movement. I ride him fast and hard, and he rests his face between my breasts with his arms wrapped around my back, holding me tightly in place. "Jesus fuck, Mia!" One of his hands slides down my back and grips my ass cheek.

I throw my head back and Mateo pulls my breast into his mouth again, clamping down on my nipple with his teeth. A surge of electricity shoots through me, right to my throbbing clit. A finger probes at the entrance to my ass, and he slides it in just as I feel myself lose control. I come, hard and fast, with a loud scream. Mateo bites down on my nipple just as another orgasm washes through me.

Now it's Mateo's turn to flip me. He pulls out and the next thing I know, he has me face down on the floor. With a hard yank, he lifts my ass into the air and enters me from behind. I'm so wet he slides right in. His thrusts are fast and with each one, he bottoms out inside me, hitting my cervix. It should be painful, but I'm still riding out my orgasm and feel another one coming. His right hand reaches around and pinches my clit as he slams into me. Every nerve in my body is on high-alert, and I've never felt such a combination of sensations all at once. Light pain, pleasure, tingles, and stinging. Every movement brings me closer to another orgasm.

I can feel Mateo harden with each plunge and with a low growl, he spills himself inside me. We both gasp, filling our lungs with air as he falls on top of me. Once our breathing slows to normal, he carefully pulls out and rolls me to my side.

"Every day, Mia. We're doing this every day. Not one day will go by that I won't fuck you like that."

I blush and press my lips to his chest.

"I'd like that," I whisper. He tangles his legs between mine and pulls another blanket off the end of the bed. He throws it over us and we lie in each other's arms, my head on his chest.

Two days ago, I was looking forward to spending a week alone in my parents' cabin. Now, I'm trapped with the man I fell in love with when he was just a boy, and I can't think of anywhere I'd rather be.

"I love you," he whispers, as he drags his fingers through my hair. His soft touch sends me into such a relaxed state that I feel my eyelids fall closed, and a sense of peace washes over me.

"I love you too, Teo." This is where I am supposed to be, with Mateo. Whether it's in New York or San Francisco, or trapped in a cabin with no electricity, this is where I belong. "Yes," I mumble, barely audible.

"Yes, what?" he responds.

"We're going to make this work."

I can feel his smile against the top of my head.

"Yes, we are."

ABOUT THE AUTHOR

Rebecca Shea is the *USA Today* Bestselling author of the Unbreakable series (Unbreakable, Undone, and Unforgiven), the Bound & Broken series (Broken by Lies and Bound by Lies) and two stand alone novels, Dare Me and Fault Lines. She has also co-written two books with her friend, A.L. Jackson, The Hollywood Chronicles: One Wild Night and One Wild Ride.

She lives in Phoenix, Arizona with her family. From the time Rebecca could read she has had a passion for books. Rebecca spends her days working full-time and her nights writing, bringing stories to life. Born and raised in Minnesota, Rebecca moved to Arizona in 1999 to escape the bitter winters.

When not working or writing, she can be found on the sidelines of her sons football games, or watching her daughter at ballet class. Rebecca is fueled by insane amounts of coffee, margaritas, Laffy Taffy (except the banana ones), and happily ever afters.

More info available at: www.rebeccasheaauthor.com

Your Everything

K. L. KREIG

"I JUST WANT TO BE YOUR EVERYTHING" – ANDY GIBB

Inscription

"And think not you can direct the course of love, for love, if it finds you worthy, directs your course."

~ Khalil Gibran

CHAPTER ONE

The hairs on the back of my neck prick as if I'm being watched.

Taking my attention from the Sterling Industries proposal I've spent the last hour fine-tuning, I lift my eyes to see indeed, I am. My employer, Richard DeSoto, leans against the doorframe of my office, arrogant as always.

Power-red Italian silk lies like blood pooled against the stark white of his starched dress shirt, easily costing a cool grand. The black, pinstriped suit is no less than seventy-five hundred. Berluti loafers add another two thousand, and the Cartier adorning his left wrist is more than most people's cars in this rinky-ass town.

He's dressed as if he's headed to a high-rise in downtown Manhattan instead of walking into a blue-collar environment where ripped jeans and plaid dominates.

His extravagance is unnecessary. It's intentional, this air of omnipotence he wears like a king's crown, though. It's meant to intimidate, control, to lord his greatness. And it has worked; I will give him that. It's what's made DeSoto Construction the unexpected empire it is today.

"Richard," I say with a slight nod. I'm irritated at the interruption and am unable to keep from hiding it.

The corner of his mouth ticks up. It's a tad sardonic. So Richard-like.

Command.

Control.

Patience.

He owns those.

Only, I do as well. I've spent my entire life learning from Richard DeSoto, so I could best him at his own game someday, because there is something of his I desperately want. Something he has too much influence over at the present.

As if he's reading my mind, Richard holds my gaze for a few long seconds, his pupils hardening. Stepping into my office, he strides over to the mini fridge and helps himself to a Mountain Dew. My last one.

He cracks the top. Takes a sip. Looks out the bay of windows behind me as if contemplating something of importance.

He's not.

I've seen this act a hundred times over. His theatrics are meant to make me uncomfortable.

It doesn't work. Not anymore.

I relax into my chair, rest my elbows on the arms, interlace my fingers, and wait for him to tell me what the hell he wants, my mind rolling with possibilities.

I didn't want to work for Richard DeSoto any more than most people in this town do. I could be anywhere. In fact, I was courted by four major East Coast firms, two starting out as a sales VP with a potential to make over half a million my first year out of grad school.

It was tempting, getting as far away as possible from the cow stink and small-town gossip that surround me here. A fat bank account was never my objective, though. I chose to come home to Dusty Falls, Iowa, population just south of six thousand belly buttons because of one reason and one reason alone. And it's not the paltry base salary Richard DeSoto is paying me. DeSoto Construction is a stepping-stone. A means to an end is all.

At last, he takes a seat. Setting the drink on my desk, he crosses one knee over the other, and hooks an elbow over the back of his chair, so his forearm dangles loosely. Classic power move. Unfazed, I lean forward, grabbing a coaster to slide under the metal that's already left a ring of condensation beading on the polished oak.

I could let us steep in the silence, waiting for him to show his hand first. I think about it for a split-second, but I have better things to do, mainly getting this proposal out the door. I may not want to work for Richard, but as long as I'm here, I'm going to prove my value. My sales closure rate is the best this company has seen in a cutthroat industry with thin margins and questionable morals. I'm proud to say that while I may butt up against that line on occasion, I pad Richard's bank account with honor and integrity.

"How can I help you this Monday morning, Richard?" I ask as an instant message from my assistant pops up on my computer screen.

"Sterling Industries is following up on the proposal due this morning. What should I tell them?"

Shit. This should have been out the door before 8:00 a.m., but I wanted to sweeten the pot, making our offer too compelling to turn down.

I'm getting ready to type a quick reply when one word from Richard's mouth scrambles that thought.

"Maverick."

My eyes snap to his.

Maverick.

Mavs.

My Small Fry.

The "something" of Richard DeSoto's I want.

And the reason I came back to Dusty Falls.

"What about her?" I ask, nonchalantly.

Her name alone makes my pulse jump, my dick twitch, but Richard is waiting for a reaction. I don't give him one. I keep every part of me relaxed, my face neutral. I finish that response to Alicia with slow, purposeful strokes on the keyboard, *"Within the hour,"* but all the while I think of her.

There is not another soul on Earth like Maverick's. No other woman has power as unique and salient. She is mouthy, spirited, and bullheaded. She frustrates me beyond belief. Makes me want to pull my hair out or put her over my knee with the crap she's pulled over the years. To this day, when I think of finding her in Robbie Reams' truck bed with his mouth clamped to her nipple and his hand shoved down her shorts, I go nearly feral. I'm not a violent man, but I wanted to kill him on the spot. Still do when I see him drive past me in that shitty, rusted Ford F150 he nearly stole Maverick's virginity in.

As angry as I was with her and that Reams shithead, though, I was angrier with myself. Letting her climb into my lap and kiss me that night was the final nail in my coffin. The way her lips moved in sync with mine, with finesse no seventeen-year-old should possess, only proved she was mine. The way her slim hips filled my palms, as her pelvis ground against mine was nearly my undoing. Heavenly perfection. And the taste of her? Nothing like it. I'd never wanted her more than I did in that moment.

But that wasn't our moment to have, so I stopped her before it went too far. It felt like a thousand shallow knife wounds, watching the passion she'd had seconds before slowly die, dulling those brilliant eyes of hers as I told her she was too young. Watching her walk away from me when I dropped her home was likely the hardest thing I've done to date in my life. The urge to jump from my car and pull her back into me was overpowering. I almost couldn't resist. I wanted to beg her to give us time. Wait for me.

But I also knew Mavs. She would have been relentless in her chase of me had I given her another opening. And it wouldn't have taken a lot for me to cave. With every year that passes, those five years that separate us become less meaningful. At the time, however, they were an impassable gorge I couldn't let us fall into.

"She's starting today," he replies, drawing my gaze from my inner thoughts back to him.

"Starting what today?"

I feign confusion, but I know exactly to what Richard is referring. I ran into Mavs at the mailbox cluster the day before last. She's matured so exquisitely over the past several years it was tough not to reach out and stroke the softness of her cheek, as she told me she'd accepted a job at an independent trucking company in Ames as a supply chain management analyst. Her father is richer than God Himself and a very connected man. With his influence, she could have any position at damn near any company she wanted, but she was adamant about making her own way. An admirable quality I love.

I admit I was disappointed she'd be moving eighty miles away so soon, but I quickly remembered she just graduated from college and needs time to find herself, and getting out of this town and out from under her father's thumb is the right step.

That's all part of the plan, anyway. The endgame. Hence why I'm currently sitting across from a man who would just as soon string me up than see me with his youngest. Richard has plans for his daughters, and my pairing with Maverick is not one of them, of that I'm damn sure.

"Starting her new job," he says casually, shifting so he can place his left leg over his right one now.

I don't understand why he's making a big production of telling me this. Is this a test of some sort? Knowing Richard, probably. Not knowing what else to say, I offer, "The first day on a brand-new job is always nerve-racking. She's bright." *She's brilliant.* "I'm sure she will do fine." *She'll blow their socks off.*

"I've no doubt." Fatherly pride beams from him.

I'm not a fan of Richard and Vivian's parenting style. Never have been. They ignored their girls' interests in favor of their own. What *they* wanted versus what Mavs or her sister, Jillian wanted. Being as obstinate as she is, Maverick rarely acquiesced, fighting them at every turn. She didn't win much, but she always gave a good fight. That Richard accepted Maverick's job choice was surprising.

"In fact, I think inside ten years she will be running this company far better than me."

"It's possible," I throw out, shrugging my shoulders. She could, though Mavs has no desire to work under her father's tutelage. It's a pipe dream on Richard's part to pass along his empire to her. "Uh, if there's nothing else, I need to get back to making you some money." My smile is tight as I point to the papers in front of me for effect.

Nodding sharply, he pushes himself to stand. He brushes his palms over the front of his trousers, smoothing out nonexistent wrinkles. "You remember fraternization is against company policy."

The fuck? What a strange conversation.

"Of course." I turn toward him fully now. I'd wager confusion is written clearly in the lines pinching my forehead.

"Violation could have . . . *unintended* consequences."

Unintended consequences? Sounds like a thinly veiled threat if I ever heard one. And one that's completely unnecessary. There's not a soul here I'd consider wetting my dick with. My only temptation is a hundred miles away.

"I'll keep that in mind, Richard."

"Good. We're aligned. I trust it won't be an issue working with her then."

"Who?"

"Maverick."

"Maverick?"

"Yes. Maverick." He punches each syllable of her name to ensure I've heard him correctly. Twisting his wrist, he glances down. "She should have been here by now. She's probably late to spite me." He mumbles the last part, though I hear it loud and clear.

My brain is working to dismantle the bomb he has dropped on my doorstep, following each wire he so intentionally exposed, when, as if this were all scripted, the timing perfectly planned, the bomb detonates, rocking the very foundation my restraint has been built on. And when the smoke clears, the "something" of Richard's I want emerges.

Maverick DeSoto. In the flesh.

And I guess the fact she's standing not ten feet away from me means her father didn't accept her decision after all. *What did you guilt her with this time, you bastard?* I want to bellow at Richard. If there's one thing that works wonders on Mavs, it's her father's guilt.

Anger bubbles inside my gut, the fury she should be following her own dreams, not someone else's ready to engulf me. Right now, though, it's dampened by waves of dreaded elation.

My Small Fry is here.

It's dangerous, this feeling rippling through me. It's a catastrophe, sure as a category five hurricane gathering force in the Atlantic, about to make landfall.

Maverick. My Achilles heel.

Our eyes lock.

My breath catches.

My God. She is so ethereal I am momentarily disoriented.

That brunette, messy hair of hers, loosely braided off to one side, is as unruly as ever, strands poking out everywhere. Long, thick, sable lashes offset orbs of jade so unique they are otherworldly. She dons no makeup besides a light pink sheen glossing her full lips, and she doesn't even need that. Innate beauty needs no window dressing.

But Maverick DeSoto is far more than a pretty face. She is wonder. She is dimension. She is a softly spoken prayer. She is grit and unassuming and witty and positively the most magical being I have ever known.

My body reacts instantly, almost violently. There's no time to think about it or stop it. It's instinctual. The quickening of my heart causes blood to pump in all the wrong places. I am immensely grateful my desk covers my lower half, or I've no doubt my balls would be twisted between Richard's bony fingers in short order.

I shift.

She smiles that smile of hers that renders intelligent men stupid. I am not immune.

Her gaze momentarily drops to my desk, the trajectory directly in line with my swollen dick. The upturn of her lips falters and she swallows hard, and we have a moment that is highly inappropriate for the company we are keeping.

God Almighty, help me.

How the hell will I deal with her being here every single day without deviating from my carefully laid plans? Without pushing her into the closest conference room, wrenching down those jeans of hers, and laying claim to the woman I've not been able to shake for years now?

I'm not. It's as simple as that.

Fuck.

I am in trouble.

Maverick watches me watch her, her father not yet aware of her presence or that we are about to go toe-to-toe in the fiercest battle of our lives. Richard will likely stop at nothing to keep us apart, but there isn't a thing he can do that will thwart the plans I have made for us. I will make my move and I *will* make her my wife, but only when the time is right. Until then, restraint and composure will be the name of the game.

Command.

Control.

Patience.

You own these, Shep. Remember that. You wield them at master levels. Use them to your advantage. To gain the upper hand. Bide your time. You've waited too long to fuck it up now.

For good measure, though, I toss up a prayer to the heavens, not because I don't believe in my own skill set, but because a man can use all the help he can get.

Satisfied her working at DSC won't throw me off track, I turn my attention to Richard, and ignore her sharp intake of breath when I say with a grin, "Appears your spite has decided to show up for work after all."

CHAPTER TWO

"Killian?"

"Mmm?" I mumble, head down.

Don't look up. Don't look up. Do. Not. *Look. Up.*

I've been pretending to be engulfed in my laptop ever since she walked into the room a few seconds ago. It's not to be rude. It's self-preservation. Every time I lay eyes on her, my craving for her grows tenfold.

These past two weeks have been insufferable. A walk straight through the bowels of hell would most accurately describe each and every second. It's left me weakened and on edge.

The iron will I thought I'd perfected has failed me miserably. My backup prayers clearly fell on deaf ears. My hand is tired, my cock is sore, and I genuinely don't know how I'll make it another day without doing something neither of us is ready for.

"Do I have a big zit on the tip my nose or something?" She says this with a half laugh that's sweet, threaded with a dash of spice. It's an irresistible combination.

"Wouldn't know," I croak. I keep my attention glued to my computer, trying not to breathe. Her perfume fills my lungs with each inhale. It's intoxicating, as if she's laced it with some sort of aphrodisiac. Not that she needs any help in that area.

To my dismay, it's just the two of us in this dimly lit conference room the size of a shoebox. Until today, I had succeeded at not being alone with Mavs. I arrive a couple of minutes late to every meeting I know she's attending and sit as far away from her as possible. I started parking in the main employee parking lot when I found out her father had given her the VIP parking spot next to mine. One day last week we were the final two in the building, and while I had at least another two hours of work to put in, I packed up and finished at home.

And yesterday, she asked me to lunch. I lied. Told her I had plans with the mayor—the big brother of an old high school buddy of mine—on a rare day when I was actually free. So, to keep up pretenses, I left the office and drove around for an hour and a half to clear my head and regain focus.

Didn't work. And I came back hungry, forgetting to eat.

"Killian?" she says again, this time with quite a bit more bite and insistence.

"Where is everyone else?" I snap impatiently.

There are a dozen people on this project, our biggest sales opportunity of the year so far, worth more than forty million dollars over a ten-year period, and yet here we sit, alone, the walls pushing us closer together with each passing minute. I can't take much more.

Why Maverick was assigned to my sales team as project manager I still do not know. No, I do. It's Karma. My penance for fantasizing about this woman for all these years.

"I didn't invite anyone else. It's only you and me."

"You . . . ?"

Fuck me. What did she just say?

The fluorescent light overhead flickers a time or two before burning faintly again. Perfect. Ignoring the hope we'll be plunged into complete darkness soon, I ask, "What do you *mean* you didn't invite anyone else?"

Now I do look up, positive I did not hear her correctly. A tongue-lashing sits at the ready, yet the second our gazes connect—no, crash—the second our gazes crash, it turns to ash, tasting of regret when I notice the shaky curl of her lips.

She's worried I'll be angry. I am. She is testing every ounce of control I foolishly thought I possessed.

"I, uh . . ." she stutters and trails off, quickly glancing at the door.

I follow, staring briefly at the slab of solid oak that's closed, separating us from the rest of the company. From my assistant. Her father. And my brother, Kael, who is right next door.

My pulse kick-starts. My thoughts race to places that are raw and rabid and forbidden in the workplace.

Not now. And definitely not here.

Taking a few extra seconds, I work for self-control. "Why?" I ask at last, my tenor a mixture of loose gravel and course sand. It sounds like an invitation for her to shed her clothes if ever I heard one. *Hell of a plan if you ask me.*

"Why, what?"

All I hear in her breathless response is, *"It's about damn time."*

I couldn't agree more, Small Fry.

Grabbing a pen, I flick it on and off for something to do with my hands, lest they end up unbuttoning the lavender cardigan she's fastened all the way to her throat. I wonder if she's wearing anything other than a bra beneath?

I picture how her perfectly proportioned breasts must look perched in white, lacy cups. Would the dark of her areolas peek through? Fuck. My mouth waters at the thought of my tongue tracing where fabric meets bare flesh, of sucking an aroused nipple through the material and the biting of her nails into my back, drawing blood.

The vibe in the room transforms, becoming noticeably charged.

She starts drawing tiny circles on the table with her index finger, eye contact not breaking with mine. Her posture softens. And the way a pink flush spreads up her neck, coloring her face as she moistens her lips, I'd say her thoughts traveled to the same place mine did.

I am insanely hard right now, and I swear to Christ if she sucks her lower lip between her teeth, I am done for. It's a nervous habit of hers that drives my thoughts to sordid places. I'm embarrassed at how many times I've imagined those teeth gently scraping the head of my cock as I dive to the back of her throat.

Concentrate, Shep. Stop thinking of her eyes locked to yours as you take her in the basest way possible.

I take in a breath, blow it out in five even counts, and pretend to relax. This is precisely why I have been avoiding her.

Command.

Control.

Patience.

Jesus, man, get a grip.

After I will my dick to deflate, I push myself away from the table and draw an ankle up atop the opposite knee. Though there are six chairs at the round table, she's placed only an empty one between us. I could reach out and touch her. How I want to, but I have got to regain the upper hand or the outcome could be dire.

"We have a lot of work to do, Mavs. We don't have time to waste with whatever games you're playing."

Fire.

Molten and scorching.

It's what's currently raining down on me from her narrowed eyes, burning my flesh in both the worst and best ways possible.

Better than the alternative, I suppose. Or is it? I'm beginning to wonder.

"I had questions about how the federal vendor vetting process varies from state ones, so I didn't miss an important step, and I didn't want to sound incompetent in front of everyone else. Since you have the most experience with both, I thought maybe you would be willing to help me understand." There is no longer an ounce of sugar in her even voice. It's a hundred and ten percent spice, particularly when she adds, "My mistake."

Chair legs scrape angrily against the floor when she stands and haphazardly gathers the papers she's spread out in front of her. Two fall on the floor. She bends down to scoop them up. They crumple when she stuffs them into the manila folder.

Yeah. I probably could have handled that better.

"Why didn't you say so?"

"I didn't know I needed to," she retorts hotly, slapping the crap out of that folder as if it were the one who wronged her. "You mentor *everyone* around here." Her eyes are liquid balls of flames. It's hypnotic. "Guess I'm the exception."

I want to mentor you, all right. But not *in the boardroom.*

Lips pursed together, she refuses to look my way as she attempts to skirt around me, which she has to do to exit.

I should let her stomp off, angry. That was my intent, after all. Only the self-preservation I've been hanging on to goes to hell in a handbasket when I get a whiff of scents elemental to Maverick. Before I know what I'm doing, my feet are planted and I'm blocking her path.

At six feet even, I'm not that tall, but I tower over her five-foot-four petite frame. It should give me a sense of dominion, this superior position I hold. It doesn't. She is the one with a power she is wholly unaware of, yet wields with native expertise.

Silence sits heavy. Her breaths come fast, hot fury needling the spot right in the middle of my chest with each ragged exhale. Those raven locks I want tangled between my fingers tickle the underside of my chin, ratcheting up my desire to bury my face in her neck, between her legs.

It's pure bliss, being this close to her, something I've denied myself for not just weeks, but years. I long to wrap my arms around her and sway as I sing the sweet lyrics of Andy Gibb's "I Just Want To Be Your Everything" softly in her ear, a favorite of hers. I want to undress her slowly and worship every curve of her body before making love to her for the first of countless times. I want romantic nights lying in the cool grass, locating each constellation in the night sky. I want arguments followed by make-up sex. I want everything I've told myself I shouldn't.

She tries to create distance by stepping back, but I gently grip her bicep, keeping her next to me. *No way, Small Fry. You're mine now.*

Command.

Control.

Patience.

All evaporate like dew on a sunlit morning when I hear the catch of breath in the back of her throat. Her chest expands rapidly, though it's no longer the hotness of anger driving the cadence. It's want.

"Move," she huffs. She doesn't mean it.

"No."

I edge a finger under her chin and tilt it up so she's forced to look me in the eyes, and when she does, the air thickens with electricity. It's potent, the sting of its voltage running on a continuous loop between us. This is the only place I have ever wanted to be, weightless within the atmosphere surrounding her.

I've felt this before, this irrefutable draw. Many times. But where I was able to shut it down when it tried to consume me, I'm helpless this time. We each feed it in equal parts now. It pulses and breathes, a living entity neither of us can control.

She blinks at me, desire the fuel lighting her up. The ache for her that's my constant companion builds to combustible proportions, and as a result, I do something rash.

"Meet me at Harbor Park tonight. Nine thirty."

"Harbor Park? But . . ." Her forehead crinkles in confusion. I resist the urge to smooth the flesh out.

And yes, I am an ass. Asking her to meet after dark implies I don't want to be seen with her . . . and I don't. I can't, but it's not because I'm ashamed to be with her. It's the only way. We cannot be found out. Not yet. There's too much at risk.

"You want to be mentored, right?"

My heart is pounding. *Talk. We're just going to talk.*

Riiight.

This is not the plan, Shep, the rational side of me chastises. *She needs time. Wings. Maturity. Worldliness beyond the confines of Dusty Falls and her father's shelter.* Yet the only logic I'm listening to is from the organ beating madly against my rib cage. The heart knows no rationality. Love follows no rules.

I drop her arm and take a half step back, breaking physical contact altogether before I put my mouth on hers. If that happens, I won't be able to stop. Not now. Not ever.

Her wrinkles deepen, now spreading down the sides of her button nose.

"But—"

"Maverick." Pinching the bridge of my nose between my thumb and index finger, I slam my eyelids shut and take a deep breath. My patience is about to snap in two. "Will you be there or not?" I ask, dropping my hand back to my side with a thud.

Say no.

Say yes.

She grips the folder close to her chest as if it's her armor, as if it will protect her from what we've both set into motion. I'm afraid it won't. It's too late for that. She gauges me hard, trying to read my intent.

It's entirely dishonorable, Small Fry. Believe that.

Her lips mash together into a straight line. I think perhaps she's going to walk out without responding when I hear a hushed "Yes" as she sidesteps me.

Elation and frustration war in conflict with each other. I'm about to grab her and shake her or kiss her, I haven't decided which, but the knob is in her hand and she has the door open before I can do either. And as my luck would have it, Kael is passing by at that exact moment.

Fantastic.

As if he can smell the pheromones pouring thick as morning fog from the room, he stops. His gaze jogs between the two of us, then over my shoulder, noting the empty room.

"Hi, Kael." Mavs tries for jovial, but her nervousness is evident as she bounces from one foot to another. He, on the other hand, doesn't even try for nice.

"Secret meeting?" His derision-laced accusation burns under my skin.

"No, of course not," Mavs replies, her short laugh. "Don't be ridiculous. We were discussing some deadlines on the I-65 resurfacing project."

"Uh huh." His jaw ticks, his teeth clearly clamped together. He doesn't take his eyes from Mavs now, trying to vet a lie. And Mavs is not a good liar. She could give Pinocchio a run for his money and win as evidenced by the telltale flush spreading like freshly painted watercolors across her cheeks.

Christ, Mavs.

"Hey, I was coming to find you," I tell Kael, shoving my hands deep in my pockets. Kael doesn't acknowledge me. He stays zeroed in on Mavs. A bead of sweat forms on her temple as if she's under a heat lamp.

"Zandeski made some changes to the indemnification clause that I think leave us too open-ended. I need your opinion."

I don't. The changes are fine and I've already approved their request, but I heard Alicia clear her throat and quickly realized we were drawing unwanted attention. Richard's office is directly across this small executive wing, his door open, and his scrutiny is the last thing I need piled atop Kael's suspicions. I'm already in shit so deep waders are pointless.

"Is that so?" Seconds tick off before Kael gradually shifts his attention my way. The tension is fork-and-knife thick.

"Do you have a few minutes now?" I ask.

I want to bark at Maverick to get the hell out of here while she has the chance, but that won't seem suspicious or anything.

"I suppose I could make time." He swings the empty coffee cup that dangles between his fingers back and forth.

"Appreciate your flexibility." I leave the sarcasm behind, though he didn't. It won't serve anyone well right now.

"I guess I'll see you guys later then."

I don't acknowledge Mavs. I pivot and walk back into the conference room, hoping Kael will follow. The way the door nearly slams shut is my indication he did. He stands at my back, unmoving, silent. Still seething, I imagine.

Before he says a word, I have the redlined contract up on my screen. "What do you think?"

I step out of the way, but Kael stays trained on me. Now I'm the one being inspected. And I don't like it, and unlike Maverick, I won't put up with Kael's backhanded bullshit.

Dragging out a chair, I take a seat. My legs fall open wide. "What?" I ask, crisply. Clasping my hands, I cock my head and wait for it.

"Cubs play the *Hitless Wonders* tonight."

Huh. Not what I was expecting.

"Sure do," I reply, not taking his bait. Kael's a die-hard Cubs fan, and he never lets me forget that my White Sox once carried that paltry label.

Nodding toward the laptop, I try to get us back on track, not interested in small talk or platitudes. I have hours of work ahead of me, and it will be difficult enough to concentrate knowing what tonight may bring.

"Thought maybe we could catch the game at Peppy's like the good ole days."

His invitation throws me. We haven't watched our rivals play in, I don't know how long. I miss it. I miss the bantering, the easy camaraderie we used to have. But those days are long gone, and I fear they can never be again.

"Can't tonight. Sorry."

"Oh?" Kael sits facing me, position matching mine, the contract all but forgotten. "Busy?"

He's fishing, and Kael's fishing skills are lacking, both literally and figuratively.

"Fuck yes." I snort. "Busiest sales season this company has seen in years. I'll be working until midnight." I should be, though that's not likely to happen.

"You're doing well."

I shrug. I'm doing all right, I suppose. I'd be doing better if I took Maverick and ran. This right here, his suspicion, the dissection of every word that comes out of my mouth, it has become commonplace between us. I know because I do the same.

"Look, I need to get back to it, so if you don't have time now, it's fine. I'll email you the language I'd like you to review."

"I thought it was urgent," Kael quips. His body language is a one-eighty from his lighthearted tone.

"I don't believe I said that. It was something I wanted to check off the list."

Kael's mouth angles down at the edges. "Okay, then. I'll watch for the email." He stands and stops, eyeing me. "You sure about tonight? Would be fun."

I hate this. The strain between us. The jealousy. The lies. Suspicions. The erosion of our brotherhood.

"Another time," I offer, wishing that were possible. Knowing it's not.

"I'll hold you to that." He has one foot in the hallway before he turns and adds with an honesty I've not heard from him in a while, "I miss you, brother."

All I can manage is a short nod. *I miss you, too*, I want to say. I don't, though. I let him walk out without a word because I know that while our relationship has suffered irreparable damage over the years, this is truly the beginning of the end for us.

We both want the same woman. We'd both give anything to have her, and though Kael is probably better suited for her, I am the one who will get her. There is a bit of ego in that statement, but it's also one hundred percent fact. There is and always has been something special between Mavs and me. Kael knows this, though he's never quite accepted it.

And from the second Maverick walked into DSC weeks ago, I'm not the only man whose rope has unraveled. Kael's has too. I see it in the way he watches her when she's not looking, or in the way he crowds her space so unintentionally she doesn't even notice. And I know he's reinstituted Thursday night darts, where he's no doubt pulling out all the stops. So, I either walk away and let my brother take her by default or I claim the one woman I genuinely believe was meant for me from the day she was born.

Some say no woman should come between brothers. Blood trumps all. Family first.

Those people have not met Maverick DeSoto.

CHAPTER THREE

Sitting in my car under the cover of darkness, I drum my thumbs against the steering wheel, waiting for the woman I've loved a lifetime to arrive. I have the game on in the background, though I couldn't tell you the score.

My mind spins with the wheels I set in motion earlier today. For a brief second, I thought about not showing up, not because I don't want Mavs but because what we're about to go through will challenge us both in ways we've not been challenged yet.

It will be impossible to start our lives here in Dusty Falls. Her father is not supportive of a romance between us, and he will make my life a living hell. He may well even fire me, citing the fraternization policy he not so subtly threw in my face a few weeks ago. Though he'd welcome me into the DeSoto family, it would be as Jillian's husband, not Maverick's.

But Richard isn't our only obstacle. Not by a long shot. At the end of the day, I don't give a shit about pissing off Richard DeSoto. That's bound to happen. Kael, on the other hand . . .

Seeing the woman he's coveted with me day in and day out will be agonizing. And I despise causing him that pain. I can't imagine how *I* would feel having to watch the two of them living happily ever after right under my nose. Well, I can. I have. It's not pretty. And it's simply not an option.

I love my brother. I do. He's the only sibling I have, and I would do anything for him. I'd lie, cheat, steal, kill, take a bullet, commit a crime, donate a kidney. All the things one brother would do for another. I'd do anything . . . except give up the woman I love to him.

I'll always remember the day our relationship shifted over the beauty we each ache to call ours.

We were sitting on the front porch steps, each with a giant slice of our mother's famous apple and potato cake. Kael was a mere fourteen years old. I was sixteen. He proceeded to tell me he was going to marry Maverick. At fourteen he already knew how he felt.

But at sixteen, so did I. I knew it the second I pulled her frozen, nearly lifeless body from a remote, icy pond behind our two houses a few months before. When she was old enough, she would belong to me, not Kael.

I tried to keep my voice even; my question *"What if that's not what she wants?"* was meant to be thought-provoking, but upon reflection I realize I came across incredibly possessive.

Yes, I was jealous of their relationship. Resentful. Still am. Kael and Mavs are best friends. They did everything together growing up, and they are still far too close for my liking. They share hobbies and memories and have secrets I am not privy to. He has parts of her I'll never have and I hate it. I want her to be *my* best friend, *my* everything, not Kael's. I'm tired of sharing my dreams with my brother. I want her for myself.

And though I've told myself countless times since then that best friends become lovers and eventually husband and wife all the time, and that Kael and Maverick's union would be accepted by all, the fact of the matter is her feelings toward Kael are platonic.

The downstream effect of acting on us, however, will be more than a trickle. It will be a waterfall. I have thought through the repercussions of this decision ad nauseum. The fracturing of two families, of friendships, of career and home.

We grew up next to the DeSotos. My father was best man at Richard and Vivian's wedding. My parents are best friends with the DeSotos and godparents to Maverick and Jillian. We spend holidays together and frequently eat Sunday dinners at their home. And in addition to Kael and me, my father also works for Richard as the CFO.

Our lives are intertwined in every way. For all intents and purposes, the DeSotos are family, though the feelings I have for Mavs are anything but brotherly. They are dirty. Raw. Visceral. Marrow deep and soundly resolute.

No. There is no going backward. No second-guessing. No more delaying. There is only forward. I simply have to manage the fallout the best I can. Regrettably my options are limited: none of them good and time is not on my side.

My gaze flits to the clock.

9:41 p.m.

She should have been here ten minutes ago.

"It's three to one, White Sox, in the bottom of the eighth," Len Kasper's distinct voice chimes through my Bose speakers. I turn the radio off, uninterested in the game or that my team is ahead. My only interest lies in the woman who is unusually late.

I glance in my rearview mirror hoping to see her pulling in behind me. Instead, the black of night is my suitor. My right leg bounces up and down. I shove my hand on my knee to stop it, but anxiety builds everywhere else to the point of heart palpitations, so I acquiesce to a childhood penchant that I detest and have tried to conquer since college. Unsuccessfully.

I let sixty long seconds pass before I dial her number.

"I'm almost there," she answers without a proper greeting. She sounds breathless. "I . . . I got hung up. I'm sorry."

Maverick loathes tardiness. Something's off, but I don't press.

"Thought maybe you'd changed your mind."

"As if I'd miss our mentoring session." I hear her smile, the teasing in her lilt. I'm hard in a blink. "Pulling in now."

The line goes dead as two bright headlights blind me from behind. Gravel crunches under the weight of tires as her car slows and comes to a stop behind me. The engine cuts and the lights fade. The click of a door opening, then shutting, rides the cool breeze through my open window.

I follow her silhouette until it disappears around the passenger side of my truck seconds before she's sliding quietly inside the cab. The overhead light extinguishes all too quickly, but the rays of an almost-full moon illuminate her perfect perfection.

"Hi." Yeah, she's breathless. Definitely breathless. And so goddamned beautiful, I am in awe.

"Everything okay?" I ask, wondering what has her flustered.

"Yeah, fine."

I can't tell if she's lying or not. I think maybe she is. I open my mouth to ask again, but that's all forgotten when she sinks her top teeth into the flesh of her lower lip and pulls it through until it pops out, plumper than before.

Sweet Jesus, Mavs. *Stop.*

Talk, I remind myself. We're here to talk. *Then stop envisioning pulling down the straps of that clingy peach blouse until her breasts are freed, asshole.*

"I just . . ." She glances out the front windshield and twists her fingers together, musing. The rush of the Iowa River fifty yards away would soothe my nerves under any other circumstances. Not tonight. Not when I'm breathing her in with every breath. "I appreciate you taking time for me. Really. I don't want to sound ungrateful, but . . . why here?" she asks, swinging her puzzled gaze back to mine.

I hate it has to be this way. Meeting undercover in the back of a park. It feels sleazy, as though we're doing something wrong when we're not. At least that's what I keep telling myself.

"Would you rather we do this at your house with your father's ear to the wall?"

"I, uh . . ." she stutters. I hear her swallow. Those jeweled irises widen until they're big and round. Lips, the color of Bordeaux, part slightly. I want to kiss them. Suck them until she's moaning my name and I hear the echo in my dreams later. She blinks fast, her breathing picking up with each passing second. "Do what . . . exactly?"

I don't respond.

Time hangs. Innuendos are unspoken.

Talk. You're here to talk.

I smirk. She squirms, and the more she squirms, the wider my grin gets. I let her off the hook, though I am highly amused.

"Kidding," I say with a wink, which makes her laugh. It's genuine. Relaxed. I fall even further into her.

For all that is holy, how is it even possible to love a woman this much?

Bringing her here was a mistake. She deserves far more from me.

My whispered, "We shouldn't be here," sounds disingenuous.

And, as Maverick is her father's daughter, she senses the opening . . . and she capitalizes.

"This is exactly where we should be," she sighs, closing the gap between us. The khaki shorts she's worn ride up even higher in the process, showcasing her tanned, toned thighs, which are now wedged nicely against my denim-covered ones.

Fuck. Me.

I'm sliding fast into every fantasy I've had regarding her, consequences be damned.

Fists clenched, I stare at the night blanketing us. "Someone could see us."

I'm grasping at strings invisible to the naked eye, fully aware that I put us in this situation. Any control I thought I would have was a fabled illusion.

"There's not another car in the whole park. And besides, it's dark and we're so far back from the road no one will see."

This night reminds me of the one so long ago where she somehow ended up in my lap, kissing me, virtually pulverizing my will. She took what she wanted then, boldly, without hesitation. She does the same now.

"Maverick," I hiss when she sets her hand firmly between my legs. Her name is a curse and a plea. A reverie.

I should stop her. Stop this.

I don't.

I *can't*.

The way she's caressing me, root to tip . . . Jesus. I grip the steering wheel, knuckles turning white, jerking violently when her thumbnail scrapes the sensitive underside of my cock. The sensation is acute. It's fucking amazing. She does it again. I hold back a moan.

Heat licks every inch of me. My head feels heavy. My thoughts war.

Stop.

Don't stop.

Take her.

Not like this.

She reaches for my zipper. God forgive me, I let her. I almost do it for her. She pops the top button with zero effort. Metal teeth separate, one by one until my fly hangs open. My dick pulsates, jumping with every rapid heartbeat. She stalls for a second . . . two . . . three. It's agonizing, the wait. I could come right now under the weight of her stare. I might when her fingertips lightly graze me through the thin fabric of my briefs, teasing.

"Maverick," I rasp. *End this torture. I beg of you.*

Torture is relative, I suppose. The sting of denial. The agony of submission. Which is worse? I don't know. I honestly don't know as she complies with my silent appeal and slips my underwear down. I'm burning up, on fire. Those slim fingers wrap around me one by one, her movements slow and calculated. Precise.

""Fuuuuck," I mumble, my eyes falling closed.

We are skin to skin for the very first time and, reverent mother of all things merciful, nothing has ever felt so erotic. Everything about her, about this moment, is better than I thought possible. The warmth of her touch, the wisps of unadulterated need fanning my cheek, the surety in the way she strokes me. She fans kisses along my stubble. Her lips are as soft as feather pillows.

It's too much. It's all too much.

Don't stop.

Don't ever fucking stop.

Pre-cum coats my head, and when she swipes a thumb over the top, gently massaging the wetness around, it hurtles me over a beam I was poorly balancing on. Every good intention I had is carried away as if it was dust in the wind.

"Maverick, Jesus Christ."

I'm done. Savage male instinct takes over. Next thing I know, I am taking and taking and taking.

Her long hair twisted in my fist, my mouth plunders, owning hers. My tongue dominates, sweeping hers in long strokes until we're both mindless and panting. I nip her jaw, kiss the hollow of her throat, tongue her collarbone. My head spins. She tastes like the sweet nectar of salvation wrapped in a delicate filament of spun fucking sugar. Exactly as I recall. I can't get enough.

I snag that bottom lip I love so much, sipping and sucking until she's a writhing mess. My free hand skims between the valley of her breasts. I cup one, pinching a protruding bud. Hard. Her strangled moans melt sweetly in my mouth, unleashing the devil in me.

I want her. All of her. In every way I've ever dreamed.

"Put my cock in your mouth," I find myself demanding hoarsely.

Is she ready for this, I wonder? For me to thrash twenty-some years of repressed craving upon her body until she breaks and begs for mercy?

I put enough distance between us so I can gauge her reaction. Will her eyes narrow in repulsion or glaze over in eagerness?

What I find astounds me. She blinks up at me with an irresistible innocence I know is not faked. Definitely not repulsion. *My earthy, humble, sweet girl. How I am going to enjoy being the man to corrupt you.*

"I want to feel you inside me," she breathes on a hush.

"And I will be inside you, Small Fry," I promise, tucking loose strands of hair behind her ear. "But I need to sink inside that mouth first. I've fantasized a thousand times over the years of you sucking me off. Don't make me beg."

The side of her lip twitches before she answers with that sass I so love. "I think I might like to hear you beg for once."

I don't think she understands that I'd give her anything; sacrifice my very beating heart and then some. And that's probably because in trying to keep the appropriate distance, I've not demonstrated her importance in my life over the years. She is my gravity, whether she realizes it or not. The promise of her has been the distant light I've walked toward for so long.

Tonight that changes. Tonight she will know what she means to me.

The timbre of my voice is barely noticeable to me when I utter words I'm happy to give her. "Please."

The droop of her eyelids is the quiet acquiescence I was hoping for. I gently guide her head to my lap, giving her time to change her mind or protest if need be. She doesn't. She only grips me stronger, then wraps that feisty, hot mouth around the entirety of me, taking me almost all the way to the base. *Fuck.* I wind my fingers through her hair and grip her scalp. She presses her tongue to a protruding vein as she travels back up and circles my tip and . . .

"Oh, Jesus, Mavs."

Nirvana.

"So good."

Nothing has ever felt better.

"Right there. Don't stop."

I don't know if I verbalize my scattered thoughts or if the words die somewhere between my brain and my mouth. I don't know much of anything but the gluttony of pleasures being lavished on me with love and complete and total deference to my gratification. I've never had a woman care this much about pleasing me. And there is something about that feeling that makes my heart swell and my head swim.

And suddenly I need to be inside of her more than I need to breathe.

Using my hold on her dark tresses as leverage, I tug her off me and slam my lips to hers, eating the protest she was trying for. I tear at her blouse, ripping it over her head. Next, I attack her bra, throwing it on the floorboard to join her shirt. I don't allow myself time to ogle her. Right now, I am thirsty, ravenous, and I gorge.

I pull a nipple into my mouth and clamp down until she gasps. I redden it before moving to the other, drinking in her flavor. I want to stay here forever, adrift in her sea, blissfully dragged under by her current, but if I'm not buried in her by the count of ten, our first time together will be a stark disappointment. Reluctantly, I move on, peppering kisses down her quivering belly, simultaneously working the mechanics on her shorts until they're gone, along with her panties.

I rise up and stare, stupefied.

She is grace. She is a vision. Mesmerizing. She is buck naked and ready for me, and as if I'm a schoolboy I don't know what to do first, one idea bleeding into the next.

I want to skim every dip and curve with my tongue.

I want my taste buds bursting with her muskiness.

I want her sobbing as she comes undone by my hand.

I want her breasts wrapped around my cock, my come coating her chest.

Her back is flush with the seat, her knees have fallen open, and the smell of her essence drifts up, but that's not what stops me cold. I realize that this—Maverick—is my homecoming. Peace and serenity begin and end with her. Every dream I have had is of her, for her. I pause, frozen, unable to rip my eyes away and I have what I can only describe as an out-of-body experience.

The moon's rays illuminate her, my angel living among mortals. Her skin glows. Her eyes sparkle. Her core is wet. She is brilliant. She is everything.

I want to capture this.

I want to freeze time.

I want to hold her and never let go.

I want it all in this moment and I want nothing, save her.

I reach out and touch her. A soft smile turns her lips as I run the pad of my finger lightly from her temple, down the curve of her face, over her mouth. My name is but a puff of air from her lips as I circle the fullness of her breast before tracing the dusky pink of her areola, puckered and aroused. Ignoring the stirring of need in her body begging me to do something, anything, I continue my trek to the top of her mound, stalling just shy of her clit. I pause, fully comprehending the weight of this moment.

It's surreal, this gift she is giving me.

"Maverick," I whisper tenderly, completely enraptured by her. Her skin glitters as if made of stardust or crushed diamonds. My gaze treks back up her body until I reconnect with her. Her entreaty is silent, desperate. A reflection of mine.

Making quick work of my own clothes, I never look away. As I discard each article, I envision a home filled to the brim with kids who have green eyes and dark hair like their mother's. How I long to make that a reality. To see her belly swell with our children. I don't dare take that chance, though. Not yet. We have a lot to work through, so I push that dream to the side, don a condom, and relish in the way she's now exploring me with her hands while searching my soul with her own.

This woman. She is so much, a vision of beauty. Infused with divinity. Setting my lips to hers, I take her breath as mine, literally breathing her in as I whisper, "The first time I come with you, it will be together." Reaching between us, I find her opening, wet and eager, and I begin to sink inside.

And fuck . . . my eyes roll.

"Oh shit, Killian," she pants.

She's tight. So goddamned tight, I wonder for a second or two if I'll be able to get all the way seated. I've never felt anything so damn good in my entire life. I can't imagine the way she'd feel with no barrier between us.

I pull out and drive back in, keeping my movements gentle and rhythmic. It's agony, holding back, but I worry I'm hurting her, so I stay tuned in to her, making sure she's with me every step of the way. With the way her lids are at half-mast and her face is drawn up in rapture, there is no doubt she is lockstep.

"Goddamn, you feel good. So good, Maverick. So wet, so tight. So . . . fuck." I can hardly breathe for wanting her, but I keep the pace methodical, holding myself in check.

"Fuck me. Hard," she begs. I almost lose it then and there. After all these years of denying her, I want to give her whatever makes her happy. Instead, I root myself and still.

"I'm not fucking you, Maverick."

"But—"

Leveraging myself on my elbows, I cup her cheeks and lay a thumb over her mouth, quieting her. This is not a quick fuck in the bed of my truck. I want to make love to the only woman I've ever been *in* love with.

"I'm going to make love to you slowly, Small Fry. I've waited too long to take you like it's a meaningless act." *I was an idiot.* "This means more to me than you can possibly know." *You're my light. My universe.* "I'm going to worship your body, love your heart, own your soul, and make sure you remember this night for the rest of your life." *Correction, the rest of* our *lives.*

She remains quiet when I remove my thumb. Her pussy pulses around me. I ache to move, bringing us both to euphoria, but I know my Small Fry. She has something to say.

It doesn't take long. Between a blink and the next breath, she murmurs, "I love you, Killian," and I hate that a sob accompanies the declaration I've waited to hear again for the last five years.

I've done this to her. Though it was with honorable intent, my continued rejections have caused her pain, and I need to make it right. I don't want her to fear telling me she loves me ever again.

I picture the rest of my life. Mountains I've yet to climb. Valleys I've yet to sink into. I can't imagine anyone I want by my side for the highest of highs, the lowest of lows, and all the mundane days traversed in between.

"I love you, Maverick. I have always loved you." *I should have told you long ago.*

Her eyes fill with tears. I wipe each one away as I love her the way she was meant to be loved. With awe and reverence and gratitude. And when she reaches her peak only seconds before I do, her sounds of ecstasy in time with my own, I know I am holding the last woman I will ever make love to.

CHAPTER FOUR

"Dinner was delicious as always. Thank you." I pick up my mother's plate on the way by, heading to the kitchen to rinse both of ours.

"I'm glad you could make it."

I should be working, but when my mother asks you to dinner, you don't refuse. I wouldn't anyway. I love spending time with her. "You know I'd never turn down an invitation for Eilish Shepard's famous Irish stew."

Her laughter follows me to the sink. I eye the fusee clock hanging on the wall above me. It was a gift from my father for Christmas last year. He had it commissioned and shipped from Ireland, my mother's homeland. She cried. I may have teared up. The love my parents share is something I aspire to. I know with Mavs I can have the same thing.

"Where's Pops?" I ask, loading the dirty dishes into the dishwasher. I remember having to wash dishes by hand because my mother refused to own a dishwasher. She didn't believe a machine could outperform a human. She still doesn't.

"Oh, you know your father. He's still at the office as you generally are at this hour."

I frown. I don't recall seeing his light on when I left a bit ago. I must have been mistaken.

"Would you care for a brandy?" my mother asks, already heading to the cupboard housing the liquor.

"I don't know." I shouldn't. I have an early morning flight to Pensacola that she doesn't know about.

"Come now. Humor an old woman."

I decide one won't hurt, wanting a few more minutes with her, knowing they're likely going to be fewer and farther between soon. "Sure. And you are far from old," I mutter against her forehead before pressing my lips to her cool skin.

Under her protests, I finish clearing the table and settle into the oversized armchair in the sitting room generally reserved for my father when he's home.

"So, are you going to tell me or do I have to pull it out of you?"

"Tell you what?" I sip the Courvoisier my mother handed me, silently cursing her special power. Eilish Shepard is many things. Loving. Giving. Fierce. Direct. And all-knowing. Her intuition is a gift. Or a curse, depending on how you look at it.

Today it would be the latter.

"Killian."

My mother's firm tone says it all.

Fuck. This is the last thing I need. My parents don't keep secrets from each other. If she knows, my father knows and my father is a worse liar than Maverick if that's possible. That means it's only a matter of time before Richard knows. And Kael, well, his suspicions grow daily. He asked me to meet him for a drink last night. Two invitations since Mavs has been back. That is no coincidence.

"What?" I reply plainly. I'm not giving her anything. She gets the slightest inkling of a lie and your proverbial goose is cooked. That lesson was learned a long time ago.

"Your father told me Maverick is working at DSC."

I smirk and shake my head. Here we go. "She is."

Short. Simple. Answer what's asked. No more. No less.

"How's that going?" My mother pours herself her own drink. Unusual, though I don't comment.

One shoulder creeps up to my ear then falls back down. "Fine."

"Fine?" She sits across from me and crosses one leg over the other.

"Fine," I reiterate.

It's been a month now that Maverick and I have been "together." Four weeks of secrets and lies and sneaking around. Attempting to treat her like she's just another employee at work has proven a challenge. And the kicker is I am happy—happier than I have ever been. Most days my heart is bursting with possibilities and plans for the future, and I have no one to share them with besides Mavs. I have to hide my contentment as though it doesn't exist. I'm tired of the subterfuge. It's exhausting.

"Why are you looking at me that way?" Mother's intuition sucks.

"What way would that be?" she asks, tipping her head a couple of degrees to the left, feigning confusion.

"Like . . ." I twirl my finger in her direction, trying to come up with the right description. "I don't know. Like *that*." Like you know that I'm in love with her and about to make the biggest decision of my life.

Her laughter breaks me down, makes those tight muscles relax slightly. "You're generally far more articulate than that, Killian."

"I know. I just . . ." I'm discombobulated. *I need my mother.*

An unusual thought for a twenty-seven-year-old man, but my mother and I have a bond she doesn't have with Kael. That she doesn't have with anyone. She knows me inside and out. And she is the best advice giver I know. I don't know a better woman besides Maverick. Having to cut her out of this huge piece of my life has been like carving a hole in the center of me.

"Maverick . . . she . . . I . . ." I stumble over my words, unsure what to say, how to say it, if I should say anything at all.

But my mother, man, she doesn't miss a beat. And her question, "How can I help?" which brims with the utmost sincerity, brings a steady sting to the backs of my eyes.

She knows. Of *course* she knows.

"I'm in love with her," I confess on a whim. Part of me wants to eat those words; the other is glad they are out in the universe. It makes them more real, somehow.

"Of course you are," is her answer, so matter-of-fact, it's like it has always been so. And it has, I suppose. "The question is, my son, what are you going to do about it?"

She has to know Kael feels the same way I do. Yet there is no judgment, no derision, no taking of sides. If there were, I'm not sure how I'd have handled it. But to have her blessing . . .

To have her *blessing* lightens this burden I've been carrying like a cross strapped to my back.

What am I going to do?

"Funny you should ask." I swallow the rest of my drink and, leaning forward with my elbows glued to my knees, I lay out the grand plan I've been working on since the moment I asked Maverick to meet me in Harbor Park.

For the next hour my mother listens to me vomit every worry, each fear. She is supportive. Encouraging, even. I tell her my concern for Pops and Kael, for those "unintended consequences" which may roll downhill. She assures me she'll handle things on the home front, leveraging Vivian's sway over her husband. I'm sorry I didn't trust her with this from the beginning.

"It won't be easy," she tells me. We stand with the front door open, bathing in the warm evening air. The cicadas are loud tonight. Their buzz vibrates in my bones.

"I don't care."

"Hmmm."

"Hmmm, what?"

Her reply is quick. "Nothing."

Oh no. It's not nothing. "It's something," I prod.

Several beats pass before she speaks again. "You care, Killian. That's why you're about to undertake these extraordinary measures. In an attempt to protect everyone you love."

My eyes burn. She knows me so well. "I'm trying."

"Yet someone will get hurt."

Kael.

My heart is heavy. I am quite sure hers is as well. Son pitted against son. Friend against friend. I wish it didn't have to be this way.

"I know." My sigh is long and weighs a thousand pounds.

We walk onto the porch and down the three front steps, neither of us saying a word. As it always does, my gaze is drawn to the DeSoto's. Maverick's car is in the driveway. How I long to see it in front of *our* home instead.

"And think not you can direct the course of love, for love directs your course," my mother says quietly.

"What?" I ask, looking down at her, brows drawn.

My mother, small but mighty, smiles up at me, all five foot one of her aglow. She sets her hands on both my cheeks, shaking them like she did when I was a child. "'Love leads us, not the other way around. The quote is a favorite of mine. Appropriate in this situation, don't you think?"

I digest my mother's wisdom, profound, steeped in experience. And always on point.

My love for Maverick most decidedly set me on a path I had could not deviate from even if I wanted to.

"Thank you, Mother. For everything," I whisper, hugging her one last time. Next to Maverick, there is not a woman on this Earth I love more than my mother. She made me the man I am today. I would move mountains for her.

"You are most welcome, Killian." I get a kiss on the cheek. "Good luck, my son," she adds as I'm walking to my truck.

Good luck. Hmm. Definitely going to need it.

Heading toward my house in town, I take my time, listening to a Keith Urban tune about not giving up on a lifetime love while I replay the conversation I had with my mother. And as I do this peaceful serenity I haven't felt before settles in my bones.

While I know challenges lie ahead, I feel good. More than good.

I feel alive.

Rejuvenated.

And for the first time . . . I feel truly hopeful that all I want is at last within my grasp.

CHAPTER FIVE

"I'm going with you."

"No. You're not," I gruff.

"I make my own decisions, you know."

To the man upstairs, grant me patience please. A lifetime of it, as long as I'm putting in my order. "This is only temporary, Mavs."

She huffs and grows quiet. That doesn't last long. "I don't understand why you have to do this."

The pattern she's drawing with her fingertip on my chest is driving me out of my ever-loving mind. I can't take it.

Rolling her over to her back, I wedge a knee between her thighs and spread them open, simultaneously pinning her hands above her head. She sets her heels on my lower back and pushes her pelvis up, fitting us together as if we've always been one. My stomach falls as I plummet into her atmosphere once again.

Dark, mussed hair contrasts against the white of my pillowcase. Satiation swims in her eyes from our last hour of lovemaking. I'm spent, yet she makes me want to dive back in. She is every man's dream, including mine. Yet somehow, someway, she has become my reality.

How have I been so blessed?

"We've already been through this, Small Fry," I groan.

Her lids narrow, her temples tick, both ever so slight to someone who knows no better. Only I do. Over the years I've mastered reading every emotion that emanates from Mavs. I've seen them all. Unfettered joy. Crushing heartbreak. Brutal anger. She feels deeply and doesn't attempt to hide it. At times I could tell you what she's feeling before she even could.

Right now, she is madder than a hornet whose nest was swatted. And I'm about to get stung. But this is the only way. In time, she will realize it too.

"Then go through it once more," she snaps. Sage irises smolder now.

"Maverick." I bend to kiss her lips, but they're stiff as a board. I don't let that deter me. "I need to make my own way." I move to her ear, biting her lobe. A hot breath rushes out, warming my cheek. "I don't want this any more than you do, but it's only temporary." Her throat tastes like candy tonight. Last night it was berries, tart and ripe. She's a mystery, a symphony for the senses.

"How long?" She's tempering, though her tone is still piqued.

"I don't know," I tell her honestly.

Last week I accepted a job at Molloy Holdings, a company that, like DSC, is in the transportation infrastructure industry, but their niche is in canal work in the Gulf. They are half the size of DSC, but they managed to beat my salary by nearly 20 percent and even threw in a few stock options that may be worth something someday. Most importantly, though, it set the second part of my plan into motion. To dismantle myself from Richard DeSoto and his interference. If I stay, I'll be fired anyway, though Mavs doesn't need to know that. She'd go to bat for me and I need to lead this battle, not her.

"A year? Longer?"

"I don't know, baby." My lips trek across the fullness of her cleavage. I stop and suck hard, knowing I'll leave a mark. Wanting them all over her as some sort of caveman reminder of who she belongs to.

I'm mapping out where I'll leave the next one when she screeches, "A year?" Her hands fly to my shoulders to push me away.

I blow out a long breath and lever on my elbows. "I didn't say a year. I said I don't know." I want to make love, not quarrel. I want to take advantage of every second we have left together before I have to board that plane for Pensacola in three days' time. "I hate the thought more than you do, Mavs."

"Well, you mustn't because you're leaving me."

What is it about a woman's tears that brings a man to his knees? "Mavs, baby." I brush my index finger to her hairline, catching a falling drop. "Please, don't cry."

"I don't want you to go."

"And I don't want to sneak around anymore."

Parks. Grain bins. Gravel roads. Hidden cars. Sneaking through back doors. Blinds pulled. I'm sick of all of it. I'm a successful twenty-seven-year-old man with a career and a home and everything to offer the woman I am in love with. To hide us this way is madness.

There is a part of me that wants to march into Richard's office and simply tell him how it's going to be. I'd be lying if I didn't admit it undermines my manhood that I don't. But I also know Richard, and I will earn his respect far more this way. So, no. This is the way it needs to be.

"That will be hard to do when you're not here." She attempts to wiggle from my hold. I tighten it. She huffs and sinks back into the pillows in feigned submission. She's still angry. It's adorable. "This is about my father, isn't it?"

Yes. And . . . yes.

"Why don't you talk to him, Killian?" she asks when I don't answer.

It's not that easy, Small Fry.

"Fine. If you won't, I will."

Stubborn as the night is dark.

"Maverick." I change into a sitting position and drag her naked body into my lap, cradling her head on my shoulder. I run strands of silky locks through my fingers until she's eased into me, her body completely pliable. "The time we've had hasn't been nearly enough for me, either, but as long as I'm working for your father, he has control of every aspect of my life." *And yours.*

She remains silent. She knows I'm right.

"He controls my career path, my income." *You.* "He can make or break me in an instant."

And the "unintended consequences" he referenced, well, I don't even go there, because I'm not yet sure how that will play out with my father or with Kael. I want to believe Richard has some measure of honor in him, but that's questionable at best.

"My father only wants to see me happy."

Sure he does. With the man of *his* choosing, running *his* company. Everything is about what Richard wants, not Mavs.

"How will that work for us if I stay and he is the puppet master?"

"I—"

"It won't," I reply firmly. "Look at me."

She does as I ask, the water balancing along her lower lids spilling over in waves at the movement. Her pain is my pain. It wrecks me. I can hardly bear the thought of leaving her.

I patiently wipe each drop away with my thumbs until they are mostly gone. It takes a few minutes, but I'd do it for hours if need be. "If I want a life with you, which I desperately do, I need independence from everything here. I need to be able to support my wife and my children on my own two feet, with no handouts or IOUs from your father."

A quick smile. It's progress.

"Your wife?" Her voice is small, her question big.

"Yes, my wife."

"And children, huh?" She bites that lower lip. Damn.

"Loads." I slide my tongue along her jawline. She giggles. I love her giggle.

"How many?"

"Five. Boys."

"You don't get to determine the sex, you know."

"Actually, I do," I chuckle, tapping the tip of her nose with my finger.

"Ha, ha," she replies dryly. "And my father doesn't do handouts, by the way."

Cheeky. There's my girl.

"Don't I know it. Look." I wrap her legs around me, suppressing a groan at the heat her pussy is giving off. I'm as hard as steel and I want nothing more than to push inside her, raw as raw can be. "I know it's not ideal, but this is the only way, okay?"

"I'm sorry," she sniffles, looking away. Her inky lashes are spiked with the remnants of her tears.

Reaching over to my nightstand, I pull a tissue from the box, handing it to her. "Nothing to be sorry for, Small Fry."

She takes it and wads it up in her fist, plucking at the edges hanging out. "I'm being childish, I know."

"Hey . . ." I wait until she lifts her gaze. "We have our entire lives ahead of us. In the scheme of things, this is a blip in time. We take things slow and get your father used to the idea of us, and I promise you, it will be smooth sailing from there."

I leave the elephant in the room, taking up way too much space for my liking. This is about her father, yes, and it's true I feel I have no other choice but to relocate temporarily, yet I haven't forgotten for a second that I'll not be here and Kael will.

I don't like it, but there is nothing I can do about it either.

Her arms snake around my neck. She presses pointed nipples into my chest, hard and taut. Ready to be punished, I do believe. I hope this means we're past the quarreling phase.

"You think?"

Think?

I can't think of anything but getting her flat on her back in seven seconds or less, giving her more orgasms than she thought physically possible. I want to wring them from her until her vision fades to black and her limbs go limp.

"Yeah, I think."

Enough talking.

My hands slide around the firm globes of her ass. I spread her cheeks apart, feathering a finger over her puckered skin, making her moan and clench up. I slip lower and gather juices, this time rimming her with a little more firmness, before breaching a place I've been dying to explore.

"Killian." Her voice is hoarse. Wanton.

"Feel good?"

"Yes." Her pupils dilate and when she starts undulating, it pushes my finger in up to the first knuckle. "God, yes." Her head falls backward, that long mane flowing to the small of her back—the sexiest part of her body in my opinion. "Killian," she breathes again.

This time my name is an overture, an entreaty. She has no need to ask twice.

"Tell me what you need, baby?" I ask. Withdrawing my finger, I lay her down, arranging her on top of my comforter. Her breasts are high, her belly is concave. She is a siren.

"You." Our eyes lock. "Just you." I waste no more time. I scoop up another condom, rip it open with my teeth, and roll it on, all the while enjoying the show she's giving me.

"Mavs, fuck," I grunt as her middle finger disappears between her center.

"Do you like that?" she pants. Spreading her legs wide, I see how much she enjoys this. She circles her clit, unashamed of what she's doing.

"Very much so, yes," I grumble hoarsely. I want to devour her, make love to her, hold her, indulge her, own her, worship her. *Marry her.* "I want to watch you make yourself come."

Her tongue darts out to wet her lips. I stroke my shaft, squeezing at the base until I feel more pain than pleasure. "I want *you* to make me come," she throws back, that smart mouth of hers in full force.

"Oh, I will, Small Fry, but I am chivalrous after all." I sit back on my knees, gesturing for her to continue. "Ladies first."

It takes two blinks, but then she grins wickedly, and my Maverick readily complies, inhibitions nonexistent. She has no idea how immeasurably sexy she is. Or how loved or how wanted.

Command.

Control.

Patience.

I was a fool to ever think I possessed these characteristics when it comes to Mavs. She is the master of those over me, not the reverse. And without a second thought, I am okay with it.

This time two fingers come out to play, and as her breaths increase and those tiny mewls of pleasure leave her throat, I can't help but join in on the fun. I thrust two fingers inside to feel her inner walls clench as we bring her to completion together not once, but twice.

Then as I hold her in my arms and sink into the only place I'll ever call home again, I think to myself, *finally*.

Finally.

It only took twenty-seven years, but I am finally where I was always meant to be, and there is not a force known to man that could tear me away from Maverick DeSoto now that she's mine.

ABOUT THE AUTHOR

Your Everything is essentially a prequel to my two-time *USA Today* bestseller Black Swan Affair. If you haven't yet, read more about Maverick, Killian, and Kael, available now.

As a *USA Today* Bestselling author, I write stories that are deeply emotional with flawed characters, because humans ARE flawed and if we read about perfect characters living in their perfect world, first of all, snoozer, but secondly, we never experience the gratification of redemption.

Outside of writing, I'm just a regular ol' Midwest girl who likes Game of Thrones and am obsessed with Modern Family and The Goldbergs. I run, I eat, I run, I eat. It's a vicous cycle. I love carbs, but there's love-hate relationship with my ass and thighs. Mostly hate. I like a good cocktail (oh hell…who am I kidding? I love any cocktail). I'm a huge creature of habit, but I'll tell you I'm flexible. I read every single day and if I don't get a chance…watch the hell out. My iPad and me: BFFs. I'm direct and I make no apologies for it. I swear too much. I love alternative music and in my next life I want to be a bad-ass female rocker. I hate, hate, hate spiders, telemarketers, liver, acne, winter and loose hairs that fall down my shirt (don't ask, it's a thing).

More info available at: www.klkreig.com

Think I'm In Love

LESLIE MCADAM

"THINK I'M IN LOVE" – BECK

♪

Cracking my knuckles, I frown, make a fist, rotate it out bodybuilder-style, pop my bicep, and ask in a deep voice, "Do you *haff* Hello Kitty tooth-brusshh?"

The room erupts into laughter.

Okay, that's not true.

Kim's parents guffaw, but Shane's facial expression remains glacial. Handsome, but so grave, like we're talking about whether he's ever going to have rhubarb streusel pie again in his life. That's his favorite.

While I've got a good idea of what's wrong with him, I table figuring out if there's anything new on his list of control-freak neuroses until after we help Kim double-check what she's packed.

If you're keeping score, I'm counting Kim in the laugh column, since she's struggling *not* to snicker.

She snaps her fingers, tilts her head, her cute, dirty-blond hair bouncing in a ponytail, and feigns seriousness. "Darn. I totally forgot." After debating whether she should make a last-minute trip to our local Hy-Vee Pharmacy, she points to a small bag. "Oh, wait. It's in there. Thanks for the reminder, Randy."

What better way to send our bestie off to Spain than to make sure she's packed a toothbrush, clean underwear, and her plane tickets, all the while doing a spot-on Schwarzenegger impersonation? At least that's what I figure.

With my spiky black hair and dark eyes, my appearance doesn't resemble Arnie by any means—especially since I'm not wielding a huge gun and I don't have on sunglasses. Still, my audience gets the point.

We're hanging in Kim's parents' living room, a place where Shane, Kim, and I have loitered together since kindergarten, a decade and a half ago. While we wait for her mom's famous corn casserole to bake and listen to her dad's jokes, we work through Kim's last-minute nerves. After all, she's taking the first flight of her life tomorrow, and it's not some puddle jumper to Chicago. Our girl's saying buh-bye to Iowa and leaving the U.S.A. like she's got an offshore account she's gotta secure before someone finds out about it.

While the tension in Kim's mom's jaw gives away her anxiety about her baby girl studying abroad for the semester, and Kim's jumpy for obvious, going-to-Spain reasons, the one who gives off the vibe of being the most ill-at-ease is the dreary moose on the couch—my other best friend, Shane.

Assuming *best friend* is the right term.

If I'm the jokester and Kim's the sweetheart, then he's the serious one—

—and the gorgeous one, with russet brown hair, chestnut eyes, and a T-shirt stretched across his sculpted chest that says, "Gamers don't die, they respawn."

Bless his nerdy little gamer heart.

Unlike me, Shane actually resembles a bodybuilder, since he's practically moved into the gym. After seeing how much time Shane spends ensuring his appearance is pristine and all the effort he expends to regulate every aspect of his life, I just don't wanna do it. Doesn't mean I can't admire his dedication, though—or his physique. Still, I'm the messy to his neat, the chaos to his structure, and the fuck-it to his earnestness. I have other things to do with my time.

Like increase my skill rating on *Overwatch*.

Anyhoo, after going through a few more essential items on her packing list, Kim confirms that she indeed has the electronic thingamabob Americans need so their gadgets don't fry in Europe, and she smiles at me expectantly. We're done making her list and checking it twice, so it's time for my punchline.

"Then, *hasta la vista*, baby," I grunt in my Ahnold voice. Everyone groans, and I clap my hands twice like *chop-chop*. "You'll be back."

My work here is done.

I take a seat in the closest unoccupied space, now turning my attention to Shane and trying to figure out the best way to make him feel better.

He and Kim have been "dating"—if you can call it that—since our junior year, but it's really more like they just know who they're going to prom with.

Me.

Kidding. I tag along. I honestly think Shane asked her out partly because it was the first year he didn't have a class with her, and none of us could go very long without seeing the other two, and partly because he didn't want anyone to get suspicious about *whatever* was building between him and me. Even if *whatever* built so slowly, it was like watching one of those time lapse painters on the internet—a few daubs of color here and there appear to be nothing at first. Then the dots and blotches of nothing form a portrait—whole, beautiful, and conveying a singular idea, and you wonder why you didn't see it before.

While I've been able to see our *whatever* for a while, I'm not sure he can.

I'll admit a part of me hopes he'll want to take a break from her and go on an adventure of his own—risking *whatever* with me, but that might require a miracle. He took the news that she was leaving pretty hard, and he's spent more time ruminating on it than I'd consider healthy—not that I'm an expert on health. I practically own stock in Cheetos.

Having Kim leave to go see the world on her own doesn't jive with his orderly life. Her trip was not scheduled, and it does not compute. He probably had her penciled in to do some activity every day for the next few years, and he's grouchy he has to plan his future all over again.

I think it's fantastic she's getting out of Iowa and studying in another country, and while I'll miss her, I'm not moping about it. I'm happy for her, and impressed she won an outstanding scholarship. She's off on a journey to the unknown.

Still, I'm worried about him. He's ignoring me, ignoring Kim, ignoring her parents. Shane's knee bounces so much, I wouldn't be surprised if he takes flight. I want to lean over and put my hand on it, but that wouldn't go over well.

In fact, just about all of my thoughts about him wouldn't go over well.

That's a story for another day.

We chat with her parents a bit more. Right as we're about to get up for dinner, Shane clears his throat. He's adorable when he does that, acting all in charge. I stifle a smile.

He stands in front of Kim, his back to me, and starts talking, his voice cracking from disuse. About how he and Kim used to play together in the river.

I was with them too, but who's keeping track?

How she helped him with his homework. I internally shrug. She helped me, too.

How she was homecoming queen to his king.

He's got me there.

"Nice speech, bruh," I interrupt, but Shane turns around and glares at me.

Something about his glare reads off to me. I tease both of them all the time, but normally neither of them take offense. At all.

With a shaky voice, he keeps talking, and as his words pour out about how much she means to him, and how much he cares about her, I start getting a bad feeling about this.

He gets down on one knee before her.

I don't realize I'm holding my breath until I gasp.

He says phrases like, "I can't imagine a future without you," and "I want to make sure you know how much I want to make that future real."

No.

He reaches in his pocket—

No.

—and pulls out a little velvet bag.

I want to scream, but I'm frozen in my seat. I can't move a muscle. This is the proverbial car crash happening right in front of me, and I can do nothing to stop it.

He tips something into his hand, and it drops to the floor.

A ring.

My heart seizes.

He isn't.

Oh no. *He is.*

I thought what was between them was just *friends*. Keeping our group together.

What the actual hell?

Heat infuses my cheeks. My stomach turns sour. I'm going to faint.

"It was my grandma's," Shane says to Kim. "I love you. Will you promise you'll come back to me?"

I can't hear the room for the rushing inside my head. He didn't just do that. Kim's mouth drops open, her hand flies to her chest, and she gasps, leveling him with an incredulous stare.

She's as surprised as I am.

Keep it together, Randy.

Yeah, I think disgustedly. Keep it together while he shits on everything you and he have shared. *Whatever.* But I can't say that.

None of us can, especially not in front of her parents.

"Oh my God, you're making her Yoko Ono," I blurt out, because if I don't say something funny, I'll cry.

Kim's head swivels to me. "What on earth are you talking about?"

"Yoko Ono broke up the Beatles," I explain, hoping I'm hiding my need to hurt someone with a nonchalant shrug.

Because I'm not allowed to feel this way. Not when our relationship—*whatever* it is—is a secret from everyone.

Or apparently nonexistent, according to him.

Now Shane's head slashes toward me, his expression controlled, but I can see fury in his eyes. "You interrupt my proposal with Yoko Ono?"

"Is that a proposal?" Kim asks with a trembling voice.

The rest of what they say gets lost in the fog that enters my brain. By the end of the night, she's wearing his ring.

And I'm suffering in silence. I don't know whether to laugh or cry, so I do neither.

While we eat dinner, I sit at the dining room table and make jokes I don't mean, knowing all the while he's chosen her over me.

♪

As I step outside to leave, I run into Shane and Kim kissing on the porch.

Dammit.

They had to pick this moment to lock lips. I rarely see them kiss, and it's normally a public peck. I'm pretty sure they've fucked maybe three times, because it's safer to lose your virginity with your best friend than the way I did it—meeting a random guy in a bar in Kansas City.

Seeing him with her wrenches my heart into a lump of hot molten metal.

"Come on you two, break it up," I say in a voice heartier than I feel. "Let's go, loverboy, before you get in more trouble. Have fun in Spain, Kim. I know you will."

I make a beeline for his car, waiting for him to join me, and fume as he says goodbye and heads toward me.

Don't get me wrong. Kim's great. I adore her as my closest friend. I want only what's best for her. But Shane's not best for her. He's for me.

If only he would stop pretending.

I mean, just last night, he hung out a little too late. A little too long. But he left in a hurry, cutting us off before things—

Is that what spurred this proposal?

He reads my mood as we pull away from the curb since it's fairly obvious—I'm so mad I can't talk, my hands clench into fists, and steam curls out of my ears. Thankfully he gives me the courtesy of not talking either. As he maneuvers the streets, his expression is more of one resigned to his fate rather than excited about his future bride. Like he was expecting a low score on a test or a guilty conviction and, yep, there it is. Getting engaged, he should be on cloud nine—or even bounding over to cloud ten—but he hasn't even gotten to cloud one.

After we travel a block or two, he says in a low, matter-of-fact voice, "Look, Randy. I had to. You know that."

I don't say anything.

We pass another block of 1950s Iowa houses with light blue and white siding. We turn down Elm and onto Central, headed to my house. Finally, when we get to Third Street, he speaks again. "I couldn't let her go so far away without some guarantee she'd come back. I had to nail her down before she leaves."

Like he spends any time nailing her.

He lets out a deep breath. "So, that's the way it is? You're gonna be childish? Give me the silent treatment?"

Again, I don't say anything, because if I do, I'm going to cry. Besides, it's not childish to be hurt, and I'm so damn hurt. He didn't just tear out my heart. He stomped on it, cut it with an X-Acto knife, and burned it with acid.

When we pull up to my house, he stops the car. Sitting in the driver's seat, he scrubs his face with his palms. "What else could I do?"

That's a loaded question if I've ever heard one, with the full panoply of multiple choice answers, including "None of the above."

A thick, ugly sob threatens to come out of my chest, but I shove it down. I don't like thinking my best friend is a coward. Maybe asking a really special woman to marry him on the eve before she studies overseas is the bravest thing he could do.

But I think it's wrong. Very, very wrong.

I pause before opening the door. It's blazing hot, with sultry, sticky August weather, but that's not why I'm hesitating.

He gazes at me. "Are you going to say anything at all? Maybe congratulations?"

I've had it. "Congratulations?" I explode. "No. I'm not saying *congratulations*. And maybe I'm an asshole, but you're a fucking liar. What the actual fuck? Did you really need to put on a big show?"

Shane blinks, and his eyes are red and laced with pain. "Randy. Whatever has happened between us? We can't do that anymore.

You're my best friend, but that's it. I'm marrying Kim."

My lungs constrict. I'm dizzy, and I'm going to throw up. The need to escape hits me hard. I get out of the car, and to my surprise, he gets out, too.

I grit my teeth. "She knows that you two aren't real, right? That you're—"

The unshed tears in his eyes almost cut me in half. He shakes his head slowly. "We are real."

"You and her? Or you and me?"

As he gets nearer, the urge to back away grows stronger. But also the urge to run to him. His next words shred my belly to ribbons. "Randy. I know I've made some mistakes with you, but I had to make a choice before she left."

"You've made some mistakes? With me?" My volume rises.

He nods, beads of sweat gathering on his lip, and he doesn't say anything.

"You're scared. You and she are just friends who hang. Not lovers." My finger shoots to his face, and I realize I'm yelling at him at full volume on my street. Any of my neighbors could hear, and I don't care. "You don't want to marry her. You double-downed on a lie when you could have freed yourself with the truth."

He gets right in my face, his meaty hand balled into a fist. He's a huge guy, although I'm not small. "You shut the fuck up, Randy."

We're so close to each other. I whisper, "Your dick's fucking hard for me. I know it."

"I'm. Straight," he hisses, slashing his head to the side and then returning my intensity. "I'm straight, damn you. This is why I date Kim. This is why I am marrying Kim. I can't date you."

"But you want to fuck me!"

"I've never done that."

"But you want to."

We glare at each other. I know his dick is hardening, because mine is too. I should just reach over and kiss him to shut him up.

"We're not having this discussion," he mutters, his fists clenched and trembling.

"We are. We've put it off too long."

Aware of all the houses with open windows around us, he shoves his hands in his pockets. "We're especially not having this discussion in public."

"It's not a discussion," I growl. "It's about to be a fistfight."

"Don't be stupid, Randy. I'd wipe the floor with you, and I don't want to do that."

"Why?" I ask, reckless now. "Maybe you need a punch in the jaw. You're ignoring the times we've been in the same bed. The times I've rubbed you off . . ."

"We were kids. Experimenting. I'm not," his voice drops to a whisper, "gay." His arms cross over his chest.

"What about last night?"

A screen door bangs behind us. "Stop it. Someone's going to call the police." And what he doesn't say, is *someone will know about us.*

I wave him off. "They'll think we're fighting about Kim."

"We are, aren't we?"

I take a deep breath. His eyes flick down to my lips, up to my eyes, then back down again. The corners of his mouth turn down, and his breathing is shaky. I know his full-staff erection grinds against his zipper, because mine does too.

This is it. The last time. I need someone who can love me back. Not someone who denies I exist. "Just get out of my sight. Leave. I can't fucking talk to you."

He pauses, his eyes watering, the anger draining out of his face. Then he walks over to the driver's side, makes a fist, and hits the top of his car. Then he opens the door, and stands before he gets in, arms listless at his sides. "Randy. You're my best friend. I want to always be your best friend. But we can never be anything more." Ducking down, he sits in his car, closes the door, and leaves.

It's not until I get in the shower that I let the tears stream down my body, mingling with the water circling down the drain.

♫

I figured out I had feelings for him when I was eleven. My Nana June invited Kim, Shane, and me to the musical *Mamma Mia*, performed by the local theatre players.

Nana must have known something before I did.

At that age, I was just excited I was allowed to stay up late. We sat in the darkened theatre, sticky with soda residue, on dusky-red velvet seats with stabby metal springs sticking out of them, the four of us pretending we were in New York City, not West Des Moines. We knew the ABBA songs because Nana played them in the car. Kim, Nana, and I sang during the entire performance.

Shane refused. Instead, he watched us with amusement in his eyes and a tick in his cheek. To mess with him, I threw a turquoise boa around his neck during *Dancing Queen*, and he wiggled out of it like it was a real snake. So, I picked it up and put it around mine. Needless to say, I rocked it, shaking my ass in husky boy's chinos. Back then, I was a big kid, so it was extra funny when I wore feathers. Like a Samoan wrestler's son wearing a tutu. Thankfully, I've stretched out since then.

During intermission, while we lingered outside drinking hot chocolate and reading the program, Shane decided to show Kim and me how he'd learned to do round-off cartwheels. Only he got too close and his shoe slammed into my face, giving me my first black eye.

Upon connection, I reeled back, pressing my hand to my face and blinking back tears. Sure, a tough kid like me could take it, I thought, but I wasn't expecting my best friend to clobber me at a *Mamma Mia* show.

His face dropped, and his eyes widened in horror.

"I didn't mean it! I'm so sorry!"

Shane threw his arms around me and held me tight, clinging like an octopus to my shoulders, not letting me breathe. He shook against me, clawing at my hair, close to sobbing. He kept repeating, "I didn't mean it. I'm so sorry."

Over and over and over again.

One of my palms pressed into my eye, the other hung uselessly at my side. I breathed in and out, experiencing the way his body touched mine. The way he clutched at me, wanting so badly to make me feel better. To not have hurt me.

Even at that age, his arms were strong. He felt like the comfort of a blue summer's day lying in green grass with a warm breeze and sunshine. Like the company of Cyril, my old ratty teddy bear. Like watching *Indiana Jones* while eating an ice cream sundae with sprinkles instead of nuts. Like everyone laughing at my joke about the potato newscaster—he's a "common tater." Like all the lists of all the things I adored wrapped into one single human being on earth.

I knew, I just knew I felt something more than regular friendship. More like, he could bruise me, rip off my limbs, make my skin bleed, and I would follow it up by laying down my life for him and/or making him laugh.

Yes, I was a little dramatic, even at age eleven.

I also knew he was good for me, even if he couldn't help hurting me. He didn't mean it. And I knew underneath it, he cared.

Summoning my voice and stepping back, I muttered, "I'll be okay, dude. You'll make a great forward on next year's soccer team. That penalty kick was epic. If you change to gymnastics though, make sure you clear the space for your landings."

His eyes searched mine—well one, the other one was shut—making sure I was okay. Then he smiled at me and nodded. "Will do."

Kim got ice. My grandma gave me an aspirin. We went back for the second half of the show. And thus began my career stuffing down my emotions so no one could see, and hiding my heart behind a joke.

Ten years later nothing's changed, except Kim's got the ring from him, not me.

♫

In the middle of the night, my phone buzzes about six inches away from my head. Guess I passed out while watching *Black Panther*.

A male voice rumbles, "Is this Randy Sanchez?"

Yawning, my face planted into the pillow, I mumble, "Yeah."

"Do you know a Shane Nichols?"

I startle, fully awake now, flipping the covers down fast. "What happened? Is he okay?" Sitting up with my feet on the floor, adrenaline courses through my veins. I rub my eyes and ruff up my hair, now impatient for the guy on the other end to talk faster.

"He's fine. He just needs a ride home. He can't drive like this. He told me to call you."

Never in my twenty-one years have I seen Shane get drunk by himself. Alcohol doesn't go with his green juice shots anyway. I'm the one who prefers beer over squats.

I'm already up and pacing. "I'll come get him. Where is he?"

"Charlie's bar."

"I'll be there in ten. Tell him to stay there." I throw on sweatpants and a thermal shirt and grab my keys, wallet, and phone. Then I get in my Camaro.

I don't remember the blur of the drive, except all I think about is him. When I arrive with my tires crunching in the gravel parking lot, I park and race in, but Shane's not at the bar or any of the tables in the dim lit room.

"Hey, look at this fresh meat," a singsong voice calls out.

I ignore him and call to the bartender, "I'm looking for Shane. Someone called me."

"You Randy?" I recognize the voice from the phone and nod. The bartender points. "He's in the john."

Tearing down the black-painted corridor, I beeline to the men's bathroom.

Shane kneels before the white porcelain, his head down in the nasty public toilet.

Eww.

As always, my heart squeezes when I see him, even after the fight we had. In most ways, he's perfect, without a hair out of place and his body a classical ideal with an inverse triangle torso and lean hips.

But when anyone is crouched over a toilet, gray and puking, they don't look so hot. He jumps when my knuckles rap on the wall. I'm struck by the beauty in his dizzy, glazed eyes. In his divine lips—that likely smell disgusting.

And even though he's shattered me, I'm hopelessly in love with him.

Always have been. Always will be.

Even when flames of anger lick up my spine. I shove them down. Rather than beat myself up, I act the best friend. Shoving an arm under his armpits, I hoist him up, businesslike. "C'mon buddy. Let's get you home."

It takes him a moment to focus on my face and process. "Randy. S'you," he slurs. "It's my best friend, Randy. Do you know I'm getting married?"

"I do." I manage to get out of the bathroom and proceed down the hall, stumbling under his weight. It's not that he weighs a lot, but with useless legs and arms, it's like carrying a statue.

"I'mmm kindah—" Shane words stick together. "The room ish spinning."

"Can I get some Gatorade?" I call out as we make our way to the front door, the eyes of the crowded room on us.

The bartender acknowledges my request with a chin lift, pulls a plastic bottle out from a glass-fronted refrigerator, and weaves his way through the tables over to us. Balancing Shane on my side, I pull out my wallet and hand the bartender a bill, not knowing what it is, and not waiting for any change. For all I know, I gave him a hundred. Nana hooked me up long ago, paying for not only my education, but my condo as well, may she rest in peace.

As I open the door, Shane buries his face against my neck and his lips skim the bare skin of my neck.

I think it's a kiss.

We stagger outside, him from drink and me from supporting him.

It's definitely an open-mouthed, wet kiss. Then he's talking against my neck, his lips smashed against my flesh, his tongue licking me. "I decideta try teh-keee-lah. Note to self, I donn like teh-keee-lah."

Oh God, this feels righteous.

Oh God, this is wrong.

And I'm pissed at him.

Facing him, trying to hold him up, I search his face for signs that someone's home despite the alcohol. Results: Inconclusive. "Noted. No tequila for you, big guy. Let's get you in my car."

He falls forward, and his mouth presses against mine.

Goddammit.

His gorgeous, hot, disgusting tongue mines my mouth, seeking my tongue.

I want to kiss him back.

I want to do more than that.

We can't kiss in the parking lot. Or anywhere. Not here. Not with him incapacitated.

And especially not after his proposal earlier today.

I extricate myself from his kiss and hold him in a hug, the habit of being there for him overriding my anger from earlier. "I got ya, Shane. I'll take you home."

A chill makes the end-of-summer night air sting, but I don't want to go back inside and see if he has a jacket, and I left without mine. If he forgot one in the bar, I'll buy him another one.

He releases his entire body weight on me as I hold him up under his armpits. Snuggling into my neck, he sighs. "You smell like buttered toast and cinnamon."

I glance around, but no one sees how far Shane is off the rails. All I can think to say is, "Thanks."

His words still blend together, making it hard to pull them apart, and he's still talking against my skin. "I jus wannened you to know. I hadta doooit. I hadta do it, man. I couldn't doannything else."

I'm mad at him. He's fucked up my life. I need to remember that.

It's hard to remember when he's completely drunk and saying what I want to hear.

With much effort, I get him in the car, then roll down the window, hoping if he pukes, he'll aim out instead of in.

"The wurld spinshh, Randeee. It's all a mess. I sosorry. I fucking fucked it up."

Is he saying . . .?

What is he saying?

I should ignore him.

Unfortunately, my damn heart still beats for him, even when I order it not to.

By the time I get in the driver's side, he's passed out snoring, and I drive in near-silence, the cold wind whistling through the car and the heater on blast. I could take him home, but since he lives with his parents and they shouldn't see him like this, I return with him to my place.

Side note, while he could live with me, he's made excuses for years about saving money by living at home, not that I would charge him rent.

Bet he was just too scared of what would happen.

That makes me shake my damn head.

I drag his limp carcass out of my car, hoist him up over my shoulder in a fireman's carry, and bring him inside. Heading to the guest bedroom, I lay him down on the bed, setting his head gently on the pillow.

He stirs, and his eyes crack open, confused.

"Take a sip of this." I offer him the Gatorade.

Shaking his head, he refuses, then winces with pain. He opens his mouth to say something, but just hazily scrutinizes my face. Then his eyes flutter shut.

I look at him with a mix of emotions. Like I'm smiling at an adorable, sleeping puppy who wore himself out by ruining my slippers.

Only what he's done is worse than using the wrong chew toy.

Sighing, I wonder what to do with him. He can't sleep like this. Carefully, I remove his shoes. Then I pause.

Taking off his clothes is something I'd rather do under different circumstances. But he looks uncomfortable, and I don't want to leave him like this. Reaching over, I unbuckle his belt and stick my finger inside his waistband to unbutton his jeans.

Just that act gives me a chub.

And makes my heart feel like it's shrinking, because he isn't mine to touch.

Steeling my nerves, I pull down his zipper, trying not to let my knuckles graze him, but noticing what a delicious bulge he's got going on. Then I shimmy his pants down to his ankles and yank them off.

He needs a change of shirt. I go into my room, grab a clean T-shirt, and on my return, pick up a bucket from the utility closet.

With much effort, I help him dress. Being so close to him makes every one of my nerves sing. His bare skin is so warm and soft, his muscles so raw and rough. Even when he smells like vomit, he's astonishingly alluring.

I want him.

But I'm not going to do anything, except get him settled and comfortable. Once his cheek rests on the pillow, I marvel at him. High, cut cheekbones. Slightly lopsided, but full lips. A jaw so square it could be used as a right-angle ruler. But with his eyes closed, he looks peaceful.

Dammit.

Bustling about the house, I place water and Kleenex on the bedside table, pull the blanket over him, and kiss his forehead gently.

He's so out of it, he'll never know.

I linger for a moment, letting his hair caress my face. Inhaling his shampoo. Feeling the warmth radiating from him.

Straightening up, I run my hands through my hair and shake my head.

Shane turns over and mutters, "I love you." Then curls up and goes to sleep, snoring loudly.

I head to my room, knowing a thin wall separates us physically, but his refusal to accept his feelings may be a deeper divide that can never be breached.

♪

Tonight's dream features him hooking his fingers in his waistband, dropping his black sweatpants like the curtain to a show, while my throbbing heart travels to my throat, where it remains.

I stare at his cock. Along the underside of his erection, red and blue veins wrap upward like rebellious stripes on a barber pole refusing to stay in the lines. His dick is hard, thick, and heavy in his hand.

It's magnificent.

In the haze, I kneel before him, ready to be subservient. The carpet abrades my knees, and my tongue readies, anticipating the pleasure I'm going to deliver. Hoping for moans and grunts and a lost, crazed look in his chestnut eyes.

My eyes travel from his muscular thighs to his deep cobblestone abs to his intensely aroused face, hoping he doesn't shut me down. *Us* down.

But no, we're good. His wide eyes barely hold in the inferno blazing behind them.

He runs his hands through his short, superhero haircut, jutting his dick toward me, and my own cock twitches.

He nods.

I nod.

I take a deep breath.

He's mine, and we're finally doing this without fear. Without being ashamed.

Together.

On my inhalation, I extend my fingers, noticing the blue veins on my dark tan skin, the individual hairs on my arms, a faint pale scar on my wrist from where I fell riding my bike.

Saliva pools in my mouth, wanting his taut muscle.

I lean forward.

Almost there.

Just this once—

But there's nothing to grasp. No one's there. My fingers fall into air.

I cry out and wake up in bed alone, sweating, thrashing, my hand around my own stiff cock. It's 4:58 a.m., and Shane Nichols will never be my lover. I roll over, but the weight in my chest doesn't move to the side. It just settles in like unformed clay, heavy and opaque.

Pumping myself violently, almost ripping my skin, the release I give myself is poor consolation.

I want the real thing, and I'll never have it.

♪

Later that morning, a sleepy, yawning Shane, wearing only his jeans, shuffles into the kitchen as I'm making coffee in my gray sweatpants and Bob Ross T-shirt.

"Morning, sunshine," I call. "You look like hell."

Actually, he doesn't. He enters the room as my Adonis with bedhead, scruff, and no shirt. In other words, perfect. How can someone with a hangover look *better* the next day? It's truly not fair. He sits at the bar and cradles the glass of water I hand him, but doesn't take a sip. A green tinge still lines his face. He avoids my eyes and keeps his distance.

"How drunk did I get last night?"

My smile feels forced, and it hurts to look at him. "Very."

He peers around the room blankly, stretching arms up, making his muscles dance.

Sexy as hell.

For fuck's sake.

"After I told my parents what I did and they were so happy, I suppose I needed to celebrate my engagement."

My breathing falters, and my stomach clenches. "Right. Do you remember any of it?"

"Some of it." He rubs his eyes with his fists, a move so charming my heart soars. *No, Randy. You're pissed.* Mid-rub, he stills. "Fuck. We missed taking Kim to the airport."

I turn my back to him and get out coffee cups. "Her parents were planning on taking her."

"Yeah, but we could have said goodbye one last time."

My throat closes up, and a headache threatens. I pour two cups of coffee and pass him one.

He steeples his hands and presses them to his lips. "Thanks for coming and getting me. I know I've been . . . I know yesterday was a surprise to you. I'm sorry we fought. I shouldn't have had it out with you, when I didn't tell you what I was going to do." His eyes are soft. "I don't deserve you."

A derisive laugh leaves my throat before I can stop it. "True. You don't deserve me."

Shane's eyes catch mine, and I see a flicker of something behind them. Indecision? Regret? Maybe I'm just imagining it. Then he chuckles, and I can't tell if it's because he's thinking of our fight or something else. "Yeah. I was going back and forth all afternoon about what to do. It was driving me crazy. Finally, I figured the only way to get me out of my misery was to just ask her."

It's not the only fucking way to deal with our whatever, *Shane.*

I turn to the fridge and take my time getting cream for my coffee. I never really thought his relationship with Kim was real. Thus, I've never felt guilty about my feelings for him. I was just biding my time, waiting for him to wise up.

But now I'm wondering if I'm even allowed to feel this way.

And I'm wondering if any of this would hurt Kim.

God, I just need to get over him.

I sit across from him. After he takes a few more sips of his drink, I get brave enough to ask questions. "When did your parents give you your grandma's ring?"

"A while ago. They've always wanted me to, uh, you know." His voice is low. "Marry her." He blushes.

I can picture the scene. Ron and Denise calling Shane into the living room and presenting him with grandma's ring to use when it came time to get engaged. Since the only girl he'd ever been linked to was Kim, obviously they meant her. They know her parents well since the Browns and the Nichols go to church together every Sunday. While her family is visible in the community due to her mom's successful weight loss business, his is prominent in other ways. Ron Nichols served as mayor twice, and Denise is on the school board.

Shane's parents are friendly people. Kind and loving. But the idea of having a non-hetero son would send them to therapy. They donate money to conservative causes designed to ensure traditional values are maintained. They actively talk about political events and their personal political views, which don't match his. He's gotten the message over the years that if he tells them, they'll disown him—and I don't blame him. I've seen it. Despite his need to face who he is, he's too scared to lose his family.

With a tight chest, I scrape my hands down my face and stay on my side of the kitchen island.

After we finish our first cup of coffee in silence, I pour him another, and he gives me a small smile. "What are you doing the rest of the day? I had plans to go to the gym. Wanna come?"

Giving him a half-hearted shrug, I pull myself together and rub my belly, always covering my true feelings with a joke. "What are you saying?" I'm no Santa, unless I puff it out, but I definitely don't have the definition he does. "This doesn't count as a washboard?"

The crinkle around his eyes and his genuine smile melt my cold, dead, irritated heart. His eyes stay on mine extra long. "I want the company, I think."

"You know it's a cold day in hell to get me to the gym."

While I should just go somewhere quiet to think, maybe getting out some frustration is just what I need.

♪

"Spot me?" I ask.

Sitting on the bench, my legs on either side, I lower myself backwards to bench press the barbell. Just the effort of slowly lying backwards wracks my nerves. Yes, I realize the bench will hold me up, but since I'm not so good with crunches, falling backwards gives me vertigo. I feel like I'm falling blindly into the void and don't know if I'll make it to solid ground. I've got no support.

Maybe this is why I don't go to the gym often. Maybe this is why I don't mind an extra ham sandwich at lunch—although thankfully my genes have kept those sandwiches from showing in my jean size. Maybe this is why the gym has always been Shane's refuge, not mine.

I'm starting to reevaluate that stance, though. As I lie on my back on the bench, my feet spread wide on the ground and hands reaching up to grasp the bar, Shane moves to my head to spot me, then takes a sip of gator-juice.

He's right there.

I can smell him—a bit salty, coppery, but also with a zesty soap scent. If I could lick, I would.

Then I frown.

His crotch is right by my face in thin black nylon shorts. My God, even his knees are handsome. The dusting of hair on his legs makes my fingers stretch to touch him. I blink and shake my head slightly, needing to focus, or I'll show how much I like having his groin in my face.

Shane bends over the bar and talks to me, his face upside down. "How many reps you going for?"

"Ahnold pump iron ten times," I say, using my Schwarzenegger impression again.

He glances down my body, his eyes lingering along my torso, but then he gets to my shoes and does a double take. "How long has it been since you bought shoes?"

"A while." I do a weird shrug while lying on my back. "What? You think I need new ones?"

"Yes."

Shane's meticulous personality doesn't allow for sneakers with the toes ripped out so badly you can see my socks. "So, like, you wanna go school shopping with me?" I ask, imitating a bored teenager.

He snort-laughs. "Yeah, sure. In the meanwhile, let's start you with a plate on both sides." Moving to the rack, he comes back with two large black circular weights, his pretty biceps bulging even though he moves ninety pounds as easily as two books.

"You got it, boss." Exhaling, I put my hands up on the metal bar. It's thick and scratchy, with a crosshatched area so it doesn't slip. While two plates should be doable for me, I don't want to embarrass myself.

And maybe I can pound out my feelings for him this way.

"Randy, you can do this. No problem."

Breathing in and out of my nose rapidly, I grip the barbell and push up, doing ten presses as fast as I can. My muscles burn, and I replace the bar and pant. "You do this every day?"

Peering down at me with those eyes, he's amused. "Normally with two plates on each side. Or more."

"You're Hercules."

He shrugs and downs some more electrolytes. I watch his throat undulate as he swallows, and it's about the most erotic thing I've ever seen.

Fuck.

After a moment, I'm ready to bench more weight. But this time, as I place my hand on the bar, Shane's pinkies brush my index fingers. Casually, so casually, he explores the space between my thumb and pointer finger, his strong finger pressing my skin.

What the hell?

I'm not imagining this, right? My head twists from side to side, checking out what's going on with the rest of the gym. No one pays attention to us, because they're engrossed in their own routines and exercise. Shane's almost absentmindedly, like he doesn't realize what he's doing, but the inside of my fingers tingle from his touch.

I look up at him. His skin is flushed, and his eyes shine. Almost imperceptibly, he inches his whole body closer to me, and I experience his *presence*. His warm, solid body so close to mine. He keeps stroking the sensitive part of my hand, and it's like he's exploring somewhere else on my body. Some other area that reacts as much as this area does.

It's so fucking naughty. Brazen, but subtle. Sensual, but chaste. If he keeps doing it, I might show through my shorts.

We have to stop this.

I can't do this to Kim. I can't do this to me.

With an exhale, regretting breaking the spell, I begin another set of ten bench presses. This set goes a little slower. At the end, when my muscles fail, Shane guides the bar back to the rack above me. As he does this, he extends his torso, and the material of his shorts falls over the top of my head.

I close my eyes in ecstasy. Or anguish. I can't think which.

It's not just the thin fabric of his black athletic shorts. I can feel *him* underneath. How full he is in his pants. How one touch would make him explode. We're in public, but lifting weights with Shane feels intimate. A cocoon of just the two of us in our own little world.

He lingers above me a moment too long, then steps back and whips out his phone, texting someone like nothing happened.

Motherfucker.

A flash of anger sizzles through my spine. I figure out immediately that Kim's texting him when he takes a Skype call from her.

And I'm helpless to do anything. Because she's my best friend, too.

With an embarrassing amount of effort, I sit up, dust my hands off, drink water and watch him talk to his fiancée face-to-face on his phone.

While wanting to throw the barbell across the room with a guttural roar.

Kim's saying how weird it is to discover this other place on the planet where there are millions of people who have never heard of her. His response is to dazzle the screen with his megawatt smile, the charming one I haven't seen in a while. "You're so weird," he says with fondness in his voice. I can't hear everything she's saying, but his voice gets deeper. "I like that about you."

How come he waits until she gets to Spain to flirt with her?

Or have I never seen it?

I'm irritated and on edge, trying to figure out why I'm torturing myself with him.

To avoid strangling him, I snatch his phone, plant my feet wide apart, and make sure my face takes up the whole screen, smiling maniacally like everything's all right.

"Yoko! *Parlez vous* Spanglish?"

Her sweet face has a broad grin, and it hurts to see her. "Hey, Randy. Did Shane finally get you to go the gym?"

To keep from showing her my clenched, grinding teeth, I let the phone pan down my torso.

"He convinced me to sculpt these gorgeous abs into the washboard of your dreams."

"I don't dream about washboards," she says.

Then why the fuck are you dating a guy with magnificent ones?

Rage pounds in my ears, and my vision clouds. Once again, I hide it. I tsk at the screen and shake a finger. "Ah, but see? Now you will."

"Give me that!" Shane yoinks back his phone, and instead of pounding a wall, I slap him on the butt. Hard. Shane's eyebrows raise, but he says nothing and focuses back on Kim, discussing her classes. He's always been interested in her studies, almost dictating what she studies. His control freakiness doesn't just extend to his precise haircut and over the top exercise regimen, but how he treats everyone.

He likes to be in charge. Orderly. Organized. Prepared. Dominant.

This is why I like him.

This is why I need to leave.

This is why he's making me so mad I'm shaking.

"Gotta go," I say, trying to still the involuntary tremors in my body. "Meet you tomorrow for Meals on Wheels."

The surprise on Shane's face registers, and he checks the time. "We've only been here fifteen minutes."

He's right, but I need to leave. I'm not getting in the middle of him and his fiancée, and I can't take another minute with him this close. Otherwise that fight we almost had will turn into a bloodbath.

♪

"Here you go, guys. Let me know if you have any issues, but the route's the same as last week."

Mandy knows we've memorized the routine. Every week since he turned sixteen, Shane and I have volunteered for Meals on Wheels. Shane started when he got his driver's license, and I started because he did. We've stuck with it because after five years, we've really bonded with the people on our route. I'm not going to ghost them just because every time I see Shane, I have to fight getting hard—and want to kick things. Mrs. Svenson and Mrs. Olafson are adorable and laugh at my jokes. They'd miss me if I didn't come for my weekly delivery. I'd miss them too.

And besides, I apparently can't stay away from him no matter how many times I vow to do just that.

Hashtag masochist.

We load up the meals and begin the route. Kim calls on Skype as we head out, but when she finds out we're busy, she ends the call. Her voice sounds different. More confident, maybe? Or determined? At any rate, I'm sure lover boy wants to talk with her later.

I crack my knuckles as we drive to our first client, Jerry, in silence.

"You ready for the new release of *Rainbow Six*?" Shane asks, his voice a croak.

I'm not sure how many hours we've spent playing the Tom Clancy tactics video game that requires teamwork and strategy. "Yeah. New missions. Cool." I stare listlessly out the window.

But I'm wondering if I need a new teammate.

"I hear the expansion pack is going to be epic."

I close my eyes briefly and open them.

Are we friends? I guess we've always been best friends. And

maybe I need to stop wanting more than he does.

Given how he was acting in the gym, though, it makes me think he wants it as much as I do. So I'm confused.

As usual.

"Yeah," I say, not sure what I'm agreeing to. But when we pull up to Jerry's house, I grab a meal and plaster on a smile.

Jerry's a thin AIDS patient who has staved off the disease this long, but the antiretroviral therapy has taken its toll, aging him faster. While we're not required to do more than wish people well, that doesn't count for him. We always stay longer.

"Good to see you, J-Man," Shane says. He grins, hugs Jerry, and hands him an extra container of soup.

"You guys are the best part of my week." With a shaking hand, Jerry invites us inside his quiet, orderly house.

Noticing Jerry's pile of books, Shane asks, "Did you catch the trailer for *Sunset*?" He's referring to the movie based on the blockbuster book.

We know Jerry doesn't want to talk about doctor's appointments, medicine, or health, so we talk about everything but. Movies, books, music, video games, history, and sports are always safe, distracting topics.

"No! It's out? I'll have to search for it."

"I'll send you the link. It was such a great read." With a few keystrokes, Shane texts him the YouTube hyperlink.

"Thanks. I can't wait to see it."

We chat a while longer and leave. I'm feeling marginally better. The perspective of delivering meals helps. Donating my time forces me to confront something other than my own problems, which is the best thing I could possibly do. My relationship status becomes insignificant compared to handing a frail, elderly man a meal because he has no other support to help him. Maybe my *whatever* with Shane can work out, or, as much as it depresses me, maybe I'll find someone else. After all, he's not the only person I've ever kissed. I did try a few girls at parties, but they weren't for me. But maybe there's another guy . . .

Ha. Not after ten years of silently falling for Shane.

I just need to accept the fact he's going to marry Kim and his feelings for me aren't strong enough to risk everything and show the world.

No big deal.

Okay, it's a big fucking deal. But apparently that isn't enough. With my next thoughts, the temperature in my body rises. Maybe I'm the one in denial, not him. I accuse him of ignoring what he feels, but maybe he genuinely wants to have a forever relationship with Kim. I need to quit whatever I've been doing. Whatever happened in the gym? That was just a mistake.

Like he said.

Back to being friends. While I don't want Shane out of my life, I don't want him ruling my thoughts either. Better to try to make things go back to normal. "Did you see that Twitter feud between . . . ?" I ask.

He grins. "No. What happened?"

I explain the latest celebrity gossip, and we continue on our route, delivering meals to Mrs. Nielson and Mr. Sternitzke. Greg. Johnny. And the rest of the clients.

As we turn in to the Meals on Wheels parking lot after finishing our rounds, I ask, "Want to come shoe shopping with me after this?"

My stomach flutters, wondering if this is a bad idea. Or if it's a step toward a new friendship.

"Sure." He parks and gets a faraway look in his eyes. "Remember when we were little and got new school shoes? They made me run faster."

"Definitely."

"That was the best feeling."

If I get new ones, am I going to be able to run so fast I can catch up to him? Or should I turn in the other direction and flee?

♪

After shoe shopping and noshing at the Mongolian BBQ place, we head to my house and play *Call of Duty* for hours. I'm happy spending an entirely normal day with him. Back to being the best friends we always were—except for the slip-ups we're not discussing.

When it's time for dinner, I talk him into pizza—he normally subsists on protein powder and macronutrients—although he skips the beer.

"I'm not touching alcohol forever. For at least a week," he vows with a wry smile.

We turn on Netflix and plop on the couch to binge watch *Vikings*. Shane slumps on one side. I lie down with my feet hanging over the other edge, my head close to his thigh.

"These guys are brutal," he says admiringly.

"I know. They just hack at each other. Swash, swash, swash. Buckle, buckle, buckle. Guess that's what happens when men are in charge. We practically kill each other rather than . . ." My voice trails off. Rather than admit our feelings. Rather than apologize. Rather than talk through what's wrong.

Instead, we don't talk about it at all.

Whatever *it* is.

Shane tilts his head at my unfinished thought, but doesn't ask anything else. He must know what I meant.

After a while, he mindlessly runs his nails through my hair.

I stiffen my back. While I want to loll like a puppy, I'm scared if I acknowledge what he's doing, he'll stop.

Maybe he doesn't know it.

Maybe it doesn't mean anything.

Maybe I need to not think about it in addition to not talking about it.

We've always been like this. Like magnets. We can't help but touch each other. Then one of us gets freaked and pulls back.

Although this is just a head scratch. Like a back rub. No big deal.

He goes from scratching my head to pulling strands of my hair, like he's giving my head acupuncture. Again, I want to sigh with happiness, but I'm holding my breath, not wanting him to know how much I like this.

I'm serious about not reading into things. I'm just gonna let him be.

His legs spread slightly as he slides farther down in the couch, and his thigh pushes against the top of my head. His fingers walk down my forehead, and one brushes up and down my nose, caressing it.

I close my eyes.

Now I know he's doing this on purpose, as his fingertips lightly outline my face, massaging it gently. Making me feel attended to. He circles my lips with his fingertip, over and over again.

"Randy," he whispers. My eyelids open and gaze at him. He's got scorching heat behind his eyes, licking his lips, then biting the lower one.

Dammit. I thought we weren't doing this. I thought he'd made his decision, and it wasn't me. I thought I'd made my decision, and I wasn't letting him toss me around like his plaything.

I thought we'd straightened everything out.

But let me tell you.

It's really hard to have scruples when the love of your life is gazing at you like he wants to kiss you.

Of course I'm getting thick down there. I'm sure he is, too.

He leans down.

He's going to kiss me.

Fuck.

Fuckity, fuck, fuck.

What do I do?

Do I push him back?

I don't want to.

Even if it's wrong.

His phone on the coffee table buzzes. We jerk away from each other. I scoot down toward my end of the couch, and he straightens, picking up his phone.

"It's," he clears his throat, "it's Kim." He frowns. "She wants to know what I'm wearing."

Oh, Shane, you oblivious fuck.

I'm going to hell for this, but I love it that he has no clue what she's doing. I grab the phone out of his hand. He'd written, *Hey. Why? Sweats.* My fingers sweep across the screen. *Oh, baby, what are you wearing?*

Kim's quick to notice the change in tone. *Randy??!!!*

Chuckling to Shane, I say, "I think your fiancée wants to sext you. Any interest?"

He turns beet red and adjusts his pants. "Uh, no. Sorry."

"I'll respond," I say. I type, *Hey, girl. Hey.*

The three dots on the screen turn to the message, *Sorry to bug you. I'll message you later.*

By my count, he missed taking her to the airport, talked to her at the gym for five minutes, and shut her down twice. All he texts her is, *K.*

I grab the phone and text her goodbye. Then we move away from each other and watch the rest of the show in silence. It's not the same comfort we had earlier today. There's a charge to the air we don't want to disturb.

Because it might explode.

We binge watch the show until I fall asleep. When I wake up, Shane's gone.

♪

The next day, I meet Shane in the student union to buy books and figure out where our classes are located. When I find him, he's in an area set up with booths for different clubs—pottery, rowing, Manga, student government, and so on.

"Hey," I say. "Wanna get some lunch?"

"Sure." He pulls out a printout of his schedule. "Most of my classes are in the Accounting Department. Where are yours? We can walk there after lunch."

We head to the cafeteria, but as we pass the pride booth, the cute guy behind the table smiles at me. "Heyyy."

I wave.

"Oh, are you two together?" He gestures between me and Shane.

Shane and I answer at the same time.

"Yes."

"No."

Gritting his teeth, Shane glowers at him.

The guy behind the table leans back his chair, unrepentant at throwing a grenade between us. He shrugs. "Sorry, I just assumed you two—"

Shane hustles so fast out of the building, I'm glad I have on my new shoes to keep up with him. He dashes over to an alcove where we're hidden in the shadows, and he starts pacing like a manic wind-up toy, back and forth. Back and forth. Wringing his hands.

"Randy. I . . . I can't do this. We can't do this. I've given Kim a promise ring."

"That you felt forced to give her."

His silence is admission.

"And you don't want to marry her."

He clenches his eyes. "She's a good friend."

"If you were a better friend, you wouldn't have asked her."

Letting out his breath, he says, "I thought it was a good idea. I thought if we made it formal, everything would work out."

My head shakes so hard I think it's going to fall off. "Face facts, Shane. It's not."

"Maybe so," he whispers. "But I can't have someone think I'm," he points his thumb toward the student union, "like that. We can't give off that vibe. Someone will figure it out. We don't live in San Francisco. It's Iowa."

I let out an exasperated yelp. "So, what? People are out all the time! It's not as big of a deal as it used to be."

"Lower your voice," he hisses. "Just because two guys can kiss on TV doesn't mean this town's ready to see us walking down the street holding hands. The default is hetero, haven't you noticed? It's still hard to be out."

"Again, I say so what? I'd be proud to be with you. We can figure it out together." I step closer to him, blocking his pacing. He looks up to me with anguished eyes that slice my guts. I scrub my hand over my face and decide just to lay it out. "Shane. I love you. I've loved you my entire life."

Emotions chokes his voice. "Look. Randy—"

Crossing my arms over my chest, I say, "Break up with Kim. You don't want to marry her, and you know it."

"I can't do it. This isn't how I've been raised." Shane winces. "My parents will disown me."

I curse under my breath. "They'll get used to it."

He grabs his hair and pulls it skyward. "What will Kim say? What will everyone say?"

My hands ball into fists, my nails scoring my palms. The pain focuses me, because otherwise I'd be yelling a lot louder. My words come out impatient and low. "I don't think Kim wants to marry you. You surprised her, and she doesn't want to hurt you. As for everyone else? If I tried to save you from what everyone would say about you, I'd never succeed. People are always going to say shit. It doesn't matter. *Whatever* we have together is way more important than what some other person says about us."

He shakes his head, scrunching his eyes closed tight.

I keep talking. "You're scared to be yourself. You need to admit who you are on your own. No one can do it for you. But if you won't admit it to yourself, you won't admit it to me. So instead, you're going to marry your sweet, beautiful 'girlfriend.'"—I have to use air quotes—"in a passionless ceremony that will be the epitome of nice, while underneath there's nothing nice about it."

His nostrils flare, and his chin lifts up defiantly. "That's not true. I love Kim."

"We both love Kim, but not that way."

I step forward, wanting to hold his hands, to hug him, to do something to comfort him. But I can't. "I've loved you my entire life."

"Randy." He's sweating, his muscles jumping under his skin. He whispers, "Even if I wanted to be with you, I couldn't."

He didn't hit me physically, but the punch in the gut feels just the same. Tears well in my eyes, and I shake my head.

I can't. I won't. No more. He needs to face it. Face us. "*Whatever this is? It hurts too much.*"

Through his teeth, he grits out, "We. Can't. Do. This." His palms press to his eyes.

My voice is barely audible. "There's only so many times I can be rejected, and I can't do it anymore. *We* can't do this to each other. Until you figure out that trying to please other people will please no one, you need to stay away from me. If you want to find me, you know where I live. Otherwise, I have to leave."

I turn and walk away.

♫

That night, I halfway expect my phone to ring with Shane drunk at the bar, but it doesn't ring. In between my tears and a good portion of a six pack, I weave into my room and open my closet. Reaching up to the top shelf, I pull out an Adidas shoe box from ten years ago.

Carefully I lift off the lid, like I'm opening a treasure trove, and breathe in the dusty, rose petal smell of memories.

Those tickets from *Mamma Mia*? They're in here, along with the program. And I think about how he held me.

My thick fingers rifle through the ephemera.

The stub from every movie I've ever seen with Shane. And we've seen a lot.

All of his school photos. From skinny kid to braces to bad haircuts to my ideal.

Printed routes from Meals on Wheels. So we remember who we've served.

Every wristband from the Iowa State Fair, although that reminds me of too much butter.

All the birthday cards he's ever given me. Every Christmas card. Every word he's written in his uppercase, neat writing, almost like an architect's font.

Prom pictures of the three of us. "Best friends forever," Kim wrote.

Yeah, right. More like two assholes and a beautiful princess.

A strip of pictures from a photo booth. He's laughing, and I'm making a face.

I sit with the memories of him until my head hurts. My body hurts. My soul hurts.

Carefully I place the lid back on and put it back up in the closet, where it will stay. While I could burn them, I won't.

I'll just lock them safely away.

That night, my dreams are a void, like I'm falling backward onto the bench press, but there's no support, and no one to spot my fall.

I start school by myself, find all my classes, and eat alone every day. Between classes, I think I see him, but I don't.

I switch my day for Meals on Wheels. When Jerry asks where Shane is, I can't answer him. I don't know.

Jerry looks at me with understanding and then talks about video games to distract me.

Days pass by, and I feel like an empty cup. I don't know if I'll ever be full again.

Every moment I go without seeing him, it's like those commercials with the dog waiting for his master to come home. I'm thumping my tail at my door longing for him to burst through.

Is it pathetic? Yes.

Do I care that it's pathetic? No.

Do I care about him? *Oh, God. Yes.*

But this time, I mean it. I've had enough of his denial.

He needs to come to me.

I'm worth fighting for.

I hope.

♪

In the middle of the night about a week after school starts, my phone rings, lighting up next to my face, which is smushed into my pillow, as usual.

Shane calling.

Why did he pick now, of all times, to try me?

Is he drunk?

My mind doesn't want me to answer the call, but my heart and body betray me, forcing my fingers to slide the button.

His voice comes through hoarse and scratchy over the line. "I'm outside your door."

I throw my hands up, and in doing so toss my phone across the room.

Pinching my lips together, I breathe in and out.

Do I want to see him?

My hand scrubs over my face. I sit on my bed. I get up. I take my time walking down the hall to my front door.

When I open it, Shane stands on my doorstep, rubbing the back of his neck. At the sight of him, all my muscles go rigid.

"Can I come in?"

I cross my arms over my chest.

If he's here to make amends, I'll let him do it. But if he's here for any other reason, I'll show him the way out.

His eyes are overly bright, his arms curled over his head. "I, uh."

Without saying a word, I just stare at him.

The pain in his eyes makes me think he's here to make amends. He begins again. "Please. Can I come in?"

Nodding, I step back. "Hey." My voice sounds raspy.

He walks in and shuts the door behind him. "Hey." Shifting his weight from side to side, his eyes lock on me, but I can't read them. "I, uh."

I don't move. I can't.

But someone has to give.

"Having trouble talking? Would it help if you wrote it down?"

While he glares at me, a smile still tugs at the side of his lips. "You're not making this easy."

"Making what easy?"

I just don't want to get my hopes up.

Shane shakes his head, closing his eyes, with that grin on his face. But his hands betray his nerves. He takes a deep breath and lets it out. "I've done some thinking. I can't marry Kim. It's not fair to any of us. I was just . . . scared." Tears glisten in his eyes. "I'm so fucking sorry. For everything. I'm sorry to her. I'm sorry to you. I'm going to tell her. In person."

"What?"

"She deserves to know as soon as possible. I'm not waiting until she gets home."

I can't say anything. I don't want to. Blood pulses in my ears.

"I surprised her. You're right. She doesn't want to marry me. She's never hinted at anything like that. She treats us both as friends. But it doesn't matter. She . . . I . . . we need to break it off. I'm breaking it off."

My heart is thumping. What does this mean?

"I, uh. I couldn't go any longer without saying it. I love you, Randy."

Now a tear really does roll down my face. He steps forward, puts his hand under my chin, and kisses me hard. It's a slow, but intense kiss. Our tongues swirl around each other like lumbering cement trucks, carrying such a weight that they're not nimble. Every move means something.

Every move does.

While our tongues lap at each other, I sense a freedom I've never felt with him.

I've never been allowed to have him. But I *feel* him giving me his true self in the way he commands the kiss.

We break apart and take each other in, panting. I think he wants me to say something, but I'm not sure what. "Okay."

"Okay?"

"Yeah, okay."

He smiles, leans in, and kisses me again. But this kiss isn't careful or slow. Instead, as I return it, a decade of pent-up emotion comes roaring out of me, and things get a little less under control.

Like, not at all.

With his brute strength, he pushes me back toward the couch, and we collapse, ending up side to side on my leather couch, the hard zipper of his jeans grinding against the bulge in my sweatpants, our hands roaming everywhere.

My chest touching his. My lips exploring his. My hands holding him to me.

He reaches down, slips his hand in my sweats, and circles his big, gym-roughened hand around my cock, jacking me hard as his tongue probes deeper.

Holy shit, that feels good.

I yank at the denim at his waistline, but it doesn't budge. Unbuckling his belt, he shoves off his jeans to give me access, and we end up on the floor, his pants around his ankles and shoes still on. Clawing at each other. Almost tackling each other.

And damn. He's mine.

With a whir of shirts overhead and legs bending, all of our clothes fall off.

We're kissing like we need each other to breathe.

His cock thumps against my belly, hard for me, and I'm so excited about it, I almost let go right then.

When I finally get to stroke his dick, it's even better than my dream—thick and strong, foreign, yet familiar, and as I milk him, he writhes in pleasure. The groans form deep in his throat, and the desire in his eyes matches mine.

The pace of our kisses intensifies. We've gone from lumbering trucks to racing NASCAR. From *oh my God we're doing this* to a frenzy of *fuck yes, we're doing this.*

Celebrating the liberty to give what we want to each other. To take what we want.

To be with each other.

To feel.

To know.

To love.

That freedom comes fast.

So do we.

"I'm gonna come," he yelps.

"Do it. I am too."

With a pump that overwhelms me, his firm grip makes me climax first. The release feels like much more than an orgasm. It lets loose fear, anger, lies, and hiding.

As my body shudders and shakes, I'm conquering all of the crap we've been through and stepping into new territory. One where we have room for a relationship.

A moment later, his eyes digging into mine, Shane gives an almighty moan of pleasure as his cock unloads. It's messy chaos.

It's love.

Lying side by side, we regulate our breath, then turn to each other and kiss and smile. I thought we'd be more shy or embarrassed, but gazing at him, all I think is, *we've only just started, because I'm nowhere near sated.* I'm sure he isn't either.

We clean up with socks, and then he follows me down to my bedroom.

As we explore each other's bodies all night long, he whispers, "I don't know what I'm doing. All I know is I want to do it with you."

I could mess with him and ask, "the fucking?" but I know he means our relationship.

"Yeah," I murmur. "Sounds good to me, too."

The next morning, Shane wakes up in my bed naked for the first time ever. His huge arms wrap around my torso as he spoons behind me. He nuzzles my neck.

"Morning," he says in a low voice, and I flop over to see his dazzling smile. The one I haven't seen for so long.

"Hey, Sunshine. You—" I want to ask him if he regrets anything. If he's got second thoughts. If he's changed his mind and is going back to Kim.

Or if yesterday is the start of something permanent.

Reading my burgeoning paranoia, he interrupts, keeping me from spiraling into worry. "I love you."

A kiss from him turns into something deeper, and he moves so he hovers over me. But instead of leaning closer, he pulls back and sits on his heels between my legs.

A-plus view, by the way, of his granite pecs and hard cock and bedhead.

He touches my thigh. "Randy, I'm not freaked anymore."

My left eyebrow hikes up to ask, *really*?

Nodding, he says, "Yeah, really. I had time to think about it, and I've decided. Once I decided, it was an easy decision. You're worth everything to me. *Everything*."

He couldn't make my heart sing more if he tried. This time I ask my question out loud, still not believing the change in the past few hours. "Really?"

This time he chuckles. "Again, yeah, *really*. The more I considered living without you, the more I knew couldn't do it. I can't live without you. Ever." His hands trace up and down my legs.

"But what about . . ."

"I have a plan. I'm just sorry it took me so long."

I snicker. Of course Mr. Control Freak has a plan.

He continues, "I saved some money from my internship. I'll fly to Spain and tell Kim about us, but I have to do it in person. It's not right to do it long-distance. Not with what I have to say."

My jaw slacks. "You *do* mean you love me."

The expression of warmth in his eyes is astonishing, but even more so, there's a determination. He knows who he is, and he's not letting anyone tell him differently.

Thank fuck.

"I do. I've had enough of hiding. This is who I am. Who *we* are. I'm making *whatever* this is official in as many ways as we can. If you're on board—"

"I'm so on board, I couldn't be more on board if there were more boards. That doesn't make sense, and I don't care."

"We've waited long enough for each other," he says matter-of-factly.

"Do you want me to go with you?"

He shakes his head. "No. Too expensive for a quick trip. I'll go as soon as I can get a flight." He grimaces. "I'll need to tell my parents too. Would you forgive me if I took some time to figure out how to break that one to them?"

"You don't wanna just rip off that Band-Aid by having me lay a big smack on your lips in front of them?"

Leaning down to kiss me, he whispers against my mouth with a smile, "That would do it."

And his lips go back to doing other things to me.

A few minutes later, Shane's phone rings and rings, and we ignore it. We're busy for the rest of the afternoon.

When he finally checks it, it's a message from Kim.

Dear Shane,
We really need to talk . . .
Kim.

"Time to book my flight to Spain," he says. "I really hope she understands."

ABOUT THE AUTHOR

To find out Kim's story, read SOMBRA, available now.

Leslie McAdam is a California girl who loves romance, Little Dude, and well-defined abs. She lives in a drafty old farmhouse on a small orange tree farm in Southern California with her husband and two small children. Leslie always encourages her kids to be themselves - even if it means letting her daughter wear leopard print from head to toe. An avid reader from a young age, she will always trade watching TV for reading a book, unless it's Top Gear. Or football. Leslie is employed by day but spends her nights writing about the men you fantasize about. She's unapologetically sarcastic and notoriously terrible at comma placement.

Always up for a laugh, Leslie tries to see humor in all things. When she's not in the writing cave you'll find her fangirling over Beck, camping with her family, or mixing up oil paints to depict her love of outdoors on canvas.

More info available at: www.lesliemcadamauthor.com

Moment of Truth

VERONICA LARSEN

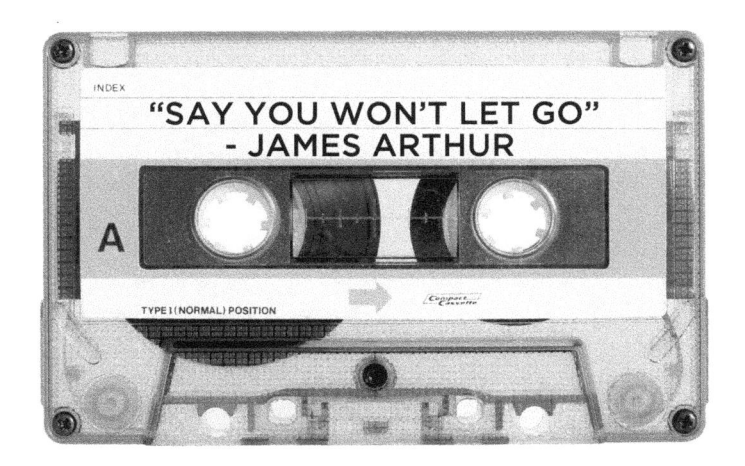

"SAY YOU WON'T LET GO"
- JAMES ARTHUR

CHAPTER ONE

Dean

If I were drunk enough, I might forget I'm still in the city.

There's the unusually warm February night, the Cuban music and the women in tiny dresses standing under the patio lights. There are men too, of course, moving like vultures past the banner that reads, *Valentine's Day Singles Soiree.*

I spot Gabby, sitting on one of the white couches. Her back is toward me but there's a bright cocktail in her hand and she's leaning into a conversation with her roommate, Remi, who's across from her.

I approach them, running a hand down the front of my button-down shirt. It's Remi who spots me first. She gives me a nervous smile, before nodding to Gabby in my direction.

"*Dean?*" Gabby says, her expression frozen with guilt. "*Hey* . . . I didn't . . . I didn't know you'd be here."

"A singles soiree? Are you kidding?" I deadpan. "Wouldn't miss this for the world."

I sit down beside her as though the air isn't suddenly thick with an awkward tension. As though this is like any other night we meet out for drinks.

Except for the sudden silence that follows my arrival.

Across from us, Remi draws the straw of her drink into her mouth and casts her gaze away from us.

Fuck this awkwardness.

I tilt my head toward Gabby and lower my voice.

"What's going on with you?"

It's loud in here, the music is competing against the rising wave of laughter and idle conversation.

"What?" Gabby shifts closer to me and her dress rides further up her thighs.

The sight makes me glad I grabbed a drink before coming to talk to her. I tilt my glass of whiskey to my lips and swallow hard.

I try again.

"You've been avoiding me."

"No, no . . . I've just been going through some weird stuff."

"When did you stop being able to talk to me?"

It's a simple question, but it seems to rattle something in her gaze. A strange struggle floods her features, like she wants to look away, but is anchored by the weight of my words.

By *our history*.

I've known Gabby all my life.

Or, at least, all the years that count.

We were eight when we met, the summer before third grade. She was a golden-haired little girl, playing in the dirt behind the trees instead of sitting delicately on the swings like the other girls. I'd been the lone boy sitting at the top of the hill, trying to hide a bruise on the side of my face by pulling my jacket hood as far down as I could.

By that point in the summer the other kids knew to steer clear of me. I had a tendency to lose my temper and get into fights—which is probably why my father stopped worrying about leaving bruises.

Reckless kids like you get hurt all the time, he'd say.

I'm sure they did. But he and I both knew that wasn't how I tended to get hurt.

That was the day Gabby came up to me for the first time, and I never understood why. Why she asked me to break off a big branch for her fort, like she knew how useless I felt that day. Like she knew how much I needed someone to not look at me like a stick of dynamite that might go off at any moment.

Even though I was.

My rage sat just under my skin in those days. And, honestly, if Gabby had been *my* daughter, I would've warned her off from befriending a kid like me. I was a bad kid. Everyone knew it.

She knew it, too.

She wasn't stupid, she was fearless.

And endlessly generous—she saw my need for an escape and

tugged me into a world of imagination. Making forts that were castles, or digging holes to make moats. We spent the rest of the summer absorbed in a world we imagined, escaping our own realities.

I never felt calmer than when I was with her.

She has the ability to ground me even now.

But tonight, my skin crawls with an urgency I can't put my finger on. All my life, it seems, I've felt right on the verge of losing her. And with her pushing me away for the past week, I've stayed up at night, wrestling a truth I can hardly admit to myself.

I have feelings for her. I don't know when I started falling for her, but I'm too far gone now to try and stop it.

I came here tonight hoping to tell her. I just underestimated how much the awkwardness of her avoidance would sting.

"Gabby . . ."

She puts up her hand, wrongly guessing I'm going to scold her. "Look, I'm good now," she says. "I just needed some time to think, and now I've got it figured out."

I frown, not liking the way that sounds. "Got what figured out?"

Remi clears her throat. "Go on, Gabby," she says from behind the straw of her drink. "Tell Dean what you figured out."

Gabby's eyes seem to narrow in warning, but Remi looks too drunk to care. She bobs her head side to side a few times, offbeat from the actual music playing.

No one talks for several moments, the sounds around us filling the silence. And somehow, Gabby and I are sitting closer than before. My arm is hung over the back of her seat.

This always happens.

We're constantly drawn toward each other by invisible threads.

Yet even as she sits beside me, she feels distant—farther away from me than ever before.

I drag my palm over my face and say, "Look, I'll go. I don't want to invade your . . . *singles soiree*."

"Wait," Gabby says with a groan. She pulls up her long blonde hair and lays the back of her neck on my arm to stare at the night sky overhead. "Please don't go."

The air is flooded with the mouth-watering scent of her shampoo. The same one she's used for years—a smell so comforting, I've come to crave it. I have to fight the urge to lower my face into the side of her hair and breathe her in.

When I glance over at Remi, there's a trace of a smile on her lips like she knows what I'm thinking. The mischievous glint in her eyes hints at her next question. "Oh, for God's sake . . . *why don't you two just screw already?*"

Gabby sits upright, coughing.

"*What?*"

"You heard me, Gabby. You heard me just fine." Remi raises her drink in mock toast.

Gabby looks flustered for the first time tonight. "*You—No, that's* . . . We grew up together—"

"And?" Remi asks.

"I wasn't always this good looking," I offer.

Gabby laughs and slaps my chest, but I set my hand over hers and flatten her palm there.

Before I realize what I'm doing, our eyes lock and there's a strange glint in hers, like she *knows*. Knows I've been coming to grips with my feelings for her. I have to wonder if she's actually considered something happening between us.

Gabby looks back at Remi, blinking.

"It's just too weird to think about," she mutters. "*Me and Dean?*" She laughs nervously, picks up her drink and gulps down what's left of it. "Anyone need another drink? Because I do. I'll be right back."

"*Run, Gabby,*" Remi sing-songs in a wispy tone, "*Run so your feelings don't catch you.*"

Visibly annoyed now, Gabby gets to her feet and edges her way around the circular table. Her dress shows off her gorgeous, long legs and I stare hungrily at the smooth skin of her inner thighs when she steps over my feet.

Then I remember Remi's watching me.

She shakes her head, laughing. "You've got it *bad.*" She drags out the last word, then stares into space for a few seconds before adding, "Seriously. I've been trying to tell her . . ."

"Hang on—you two talk about this?"

Remi answers with a non-committal, "*Mmmmm.*"

"Remi . . . tell me what you know."

She narrows her eyes. "I was sworn to secrecy."

We have a silent standoff, staring at each other and daring the other to speak. To confess.

But Remi, clearly drunk, seems to forget about the standoff after just a few seconds. She leans in and lowers her voice.

"Gabby's been having dreams about you."

I tilt my head. "Dreams?"

"*You know* . . ." Her smile widens.

I stare at her, not daring to take her seriously just yet, because she's been known to mess with people for sport. But Remi nods at my incredulous look and says, "*I know* . . . crazy she's just now having them—I've been having sex dreams about you since the day we met. I'd fucking *destroy* you." She snorts. "Don't tell Gabby I said that. But seriously, mine are innocent compared to hers."

"Wait—" I hold up a hand, sure I've heard her wrong. "Gabby's having sex dreams about me? Why wouldn't she tell me?"

"Isn't it obvious? They're fucking with her. Why do you think we're here? She's trying to get them out of her head."

Remi raises her free hand at our surroundings. Just then, a guy walks by our table, his eyes fixed so squarely on the plunging neckline of Remi's dress he nearly trips over his own two feet.

The humor of the situation evaporates from the air when I realize what Remi is trying to tell me.

"Are you saying she came here to find someone to sleep with?"

"Someone who isn't *you*. She wants everything to go back to normal." Remi pauses to slurp back more of her drink, then flicks her gaze to the ceiling as though she finds this whole situation trivial. "Gabby's super attached to you, Dean. You know that. She's not going to risk making things weird between you."

"Shit's already weird," I say, leaning back in my seat.

I'm staring at Remi. This is a lot to process.

Remi snaps her fingers in the air in front of me to get my attention.

"Dean? You need to stop pretending you're okay just being friends. You guys are not getting any younger and—" Remi stares past me, in the direction of the bar, and frowns. " . . . it's only a matter of time before someone else swoops in."

I follow her gaze and my throat goes dry.

Gabby is standing at the bar with a dark-haired guy. He's got his hand on her arm and she's smiling at him. The chemistry between them is undeniable.

"Who is that?"

"He's been flirting with Gabby all night. I think she actually kind of likes him. But look at him—I wouldn't trust a man who parts his hair on the side like that . . . Looking like a goddamn IRS agent. Fuck that guy."

I can't hear Gabby's conversation, but it looks like the guy is sweet talking her into giving him her number. She takes his phone in her hand and starts punching numbers in.

Gabby's not one to give random guys her number. She's either genuinely interested in him or too tipsy to care. Either way, these guys are goddamn predators. No way in hell I'm letting him or anyone else put their grubby hands on her.

"Where are you going?" Remi calls after me, but I'm already halfway to the bar.

I catch the tail end of Gabby's conversation.

The guy is saying, " . . . maybe sometime this weekend? Tomorrow?"

"I don't know . . . maybe."

She's smiling in a way that makes me want to throw her over my shoulder and take her the hell away from here. I set my hand on her lower back, instead. She turns defensively then relaxes when she sees it's me.

"Let's go dance," I say.

Her eyes go wide. "*Dance?* But you never want to dance."

"I do now."

"Excuse me," the guy says. "We're in the middle of a conversation."

I look him dead in the eyes. "Yeah, and now it's over."

He straightens and for a brief second, I think he's about to take a step toward me. But he sizes me up in a glance and seems to think better of it.

Gabby lets out a small drunken laugh and sets her hand on my chest, as if to calm me.

I'm fine. I'm not worried about this guy.

Gabby downs the shot she just ordered and says, "I gotta go, Ron."

But the guy frowns after her. "It's *Jordan*."

Gabby gives Ron-Jordan a thumbs-up as I guide her away. We step back inside from the patio, to where the music is loud and the floor crowded with people dancing.

"I love this song," she says. With her hands up in the air, she moves her body to the rhythm.

And I stare after her.

I've seen her dance before. But there's something different about tonight. Maybe it's the low pulsing of the lights overhead. Or the people crowding around us. Or the way she's completely unaware of me staring at her ass as she swings her hips to the music.

Or is she moving like this because she knows I'm watching?

I take a step toward her and lower my lips to her ear. "We need to talk."

Her body goes still, then she spins around to face me.

"Talk? I thought you wanted to dance."

"Not until we talk about your dreams."

Her eyes round and she quickly brings her hands up to cover her face. From behind her palms she says something that sounds like, "I'm going to kill Remi."

I take her hands in mine and gently pull them away from her face. She still avoids my eyes, instead staring squarely at my chest. All around us, people are dancing, but we're standing still, somehow knowing we're at the edge of an abyss and neither dares to look down.

The music makes it hard to think. But maybe that's for the best.

Slowly, Gabby's light-brown eyes peer up at me, her face flushed with color.

"I don't want to talk about it," she says.

"Why?"

"Because, Dean, I love you."

My heart stops, just for a moment, before I realize she's not saying the words I think she's saying. She's not confessing being in love with me. She's reminding me she loves me in the way I've always known she has . . . *as a friend*.

I swallow.

"I know, Gabby. I know."

"I don't want things to be weird . . . I can't imagine a world where you aren't in my life," she sighs, then puts her arms around my shoulders. "Can we not talk about this? Can we just dance?"

I move in close, setting my hands on her hips. Tilting my face down, I press my forehead to hers.

She shuts her eyes.

The way her scent stirs in my chest scares the shit out of me. Because I want to sink my hands in her hair and pull her lips to mine.

We dance. Too slow for the music. Too slow for the crowd. We dance to the strange silence between us, where neither of us is quite telling the truth.

Finally, I move my lips to her ear.

"I want you, Gabby. I want to *be* with you."

The words escape my lips in a soft whisper, but they leave a burning behind in my chest.

Gabby shakes her head. But she doesn't pull away. She leans into me, bringing our bodies flush together as we sway softly to a different tune than everyone else.

This has always been us, creating our own reality, far from the reach of the world.

But Gabby doesn't respond to my words. Even with her arms around me, even with her body pressed to mine, her silence stings. I swallow back my disappointment. Then I remember she's had too much to drink.

This isn't the time.

This isn't the place.

So, we dance.

I try to focus on the here and now. How she feels incredible in my arms. How I've said the words I was afraid to say, and yet I haven't lost her. Even though she's still not mine.

God, I want her to be mine.

But her delicious scent is shrouded by the smell of liquor and after we dance for a while, Gabby stumbles off for another drink. She's trying to avoid the conversation, I know she is. But she's going to make herself sick.

Finally, I say, "Let's get you home."

We go find Remi, who tells us she wants to stay longer.

Gabby holds onto me as we make our way back through the dance floor and out of the bar to flag down a cab.

It's on the ride home Gabby does something crazy.

She stares at me. Hard. Her eyes reaching into mine, eclipsed by a lust I've never seen on her before. An intoxicating look that makes me want to fuck her right in the back of this cab like a goddamn animal.

"Fuck it," she whispers, moving in on me.

"Gabby . . ." I suck in a breath.

One of her hands is on the back of my neck, keeping my face on hers, but her other hand is smoothing down the front of my shirt, wandering dangerously close to the belt of my pants.

In a far-off voice, she says, *"Let's do this. Right now . . ."*

She's drunk, so far gone.

I take her hand in mine to stop her from reaching too low.

Even as the world spins from the rush of her touch. The way she's staring at me.

Goddamn it.

The cab comes to a stop at her place. I walk her to her door and help her find her keys in her bag.

The street lamp overhead casts her perfect face in beautiful shadows. I want her so bad it's ripping me at the seams not to take her right here on her front steps.

She brings her arms up around my neck and presses her body against me again.

"Don't you want to?" she asks. "Don't you ever think about us?"

I don't know how long we stand there, bodies flushed and pulses racing.

I swallow back my hesitation.

"You're all I fucking think about, Gabby."

Her reaction is slow, like she isn't sure if she imagined me saying it. But I can see the moment the words click into place. Her eyes light up the night. She pulls up on her tiptoes and tries to kiss me, but I take her face in my hands and lower my forehead to hers.

This isn't how I want our first kiss to be.

A drunken mistake on her doorstep.

"You're drunk, Gabby."

"I'm fine, I promise," she breathes. "You should come in."

I have to shut my eyes before I answer.

Because . . . *fuck*, I can't believe I'm about to turn her down.

"I think you should get some rest."

She looks like she might argue with me, but she doesn't. I keep my hands deep in my pockets as she opens her front door and walks into her entryway.

When she turns to look at me one last time, there's a tangible promise in the air between us . . .

It's not too late to change your mind.

I want to come in. So fucking bad.

There's something about her tonight, about the uninhibited way she's looking at me, that's ripped open a possibility I don't want to touch if it means it won't ever go beyond just one drunken night.

I'm in love with her.

I've known it for a while.

"Goodnight, Gabby," I say.

I head back to the waiting cab, telling myself nothing will change come morning time.

I'm going to show her what we can be.

One night—that's all this is.

Except it's not.

I had no way of knowing as I walked down her front walkway, I was about to lose her to someone else, forever.

CHAPTER TWO

Dean

I walk down the hall, loosening the knot of my tie one millimeter at a time. Not that it makes a difference—it's not the collar of my shirt strangling me, or the fact I'm wearing a suit in the middle of the summer.

It's the idea of seeing Gabby in a wedding gown.

I'm halfway to her suite when a shadow crosses my peripheral and Jordan appears in front of me, frowning in his four-piece suit.

"Where are you going?" he asks.

"I'm going to see Gabby."

He straightens. "No, I don't think so. You can't just go in there and—"

I take a step forward and Jordan pulls back a fraction.

"Get out of my way, Jordan."

"No." He sounds firm, but his Adam's apple bobs in a swallow, making the teal bow-tie he's wearing quiver.

My hands are curling into fists at my sides. I can't help but consider how good it would feel to drive my fist into the side of his weak jaw.

Down the hall, a door clicks open and Remi comes running toward us in a long, bright dress. She rushes to stand between us.

"*Whoa*, what's going on here?"

"Jordan was just about to get out of my way so I can go check on Gabby."

"If something is wrong with Gabby, I'll be the one to go check on her," Jordan says.

Remi sighs, running a palm over the back of her neck. "Okay, listen. Jordan—you can't go in there. You're not supposed to see her before the ceremony, it's bad luck. It's best if Dean goes in and talks to her for a few minutes. She needs her best friend."

Jordan's frown deepens. "What exactly is going on with her?"

Remi's mouth opens, but she hesitates.

"Uh, you know. Just the normal jitters . . . feeling ugly and all that . . ."

She's not convincing anyone.

The worry creeping across Jordan's face tells me we're both thinking the same thing.

Is Gabby having second thoughts?

I've spent the last few months parsing every word she spoke, hoping to find evidence she's not as happy as she seems. That Jordan isn't as fucking perfect as he seems.

But he is.

The guy's a goddamn saint. He treats Gabby like a queen and has the means to give her everything she deserves.

And that's where all roads lead . . . Gabby deserves *everything*. And if she's truly happy—I'm not going to be a selfish bastard and try to stand in her way.

There's only been a single point of contention in Gabby and Jordan's relationship.

Me.

He's bent over backwards to give Gabby the wedding of her dreams. But when she begged him to let me be in the ceremony as one of the groomsmen, he resisted and it caused an argument between them. Gabby only let up when I convinced her I was fine with not being in the wedding party. Secretly, I was relieved not to be. I can think of a dozen torture devices I'd find more pleasant than standing a few feet from Jordan as he marries the woman I love.

Now Gabby's freaking out? Does this mean she's having a change of heart? I try and fail to push down an idiotic surge of hope.

Remi sets a hand on Jordan's arm and gives him a reassuring look. "It's going to be fine. This is all normal. Get back to your room and trust me. Okay?"

Jordan's gaze moves toward me and hardens. But Remi gives his arm another little squeeze and he nods. "Fine."

He turns and walks off in the opposite direction. Straightening my suit, I follow Remi to the bridal suite.

The sitting room is full of women in teal dresses, lounging on any surface they can. Some doing their makeup, others scrolling through their phones.

"Where is she?" I ask.

Remi leads me to a set of doors.

An older woman wearing a teal suit runs up and sets her hand on the door handle.

"Excuse me, where is he going?" she hisses to Remi.

I recognize her. She's Jordan's mother.

"Gabby asked for him," Remi hisses back, clearly nearing the edge of her patience.

The woman takes a step back, her face and neck flushing. "It looks inappropriate for another man to—"

"Oh, for God's sake." Remi pulls the door open. "I'll be in there too, okay?"

We step in and Remi closes the door on the woman's red face.

This room has a king-size bed and sweeping views of Central Park. Gabby is nowhere to be seen.

Remi sits on the edge of the bed and nods toward the bathroom. "She's in there."

The bathroom door is open just a sliver. I rap my knuckles against it, gently.

"Gabby? Can I come in?"

There's a soft sigh, then, "Yeah."

The bathroom has so many mirrored walls, I'm not sure what I see first. Reflections of tiles, sinks and tan walls. Then comes a small voice from the corner of the room.

"Hey."

Gabby is sitting in the empty bathtub wearing a white robe.

I unbutton my suit jacket, tug it off and fling it over the white granite counter.

"Hey . . ." I say.

Kneeling beside her, I take in her appearance. That's my first mistake.

I've never seen her look so gorgeous. Maybe it's something

about her skin set against the white porcelain of the tub and the white robe, but she looks velvety tan, with a breathtaking glow. Her blonde hair is gathered up in an elaborate hairstyle I couldn't describe if I tried.

She looks regal.

Like a fucking queen.

She's not looking at me, though. She's staring at her manicured hands. A single leg peeking out of the slit of her robes.

"Gabby, what's going on?"

She shuts her eyes. "*Fuck*. Dean, what I am doing? Am I ready for this?"

My body goes cold.

Stupidly, it hadn't occurred to me she would need me to convince her this wedding is a good idea.

"You can't ask me that," I say, reaching in to sweep a stray hair from her forehead. "You're the one who needs to stand up there and say those vows."

Gabby takes a deep breath, then another. Then another. I realize her breathing is picking up and not slowing down. She brings her hands up in front of her and starts shaking them as though to ward off her thoughts.

"Fuck. Fuck. I'm freaking out. This is normal, right? Remi says it's normal. He's a great guy, right?"

She casts her gaze up at me for the first time. Under a pair of thick, dark lashes, her typically light-brown eyes shine an electric caramel color.

They're like a punch to my stomach.

"Move over," I say.

"*What?*"

"That tub looks like it's big enough for both of us. Move over."

It is. I kick off my shoes and move in beside Gabby, pulling an arm around her. She curves around the side of my body and settles her head comfortably on my chest. Her scent envelopes me, lifting me inches from the earth. I resist the urge to close my eyes, resist the nagging fear this may well be the last time we can do something like this.

"Remember when we were ten," I say, "and you dared me to ride my bike over to the creepy house down the block?"

She shakes with a small laugh. "Yeah, you almost got caught stealing flowers from their backyard."

"Not just any flowers. Big yellow ones you needed for your special magic spell."

Gabby covers her face. "Oh God. I seriously thought I could do real magic from a random website online. It seemed so legit."

"I bet you don't remember what the spell was for."

"I do. It was supposed to grant me a wish. So, I wished for my perfect future. The perfect husband, eight kids, a big house with a barn and horses—you think I can find all that in the city?" She snorts.

We grow silent for a minute, like we're both imagining the same thing. Two little kids, crushing flower petals in bowls and whispering nonsense words under our breaths.

"Hey, Dean . . . I can't remember what your wish was."

I look down at her face, but she's staring straight ahead, as though our memories are projected onto the white tiles of the bathroom.

"I wished for your wish to come true."

Gabby lifts her head to look at me, her eyebrows arched. "Seriously?"

"Yeah. All I remember, even back then, is I wanted you to be happy. I really do, Gabby. I want you to be happy. No matter what. That's always going to be my wish."

Gabby blinks a few times. "Stop it, you're going to make me cry. Do you know how emotional I am today?"

I kiss her forehead, my chest aching.

There's a beast clawing its way from inside of me, desperate to make its presence known.

It's the part of me that's made me reckless and impulsive in every other aspect of my life except for my relationship with Gabby.

She's the one thing I couldn't bring myself to risk—and that's the reason I lost her.

Gabby lets out a breath. "I know I'm being ridiculous. Jordan is great. He's going to be an amazing husband."

Her words hover overhead and seem to slowly lower on me. Two months ago, my grandfather was on his deathbed. He was the only person who knew how I really felt about Gabby. I told him I was going to tell her how I felt, that very night. The words he spoke, which were among his last to me, shattered me.

Let her go, Dean. She's happy.

Let her be happy.

There was a part of me that hoped my grandfather would offer me one last rallying cry, pushing me into the arena. But he didn't. Even he couldn't imagine a world where I'd be able to give Gabby a better life than Jordan could.

Perfect Jordan.

He has the money, he has the connections, he has the reputation of being a nice guy. Me? I have none of those things. I've never wanted any of them until I realized they were the things Gabby wanted. She knows all my flaws better than anyone, she's traced all of my cracks. If I were really the one she wanted—wouldn't she already be with me?

Goddamn it.

I can't do this. I can't watch her get married to someone else.

Why am I going to the wedding, at all?

It's clear Jordan and his family don't want me there. Would Gabby even notice?

Perhaps. Perhaps not.

Regardless, I realize in this moment, there is no reason for me to torture myself.

I'm not going to the ceremony.

I'm going to leave this bathroom, get on the subway and take the train to the last stop. Fuck it. Coney Island it is.

Gabby's looking up at me, frowning. Maybe she sees something in my eyes.

Her mouth opens in the wake of a question—but the door to the bathroom opens and Remi storms in.

She starts to speak then stops when she sees us in the tub. "What in the—you know what? Never mind that—we, uh, we have a small problem."

Gabby and I stare at Remi, who's wringing her hands together.

"Donald isn't going to make it to the ceremony. He's not in good shape."

Gabby shoots up to a sitting position and climbs over me to get out of the tub.

"Is he okay?" she asks of her step-father.

"He's sick to his stomach—something he ate last night."

"*No, no, no . . .*" Gabby starts pacing. "Who's going to walk me down the aisle?"

I get to my feet and step out of the tub as well, my heart pounding. Remi's looking at me. My blood runs cold when Gabby stops pacing and looks at me, too.

"Dean? Do you think . . . I mean, I know it's last minute—Could you?"

No.

Get the fuck out of here.

Fuck no.

Hell no.

That's what I would say, if it were anyone else. But it's Gabby.

Gabby.

The same Gabby that held my hand on walks to school. The same Gabby that took the blame when I broke my dad's flat screen TV because she knew he'd beat the shit out of me.

The same Gabby that's been there for me through every up and down, every goddamn mistake I've made and has never once looked at me any differently.

I've never had much to offer her. But I've never hesitated at giving her everything I could.

"I'll do it. I'll walk you down the aisle."

CHAPTER THREE

Dean

The murmur of the wedding guests dies away as the music signals the beginning of the ceremony.

I stand just outside of the huge oak doors as the wedding party passes me to head down the aisle.

I avoid making eye contact with Remi as she walks by in her teal dress. She had only one thing to say to me right before I left Gabby's suite earlier.

Don't fuck this up for her, okay?

That's all she said.

No context.

Because Remi and I both know I'm still in love with Gabby. And we both know I waited too long to tell her.

There was one night . . . one night, where Gabby seemed to warm to the idea of risking crossing the line. I should've stayed with her—even if I slept on her couch—just to be there when the sun rose. Because come morning, my words were lost in a cloud of intoxication. I called Gabby, but all she talked about was how hungover she was. She didn't remember the moment we shared at the end of the night.

How was I to know she met her future fiancé earlier that night?

I didn't take Jordan seriously until it was too late. Until a giant diamond sat on Gabby's finger and her beautiful eyes begged for me to be excited.

Fuck.

I can't see him from here, but I know Jordan's standing at the end of the aisle, staring at these very doors, waiting for his bride.

And here she comes.

Gabby's walking toward me.

Time crawls to a near-stop. She's all glow and lace, the long tail of her dress flowing behind her as though it has a life of its own.

I can see it now—the future she wished for all those years ago plays out before me.

Gabby with a round stomach, standing barefoot on a lush green lawn that stretches out before her. Two little golden-haired kids run around, their little giggles peppering the air. I walk out into the backyard and wrap my arms around Gabby. She lets out a sigh of relief, smiling with an effortless ease.

Only it's not me. It's Jordan.

He gives her this life. And her life is good.

Her life is everything she deserves.

She's happy.

Let her be happy.

The vision flickers and Gabby comes into focus in front of me.

She looks nervous, but she's smiling at me.

I can't talk.

But if I could, I'd tell her she looks stunning. I'd tell her I wish she was mine.

"Are you ready?" she asks.

I'm not.

She loops her arm around mine and faces the entryway.

This might just be the hardest thing I'll ever have to do in my life.

We wait, and when the organ starts playing, we walk down the aisle to the ominous tune of the wedding march.

My mouth dry, I stare straight ahead, somewhere over the podium. From my peripheral, I catch Gabby looking at me a few times. But the rest of the time, her eyes are on Jordan, who waits at the end of the aisle.

I don't know how long we spend walking toward Jordan, but it feels like an eternity. Long enough for me to think about all of the wasted opportunities.

The years I took Gabby for granted, thinking she'd always be in my life. The times I was too scared to admit my feelings for her had grown beyond friendship. And the times my fear of losing her paralyzed me from telling her the truth.

The night I told her the truth, but it didn't make a dent.

Finally, we reach Jordan.

I barely look at him. Not that he notices. He takes Gabby's hand and guides her forward.

I turn and look out onto the wedding guests. I don't remember sitting down, but the next thing I know, I am.

My ears ring, clogged with the echoes of thoughts that don't really matter anymore.

Don't fuck this up for her, okay?

Let her be happy.

The minister begins his spiel, his words bouncing off the vaulted ceiling and raining down around us.

I don't catch a single one.

My eyes are fixed on Gabby.

And her eyes are fixed on Jordan.

She looks nervous, self-conscious of the hundreds of people watching her.

Then again, he looks nervous too.

From beside me, someone sets a soft hand on mine and squeezes. It's Gabby's grandmother. She beams up at me, her eyes glossy with emotion. She's the only one in Gabby's family who liked me when I was a kid. Maybe because she saw the real me—the me only Gabby managed to bring out.

I look at the glee in the old woman's eyes and I forget, for just one wild second, that I'm watching the woman I love marry someone else. Instead, I see what Gabby's grandmother sees. Her little girl, all grown up in a beautiful gown. The same golden-haired girl who spent hours making boats for ants to cross puddles in after a rainstorm.

The girl who took in every cat. And every stray dog, even when her mother punished her for it.

The girl who couldn't stand to see someone abandoned or hurt or in need.

The girl who saved me.

Saved me from who I was going to become.

Fuck.

Fuck.

I blink several times. The burning in my chest now pairing with the burn in my eyes.

I tug on my tie, hardly able to breathe. And all I can think is . . .

I can't let this happen.

I can't let Gabby marry this man.

She's supposed to be with *me*.

I still can't hear a word the minister is saying, but I'm staring hard at Gabby, silently begging her for a sign.

One look.

One look and I will bring this whole damn thing to an end.

Will she ever forgive me for interrupting her wedding?

Will I be able to live with myself if I don't?

My hands clench to fists and I rush to my feet. And in this exact moment, sound comes rushing back and I hear Gabby's voice hurls toward me like a spear.

Her eyes still on Jordan, she says, "*I do.*"

CHAPTER FOUR

Gabby

I see him from the corner of my eye—Dean, getting to his feet in the front row. My heart plunges into my stomach as the words I just spoke echo in my mind.

I do.

I do.

I do?

But Dean . . . is *Dean waiting for me to look at him?*

Time shutters before my eyes and a strange sensation floods over me, like I've been submerged in water.

I'm frozen, unable to breathe. And all I can hear is my pulse, which draws out impossibly slow—*thump-thump.*

Thump . . . thump . . .

The minister's mouth is moving, but it too, is moving in slow motion. My breathing is jagged as fear grips me.

I think I'm going to be sick.

Jordan's trying to hold my gaze. My expression seems to hint to him something is wrong because his brows pull inward.

All my focus is going toward resisting the urge to turn my head. Just an inch—a fraction—and I will see Dean's expression.

No one in this room knows me like Dean. And for months, I hoped he knew me well enough to see how terrified I've been of this moment.

The finality.

There's no doubt in my mind Jordan loves me. No doubt he means every single word of the marriage vows.

But as his lips part to finally form the words, *I do,* I wonder if he feels the intense dread I felt when I spoke those same words.

In good times and in bad.

What bad times have we had?

He wasn't there when my father was sick. When everyone

thought I would collapse from exhaustion because I refused to leave his bedside. It was Dean who took time off from his job just to make sure I was eating and getting some sleep.

In sickness and health.

Would he really stick around?

I'm a horrible sick person—groaning and whining any time I have a cold. The only person who I let see me in that gross state is Dean, and only because he's never given me a choice.

Until death do us part.

Death? Why does *this* feel like a death? Why does this very moment feel like a funeral to me?

I try to picture my deathbed—next flu season, for all I know. Jordan's not there. There's Remi. There's Dean. But Jordan? How long will he really be around?

Where the hell are these thoughts coming from?!

Stop it. Stop it.

Jordan is a good man.

The *perfect man.*

There hasn't been a moment where I haven't been reminded by everyone around me how lucky I am to have him.

Lucky.

Why don't I feel lucky?

Why do I feel . . . trapped?

"I do," Jordan says.

I'm very aware of Dean still on his feet. He hasn't said a word, though several minutes have passed. He hasn't even moved. But the fact he's still standing, as though waiting—*hoping* for me to look at him, sends shockwaves through me.

What will happen if I *do* look at him? Will I be forced to admit I don't really want to marry Jordan?

I just did.

Time lurches back to normal speed and the minister's voice drums over me.

"And now . . ." he begins, as my pulse surges up to warp speed. "By the authority vested in me by the State of New York . . ."

Oh God...

"I now pronounce you..."

"*Wait!*" A desperate voice calls out, making the minister's mouth snap shut in surprise.

I finally turn my head and look at Dean.

Dean.

There are a few people throwing nervous glances his way, too. No doubt fearing the moment he'd shout out in protest. It seems as if he was waiting for the moment the minister would ask if anyone objected to this union. But that moment never came—we requested the minister omit that part because it's always an awkward moment at weddings—the tense silence.

The truth is . . . there was a part of me that feared *I* would be the one to object.

And now, the ceremony has come to a halt right at the last few moments. Because someone did object. But it wasn't Dean.

The desperate voice that called out for the minister to stop . . .

It was *me*.

Not a single person stirs, everyone seeming to hold their breath at once.

All eyes are on us.

Waiting.

Cringing . . .

"Gabby," Jordan hisses, forcing my eyes to lock onto his. He's grown pale and his lips barely move as he speaks. "*What are you doing?*"

A haunting, dizzying silence closes in around me.

Over Jordan and me.

Every millisecond goes on for hours.

Oh my God.

I don't want to hurt him.

I don't want to embarrass him.

I don't want to disappoint the hundreds of people who flew in from around the world.

But I also don't want . . . to marry him.

I can't process a single thought beyond the desperate need to get away from here.

Right now.

"I can't do this," I whisper.

Jordan closes his eyes. I can almost hear his heart break.

Mine does, too.

"I'm sorry," I add, my eyes burning.

Clearing his throat, Jordan looks at the minister and says, "We need a few minutes."

A wave of murmurs moves through the crowd of wedding guests. People turning to look at each other and whisper behind their hands.

"No, Jordan," I blurt out.

He's eyeing the nearest door. There's determination in his eyes.

He wants to take me aside and talk some sense into me.

I'm terrified he will.

Because this isn't at all something I'd do.

This.

This . . . scene.

This . . . mortifying moment belongs to someone else.

Jordan takes my hand and tries to guide me to the side.

"*No,*" I say again, yanking my hand away. "I can't. I'm sorry."

The room is spinning.

Footsteps echo behind me and before I know what's happening, Dean is at my side. It's not until he takes my hand in his that I finally take a breath.

He gives me a look, a look I can read loud and clear.

Say the word and I'll take you away from here.

Dean.

His face is one I know better than my own—it brings me comfort. Even his blue eyes, churning and wild, and struggling to contain his demons, give me strength. And the scar across his left eyebrow is a reminder of the many times he literally fought for me.

To keep me safe.

The look we share lasts a split second, but echoes decades of stories and trust. I know, just like I always do, I won't feel safe with anyone else but Dean.

My voice breaks with a shaky breath as I say, "*Get me out of here.*"

"What—Gabby, don't . . ." Jordan warns under his breath.

Dean doesn't skip a beat. "She's coming with me."

I couldn't stay if I tried—that's how desperate my urge to flee is. But the hurt in Jordan's eyes shreds me. I know it should've never come to this. I should've been strong enough to know what I wanted before stepping in front of everyone we know.

"I'm so sorry," I say, my voice breaking.

Then I let Dean lead me down the wrong side of the aisle, past a chorus of gasps and a blur of mortified faces.

Dozens of people get to their feet to watch us go.

In what sounds like a distorted, far off voice, someone—maybe my mother, or my grandmother, or Remi or even Jordan—calls out my name one last time.

"*Gabby!*"

But I don't look back.

CHAPTER FIVE

Dean

The tail of Gabby's dress is now a giant ball of fabric between her arms. She runs past me and heads toward the doors like the floor is crumbling into a crater behind us. I follow, not bothering to look back as the confused mutters from the guests erupts into a full-blown commotion.

We push past the large oak doors and by the time we're halfway down the hall, footsteps begin to echo behind us. People are following us out, no doubt entranced by the train wreck playing out before them. Gabby reaches the exit doors first. She runs out onto the street and comes to a stop a few paces ahead. The moment I step out beside her, I can see why.

The city's alive around us, bustling and loud, cars honking and engines purring, people moving quickly past us on the busy Manhattan street. Only a few people spare a glance at Gabby, flustered in her large wedding dress, but for the most part no one seems to notice what's just happened.

It's a heist—I've stolen the bride.

I scan the street and line of traffic in search of a taxi.

Gabby looks more panicked than ever, her chest is rising and falling at quicker and quicker intervals. She's clutching the material of her dress tight against her chest and looks like she might faint.

"I can't stay here," she says, glancing back.

People from the ceremony are starting to trickle out of the building. And with every passing second, the city is becoming aware of the chaos following us out onto the sidewalk.

"Come on," I say, taking her hand again.

We head down the block to the entrance of the 81st subway station. In our rush down the stairs, Gabby almost trips. As far as I know, no one's chased us down the block—yet there's a frenzied energy about the way I swipe my metro card for Gabby to get through the turnstile. Her dress snags twice before we are both able to clear onto the upper platform.

Once again, she comes to a stop, seemingly frozen with indecision.

"Oh God, Dean. I can't go home. Where the hell am I going to go?"

I take her hand again. "Don't worry. I got you, okay? Don't worry."

We head down another flight of stairs to the lower level of the station. The C train comes to a stop at the platform, its doors barely begin to open when Gabby shoves inside the subway car.

We're met with stares from nearly all of the several dozen people sitting inside. Their looks of pleasant surprise melt away to apprehension—because neither Gabby nor I are smiling.

I spot two seats in the back.

"This way," I say.

Gabby sits beside me, staring blankly ahead. "Did . . . did that just happen?"

My heart's still pounding, but relief floods me so suddenly—I laugh out loud.

The sound is met with awkward silence.

Overhead, an AC vent kicks on and icy air blows over us. I shrug off my suit jacket and pull it around Gabby's shoulders. She sits eerily still beside me.

The train lurches into movement and rumbles away from the stop.

Away from Gabby's wedding.

From the future she planned.

"Are you okay?" I ask.

I regret asking.

Gabby's face turns toward mine, slowly. She nods once, twice, then switches course and starts shaking her head, her eyes brimming with tears. She releases the bottom of her wedding dress and lets the lace material pool at our feet like milk.

"Oh my God," she whispers. "The look on his face . . . all those people. This is awful . . . *I'm awful.*"

There's a dizzying swirl of emotions in her expression.

Guilt. Pain. Embarrassment.

It's all the opposite of what I'm feeling.

I'm relieved. Elated like a man who had a brush with death.

But I know better than to let any of it show. Gabby's going through a completely different experience than me. She could've ran halfway across the globe and it wouldn't make her problems disappear. Her last-minute decision to stop the wedding has undoubtedly ignited a tornado of drama she's going to have to face.

Jordan.

His family.

Her family.

The three hundred plus guests that witnessed her flee the altar.

Everyone is going to want answers. She knows it's only a matter of time before their questions, anger and judgement pours down on her.

I can't stop it and I can't fix it.

"*Shhhh*," I say, putting my arm around her.

She settles into my embrace without hesitation, the way she always does.

And I shut my eyes, savoring the stirring in my chest when she lowers her head onto it.

Can she hear my heart beating?

It's where she belongs.

With me.

She goes quiet for a few seconds as the train rumbles along the tracks. I know she's crying, but she's trying hard not to make a sound, except for the occasional sniffling.

"I kept waiting for the feeling to go away." She wipes a stray tear creeping down the side of her nose. "The nagging feeling . . . the . . . the *fear*. Everyone told me it would go away. But it didn't. It got worse. I couldn't breathe toward the end. I got . . . I got so panicked I felt like I was going to drown if I didn't say something. I just couldn't . . . I couldn't marry him."

"Do you love him?"

The beat of silence that follows my question makes me brace

for impact.

"I care about him, so much." Gabby shakes her head. "But . . . no. I realized standing there in front of him that I'm not in love with him. Not how I want to be. Not how I dreamed I'd be. What is *wrong* with me?"

I want to kiss her. Her red nose. Her tear-streaked cheeks.

I want to kiss her and take away every ounce of pain she feels.

And it's like she can read my thoughts because her gaze lowers to my lips.

The questioning gazes of the strangers around us disappears into a fog.

It's just us—just Gabby and I. Nothing else matters—nothing else ever does.

"Look at me," I demand. She turns her face up toward mine, her eyes wide at the sudden force of my voice. "There's nothing wrong with you. Do you hear me? Sometimes we're placed in a horrible situation, where doing the right thing for *us* means hurting someone else."

CHAPTER SIX

Dean

I take Gabby to my place and set up the guest bedroom for her. It takes hours for her initial shock to wear off. In that time, I help her out of her wedding dress and shove it into my entryway closet like it's a bag of money we're trying to pretend we didn't steal.

I make her food and let silence settle between us when it needs to and listen when her thoughts flood over. There's a heaviness in the air, an acknowledgement we're sitting in the eye of a storm. Gabby's emotions swing from relief to guilt and back again. She'll laugh out loud one minute, then grow silent for several more.

I'm not sure what to do except sit with her.

I make French toast for her after she admits she hasn't been able to eat in two days from nerves. I watch her carefully, wondering if she will wake up tomorrow regretting what she did. Whether she will regret leaving with me. Her phone buzzes endlessly in her purse and we pretend we can't hear it. I suggest she turn it off, but she's against the idea. It's like she wants to torture herself by knowing everyone's trying to reach her.

At one point, she says, "I'm going to have to see him. And apologize."

"Yes," I tell her. "But not tonight."

She nods, seemingly relieved.

Tonight, we settle in with the tense energy, the prickling sensation that comes from knowing you've hurt someone, and try to drown it out with action movies. My thoughts drift and I find myself not really paying attention to the screen. The sky outside my apartment windows grows dark and Gabby falls asleep beside me.

The last thing I remember thinking is I should carry her to the guest bed.

But I fall asleep next to her on the sofa, too.

The next day is hell for her. And for me.

Because I have to watch her pacing my apartment with her phone clutched to her ear as she tries to get a word in edgewise. Loud voices come from the other end. Her mother. Jordan's mother. Even Remi seems to be demanding an explanation from her. It takes everything in me not to snatch the phone from her and tell them to back the fuck off.

The one person who deserves an explanation is Jordan, but he refuses to speak with her. Angry and embarrassed, he sends all of her calls to voicemail. His mother tells Gabby to give it time. And she does.

Gabby stays with me as the hellish days go by. I try hard to take care of her, making her feel as comfortable as possible. Someone has to. She's become everyone else's emotional piñata. Everyone seems to think since she's the one who left, she can't be the one in pain.

I'm the one witnessing the color drain from her face as her friends and family call to hound her with questions and insinuations. I'm the one watching the quiet way she puts down her phone and carries the energy with her for the rest of the day.

Gabby holes up at my place for several days. By the time Remi comes to see her, Gabby's boiled down her decision to a simple explanation. She explains how trapped and crazy she felt for not wanting what everyone assured her she should want—what she herself was so sure she did want.

Gabby also manages to bring her mother around to accept her decision. But Jordan's mother won't be swayed. The woman's dislike and anger only grows as the days go by. It doesn't help her son seemed to fall off the face of the earth for over a week before resurfacing and agreeing to meet with Gabby.

I want so badly to come with her, to stand between them like a protective barrier. Not because I'm afraid she'll go back to him—at this point it's clear she knows she made the right decision—but because I know how much he's going to play on her guilt. Beat on it until she's standing squarely in the space of the villain and he as the victim.

But when she returns from seeing him, she's visibly lighter, like a thousand-pound weight has been lifted from her chest. She tells me how awful their meeting started, how angry Jordan seemed. But how by the end of it they both started crying and he ultimately admitted a part of him knew she didn't really want to be with him.

It seems denial is a widespread phenomenon.

That night, I catch her looking through pictures of her dad on her phone.

He died right after we graduated from college and left a rip in her heart.

I sit beside her, silently looking over at the pictures she's scrolling past. Pictures of camping trips and Christmases. Pictures of ski trips upstate and tropical beaches in the Florida Keys. Every once in a while, she'll pause over a picture and we'll share a laugh. She'll tell me the story behind it. Or, in the pictures I happen to be in, we'll recall some ridiculous detail of the day that makes us smile.

Gabby's scrolling begins to slow when she reaches pictures of her father in a suit and her mother in a wedding gown. It's from the time the two renewed their vows back when Gabby and I were in college.

She stops at one of the pictures, where her parents are standing at the altar, hand in hand, staring at each other. Gabby's in the picture too, standing off to the side with a bouquet of flowers in her hands and a look of awestruck wonder in her eyes.

"I miss him," she says quietly.

Setting her phone down, she goes still and quiet for several seconds. Then . . .

"Dean?"

"Mmm?"

"Do you think I'm a horrible person?"

Her tone is serious, the type you use on a friend so they know you want the truth.

I stare at her.

"Are you kidding? You're the most incredible person I know. Gabby, what you did? It was brave. Some people would rather spend their lives living a comfortable lie than face the backlash that comes with the truth."

I lower my lips to her forehead and plant a kiss on her smooth skin.

She stares up at me in stunned silence, though she has no way of knowing I'm talking about me. About my feelings for her. About the tight ball of unspoken words coiled up in my chest since the last time I spoke them.

Next time I tell her how I feel, I'm going to make damn sure she doesn't forget.

CHAPTER SEVEN

Gabby

If I'd gone through with the wedding, I would've spent the past few weeks on a honeymoon in Aruba. Lying on the beach, sipping coconut mojitos and staring at the wedding ring on my finger. It's a reality I pictured vividly while planning the wedding. But now the fantasy has an eerie sheen to it, like a treat that was too disgustingly sweet to eat in the first place.

Instead, my days have been spent at Dean's place. Settling in for the long haul, letting Dean's familiar nooks and crannies wrap me with a sensation of safety. This feels more like home than anything Jordan and I had.

Dean has never mentioned it, but there's no logical reason for me to still be staying here. Jordan left our shared apartment days after our would-be wedding.

I stay because there's nowhere else I'd rather be.

In the mornings, Dean's apartment smells of sugar and cinnamon as he makes me my favorite breakfast before he heads to work. He refuses to let me help, insisting I sit behind the counter and let him work. He's always loved cooking, putting so much effort and focus into making the perfect French toast. He looks damn good doing it, too. The button-down shirt he wears to work rolled up at the elbows, and he'll occasionally bring the tip of his thumb to his lips to suck away powdered sugar.

And I stare, much longer than I've ever allowed myself to.

He's here. He's always been here, yet I feel like I've been asleep the whole time.

Dean and I have been through hell and back together. It seems one of us is always going through some crisis, and we take turns leaning on each other.

When I look at him, I'm relieved I didn't marry Jordan.

Everything would've changed.

Dean and I never admitted it out loud, but we both knew our friendship would change forever after the wedding. I shudder at the thought. How did I ever think I could live without this? Without Dean.

He's home to me.

He brings my thoughts fluttering to a standstill with his touch. The smell of his shirts. The way he holds my head to his chest and drowns my thoughts out with the beat of his heart.

A life that takes me away from Dean feels like a life without oxygen.

I'm so grateful for this man.

This beautiful man who's been there for me through everything.

Every damn thing . . .

I let these thoughts settle in my chest long after he sets breakfast in front of me and we eat together in a comfortable silence. I know he'll let me stay here forever. A part of me wants to. Dean knows me well enough to know when to give me space, and how much of it to give. He knows when I need silence and when I need to be distracted from my thoughts.

He's the way out of the mess I've made for myself. He's always been the anchor in the storm. I ran away from more than just Jordan at the altar. I ran away from the version of me tethered to the opinions of my friends and family. The part of me that cared more about their peace of mind and happiness than my own.

What happens when you suppress what you want for so long you can't even find it anymore?

That's how I feel. On the cusp of possibility. Like the moment right before the clock ticks to midnight on New Year's Eve and an exciting new beginning awaits.

My subconscious is nagging me. Every night, I find myself looking through the pictures on my phone of my parents' vow renewal ceremony. There's one picture in particular I keep hovering over.

It's a picture of the wedding reception, my parents are in the middle of the dance floor, my mother's hand pressed to my father's chest, her head tilted back in a wild laugh. The way my father is looking at her, a small smile on his lips, brings butterflies to my chest. Off in the distance, almost out of the frame, Dean and I are sitting at a table.

I go back to the photo several nights in a row. One night, Dean sits beside me on the couch and points at the picture.

"Look at you," he says. "You look so cute staring at your parents. That was a fun night."

I nod, keeping my eyes on my phone screen.

The me in the picture is smiling as she stares at the couple on the dance floor. But it's the smile on Dean's face in the photograph that I can't stop looking at. He's looking at me with a warm, satisfied smile that's too familiar.

The same smile that's on my father's face.

The longer I stare at the picture, the quieter Dean becomes. It's like he's starting to hear the thoughts whirling in my head, churning alive like a rusty engine.

"Dean? Why did you stand up in the middle of the ceremony?"

His gaze locks with mine.

"I think you know, Gabby."

I shake my head, though a part of me knows he's right. I do know. I know in the same way anyone knows the truth. It's always been there, just below the surface. All we need is permission to pull it out.

Dean looks down to my lips, then back to my eyes.

Is he . . . is he going to kiss me?

The room grows warmer and for the first time in a long time I'm fully conscious of how close we're sitting.

Swallowing, I try to stall. "I . . . I don't know."

"I think you don't want to know. I think knowing scares you. Because if you think back to that night last year, the rooftop bar on Valentine's Day . . . Do you remember the words I said to you?"

That was the night I met Jordan.

I'm uncomfortable now, but resist the urge to shift away. It's a foreign feeling for me to have around Dean. I'm usually more at home around him than I am in my own skin. But right now? Every part of me is resisting the memory he's tugging out with his words.

The words he told me?

I shake my head, but even as I do, my heartbeat picks up. Because I know . . . somehow, I know something happened between us that night. Dean was different for a few days after, disappointed in me for reasons I didn't understand.

Then I remember why I went out to a bar that Valentine's Day to begin with.

I was looking for ways to chase my thoughts away. Thoughts of Dean I didn't want to have because I was sure they'd ruin our friendship. I'm frozen now, looking into his beautiful blue eyes and wondering if he can see the images flashing before mine. Dreams I got good at pretending didn't matter.

Dreams that still happen every once in a while, and leave me flushed and breathless. Of Dean's hands running up the skin of my back, then tugging me down onto him. Of me, writhing over him. Of our mouths opening in wild breaths.

I never told him about them.

At least . . . I don't think I did?

Something inside of me stirs, a memory flutters to the tip of my tongue. I open my mouth to say it aloud, but it slips again.

The words he told me . . .

The window at the end of Dean's living room faces the street, where a streetlamp flickers every few seconds. Like the lamp that was outside of the apartment I used to share with Remi.

And there, a memory slithers free. A cab waiting on the curb. Dean standing on my front steps with his hands in his pockets. He's looking at me in a way that makes me forget to breathe.

Words he said to me were still fluttering around my head, making me feel drunker than I was.

I want you, Gabby.

You're all I think about.

He looked down at me, his eyes bright enough to cut through miles of darkness. I thought he was going to kiss me. I *wanted* him to kiss me.

That night was the night . . . something almost happened.

We almost . . . were.

Dean sets a hand on mine, and I blink away the memories. But they leave me staggered, mentally trying to find my footing. I was brave that night. Brave enough to be reckless.

And that's what it takes, sometimes.

One reckless move to change your life.

I remember the feeling so vividly. Feeling like I was sitting at the edge of a well, staring down and wondering how deep it was. I wanted to jump in, but only if he was going to jump, too.

I didn't want to fall in love with him if he wasn't going to fall in love with me.

Stupid girl.

I thought I had a choice.

And my thoughts are spilling over, infiltrating reality, because Dean leans into me, close.

Too close.

"I know you remember," he says.

"I . . . I do."

He smiles his beautiful smile. The one that lightens up his whole face. One of his hands comes up to the side of my face, forcing me to look directly into his eyes.

"You never belonged with Jordan . . ." He trails off, his fingers sliding down my jaw, tilting my face up to his.

My skin is on fire and my thoughts freeze in place.

He's going to kiss me.

Oxygen rushes to my lips and I suck in a breath, but Dean's mouth moves over mine to steal it again with whispered words.

"You belong with me."

CHAPTER EIGHT

Gabby

Dean's kiss is sudden and intense.

It carries with it a jolt that wakes me from a coma of lies. How long have I pretended I didn't want this to happen? There's no point pretending now. Not when our desperation singes the air between us.

I forget why I held back for so long, why crossing this line always felt so wrong.

It doesn't.

This kiss is the most honest thing I've ever done.

Nothing in my life has felt this right. Or this inevitable.

He kisses me with a fierceness I never knew he was capable of. But there's familiarity there, too, like he's memorized the shape of my lips and has been preparing to make them his for a long time.

The kiss lasts somewhere between a second to a lifetime. When we finally pull back, our lips linger a hair's width apart as we breathe desperately against each other's mouths.

Words hang in the air all around us. But our hands are doing the talking now. Mine are shaking as they work to unbutton his shirt, his are tugging away at my jeans. Impatient, we get to our feet and fight against buttons and zippers, undressing like our clothes are suffocating us.

And in a way, they are.

The truth we're dying to speak is written on our skin, it has been for years. Maybe that's why nothing else has felt right. I've been swimming upstream, resisting this.

Resisting us.

My heart is throbbing madly in my chest when I realize we're standing naked in front of each other.

Holy shit . . .

There's no denying how turned on he is.

This is really happening.

Dean's gaze travels up my body, mentally tracing all my curves like he's drawing a map. When his eyes reach mine, his lips curl into a smile. "Come here."

The way he says that sends a delicious thrill down my spine.

I close the gap between us as he eyes me hungrily. He picks me up in his muscular arms and my legs wrap easily around his waist. Our lips find each other again.

Our kiss is slow now, relishing every moment.

There's no hesitation, no pretending.

We both ache for the same thing, both starving to confess.

We kiss the whole way to his bedroom. He sets me down on the bed, and I fall back onto my elbows. My breath catches as I watch his large hands spread my legs apart.

He lowers his head between my thighs, then pauses to peer up at me, eyes dancing.

"I've been dying to taste you for so long."

The sight is electric, his face between my legs, his hands gripping my thighs. But then his face lowers and his tongue finds the spot where I'm aching with need. My eyes shut and my lower back arches from the bed at the delicious jolt he sends through me.

Dean's lips and tongue move in maddening patterns, sending tantalizing waves up my body. My hands ball up the sheets around me into my fists.

"*Oh,*" I breathe out.

Again and again.

His tongue's caress grows rougher and punishing and my breathing more and more erratic. He doesn't stop, even as delirious whimpers lift from my throat and I start squirming away from the intensity of the sensations. His fingers dig deeper into the skin of my thighs, holding me in place as my moans grow louder. My hips jerking, I grind myself straight into an orgasm that splinters me.

Wow.

I've never had a man taste me like this. Like he was getting even more pleasure from it than I was, like he could do it forever and never come up for air.

My heart's beating a hole through my chest when Dean moves over me, his perfect face appearing overhead. He smirks and mutters something that sounds like, "*fucking delicious.*"

I reach up to touch his face, and wipe his lips with my thumb.

All the while, I can't believe this is Dean.

My Dean.

Would I have been able to lie to myself for so long if I had known he could do this magic with his tongue?

Our eyes lock and he winks at me. It's a familiar gesture for us, one he does whenever he's reminding me everything's going to be okay. But there's a twist to it now, a sort of promise for what he's going to deliver.

Everything's going to be more than okay.

He's promising to blow my fucking mind.

I hold my breath as he positions himself between my legs.

He keeps his eyes on me, but his gaze is far off and cloudy, like those pictures of celestial clouds you only wish you could touch. They exist somewhere between everything and nothing. And that's what this moment feels like.

Too big to wrap your head around.

Too striking be real.

His forearms lower on either side of me, allowing his hands to touch my face as his body hovers just over mine.

I tense when he pushes inside of me, and he curses under his breath.

For a second, he holds still, neither of us moving. I can feel myself squeezing around every inch of him. A wild need erupts in me to feel him stroking me from inside, to feel his length again and again with every thrust.

But for a second, he doesn't move, he lowers his lips over mine and plants a sweet kiss. Then he whispers. "I'm so in love with you, Gabby."

The words threaten to disintegrate my heart, from the amount of emotions that erupt from it. But he doesn't wait for my response, he starts weaving in and out of me with a mouth-watering tempo. His pace increases slowly, and every stroke is spine-tingling, every cell in my body alive with bliss.

I swear, I can stay like this forever.

I've never felt this full.

This complete.

I'm sure I will never get enough of this man.

Every move he makes overflows with a blazing passion I've never known. It's too hot to touch, our skins burning against each other. His tempo quickening to a controlled turbulence that shakes my entire body. All the while he watches me, watches my eyes roll upward, watches me shake beneath him

I breathe out sounds I've never made before.

Desperate pleas for more, even though more would never be enough. I'm starving for him, insane with longing. So far gone off this intoxicating experience, I lose track of time and space. My body moves to scratch every damn itch that arises. And Dean takes me in as many ways as he can. Spinning me over to my stomach, pulling my hips up and grabbing hold of my ass as he drives me completely insane with desire.

We fuck, we screw, occasionally we slow to a sweet love-making, then he turns me over and fucks me some more. We make up for the years of denial, the years of fantasizing. The pent-up need.

I give up on resisting the explosive pleasure, letting it shatter me again and again until all I know is delirium.

Who knows how long we go at it? The sky outside grows dark and we can't seem to get enough. Falling off the bed and finding ways to continue on the floor until a mind-numbing orgasm shakes my entire body.

Dean's dripping in sweat and exhausted when he collapses on top of me, with a long, satisfied groan.

I wrap my arms around his body and lay there on the floor with him. Silence engulfs us. The best kind. The sweet, comfortable kind that can last forever.

I want this forever.

Just him and I.

Just like this.

"Dean?"

He lifts his head to look at me, eyes smiling like he's well aware he's just screwed my brains out. But it was more than that and we both know it. It was more than gluttonous lust, it was a searing need that could no longer be contained. It was years of us denying we belonged together.

His voice is soft when he responds, "Yeah?"

"I think I've loved you my whole life."

He lets out a small breath, so small I almost miss it.

"Gabby—I've loved you since before I knew what it meant to love someone."

I bite my lip, a stampede of sensations erupting in my heart. "So, what the hell took us so long?"

"We were clinging to our friendship because it was what kept us steady. It was safe. But safe isn't worth the price of missing out on this. Because this?" He smiles at me, his blue eyes twinkling in the dark. "This is where our lives begin."

ABOUT THE AUTHOR

Veronica Larsen began writing around the age of seven, scribbling Nancy Drew-like stories between the margins of composition notebooks. Her journey into the romance genre began once upon a long military deployment when she penned a steamy romance for her husband, a US Marine. This story eventually turned into her debut novel Entangle. She fell in love with writing romance and hasn't looked back since. Her novels are known to feature engaging story-lines, relatable characters, heart-tugging truths, and tangible chemistry that builds throughout the story. She holds a Bachelor of Science in Psychology, which has come in handy in resolving the messy lives of the fictional people in her head.

More info available at: www.veronicalarsenbooks.com

*Cerys,
Enjoy babe!
♥*

Lush

MARNI MANN

"S+M" - RIHANNA

CHAPTER ONE

Pepper

As the owner of Lush—the hottest, most exclusive chain of sex clubs in the world—I saw some incredibly handsome men come across my camera feed. That was because I had over three hundred cameras in our LA and Miami locations, giving me the ability to see every person inside.

And I saw them at every stage.

When they placed their hand on the security tablet at the front entrance, when they walked into the mouth of the club. As they wandered down all the different hallways, stopping to view the fetishes taking place inside each room.

There weren't any secrets at Lush.

I designed it that way.

So, when Bale showed up at my LA club, I noticed.

It had been three long weeks since I'd heard from him, after he disappeared in the middle of the night, leaving only a note on my pillow.

Four lonely words had been written on the small piece of paper.

Don't look for me.

I immediately flagged his membership, so I would be alerted if he ever tried to enter the club. The second his fingerprints were taken at the front entrance, a notification came across my screen.

The one I was staring at now.

My relationships didn't usually last long, not with the business I was in. But everything with Bale seemed perfect.

I didn't understand why he left after spending four perfect months together.

And I certainly didn't understand why he came back at two in the morning on a Tuesday, dressed in a suit, staring at the front entrance camera as though he knew I was watching the feed.

I reached toward my nightstand to turn on the lamp before I climbed out of bed. After grabbing a robe from the bathroom, I crossed the silk over my naked body and made my way to the other side of the house. When I reached my office, I sat behind the large glass desk and shook the mouse to turn on the monitor.

I entered a series of security codes that got me into the system, and I chose a feed that would show me the progression of Bale moving through the club. As I watched him, I leaned into the edge of the desk, moving closer to the screen.

"Where have you been, Bale Pierce?" I whispered, zooming in on his face.

I stared at his lips while he stood at the bar and asked for a drink.

Tanqueray and tonic.

The same cocktail he always ordered.

Once the tumbler was in his hand, he turned around, pushing his back into the edge of the counter and he gazed at the camera across from him.

His skin was tanner than it had been three weeks ago. His golden-brown hair was a little longer, tucked behind his ears, the ends curling around his lobes.

"What in the hell have you been up to?" I said softly.

He smirked at the camera and pushed himself off the bar, moving toward the left side of the chamber and down the last hallway, where the club's private room was located at the end.

Out of all the spots in the club, that was the only one I would use.

The one I'd designed specifically for myself.

My heart began to pound.

Wetness dampened my pussy.

Bale had my attention.

I could swear he knew that.

And I could swear that was what he wanted.

He stopped outside the last door, and his hand went into his pocket. He took out a key, pausing right after he slipped just the tip of it into the lock.

Slowly, he looked over his shoulder at the camera that was right above him. "Ten minutes," he mouthed.

In eleven minutes, the punishments would start.

That was what he was telling me.

But he knew it took eight minutes to drive to the club from my house in the Hollywood Hills. It would take another minute to park and walk inside, assuming I could get through the door without every employee stopping to speak to me.

He didn't care.

He wanted me there.

Now.

He pushed the key the rest of the way in and went into my private room. There was a table in the center. One I'd been tied to many times before.

Each of those times by Bale.

He stood behind the table and ran his hand over his neatly trimmed beard. His gaze locked with the camera in the corner of the room. He gave it a look I knew all too well.

"Fuck," I gasped, pushing my chair away from the desk.

Seconds ticked by and his glare deepened.

His eyes were commanding me to submit.

He believed he still had that kind of power over me.

The truth was . . . he did.

CHAPTER TWO

Bale

The men who were granted a membership at Lush had to meet certain requirements. They had to have excellent credit, a clean background, and a job that earned them over a million a year.

On paper, I had all three.

And after ten months of being on their waiting list, I was finally given access.

But, in reality, the person on that application wasn't me. It wasn't my social security number that Pepper's team had thoroughly researched and I wasn't a hedge fund manager, even though they confirmed my job.

Bale Pierce was a persona my team had created to get me inside of Lush. To put me in a position where I could get the information I'd been hired to find.

As a fixer, that was my job.

I could make anything happen.

I could make anyone disappear.

What I wanted from Pepper Michaels was answers.

Before I confronted her with those questions, I first had to learn everything about her. Her habits, her likes.

What made her cunt wet.

That took some planning because she didn't go into either of the clubs that often. So, my team hacked into her security system, and I memorized the placement of each camera. I studied the feeds she spent a majority of her time watching.

And I figured out how to lure her in.

It only took seven days of hooking up with other members, showing her how torturous my tongue could be, before she came into the club and sought me out.

Orgasm denial.

That was Pepper's fetish of choice.

I became a fucking expert at it.

But something happened I hadn't anticipated. Something that, in the ten years I'd been doing this job, had never happened before.

I fell in love with my mark.

I spent every night with her. I talked to her about a future.

I told her I fucking cared.

And I did.

But after four months together, I had to go. It wasn't what I wanted. I just couldn't put it off any longer, not with my partners wondering why I hadn't returned or my client threatening to fire me.

I left in the middle of the night, giving Pepper no notice, no explanation, no way to get in touch with me. Once I was gone, Bale Pierce no longer existed. He vanished on paper as quick as he had been created.

The client paid me half a million for my services, and I was on to the next job.

That was three weeks ago. In that time, I'd thought of her non-stop, I craved her. My goddamn hands twitched for her.

And now that I was back in LA for another job, it was impossible to stay away.

So, here I was, standing in *our* room, running my fingers over *our* table.

I had eight hours until my private plane would take me back to the East Coast.

Eight hours to do anything I wanted.

Eight hours to devour Pepper.

When I put my hand on the tablet at the front entrance, I expected to be turned away, that Pepper had revoked my membership.

When that didn't happen, I knew she still wanted me.

I knew she'd be notified of my arrival.

And I knew it would take a little convincing, but I had the power to get her here.

Due to the time, I suspected the alert would wake her. She'd check her phone and wouldn't be satisfied with the image, so she would go into her office and use the large monitor to track my progress through the club.

    She'd watch me order a drink.
    She'd follow me to the private room.
    She'd get wet as I stuck the key in the lock.
    Now, as I stood behind the table, I stared at the camera.
    And I counted the seconds.

CHAPTER THREE

Pepper

I opened Lush because there wasn't a sex club in LA that gave me everything I wanted—a safe place to explore my fantasies, an environment that was as sexy as the people inside of it, and exclusivity. Just because someone liked to play didn't mean they should be allowed through the door. There had to be rules, and I found that most places didn't have any.

My club would be different.

It would be full of wealth.

Power.

Dominance.

Submission.

Memberships would be given to those who hungered for them, but there was a limited amount. Each candidate was thoroughly researched and certain criteria had to be met.

The LA location had been open for seven years, Miami for five. New York, Vegas, and London facilities would be opening in the next two years.

What started as a passion had turned into a business, and I treated it as one.

That meant I didn't fuck at the club. In fact, unless it was for a professional reason, I didn't mingle with the members in any of the main or private areas. I stayed in the office upstairs instead.

Sexually, I got what I needed, I just didn't get it there.

Until Bale.

I remembered when I saw him for the first time. I'd just grabbed some dinner from the fridge and returned to my desk. I was working late and planned to be there well through the night. An alert had come across my computer that showed me Bale had entered the club. The system was set up to do that for new members and to track them, so they could be monitored during their first few visits.

I wanted to make sure they followed the rules and were mixing in well with the others.

Bale came in wearing a suit similar to the one he had on tonight. His hair was shorter, his beard trimmed and edged. He walked with a confidence I didn't see often. His smile was a little sinister. His presence demanded my attention.

I liked everything I saw.

A little too much.

To the point where I couldn't look away.

He'd walked down one of the hallways and stopped in the first doorway. Inside the room, a woman was tied to a chair. She was blindfolded with a gag in her mouth.

She'd been in there, waiting for someone to come in.

Without saying a word, Bale walked over to the armoire that was in the corner and he chose a long feather from one of the drawers. As he brought it over to her, my pussy began to tingle. My clit pulsed as he ran it up and down her naked body.

I couldn't stop watching.

I couldn't stop fantasizing that feather was on me.

Over the next few hours, I'd watched him deny her an orgasm.

Minute after minute of pure lust.

Need.

A slow torture that had three of my own fingers thrusting inside my pussy, my wetness dripping all the way down to my wrist.

She never came. He wouldn't let her.

He was the partner of my dreams.

The next night, I watched him do the same thing to a different woman.

The third and fourth evenings were identical.

After a week, I couldn't stand it anymore, I had to experience Bale for myself. So, I went downstairs shortly after he entered the club, and I followed him to the archway of one of the rooms where he had stopped to watch two of my members. The scene involved a sex swing that was extended several feet up in the air.

While he stared at the couple, I looked at him.

And I continued to do so until his eyes moved in my direction.

It took one second for our gazes to lock. For my body to respond. To know this was the man who was going to give me a level of pleasure I hadn't ever experienced before.

And he did, night after night, until he walked out of my house and didn't return . . . until this evening.

Now, as I walked down the same hallway I had the first time we'd been together, I found my body reacting to the anticipation of seeing him. My hands were tingling. My pussy was dripping.

My heart was torn between anger and an ache so deep it was hard to catch my breath.

A quick glance at my watch told me it had been nine minutes.

I had thirty-six seconds left.

So, I paused outside the locked door and I took a breath. I straightened my shirt and tucked a small chunk of hair behind my ear. I tightened my fingers around the key that was in my pocket.

I didn't have to go in.

I could go upstairs to my office and watch his reaction from the camera feed when it hit ten minutes.

I could completely wash Bale Pierce from my life.

But I knew that wasn't possible.

My body wouldn't allow it. Neither would my heart.

So, I stuck the key in the lock and his eyes caught mine the second I opened the door. His stare followed me to the table where I paused on the other side.

Six feet separated us.

"What are you doing here, Bale?" I had so many questions, but this was a safe start.

"I missed you."

I laughed. Not from the edge in his voice, or the way he looked at me like I was a medium rare ribeye, his favorite temperature and cut of meat. I laughed because I could tell he was being honest, and that wasn't something I wanted to hear.

I wanted a lie. One after another of why he'd left, why it had taken him this long to return. Why he hadn't called. Why he was here now.

The truth hurt.

The look in his eyes hurt even more.

"Why?" My question didn't just apply to his last statement. It covered the last three weeks, the reason he had disappeared, and the cause of him coming back.

"You don't want to hear the answer to that."

"No?"

He tilted his head a little to the side, his stare dipping down my body, before slowly lifting to my face again. "No."

"Why—"

"I have eight hours until I have to leave again, and I don't know when I'll be back. Do you want to waste that time arguing about something I can't change? Because I can't discuss why I left, but you already know that." He paused for a second, continuing before I had a chance to respond. "I know you looked for me even though I told you not to, and you hit a dead-end. Bale Pierce disintegrated the moment I walked out of your house."

He was right; I'd looked.

I had my entire fucking team look.

But Bale was gone—from my house, from the internet, from any documentation I had on him.

The only crumbs he left behind were memories.

And I had so many of them in the short time we'd been together.

His hands dropped to the leather cushion, his fingers wrapping around the edge of the table.

"I know what you want," he said, even though I still hadn't responded. "I know what you need." The tips of his nails turned white. "Don't stop me from giving it to you."

I didn't answer.

I just stared—at his lips, at his hands, at the length of his body that was more powerful, more dominant than any man I had ever been with.

God, he was so achingly handsome.

"Bale . . ."

"Don't," he warned.

I had a choice. He was just reminding me which one I should make.

"I want you to remember something, Pepper." He leaned forward a few inches, as though getting closer would emphasize his words. "I want you to remember what my tongue is capable of."

CHAPTER FOUR

Bale

Pepper was the type of woman who needed to be reminded of things. She had a tendency of focusing on what she couldn't change instead of appreciating what was right in front of her. And that was a man who wanted to lick her cunt.

I didn't want her heart involved in this conversation.

I wanted her to think with her body. I wanted her to listen to her pussy.

I wanted her to take off her clothes and get on the table, so I could tie her wrists and shackle her ankles. And besides, *"Yes,"* the only other things I wanted to hear were her screams and moans.

"I know you want this," I said when she still hadn't responded.

She didn't move. She didn't say a word.

I walked around to her side of the table, put my hands on her waist, and turned her toward me.

She faced me without a fight and stared into my eyes.

Heat radiated off her body.

I felt her need pulsing through her skin.

"You've never disobeyed me in this room," I said, placing two fingers underneath her chin and tilting her head up. "Don't start now."

I'd missed her lips.

And that fucking smile.

I ran the pad of my thumb across her mouth, the softness brushing against my skin. "All I can think about is getting you flat on that table and having you stay perfectly still. I don't care how hard I'm licking you or how badly you want to come, the only movement I'll allow is the goddamn rise and fall of your chest." My hand dropped, and I caged her nipple, squeezing it until I saw a change in her eyes.

She didn't need to be convinced. I'd already done that.

I could tell by the way she was breathing. By the look she was giving me, how she was taking me all in.

The reason for her silence was to punish me.

I guessed I deserved that.

That was the only reason I didn't put her over my knee and slap her ass until my hand was printed on it.

But that didn't mean I was going to wait forever.

So, while she still played hard to get, I refamiliarized myself with her body, knowing the sensations from my fingers were going straight to her pussy. And with each second that passed, those feelings were building.

Slowly, I went lower, halting when my palm was at the top of her pussy. I tilted my wrist back and slapped her clit. She had jeans on, but they were thin enough she could feel the sting. The friction.

I did it again.

On the third time, I cupped her cunt. So much warmth came from it, my skin was burning. "I'm not going to wait. I want you naked. Now."

She let out a long, sensual sigh.

That was when I pulled my hand away and moved to the other side of the table. I gripped the edge of it and locked our eyes.

"You've made your point, and I've been lenient long enough. Take your fucking clothes off, Pepper."

CHAPTER FIVE

Pepper

I couldn't ask Bale the questions that were burning inside of me, nor could I tell him how badly he had hurt me. Conversations like that just couldn't happen at Lush. Not when every word spoken within these walls was recorded and the girls in my office had full access to the feed.

Physically, I had no secrets.

But emotionally, the girls knew nothing about my relationship, and I wanted to keep it that way.

A discussion with Bale would happen later. Right now, we both needed something I'd put off long enough.

"Bale . . ." I started.

His brows rose.

His lips parted.

"I want you to promise me something," I said.

"I'm listening."

I reached toward the bottom of my shirt and gradually lifted it over my head. I held it in my hand for several seconds before I dropped it onto the floor. "I want you to promise you're not going to be easy on me."

"Fuck," he hissed, his teeth gnawing into his bottom lip.

"Because for the last three weeks, I've thought about your tongue . . ." I kicked off my shoes, my pants, then my panties and bra, and I crawled onto the table. "And I haven't been able to stop touching myself."

"No one has licked you since me?"

I shook my head. "I was waiting . . . for you."

Now that I was on the table, I spread my body across the leather, separating my legs as far as they would go without crossing the edge of the cushion. I did the same with my hands, anticipating the material he was going to use to secure them.

"You know I'm going to reward you for that."

I didn't know.

I'd just hoped.

He turned his back to me and walked to the armoire in the corner of the room, where there was an entire section of shackles. There was rope and twine, handcuffs and ties. I never knew what he was going to choose and that was part of the excitement.

Before Bale made his selection, he took off his jacket and tie and hung them over the corner of the Tantra Chair. His button-down was fitted and it showed off the muscles in his chest and arms. I wanted to rub my fingers over them. I wanted to feel their power. I wanted to slide them through the thin, dark hair on his pecs and the trail that ran straight to his cock.

His cock.

Fuck.

God, he was one delicious, dominate man—perfect to stare at, to fantasize about.

With his back to me, he opened one of the drawers, and removed something. When he turned around, I saw it was rope. The material was thick, white, and extremely rough. It would burn my skin and leave marks the harder I fought.

I loved it.

"Yes!" I roared as he wrapped the rope around his fist and moved closer. Once he reached me, he tied it around my hand and I moaned.

"Is your pussy wet?"

It wouldn't stop clenching.

It wouldn't stop dripping.

I hadn't been this wet since the last time he'd touched me.

"Yes," I answered.

"I want to tie you so tight you'll be on the verge of bleeding."

"*Yesss.*"

He slapped my breast and I yelped, even though it felt amazing.

"Yes, what?"

"Sir," I breathed. "Yes, sir."

"I've been lenient, Pepper. That's going to stop right now, do you hear me?"

"Yes, sir."

He traced his fingertips around my breast, soothing the skin he'd just whacked. "You're such a good girl."

My clit throbbed, and I clenched my fingers together, waiting for him to move to the next wrist, where the added friction would only build the need that was pulsing through me.

When it finally came, when he had it as snug as the first knot, I almost tried to close my legs.

But I couldn't.

I wasn't allowed.

When I was on this table, I was Bale's. I had to follow his rules and instructions. If he wanted me still, that was the way I had to remain until my feet hit the floor.

Once both wrists were secure, he moved to my ankle, looping the rope around me, and then through the hole in the corner of the cushion where he tied it underneath.

"*Ahhh*," I breathed when it tightened against my flesh. I made the same sound when he repeated the action on my other ankle.

Now that he was done, he took a step back to admire his work.

I was spread wide, vulnerable, completely at his mercy.

I wouldn't want it any other way.

Despite Bale disappearing, I still trusted him when it came to my body. He knew what I could handle and what I enjoyed. We had a safe word we were both comfortable with. And he was the type of lover who only focused on my pleasure, who consumed every one of my senses while taking care of needs I never even knew I had.

His absence hadn't changed that.

If anything, it made our desires grow stronger.

Still standing at the foot of the table, his eyes roaming my body, he groaned. "You're so fucking gorgeous. I don't know how I'm going to get on that plane tomorrow."

"Then don't."

His lids narrowed. "Do you know what would happen if I didn't return?"

I shook my head, my heart aching at the thought of him leaving again. And this time, I had a feeling he wouldn't be coming back. That the four months we'd spent together was all I'd ever have with him.

That stung worse than the rope biting my skin.

He walked to the other side of the table and leaned into my ear. "My partners would find me. And they would kill me," he said softly, since he knew he was being recorded.

I sucked in a breath and held it.

"People can't quit what I do, Pepper," he continued. "You retire when you're too old or you die. Those are the only options. So, I want you to enjoy tonight, because it's all we have."

His words echoed inside my chest.

I knew how to push them away. This club had trained me to do that. If emotions seeped through these walls, I wouldn't have a business. My members were here for one thing. And tonight, Bale and I were here for the same reason.

That didn't mean it was easy.

I just couldn't allow it to ruin the time we had together, so I focused on his presence, on the way his mouth moved away from my ear, how his teeth nipped my cheek.

His face hovered directly over mine and I saw a change in his eyes. They turned hungrier. Feral.

He was back in the moment.

And he was ready.

His hands pressed against my face. "While you've been thinking about my tongue, I've been dreaming about your cunt." He dragged his tongue across my lips. "All I've wanted is to lick it." He moved down my chest, the wetness he left behind on my skin turning cold from the air conditioning. "And to do this . . ." He went to the side of the table and put his nose on my clit. He inhaled. Not just once. These were long, deep breaths he took in and didn't immediately release.

"That fucking scent," he moaned. "It's consumed me these last three weeks."

"Oh God," I hissed.

He wedged in deeper, his nostrils now between my lips while his hands surrounded my pussy. He was spreading me wider to get a better whiff.

It was so incredibly hot to feel his air shoot across me.

It was even hotter to know the hard-on that was bulging through his suit pants was because of me.

I was doing everything I could to stay still.

But it was becoming impossible.

He pulled his nose away, but he didn't leave. Instead, he replaced it with his tongue and a long, pent-up scream came pouring from my lips. "Bale . . ." I gasped as his tongue swiped me.

"*Mmm.*" It was a growl much deeper than the other ones he'd made. "That fucking taste is better than I remember."

He licked again, this time covering my entire clit. He stopped at the very top to suck it into his mouth. While I was surrounded by his heat and wetness, he flicked, using just the tip of his tongue.

"Fuck!" I shouted, doing everything I could not to wiggle, not to fight against the ropes.

The build was there.

It came on immediately.

It threatened to burst through my stomach.

And then I started to come down because he moved his mouth away and stared at me with eyes that belonged to a savage.

The air was almost enough to get me off. I knew if I could just hump my hips a few times, the orgasm would be exploding through me. But I couldn't do that. I had to stay frozen or he'd never let me come.

"It's been too long," he said, and I knew he was referring to the time that had passed since he'd gotten me off.

"Yes, sir. Far too long."

He stuck his tongue out and made slow, exaggerated movements. "I could taste how close you were."

The build had returned. It was dull, but it was there. And it intensified as he traveled the length of my clit, back and forth, adding more pressure with each lap.

"Bale . . ." I gasped.

He pulled away and moved to the foot of the table.

The cold air was like a punch to the face. A reminder that I wasn't going to get what I wanted.

At least, not yet.

He got on the table, his hands now on my thighs, and his mouth dove into my pussy.

I was there.

It came on even quicker this time.

And it came on even harder, as his tongue moved at a speed I didn't think he'd ever given to me. It was as though a battery was hooked up to his tongue and he'd turned it on high.

"*Ahhh!*" I shouted.

I screamed again as he went in a little harder, thrusting two fingers deep inside of me.

"Yes!" I yelled.

And then the air was back, the freezing reminder he was no longer touching me.

But suddenly I felt him, and it came with a searing pain that shot straight through me. He'd slapped the top of my pussy much harder than he had before.

He immediately did it again.

And a third time.

And a fourth.

My eyes opened, not even realizing I had closed them.

When our stares locked, he snarled, "You know better than to get that close."

There was wetness all over his lips. It was a sight that was as beautiful as it was erotic.

"I'm sorry, sir. It just felt so good."

"Do you want me to take all the pleasure away from you?"

I didn't even dare shake my head. "No, sir."

"Then, don't do it again."

His fingers were still inside me and he began to move them.

Slowly. As deep as he could get them. I could hear how wet I was. I could feel the walls of my pussy clenching against him. The sweet, agonizing build was back with a vengeance, starting at the base of my stomach.

"Yes, sir," I promised.

He swiped his tongue on my slit and stared into my eyes. "You're going to have to endure hours of this, Pepper. I told you I have eight before I have to leave. So, my mouth is going to be down here for seven of those."

"Seven . . ." I repeated.

He'd never gone that long before.

Five hours was our current record.

And at the end of them, I thought I was going to die. I thought my lungs were going to stop taking in air and my heart was going to quit beating.

I didn't know if I'd survive two more hours.

But I wanted to try.

"Sir?"

"Yes."

"What's going to happen after the seventh hour?"

He lifted his face, so I could see all of it, and he smiled.

God, he was so handsome.

"I'm going to fuck you."

I wanted to squirm.

I wanted to force his tongue between the lips of my pussy and ride it until I came.

"Not your pussy, though." He pointed the tip of his tongue and rubbed it over my clit. "I'm going to fuck your ass."

CHAPTER SIX

Bale

I stood by the armoire and stared at Pepper as she rested on top of the table, and I watched the rise and fall of her chest. She was exhausted. Her pussy and inner thighs were bright red. Her face was sweaty, the hair around it sticking to her cheeks. Each inhale sounded more like a pant. Each exhale was a sigh.

I'd promised her seven hours and that was what I gave her.

I hadn't used my mouth the entire time. I'd also used several of the toys in the chest behind me—the flogger, whip, vibrators, and plugs.

Seven fucking hours and she hadn't had an orgasm.

She'd gotten close. I'd felt her start to shudder and the walls of her cunt tighten around my fingers. But that was as far as she'd gotten before I pulled away. I'd give her a few seconds to calm, and then I'd return to her clit.

I wanted this night to stay with her for the rest of her life. I wanted her to always remember me.

After everything I'd done, I was positive she would.

When the timer on my phone had gone off, I untied her wrists and ankles, and moved to the back of the room, where I'd been standing for the last few minutes. I watched her come down and find her breath again, and try to regain the feeling in her body.

Now, she was in a space where she needed an orgasm. Where her body had been built up so many times, dangling on the edge for hours, it would take almost nothing to get her off. Once we were done, I would make sure she had food and water and a bed to rest in.

But first, she was getting my cock.

I moved to the edge of the table and ran my hand over her leg, staring at her pussy. The redness had faded a little, but it was still bright, and it still covered most of her skin.

It didn't matter what color it had turned or that it had been the only thing I'd focused on all night.

It was still beautiful.

In fact, there was nothing in this world as perfect as Pepper's cunt. The smell, the feel, the temperature, the tightness. I'd never felt anything like it. And I knew I never would again.

I brushed my thumb over her clit and her eyes flicked open.

She was still so wet.

"Do you want to come?" I asked.

She didn't need to answer. Her eyes were pleading with me. But she still said, "Yes, sir."

So submissive, even after seven hours of torture.

God, I'd miss this fucking girl.

My thumb went to her clit again and I rubbed it back and forth, giving her just enough pressure. "Come."

It took only a few flicks before she was quivering beneath my hand, ripples of pleasure passing through her stomach, the loudest moans emptying from her mouth. Her head leaned back into the table, exposing her whole neck, and I watched the groans vibrate through her throat.

Once she stilled, she looked at me again.

Most women would be satiated, an orgasm the only thing they needed before the tiredness in their body caused them to pass out.

Not Pepper.

She was just getting started.

And so was I.

"Get on your knees," I ordered.

She slowly sat up, knowing the rush she would feel when she finally moved from the table, and she gradually got in the position I'd requested. As I walked around the table, I saw the burn marks on both wrists and ankles—they were even redder than her pussy. I saw the creases the leather had left on the backs of her legs. I saw the hardness of her nipples. I saw the wetness on her cunt and her inner thighs.

While I took her in, I unbuttoned my shirt and dropped it on the floor. My pants and shoes came off next and when I reached the back of her, I was fully naked. Now that she was on her knees, I could see the fold of her lips and the puckering of her ass.

Both were so fucking tight.

And both I wanted to be inside of.

Pepper hadn't been the only one who had been denied an orgasm. My hand hadn't touched my cock since I'd walked into this room. Her lips hadn't wrapped around my crown either. Plenty of pre-cum had leaked out of my tip, but that was the only bit of pleasure that had left me.

I was as pent-up as she was.

And I needed a release as badly as she needed a second one.

"Move to the edge of the table," I demanded. I gripped her thighs as she slid several inches closer, her pussy lining up with my hardness. I growled as she got closer, positioning her cunt directly in front of me.

She knew not to move. Not to slip even the smallest amount of me inside of her.

That was my job.

And as much as I wanted to continue teasing myself, imagining how good she would feel when I finally plunged in, I couldn't wait another fucking second.

I reared my hips back and stroked in.

"*Ahhh*," she moaned.

Her wetness coated my cock. Her tightness sucked me in. Her warmth made my body tingle.

"Fuck, you feel good," I hissed, holding her hips and using them as leverage.

I fucked her with every bit of energy I had left and just as I was about to come, I pulled out.

"No!" she cried. "I want more, sir."

I agreed with her. It was goddamn torture to stop. My balls were fucking screaming because of it.

But her pussy wasn't where I wanted to drop my load.

"You're going to like this even more." I leaned my face into her ass and I spit. I did it again, making sure the area was nice and wet before I moved back and placed my tip there. I swiped my fingers across her pussy, gathering some of the wetness and I lubed it over my crown. I pumped it several times before I pressed it against her ass and gently worked my way in.

"Motherfucker," I groaned, the tightness taking over me.

She had stretched to fit me, but had closed in again, and she was milking me with every stroke.

"Your fucking ass . . ."

"Bale," she breathed. "Oh God, I can't hold it off."

I reached around and found her clit, squeezing it between my fingers as I rocked in and out of her ass.

"Yes!" she screamed, and I felt her start to come.

Her clit hardened.

Her ass clenched around me.

She was so fucking wet, so snug, I knew I couldn't stop myself from coming either.

"Ride me," I demanded.

As she screamed, as her entire body shuddered, she bounced over my cock. She moved to my tip before her ass squeezed all of me back in. When I was buried, she clutched my shaft until the whole process began again.

It only took a few dips before my orgasm took hold of me.

The feeling started in my balls, tightening them, bursting through them, before it ran through my shaft and down my goddamn legs. "Harder," I ordered as the first load shot into her ass. She did as I asked, bobbing on my fucking dick, forcing the cum out of me.

She emptied me, hard and fast.

She made me moan, "Pepper," so loud, it echoed in the room.

And just as the last pump came out of me, I felt her come again.

"Yes!" she yelled. "Fucking yes."

When there was nothing left inside of me, when the only sounds in the room were our breathing, when our bodies were completely still, I pulled out. I wrapped her around me and lifted her into the air. Then, I turned us around and sat on the table, cradling her against my chest.

I didn't have to look at my phone to know I only had about thirty minutes before I needed to be at the airport. But I needed these few minutes with her. I needed to feel her without my cock being inside of her.

I needed her to know I really fucking cared, and I hated leaving as much as she did.

"Is this goodbye?"

Her voice was quiet, but her words filled my chest.

I didn't like the way they felt.

I didn't like that tomorrow night, she wouldn't be in my arms the same way she was now.

"I don't live on this coast, Pepper. I can't spend the amount of time here that I want to."

"How about Miami? I have a place there, as you know." She paused and then added, "Are you anywhere near Florida?"

She sounded hopeful. She shouldn't.

"No."

Her fingers traced over my chest. "Long distance never works."

I nodded, knowing how true that was.

I'd tried it once, living in Boston while my girl was in New York. It lasted two months. I wasn't willing to try it again.

Not even with Pepper.

"How often are you in LA?" she asked.

"I never know where I need to go until about a week before I'm scheduled to fly out."

"And when you're here, how long do you stay?"

That was a tricky question.

Four months was the longest I'd worked on any job. That was because I'd dragged it out, not wanting to leave Pepper. But normally, I was quick. I got in, did what I needed to, and I got out.

"Couple days," I answered. "Or as short as a few hours."

She turned her face, so our eyes locked. "I have so many questions."

"You're never going to get those answers, so put them to rest."

I could be tortured, and I still wouldn't give up that information. I would take death before I shared those secrets.

It was the oath I took when my partners took me on.

An oath we all took.

But as I looked into the eyes of the woman I loved—because I'd fallen for her so fucking hard—it was impossible not to feel guilty about the information I'd stolen from her. About the file I'd passed on to the client who had hired me. How the data on those sheets of paper were going to affect Pepper.

The client wanted numbers.

Dollar amounts.

Names of every client.

Locations of future clubs.

Some things, we couldn't hack. Some required us to log in and download straight from the source.

That source was Pepper's home computer.

And I'd gotten everything I needed.

But now, she was vulnerable. Her business was on the verge of collapsing because my client was going to steal her members and build a club that was even larger than hers.

And it was all because of me.

I didn't deserve this girl and that was part of the reason I stood from the table and set her on top of it. I found my clothes and put them on my body, and once I was dressed, I moved back over to her. My hands went to her face and I cupped her cheeks, pressing my mouth against hers. "I have to go."

"I know, and I hate that."

I breathed her in. I memorized the feeling of her skin and her scent. I heard her sigh and I devoured it with my mouth.

"I don't want to go. You need to know that, and you need to believe that."

"I do." Her hands went to my stomach and she ran her fingers over my abs. "I'm not going to revoke your membership. You're welcome here any time. I'm hoping that's enough to entice you to come back often."

"I'm not here for the club, Pepper. I'm here for you."

She inhaled and didn't release the air. Instead, she held it in, her eyes softening as they roamed over me, eventually locking with mine again. "If that's true, then don't stay away too long."

In a different world, I wouldn't leave. I would put a ring on her goddamn finger and I'd spend the rest of my life with this woman. She was everything I wanted. Everything I needed.

But my life was in Boston and I'd betrayed every bit of trust Pepper had in me.

It couldn't work, no matter how much I wanted it to.

I held her face tightly and kissed her one last time, dipping my way into her mouth, sucking the end of her tongue. After a few seconds, I pulled away.

Her eyes slowly opened. I immediately saw all the emotion in them.

"I want you to go get yourself some food and water," I said. "And then I want you to go straight to bed, do you hear me?"

She nodded.

"After everything I did to you today, you need to replenish your energy, and you need lots of rest."

"I know."

Of course she did.

This wasn't her first rodeo.

I put my hands on her thighs and I moved my face away, taking hers in one final time.

"You be good to yourself, Pepper. You deserve it. And you keep fighting, no matter how hard it gets."

One day soon, those words would come into play and she'd remember them, and I hoped to hell they'd keep her motivated.

"I want you to remember something," she said. I held her chin as I waited for her to continue. "You deserve to feel love. I want that for you, even if it's not with me."

I pressed my lips against her cheek, gently kissing it, and then I left.

I was a killer.

I destroyed lives.
I crushed futures.
None of that affected me.
But walking out of that club was the hardest thing I'd ever done.

CHAPTER SEVEN

Pepper

Unknown: Fuck, I miss you.

Me: Who's this?

Unknown: Logan.

Me: Logan?

Unknown: That's my real name. It's time you know it.

Me: But I thought yesterday was our goodbye?

Logan: Is that what you want?

Me: No.

Logan: I'm going to be in LA again next week.

Me: Does that mean I'll get to see you?

Logan: I'm giving you my number. Use it. And I'm giving you my name, so the next time my tongue makes you scream, I want you to call me by the right one.

ABOUT THE AUTHOR

Best-selling Author Marni Mann knew she was going to be a writer since middle school. While other girls her age were daydreaming about teenage pop stars, Mann was fantasizing about penning her first novel. She crafts sexy, titillating stories that weave together her love of darkness, mystery, passion, and human emotion. A New Englander at heart, she now lives in Sarasota, Florida with her husband and their two dogs who subsequently have been characters in her books. When she's not nose deep in her laptop working on her next novel, she's scouring for chocolate, sipping wine, traveling to new locations, and devouring fabulous books.

More info available at: www.marnismann.com

Kiss Me

LYNDA AICHER

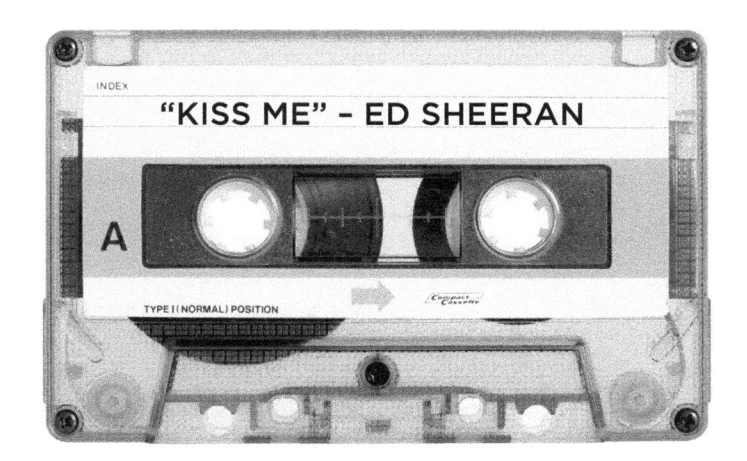

"KISS ME" - ED SHEERAN

CHAPTER ONE

The pulsating warmth soaked into Tara McTavish the second she stepped through the doorway, the brisk autumn chill shoved aside by the heady beat of music, chatter and life. Damp heat pressed against her skin with the weight of expectation. Sex, lust, a start—everything was possible at the beginning of a night.

A sigh blew from the depths of her exhaustion, draining the tension from her shoulders. God, she needed this.

"There's a table," Stacy said, stretching on her tiptoes and pointing to a four-top on the far side of the crowded bar. She took off, weaving her small frame through the people with a focused intent that brought a smile to Tara.

"I love going out with her," Jen said as she followed their resident table-spotter, leaving Tara behind.

She sucked in a bracing breath and made a quick scan of the room. Suits, smart dresses and heels were the predominant dress code with a collection of casual hip and sex kitten thrown into the Friday night crowd. The impression of overworked overachievers meshed with the upscale steel-and-wood décor to make it the hot spot for the successful and climbers—or the blatantly exhausted who wanted to blow off steam after a sixty-hour work week that wasn't over.

Her gaze caught on a man leaning against a pillar near the sunken dance floor; a sweep of black hair cut short yet stylish, a black suit fitted to his broad shoulders, a square jaw highlighted by end-of-day stubble, cheekbones to die for beneath eyes that could darken when intense, or spark with laughter.

Tall, dark and too damn hot to be anyone's boss—but he was.

He'd been *her* boss until twenty-four hours ago.

Her heart slammed into her throat in time with the deep dive of her stomach. Her last glimpse of Daniel Marks had been the formal handshake and nod that had accompanied his words of regret. Three years of blood, sweat and tears for a company had ended with a *thank you, and don't let the door hit you on the ass as you leave.*

Anger and resentment bubbled over to cover the hurt and betrayal, which were doing a piss-poor job of hiding the underlying embarrassment from being let go. The mass layoff that'd swept across the company in a broad stroke of indifference burned her pride and laughed at her gullibility.

She'd trusted Daniel. She'd thought of him as a friend—forgetting he'd been her boss. Stupid of her, really.

The urge to run, to fight, to cut loose with the string of curses she'd been too professional to set free yesterday, rushed up in a jumble of inaction.

She wasn't new to Corporate America, wasn't naive enough to believe a company—any company—regarded its employees as more than marks on a spreadsheet, but she'd been good at her job, and she'd thought he'd agreed with that assessment.

Apparently, she'd been wrong.

Her ex-boss stood by himself, a drink in his hand, his expression neutral but piercing in that direct way of his until the corner of his mouth hooked up in a half-smile. Her breath hitched. His focus was locked on her, exactly like hers had been on him—for way too long.

She jerked her gaze away, immediately flashed it back along with a smile of forced acknowledgement before she eased between two men still dressed in their suits with a mumbled "excuse me." Her mood darkened as she skated past a full glass of beer that'd been swung into her path on the end of an exuberant gesture. *This* was *not* what she needed.

Her pulse drummed in her neck, every step she took a show of control she was far from feeling. She refused to look his way, yet the back of her neck burned with awareness, that sense of being watched prickling over every nerve ending.

He was the last person she wanted to see, especially on the night that'd been dedicated to drinking away the problems he'd delivered.

"There you are," Stacy chirped when Tara finally made it to their table. Short, blond and perpetually happy, Stacy could run into the grumpy man on the corner and leave him thinking they'd been friends forever. "Where'd you go?"

Tara dropped her purse onto the table, the back of her neck still itching with the telling sensation she couldn't ignore. Oh, she could. She probably should—but that wasn't her.

"I'll be right back," she told her friends before she strode away. Their mutual calls of concern blended into the noise and pinged her guilt. She'd explain after she confronted her ex-boss. She had no clue what she was going to say to him, but doing nothing screamed of complacent acceptance or cowardice, and she refused to show either.

The sultry beat of the music mocked the casual pretense she tried to maintain as she wove her way around the edge of the dance floor. He didn't move other than to lift his drink to his lips. His gaze was still locked in her direction, intense, studying and too scorching to be casual.

That damn awareness sunk deep, where it sizzled and hummed. It was an all-too-familiar sensation when it came to him. She usually ignored it, had refused to acknowledge it when there'd been no point to it.

Her heart did a small flutter she failed to control. Why was he here? Why was he staring at her? What did he want from her?

He'd been her boss—her boss's boss, actually. Two levels above her and so far out of her dating pool, both ethically and socially, she hadn't even sniffed in his direction. But in addition to being attractive, he'd been nice. Kind. Complimentary and less overbearing than her direct manager. His rich laugh could defuse a tense situation, his sharp mind quick to see through bullshit. He'd worked beside her during months of late nights until he'd become a vital part of her day.

And then he'd fired her.

Prick.

Yes, she was being irrational. Her sense of betrayal wasn't based on logic. He owed her nothing more than he'd given her, just like every employee under him. Yet, it still stung.

His secret smile, the one that turned up the corner of his mouth when he let his guard down, had meant nothing. Just like the rave reviews in her HR file and the late-night conversations they'd shared over Chinese take-out.

He shifted away from the pole, set his glass on a random table. Music pulsed through the room and flooded the space with an erotic intent that matched his movements. Direct, composed, a purpose to his stride as he moved toward her.

Her feet stalled, along with her heart. She couldn't look away. Hell, she couldn't even blink. His suitcoat was open, tie gone, collar unbuttoned. He was pure, dark sexiness stalking his prey.

She wet her lips, trapped by the want that blazed unchecked from him. Could that really be for her? He'd been her living wet dream for the last year, and not once had he indicated he had any interest in her outside of work, especially sexual.

But the smoky, scorching heat in his expression now was definitely not professional.

Warmth blew through her, leaving her breaths short and her muscles clenching around the lust she'd buried for so long.

He didn't spare a glance for anyone before he stopped in front of her. He stood too close to be impersonal, too far to be intimate. He didn't touch her, but his presence wrapped around her and lit up every cell that ached for him. "Tara." The deep rumble of his voice was hauntingly sexy and far from his office tone.

"Daniel," she managed through her tight throat. They'd dropped the professional formalities when he'd rolled up his sleeves and dug into the Haskin project alongside her, only now it felt way too personal. Especially when his eyes were filled with longing and the same hunger she'd suppressed since he'd walked into their department, the shiny title of VP stamped on his new job.

She knew better than to trust the hope that flooded her, but she was powerless to stop it when the message he was sending was clear.

Daniel Marks wanted her.

CHAPTER TWO

Daniel studied his former employee, their surroundings vanishing until every thought, longing and suppressed desire boiled in his groin and hammered at the wall of resistance he'd stood behind for months.

Months of wanting what he couldn't have. Of admiring her intelligence. Of relying on her capable efficiency and dedication. Of getting lost in her smile that could light up a room. Of yearning for her full laugh and breathy sighs. Of wanting to rub the tension from her shoulders, brush the exhaustion from her brow, kiss every emotion from her lips until she forgot everything but him.

But she wasn't his employee anymore.

His restrictions were off. His restraints severed. The freedom to pursue her pulsed in time to the slow, sultry music. It vibrated up his legs and into his groin on a beat meant for long, slow fucking.

"Dance with me." He held out his palm. He didn't ask. He should've, but he was so damn tired of holding himself back.

A dance was only a start, an introduction to what he really wanted—if she was willing.

Her eyes widened. Her lips parted just enough to have him longing to run his tongue between them, to taste the sweetness that cuddled next to the fiery passion she was struggling to hide. Her hair flowed loosely over her shoulders in a wave of silky brown. Was it as soft as it looked? Would her eyes flutter if he ran his fingers through it? Would the tension drain from her shoulders if he cupped the back of her head and drew her in?

He tracked her tongue as it made a slow pass over her bottom lip. She swallowed, indecision flashing beneath the want in her eyes. She hesitated just long enough to constrict his heart and have him cursing every corporate rule and moral code that'd prevented him from showing any sign of personal interest in her.

He'd held strong against the temptation she'd presented, until he'd let her go in a wave of dismissals that'd cut corporate expenditures by thirty percent and gutted productivity by sixty. A stupid, short-sighted, budget-focused move forced on him by imbeciles who'd dismissed his concerns and suggestions.

Her throat bobbed with another hard swallow before she laid her palm in his hand. "Okay." Her consent brought a wave of relief that opened the door to possibilities.

He didn't give her a chance to rethink her response or question his intent. He wanted Tara to himself. Now. Tonight. Tomorrow.

For as long as she'd let him have her.

He led her to the middle of the dance floor before he pulled her close. Her sweater was soft beneath his palm on her lower back, her hand warm where she clasped his. Questions flew over her expression. It didn't take a mind reader to decipher her confusion. Twenty-four hours ago, this would've been taboo.

"I've wanted you since that first department meeting when you told me why the quality process was bloated and illogical," he told her, inching her closer as he made a slow turn. "You were the only person willing to speak honestly and that never changed. I respect that. I respect you." He lowered his voice, shoving every ounce of honesty into it. "And I want you even more."

Her mouth formed an O that wasn't quite surprise. Her hand twitched in his before her lips curled up in a confused smile. "I didn't know." Her voice was throaty and layered with sultry wonder. It eased through his chest and wrapped around his heart as she relaxed a little.

"I couldn't let you know." Not when she'd been his subordinate.

"And now you can?"

He leaned down until her hair tickled his nose and her soft floral scent teased every erotic thought that spun in his head. "Yes," he whispered by her ear.

A subtle shiver vibrated down her spine and into his palm. She turned her head toward his, her lips so close that he could almost taste them. Did she know how much she'd tortured him? How he'd memorized every dip and curve of each expression? How he could measure her emotions on the arc and fall of those very lips?

"You're serious?" She searched him, her doubts and hesitation displayed in the depths of her deep blue eyes. He knew those too. How they lightened when she was happy and darkened when she was deep in thought.

"Very," he assured her. Another turn, and he brought her closer. His dick ached for contact where it lay hot and hard beneath his briefs. "Do you believe me?"

A low laugh tumbled from her. "I don't know." But there was amusement in her eyes, a hint of "yes" that overrode a possible "no."

The slow, steady beat of the music taunted his imagination with the many ways he could prove he was speaking the truth. "I'm hoping you will."

"It's a little hard, given you fired me yesterday."

His grin stretched wide in appreciation for her directness. She waited, a brow lifted in challenge that was so her. He forced his laugh into a stunted chuckle. "I see your point." He'd been that bastard. The one who'd stood at the head of a conference room full of people and calmly told them their employment had ended. Who'd watched the shock and disbelief overtake some, the anger and resentment on others. And a few, like Tara, had simply left, no emotion shown—at least to him. "I'm sorry about that."

"Are you? Really?" Her spine stiffened as she stopped all pretense of dancing. "Do you honestly care about the people you fired?"

That challenge remained, reinforced by a fiery defiance that covered the underlying hurt she was trying to hide. But he saw it. Felt it. In the dark pain in her eyes, the pinch of her lips. The slight tremble of her hand before she curled it into a fist on his shoulder.

Her doubt added to the bitter disgust that'd festered since the reduction order had come down. The fact that she could ask him that question, that she thought him that heartless, gutted him.

Objections piled up in his throat, but he swallowed them back. They were nothing more than his own anger at being put in that position. He'd disagreed with the decision but had been forced to implement it anyway. Did that make him a coward or a survivor?

He released her hand so he could slide his palm along her jaw.

Her breath hitched in a quick inhalation. "You know I am." His tone left no room for doubt, opening himself up to her scrutiny. "I would have hoped you knew me better than to think I don't care."

Guilt and regret flashed in her eyes before she closed them, her head falling forward. The knot in his stomach cinched tighter as he questioned each step that'd led him to this point.

"I do care," he told her. "Too much." If she only knew how much.

He shifted her the last few inches until her head rested on his shoulder. Every inch of him ached for her touch. She didn't resist or protest, instead melting into him, her free hand settling on his chest.

A sigh blew through him, his heart expanding to absorb the perfection. He started moving again, small steps that simulated dancing but were barely movements. Her hair teased his cheek, the light undercurrents of her perfume tempting him closer, holding him captive. His desire simmered with the slow unpinning of possibilities.

Her low hum reached him on a husky rumble. "Daniel?"

"Yes?"

She lifted her head. Her eyelids were lowered, lust edging her deep intake of breath. He understood every question this time. *What is this? Is it real? What are we doing? Why now? Why me?*

"Trust this," he murmured. He pressed his lips to her temple, savoring her small gasp and slow sigh. His eyes fell closed as the pure sense of rightness hit him. "Something this strong can't be wrong."

Not when he'd waited thirty-six years to find it.

CHAPTER THREE

Something this strong can't be wrong.

Tara didn't have the will to contradict him. Not when his head was slowly dipping toward hers. Her lips parted, breath stopping in the single beat before his mouth brushed over hers. She closed her eyes, savoring the first touch, the glide of innocence that hinted at the passion burning so close beneath. It ignited the ragged wonder she'd long ago crushed and stunted her doubts.

That simple brush of lips warmed every inch of her down to the tips of her toes. How? This man. Her boss—former boss—was kissing her, and it wasn't enough.

Her heart caught when he eased back. His breath feathered against her oversensitive lips, teasing her with everything he was holding back. She glanced up, unsurprised to find him watching her. Desire flowed in a checked ripple that pulsed and tempted her with its siren strength. Yet there was more at play than a night of passion. He hadn't said that, but the truth writhed in her chest beside the panic scrambling to break free.

He slid his hand up her back, then down, pressing until her hips were locked to his. His leg grazed her thigh as he made a slow turn, his eyes holding hers as firmly as the hand along her nape. Liquid heat raced up her inner thigh to taunt her pussy with promises and awaken a hunger that left her aching for more.

She refused to put words to the emotions fluttering around her heart and twisting in her stomach. It was too much, too fast and somehow still right.

The tiny lines between his brows only appeared when he was intent on something. She'd studied those lines when he'd been focused on reports, caught in the matching flex and pull of his lips, just like now. Add in the dark coffee color of his eyes that only occurred when he was passionate about something, and she could barely breathe.

To have all that intensity leveled on her was overwhelming.

"This scares me," she whispered, more to herself than to him. She'd dated plenty, but nothing had ever felt this . . .dangerous. It scratched beneath her skin in warning yet lured her closer.

The slight flinch of his hand on her neck was the only sign that he'd heard her before he shifted back. The loss sucked at her fear, her pulse jumping in an erratic beat in her neck. His lips pressed, soft but firm, to her temple once again, the tension a living thing that wound around them. It insulated them and drew her in until there was only Daniel. Only this dance. Only the two of them despite the crowd surrounding them.

The music shifted to something faster but just as sensuous. Thoughts of hot, passionate sex curled through her mind. All the things she'd kept herself from imagining, from even thinking of, unwound to burn her from the inside out.

He swung his hips in a slow grind that left no doubt to his thoughts. The hard line of his erection rode her hip with each roll that could've been simple dancing but wasn't. Her groan rumbled in her throat as she pressed her lips to his neck in a naked plea for answers. For help?

No.

All she really needed was strength and the courage to leap when she was programmed to run.

She didn't know why, didn't understand what had made her dodge and sabotage every relationship until now. There was nothing in her background to give her a fear of commitment, but she had run whenever that sick, squirming, stomach-turning sense of entrapment—of wrongness—had overtaken her.

But the jumble of emotions tumbling around inside her right now were different. They weren't shoving her away but drawing her closer.

She breathed deep, held it. Stubble tickled her lips, the salty lure of his skin tempting her to taste it. The haunting undercurrent of his aftershave swirled with the longing he'd ignited until she was lost to the feel of him against her.

His breath warmed her temple. The rapid pace of his pulse

thumped just below her bottom lip in a telling beat. She flicked her tongue over his neck, catching that hint of salt and scratch of stubble. His chest hitched. Shivers tracked the trail of his hand as it slid down her neck in a caress that spoke of everything he wasn't saying.

He wanted her, but foremost, he had her. He could've pushed this attraction long ago but he hadn't. Not while he'd been her boss, when he'd had the power position over her. He'd waited until they were equals. The gentleman who opened doors, paid for lunches and bought toys for his assistant's kids had honored the boundaries that came with authority.

That meant so much.

She shifted her hand to the back of his head and drew him down. He came easily, longing burning in his eyes. He tensed, waited. Expectation crawled in her chest until she finally whispered, "Kiss me."

CHAPTER FOUR

Her whispered words hung between them for an extended pause. A dozen scenarios of right versus wrong ran through Daniel's head before he gave in to his base desire and followed her demand.

He should've been prepared for this kiss, for the tender feel of her lips. For her breathy inhale and sigh. Should've . . .

Her lips were warm velvet beneath his as she welcomed him in. His groan caught in his throat, his thoughts scattering with the first swipe of her tongue over his. The haunting taste of her triggered a visceral reaction almost as strong as her floral scent. It curled around him, drawing him in until he wondered how he'd lasted without this for so long.

He wanted more. Of her. Of this. Of where they were heading.

He tried to remain gentle, tried to hold back the urgency that pressed on his need. Fire whipped through his groin so quickly, he groaned at the wild hunger it unleashed. He struggled to hold back when he wanted nothing more than to sink into her, to feel her wrapped around him, taking him in.

Her fingers dug into his nape, her response unrestrained. Her open desire merged with his, tempting him to lose all track of where they were. Each hot, desperate pass of her tongue over his pushed him closer to forgetting why he needed to stop.

A last deep swipe, a nibble, a small brush that screamed not enough, and he pulled back. His head spun with so many thoughts, but none of them clear. She was freedom and freefall all in one. The terrifying sense of spinning wildly out of control was grounded by a belief that she was in the same state.

Her eyes lifted, her lips still parted as she tried to draw him back down. God, how he wanted to let her.

He brushed his thumb down her jaw, marveling at the flutter of her eyelids. She turned her head into his touch, her lips opening further. His stomach pitched with the knowledge that his life was changing, that she was changing it in ways he'd never fully imagined.

Their surroundings pressed in when someone jarred his back. The music was suddenly overly loud, the crush of bodies claustrophobic. They'd come to a stop in the middle of a sea of movement.

"Come home with me." His pulse seemed to stall as he waited for her response, every muscle tense. He was pushing. Things were moving at lightning speed, yet in some ways he'd been waiting forever.

She lifted until her lips hovered near his. Her eyes had darkened to a molten blue that spoke to everything he was feeling. The promise of "what if" hovered between them like a tangible thing before she whispered, "Yes."

Relief unwound the tension holding him stiff before she grazed her lips over his. His muscles constricted tenfold at her tender touch, the light confirmation more powerful than any wild plundering.

"Let me grab my purse," she said, stepping back. She trailed her hand down his arm, a promise wrapped in the curl of her fingers around his. "I'll meet you outside."

He swallowed his instant objection to her departure, instead nodding as she turned away. He tracked her slow escape from the dance floor until she glanced over her shoulder, her smile both a promise and a question. His grin was instantaneous before he found his wits and made his own escape to the exit.

The urge to stay at her side was too foreign for him to dissect. Tara did that though. Wound him in knots before she slowly unraveled them with a smile or a simple glance his way.

The brisk outside air was a solid reminder that this wasn't a fantasy. Tara was coming home with him.

The valet had the car at the curb, the engine idling, when she stepped outside. Her soft V-neck sweater and mid-thigh skirt were both sexy and modest. Her style had never been blatantly anything, yet she wore everything like it'd been tailored specifically for her.

He held the car door open, enticed by the flush on her cheeks and the secrets hidden behind the faint curl of her lips.

"Thank you," was the only thing she said before she slid inside. No questions on where they were going. No sudden doubts or hesitation.

Yet another thing about her that captivated him.

His low chuckle rumbled out as he rounded the car to the driver's side. At this point, there was little that didn't draw him to Tara. She was a force he had no ability to resist.

And zero desire to do so.

CHAPTER FIVE

"Did you fire me simply to get me into your bed?" Tara laid the question down with only a small slice of accusation in her voice.

He jerked his head toward her, his glare hard and unwavering. The streetlights flickered over his face in a show of shadows and highlights that displayed his sharp scowl, which held irritation more than anger before his gaze returned to the road. "What if I did?" Light amusement underlined the speculation in his voice.

Her laugh burst free, sharp and abrupt before she clamped her mouth closed. She recognized that playful yet taunting tone he used to draw out answers before he gave his own.

She shook her head, her eyes closing. The absurdity of him firing her just to sleep with her was too much to handle. There's no way he would've done that. For one, he was too ethical. Secondly, she couldn't possibly be worth the risk if anyone found out.

"I'd still be right here," she finally admitted. Her stomach contracted with that truth. Even now, snuggled into his leather seats, heat warming her bare legs, his scent filling the car with hints of wicked ecstasy, she couldn't believe she was really there. That this gentle yet strong man could really want her. Most likely, she would've been right here if he'd asked when he'd still been her boss. Apparently, her ethics weren't as strong as his.

His soft laugh rolled through the interior to ease the tension that'd sprung up. He grabbed her hand, squeezing it. "I didn't."

Her shoulders fell, the relief a surprise. "Good to know."

He brushed his thumb over the back of her hand before he let it go. The shiver that tracked up her arm hugged her chest and filled it with promises she wanted to trust.

"Do you want to talk about it?" she asked.

"What?"

"Yesterday. The layoffs."

His sarcastic huff forecasted his response. "No." He scrubbed a hand through his hair, the black strands falling back into place as if he'd willed them to. "Do you?"

Her brows whipped up. Did she? Not really. The layoff stung her pride, but holding him responsible was stupid. "Can I ask you one thing?"

"Of course."

"Am I better off being out of there?" The tension within the company had been building for a while. Sales had dropped, and the whispers of a power struggle at the top had fed the discontent among the employees.

He'd exited the highway and was winding through the quiet streets of one of the sprawling suburbs that extended from the city. His weighted sigh pulled on his shoulders. "In my opinion, yes."

His answer didn't surprise her, yet he still worked there. "Is that the VP talking or the guy trying to get me into bed?"

His smile was quick, the gleam in his eyes deadly when he glanced her way. "Both." Her mouth went dry. A rush of warmth coated her cheeks before he looked away. "But my answer has nothing to do with getting you into bed."

"No?"

"No." The corner of his mouth hooked up in a quick smile. "Not even a little." He turned into the driveway of a house set back behind a sprawling front lawn and mature trees before she could ask him anything else. The two-story home fit into the suburban neighborhood that seemed more family-friendly than executive-stuffy.

She quickly typed in his address and sent the text to her friends as he pulled into the garage. He hitched a brow in question after she clicked the screen off. She shrugged. "You can't be too safe."

"No," he agreed. "You can't."

Something like pride simmered in his voice and charmed her for no explainable reason. All thoughts of work and safety fled when she caught the heat in his gaze. She wet her lips, forcing herself to look away. The intensity was too much and not enough, if that was possible.

They entered his house through the garage door that opened into a laundry room. She caught a brief glimpse of the kitchen before she was in his arms, his mouth seizing hers. *This. God . . .*

She melted into his urgent touch, into the possessiveness that swelled with each demanding brush of his tongue. The kiss was everything she'd dared to imagine and had thought impossible. It curled through her on a sensuous path to her core, stroking the desire bursting to break free.

She was falling, hard, fast and so out of control that she could barely scramble to hang on even though her hands were around his neck, one buried in his hair in a frantic rush to get closer. To finally take what he was giving.

Her head spun, the lingering taste of scotch tempting her on every swipe of his tongue. Want stormed through her and set her skin on fire. Her sweater was suddenly cloying, her cheeks burning.

Her back hit the wall, and her purse fell to the floor. The solid thump of it striking the tile barely registered above the persistent rap of her heart. He slid his palm beneath her sweater, igniting a shock point of awareness that burned into her side. That first illicit contact sparked another rush of unhinged desire. It was fierce yet tender. Intense yet right.

A trace of panic skittered up her chest, which only served to clarify the moment. She wasn't just falling for him, she was close to being gone. She tore her mouth from his, her weak cry cutting through the room. How had they gotten here? What did it mean?

He trailed a line of kisses up her jaw, his hand gliding up her ribs on an ascent she didn't want to stop. No, she didn't want to stop any of this.

"Don't hurt me," she whispered. The words were more air than sound, but it rose from her heart to hang between them. A warning, or a plea?

His hand stilled beneath the curve of her breast. Her chest rose and fell in quick beats that matched the rapid pace of her breaths as he shifted back.

The room was dark, lit only by the pale glow of the appliances and the dim light of the moon. His face in shadows, she felt more than saw his concern. His touch lightened. The tips of his fingers trailed down her jaw. Her eyes fluttered shut on the tenderness communicated by that one simple caress.

So soft. So . . .honest.

"I'll try not to." His fingers feathered over her tender lips, his words touching too close to the want growing in her heart.

He'll try not to. Not a false promise but an honest admission. She smiled at the statement that was so him. Direct, when others would've used flowery words to appease her. Truthful almost to a fault.

She drew him down to take another kiss before he exposed every vulnerability she tried to hide. He'd already exposed so many. Too many.

But there was no reward without risk. Maybe that had been her problem all along. The thing she'd been avoiding without conscious thought.

She had to risk her heart in order to claim another's, and no one had been worth that risk—until now.

CHAPTER SIX

Hurting Tara was the last thing he wanted to do. In fact, it was why he'd resisted her for as long as he had. So he wouldn't hurt her.

So he'd be free to love her.

He didn't hide from that truth, not when it pulsed in blinding clarity from his heart.

She took his mouth with the same open passion he poured into her. Every nip and dip, each stroke of her tongue and soft hum, told a story close to his own. Her skin was tempting silk beneath his palm, the curve of her breast an inviting tease.

The urge to swing her around and take her on the kitchen island clamored beside the desire to savor this moment. To show her how much she meant to him, how different she was from other women.

Even if he couldn't stop touching her . . . kissing her . . .

He dragged her bottom lip between his teeth, let it slip out as he pulled back. The darkness closed around them to provide the privacy he'd longed for, only now he wanted to see everything. Catch the shift in her eyes, the parting of her lips, the blush that stained her cheeks and bled down the valley between her breasts.

The promise of so much more motivated him to step back. Her eyes opened to watch him beneath lowered lids. Her brows dipped in question until he took her hand and led her from the kitchen. The path to his bedroom had never seemed so far. The stairs ended at a small landing that curled back to reveal the rooms off the hallway.

Their shoes tapped lightly on the hardwood floors, the clicks loud in the quiet anticipation. It prickled over his skin and tightened in his groin as she followed him into his bedroom.

The room was cast in shadow from the moonlight, adding to the sensual mood humming in his blood. He captured her mouth in another long kiss, one that curled through his chest before it wrapped around his dick. He'd been hard since she'd stepped into his arms on the dance floor, but the demand had been mellow, almost patient until now. The urgency spread in little snips that licked through his stomach and peppered his chest with increased hunger.

Her gasp sucked the air from his mouth, her muscles tensing for a long beat when he finally cupped her breast. His groan tore through him as the mound filled his palm, the soft silk of her bra the final barrier to the flesh he wanted to worship. And that was just the beginning.

Did she have any clue of the power she held over him? Of how he longed to explore every inch of her?

The hard nub of her nipple teased his thumb beneath the material, upping the desire that'd become entangled in the prolonged anticipation that continued to circle. Need clawed up his spine at a pace that only heightened the wait. He grazed his teeth down her jaw, nipped her earlobe as he skimmed his thumb back and forth over the tip straining beneath her bra.

Her whimper held the same tempered need that wove through him. Her fingers tightened on his shoulders, her head tilting as her chest lifted into his hand. He hummed his agreement into the soft side of her neck. This dance of theirs was so damn amazing. Perfect in ways he'd never imagined, had never dreamed possible.

Not for him.

The workaholic perfectionist who'd dedicated his life to getting ahead, only to realize he had no idea where he was going. Tara had changed his outlook, while highlighting what he was missing.

She worked her hands beneath his suit jacket and ran her palms down his chest, her nails dragging over the material to score the skin beneath. His stomach clenched against the hit of shallow pain. It tugged his desire forward and laughed at his show of control.

Their mutual groans vibrated into the darkness. His erection pressed hard and prominent into the firm plane of her stomach and spurred the desire he was barely holding back.

"God . . .Tara . . ." He tore himself away under the promise of more. Better. Getting her naked—getting them both naked—had become a necessity.

Her expression was indistinct in the dim lighting, but her touch held nothing back. She shoved his jacket from his shoulders, and he let it fall down his arms, catching it on his fingertips before it tumbled to the floor. He sensed more than saw her grin. It'd be that devilish one. The one that could tease a laugh from him or warn of something to come.

He tossed the jacket over the back of a chair and flicked on the bedside lamp. Light bloomed through the room and brought everything into focus. The moment. The importance. The significance of having Tara there.

Her hair spread over her shoulders and down her back in a tumble of brown curls that she usually contained in a bun or clip. The corner of her mouth hooked up in a teasing smile as she reached for the hem of her sweater. He was there a second later, replacing her hands with his own to draw the material over her head.

His swallow was thick as he got his first glimpse of her. Her breasts were smaller yet full. They rounded beneath the cups of her bra to display an enticing line of cleavage. The unexpected sexiness of her bra had that hunger tearing at his chest. Her preference for high necklines and modest clothing made this discovery all the more attractive.

What else was she hiding?

He tossed the sweater onto the chair with a blind throw, his focus never leaving her. "You are so beautiful," he murmured. Beyond beautiful.

Her head dipped, embarrassment edging her weak smile. Did she really not get it? She'd been the most beautiful woman in the room since the first time he'd seen her.

He ran his fingers down the edge of her bra, over the curve of her breast to the bow at the V before he followed the material up the other side. Her shiver trembled down in a tiny wave as goose bumps dotted her chest and upper arms.

"You're killing me," she said on a breathy laugh.

He held back the boorish growl that demanded freedom and ignored the damp spot growing on his lower stomach. He eased her bra strap down her arm, ran his fingers back up and over her shoulder to lift her chin up. Her eyes were wide, yet heavy with lust.

"Then we're even." His words broke over her lips before he claimed them again. Heat ignited instantly, his fever crashing through the barrier held in place with his restraint. Need overtook everything in the quick intake of breath and the desperate tug of her hands.

He stopped thinking the second she palmed his erection beneath his pants. A tortured groan ripped up his throat. *Christ.* She really might kill him. His dick pulsed under her touch, his balls drawing up in a prewarning that spurred him into action.

His hands seemed to move on their own, skimming up her back, over her sides, around to her breasts. Her bra came off with the quick flick of his fingers, and then her nipple was in his mouth. Her shocked cry echoed through the room and shimmered down his spine. He sucked the hard tip between his lips, trapping the other with his fingers. One long, hard pull was all he allowed himself before he straightened, plunging his tongue into her mouth to swallow her erotic sounds.

She struggled to free the buttons on his shirt with the same frantic edge that he yanked the zipper down on her skirt. One shove had the annoying barrier dropping to the floor. He shoved his hands beneath her panties and cupped the soft curve of her ass in the next instant. She lifted on her toes, one of those desperate whimpers of hers grinding in her throat. The hunger seemed to bleed into their kiss, the taste coating his tongue with a frantic freedom.

He found the warmth that hid between her legs. His breath stalled at the first swipe of his finger through her folds. Wet, warm and so silky soft. There was nothing like it. Nothing that ever imitated the distinctly erotic feel of a woman's pussy.

Her head fell back, her chest heaving as he searched out her secrets by touch alone. The nub of her clit was already firm and sensitive. He circled his find, pressing just enough to draw out the desire pooling beneath.

Tension clung to her muscles and matched the quick hitch of

her breath. She squirmed in his arms, wrapped her leg around his thigh, drawing him closer and opening herself to him. He buried his face in her neck, her scent drugging his thoughts despite his intense focus on the slick heat encasing his fingers. He plunged them deep within her, stunned at how good it felt.

She jerked, groaned and clenched around him until he swore he was drowning in the pure wonder of her. It defied logic, but then, nothing about this was logical.

Love was never about logic.

The rough growl that escaped him emulated the passion raging within him. His dick strained to feel the heaven of her. The slick sounds of her wetness became the carnal backdrop to the images spinning freely in his head.

He moved them, never once breaking his hold until the bed beckoned behind her. She sagged in his arms when he withdrew his fingers, her tongue making a slow swipe over her lips. The invitation was almost too much to resist. Tasting her was all he wanted to do.

Her smile spread as he lifted his slick fingers to his mouth, licked them clean with a deliberate, slow suck. Her heady, rich flavor swarmed his taste buds, leaving him ravenous for more. There was nothing about her that he didn't want more of.

His next kiss was hard and demanding, edging on ruthless. He forced her back and followed her down as she tumbled onto the mattress, still clinging to him. He straightened and took a long, slow sweep over her sprawled on his bed. His stomach contracted, his dick pulsing with wild, crazed want.

She was . . . everything.

Her skin glowed beneath the soft lighting, every dip and curve an extension of the beauty within her. Her hair spread in a dark pool against the gray bedding. Her nipples were deep-rose tips on rounded mounds. Tiny, pink panties hid her last secrets, the barrier adding to the sensual image instead of hindering it.

Sultry longing flowed from her eyes when he met them. She hid nothing, and in return, he would give her everything.

He could do nothing less.

CHAPTER SEVEN

Tara had never wanted anyone or anything more in her life. There wasn't even a close second.

Daniel looked down at her with something close to . . . reverence, maybe? Whatever it was, it burned her without a touch, enveloping her in a sense of security. This wasn't a man out for a quick lay or even a temporary fling. The truth of that hugged her heart and kept her strong.

"I don't deserve you," he mumbled. He tore through the buttons on his shirt with precise flicks of his fingers before he tossed it aside and yanked his undershirt over his head to reveal the firm expanse of his chest.

Her mouth went dry, want racing up to feed her lust. Her hand fluttered at her throat, mindlessly rubbing the ridge of her collarbone as she appreciated the view. She slid back on the bed when he reached for his belt buckle. He shoved the last of his clothing to the floor, stooping to rid himself of his shoes and socks before she could get a good look at all of him.

Intent blazed when he raised his head, every inch of her skin between her toes and head scorched from his gaze. She bit her lip to keep another of those whimper sounds from escaping. They gave away too much when she already felt so exposed.

He skimmed his hands up her legs, stopping when he reached the last piece of clothing that stood between them. He traced the edge of her panties, her stomach clenching at the feather-light touch. "These are sexy as hell."

Her disbelief surfaced in a breathy shot of amusement. The cotton bikini underwear had been chosen for comfort over enticement. Practical to the bone, her forte had never been seduction, and that included her wardrobe.

His brow hitched, speculation dancing. "You don't believe me?"

She swiveled her head, but who was she to contradict the man who was currently naked and snuggled between her legs? "If you say so."

"I do," he rumbled, leaning in.

Her back arched with the sudden hit of warm air on her pussy. Her stomach contracted. Her eyes rolled back when his second dragged-out exhalation set her pussy on fire. Perspiration dampened her nape and flushed across her chest with the quick puckering of her nipples.

He'd done that to her with nothing more than a breath.

She tried to wrap her mind around that and couldn't. Not when he added his mouth to her torture. The wet slick of his tongue soaked her panties, the barrier increasing the erotic sensation. He moved his mouth over her clit and then prodded her opening until she squirmed for the fulfillment blocked by the material.

She laced her fingers in his hair, the strands just long enough to grip. His chuckle became another tease as it vibrated over her clit and into the need coiling beneath it.

"You . . ." Daniel whipped her panties down her legs, a fierceness barely contained, " . . .will kill me," he insisted, pausing only briefly to force her knees up, opening her even more before he dove back in. The first, hot lick of his tongue ripped a cry from her. Her fist curled in the bedding as the heaven that was his mouth became her world.

There was just him. Just this. Just . . . his tongue driving her insane.

Her orgasm crested so quickly, she barely had time to acknowledge it. "Daniel." Her weak plea was indistinct in its request. She had no idea if she was begging him to stop or continue. It was so good, so slick. He worked her clit, his fingers filling her in a steady pump that met her need yet left her longing for all of him.

The sudden force of his bite on the inside of her thigh shoved her orgasm back and ripped a shocked cry from her. Confusion muddled her thoughts before the residual pain eased, spread and then throbbed over her pussy in a crazy demand for more. *Oh my God.* Her lids were weighted when she tried to lift them.

The sight of him rolling a condom down his thick erection was so damn hot. He was pure man beneath his tailored suits. Firm, toned and studying her with a hungry, predatory air that made her toes curl. The muscles in his arm flexed with the two quick strokes he gave himself before he kneeled between her legs.

She tracked the progress of his kisses up her thigh, over her abdomen to the valley between her breasts. Each touch of his lips added another kick to her racing heart. She dragged her hands through his hair, but she had no desire to hurry him. Not when everything felt so good.

The teasing swirl of his tongue around her nipple drew out the tension that'd been so close to bursting just moments ago. Anticipation danced over her chest and twisted in her stomach until he finally pulled the tip into his mouth. Her moan was pure pleasure that raced back to her halted orgasm. The ache grew to a harsh demand as he sucked, nibbled and tweaked the bud until it pulsed in time with her heart. Only then did he shift to apply the same dedication to her other breast.

She was officially lost to him by the time his mouth closed over hers again. She clung to him, throwing everything into the kiss that she wasn't ready to say.

He broke away with a pained groan that trembled over her skin like an erotic purr. He pressed his lips to her temple, deep breaths gusting out through his nose. His muscles strained through his back and arms in a telling display of restraint. His erection lay heavy and thick on her mound, tempting her until she could barely breathe. His pulse raced beneath her lips on his neck, the heady scent of sex and him drowning her senses.

She wrapped her legs around his hips. Lust, need and something so much deeper burned in his eyes when he shifted, his dick grazing her pussy. Everything seemed to clench, wait, pulse with the expectation he'd been building since she'd stepped into his arms on the dance floor.

The slow, final push of him into her was amazing. Her breath caught, emotions colliding, then settling. Rightness, mixed with awe, eased through her. It pulsed beside the desire and urgency thrumming in her blood. He filled her completely, her walls clenching around him in a desperate attempt to get closer. Wonder clogged her throat and locked around her heart where it beat so close to his.

His eyes closed, his mouth parting. "Tara." There was more than desperation blended in his tone. Disbelief. Restraint. Reverence. She couldn't pick them out, but they struck a matching chord within her.

She framed his face, stunned by the emotions he'd exposed, both his own and hers. She drew him into a kiss so tender, so weighted with promise, she almost wept. Tears burned her sinuses and prickled at the backs of her eyes for no discernible reason. He moved then, pulling out on that same slow pace that'd embraced the moment.

The roll and slide of his hips became a gentle tango of building need and denied urgency, every thrust a declaration and confirmation in one. Love collected in her heart with each tender stroke. She'd never expected this, had never expected him.

The build was a slow, luxurious climb that allowed the knot in her core to twist and grow until the hunger sizzled over every fiber. His breath warmed her neck, his skin smooth beneath her palms. Heat melded his chest to hers, the pace almost lethargic in a way that intensified everything. They moved as one, her hips rising to meet his, their lips grazing in almost-kisses that spoke louder than words.

His back arched beneath the drag of her nails down his spine, his breaths increasing. His strokes became harder, each one ending with a distinct slap of skin. The sound was just one more piece of the dance that wound the tension tighter.

"I—" Her words were lost in the almost brutal kiss he claimed. He swallowed her whimper, his tongue searching every inch of her mouth before he reared back. His eyes had gone so dark and fierce she could barely distinguish the color. They ravished her as thoroughly as his body when they raked down her chest to where they were joined.

"Yes." Her choked confirmation scratched over her dry throat on his next quick descent. Her legs contracted around him, every drive bringing her closer to the ending she craved yet resisted.

He spread his legs wider, his hips driving hard until she could only hold on and take. God, she could take it. She wanted more of him. More of the wild, frantic need he'd built. More of his scent and touch and the feel of him over her.

Her breath caught, her gasp silent as she rode the edge of almost. Her nails dug into his shoulders, his grunt sharp. His curse had the texture of coarse gravel when it hit the air.

He crushed her to him, an arm wrapped beneath her shoulders. His lips buzzed her ear, each raspy breath abbreviated like her own. The first touch to her clit sent stars exploding behind her eyelids. He rubbed, hard and quick, timed with his powerful thrust.

She tensed, her skin burned, and then she was coming. Her breath was trapped in her lungs for the first harsh wave. It released on an aching cry that shattered her thoughts, only to have her gasping at the next hard pulse. Her toes tingled; every cell vibrated until it slowly fizzled into stunned relief.

His rough groan broke through her haze as he shuddered, his hips slowing to a firm, grinding finish. He grunted a string of sounds that could've been words, but she had no clue what he said.

His heart pounded against her chest, the pace equal to her own. Silence shrank in to hold them close in the aftermath. The sex hadn't been wild or extreme or out of control, yet it'd been the most passionate experience of her life.

She held him tight, her fingers threaded into his hair in an attempt to trap the peace that teased her heart into feeling things it had no right to feel.

But she did feel them. It was ridiculous and terrifying and illogical—and none of that mattered. She couldn't stop herself from loving him. Not when he'd proven himself to be so honorable.

She could only hope her trust and love wasn't misplaced.

CHAPTER EIGHT

Daniel stayed where he was for as long as possible.

His face was buried in the crook of Tara's neck, her scent mixing with the heavier layers of sex and come to create a telling aroma he never wanted to forget. His pulse had decreased from its wild pace as the lethargy overtook his muscles and dulled his thoughts.

He didn't want to think, not when Tara was wrapped around him and he was still buried deep within her. He'd never imagined anything could feel so good and . . . right.

He'd guessed. He'd hoped. But he'd never expected it.

He held out for as long as he could until he gave in to the inevitable. He pressed a kiss to her temple and then shifted away, her legs and arms falling to her sides. The loss was startling and yet another unexpected sensation.

He rolled off the bed and headed to the bathroom. His movements were automatic, his thoughts erratic. He was so far in love with Tara, he was amazed he could think at all. She had him wrapped around her finger, and she didn't even know it.

Fear tiptoed in before he could shut it down. *Fuck.* His head fell forward, the counter's edge digging into his palms where he braced them. Exposing his heart was far more terrifying than standing up to the starched faces that'd filled the boardroom. They'd held nothing over him, unlike Tara.

The air chilled his skin by the time he returned to the bedroom. The sight of Tara sliding her sweater over her head, her cute little panties peeking out below the hem in a too-sexy way, inflamed and froze him.

"What are you doing?" His tone was curt, harsher than he'd intended, but her quick departure nailed his chest and took a hatchet to the false hope he'd raised.

She spun around, her hand landing on her chest, mouth wide before she snapped it shut. Guilt flashed before hurt overtook it. Her brows dipped, her mouth curling down as she looked away.

Her eyes closed with her slow inhalation.

What had happened?

Calm restraint was in place when she looked back to him. The cool reserve whipped out to chill him further. "Office gossip spreads quickly." Her flat delivery held the hurt she was trying to withhold from him.

"Ah." He refused to take the guilt she was trying to shovel on him. A quick glance to the bed showed her phone, the screen lit up with text messages. "Of course, it does." He should've expected it, but he hadn't thought the news of his departure from the company would spread this fast. He crossed his arms and leaned against the doorframe, uncaring that he was still naked. Defending himself seemed pointless, especially after what they'd just shared.

She studied him, the tension shifting from frustration to annoyance. She shook her head, a bemused sigh gusting out. "All right." She dropped onto the bed and met his gaze with the determined one he'd grown to love. "Tell me why I shouldn't walk out the door."

His scoffed laugh cut between them. There were a hundred reasons why she shouldn't go. Hell, a thousand. He scrubbed a hand over his face, dragged it through his hair. "Tell me why you think you should," he countered.

Her eyes narrowed. "Why didn't you tell me you quit today?"

"Why does it matter?"

"Because it's deceptive."

"How?"

She threw up her hands. "Don't you think it's relevant, given you were my boss yesterday?"

"How is it relevant?" He wasn't that blind, not truly. But he kind of enjoyed seeing her riled. It brought out the fire in her eyes and that stubborn streak when she believed in her point.

She flopped back on the bed with a groan, all pretense of leaving gone. She turned her head to glare at him, but she didn't offer up a counter-argument.

A smile tugged on his lips. Her scowl deepened. She probably wouldn't appreciate it if he told her how cute she was right then. His gaze tracked to the width of bared stomach between her sweater and those tiny pink panties. Sexy, too. "I resigned from my position this afternoon," he relented, shoving away from the wall.

"You didn't think to do that *before* you laid off half the department?" Sarcasm dripped from her words.

He moved toward her, his prey so sweetly unsuspecting. Her eyes widened with each step he took, but she didn't shift from her vulnerable position on his bed. "The board was set on that course," he told her. "No matter how hard I tried to show them the error in their thinking, they wouldn't listen to me. The layoff was happening whether I was there or not." He braced his legs around hers. The simple brush of her skin against his sent a trail of longing up his inner thighs to his groin. "I thought it was kinder," he paused, "smarter, maybe, to see that through."

"Why?"

There was the big whammy. *Why.* He dropped every wall and let her see the truth in his next words. "For one, it was my responsibility, even if I didn't agree with it. I wasn't going to dump that on someone else. Second, I had the knowledge of the people, their skills, contributions, potential and exposures." He shrugged. "I tried to be fair. I tried to think of what was best for the individual, not just the company. I tried . . ." He blew out a breath, releasing the weight that'd settled on his shoulders. "There are some who will find new jobs with little trouble, and others who wouldn't fair as well. I took that into consideration as well."

Her expression softened, the last traces of anger fading away. "Hence, why I was let go, and Gary with four kids wasn't."

He was grateful he hadn't had to spell it out for her.

She studied him until he swore she'd dug through every thought and exposed every secret hidden inside him. He let her see it all. He had nothing to hide from her. Nothing he wanted to keep from her. Not anymore.

"And then you resigned, after seeing that everyone was taken care of," she said, the tenderness in her voice an offer of understanding.

He gave another shrug. He didn't believe in the direction or choices the company was making. Job satisfaction outweighed a paycheck for him, and he was fortunate enough to be in a position to make that choice. Not everyone was. Like Gary. Or Rupert, who was five years from retirement. Or Lucinda, who was raising two kids on her own.

"I did what I could, which wasn't nearly enough." Not for everyone, at least. He honestly didn't know if the remaining people were better off or not. But they had a warning now and time to hunt for a new job if they wanted to.

A smile unfurled over her lips, her gentle amusement releasing the worry that'd held him tight. She beckoned him closer with a curl of a finger, her naughty tease drawing him in as much as the gesture.

Relief was becoming all too familiar to him when it came to her. He leaned down, bracing his hands on either side of her shoulders. She framed his face in her hands and urged him closer. Her eyes had darkened with the emotions swirling within them, things he wanted to believe, yet were still too soon to voice. Things within himself that were still too new to risk breaking with words.

"You are something else, Daniel Marks," she whispered.

"I hope that something is good."

"It's very, very good," she said, drawing him down. "At least so far."

Her last dig tickled his lips before her kiss swept away his rebuttals. She was still there, teasing him, holding him close, claiming his mouth like she owned it. He gave it all right back, every swipe of tongue and caress of skin until he was lost in her.

Tara was finally his, and now that he was free to show her, she'd never doubt his intentions again.

EPILOGUE

Tara raced through the patio door, her laughter echoing through the kitchen. She dodged a dining room chair and ducked around the wall in her wild sprint for safety. Her heart raced, adrenaline spiking it higher. Joy bubbled over when she risked a glance behind her. Daniel was hot on her tail. His determined grin held a promise of retribution when he caught her.

His arm snagged her waist moments later. Her peals of laughter overrode the warning bells going off in her head. He dragged her to his chest. His soaking-wet shirt chilled her skin and bled through her thin tank almost instantly. "You thought you could run away?" he growled into her neck, spreading the wetness further.

Her protests were lost when he nipped the tender side of her throat. Her head tilted, a strangled moan falling out. Her struggles stopped, along with any pretense of getting away. She was powerless against him when he touched her, even when he was drenched in water from the hose she'd aimed his way.

She turned and wrapped her arms around his neck. "I beg for mercy." A quick flutter of her eyes and an innocent smile was a weak ploy she still tried.

His fake frown failed to mask his humor. "Why should I give you any?"

"Because you love me," she said. Her smile spread as his expression softened. Warmth spread outward from her heart as the knowledge settled firmly within her.

The past months had been a dream that consisted of a dizzying yet gentle tumble into a relationship with Daniel. They'd both secured new jobs, and she'd officially moved into his home a few weeks ago. It'd been almost natural, their lives blending with barely a hitch until she couldn't imagine life without him.

"I do," he confirmed before he closed his mouth over hers. His tongue played with hers, the gentle glides and tender swipes displaying what words lacked.

Her breaths were short when she eased her lips from his. "I love you, too," she whispered. So very much. More than she'd dreamed possible.

"You still deserve to be punished," he joked, slapping her bottom lightly.

Her brows hitched up. "Really?"

His serious nod was anchored by a stern expression.

"In that case . . ." She shifted, pausing when her lips were over his. "I guess you'd better take care of that."

His tortured groan blew over her before he took command of her mouth. The urgency swept in, every pressing dip and swipe merging into a symphony of want.

She trusted him with everything. Her heart. Her happiness. Her dreams. She'd found love where she hadn't been looking. Or maybe it'd found her. Either way, her being laid off had freed them both to find something far more precious than any job.

And she would treasure that forever.

ABOUT THE AUTHOR

Lynda Aicher is a RWA RITA award finalist, RT Reviewers' Choice Winner and two time Golden Flogger award winner who loves to write emotionally charged romances. Prior to becoming an author, she spent years traveling weekly as a consultant implementing software into global companies until she opted to end her nomadic lifestyle to raise her two children. Now, her imagination is the only limitation on where she can go, and her writing lets her escape from the daily duties of being a mom, wife, chauffeur, scheduler, cook, teacher, cleaner, and mediator.

You can find her online at: http://lyndaaicher.com

Thank You

Thank you so much for reading! We hope you enjoyed the anthology. If you did, would you be so kind as to post a review on a retailer, Goodreads, or BookBub? A few words can help tremendously!

This anthology would not be possible without the help of the amazing editor/admin duo of Andrea Lefkowitz and Nikki Terrill, Heather Roberts and L. Woods PR, and Nina Grinstead. Thank you so much, ladies!